RASSKAZY

RASSKAZY

NEW FICTION FROM A NEW RUSSIA

Edited by MIKHAIL IOSSEL and JEFF PARKER

TinHouseBooks

Published by Tin House Books, Portland, Oregon, and New York, New York
Distributed to the trade by Publishers Group West, 1700 Fourth St.,
Berkeley, CA 94710, www.pgw.com

Library of Congress Cataloging-in-Publication Data

Rasskazy : new fiction from a new Russia / edited by Mikhail Iossel and Jeff
Parker. -- 1st U.S. ed.
p. cm.
ISBN 978-0-9820539-0-4
1. Short stories, Russian--Translations into English. 2. Russian fiction--
20th century--Translations into English. 3. Russian fiction--21st century--
Translations into English. 4. Russia (Federation)--Fiction I. Iossel, Mikhail. II.
Parker, Jeff, 1974–
PG3286.R37 2009
891.73'010805--dc22   2009019417

First U.S. edition 2009
Interior design by Laura Shaw Design, Inc.
Printed in Canada

www.tinhouse.com

Thanks to the editors of the following publications, in which some of
the stories in this collection appeared: "Spit" in the *St. Petersburg Review*, "One
Year in Paradise" in the *Virginia Quarterly Review*, and "They Talk" in *Absinthe*.

CONTENTS

NOTES ON THE TEXT

For transliterated Russian names and words we have opted to use the closest phonetic approximation and that preferred by the individual author and translator rather than follow the Library of Congress's transliteration standards.

Diminutives of Russian names—such that both Alexander and Alexandra become Sasha; Mikhail becomes Misha; Dmitry, Dima—are very common and appear throughout this book. Further permutations are also possible, usually made by the addition of suffixes to the name or the root of the name, including -yusha, -ya, -ka, -enka, -chik, and others.

The title of this book, *Rasskazy* (or **Рассказы**), means *stories*.

FOREWORD

"I do not tell you, but I sadly note to myself that the
newly acquired country that I'd dreamed of seeing appeared
in the dream not at all as it should have."

—"The Pleshcheyev Lake Monster"

The authors included in *Rasskazy: New Fiction from a New Russia* are
part of the first generation of Russian writers born in the twentieth
century who have spent their entire adult lives in post-Soviet circumstances. The developments in Russia's political sphere during this
time and under Vladimir Putin's rule—total consolidation of power
in the Kremlin's hands, airtight censorship in the electronic media,
the wholesale institutionalization of corruption, the all-out ascen-
dance of former KGB personnel (especially the Leningrad KGB)
to prominent posts throughout the government, the near silencing
of political opposition, the open fomenting of overtly xenophobic
and nationalistic sentiment in a society still traumatized by the
grand geopolitical defeat and subsequent disintegraton of the once-
indestructible Soviet Union ("Russia is rising from her knees"), even
the restoration of the Soviet National Anthem—have in many ways
turned back the hands of Russia's sociopolitical clock. However,
Russia has also experienced its share of undeniable successes: the
strengthening of its currency; the steadily rising living standards of its
citizens and the emergence of a bona fide middle class; its resurgence
on the international stage as a global power; and so on. Some of these
successes were woefully short-lived given the Russian economy's
reliance on oil prices. It is during this complicated and conflicted

moment in Russian history that this new generation of Russian writers wrote the stories presented in this anthology.

Although the Soviet Union did not technically cease to exist until 1991, its disintegration was a fait accompli even before the Berlin Wall fell two years earlier. These writers don't remember Soviet life all too well, but its genetic code is stored in some dormant memory cell in their brains that is activated when the curve of modern-day Russia hews too closely to the former Soviet matrix of societal atmosphere. They recognize the air they've never breathed before, and they come alive within this condition of borderline nonfreedom. They're free people, but they're also Russian writers, and Russian writers need a measure of nonfreedom to feel free, to realize their relevance.

This relevance was called into question some two decades ago, when the dissolution of the Soviet Union seemed to signal that the long tradition of dissident literature in Russia no longer had a countervailing ideological force—and the brutal physical force of a political regime behind that force—to oppose it. In fact, the only opposition the heirs to this tradition faced was the formidable capitalist free market, which, in a very short time, drowned out their voices with the roaring torrents of Western mass culture—lowbrow literature, pop music, American-style TV game shows, video games—suddenly flooding the previously empty vistas of Russian public space.

The lack of the power to be heard by the broad swaths of Russia's populace, the dearth of mass-media's *Urbi et Orbi* transcountry reach, has its advantages and privileges. Today the written word (both printed and electronic) has become, to a large extent, the only form of art in Russia not subject to censorship or (no less important, and much more pervasive) self-censorship out of fear of reprisal on purely political grounds. This is due to the simple circumstance that, as a mass-communication medium, serious (and we use this term judiciously here) literature is dwarfed to an untold degree by the two channels of all-Russia television and the mammoth, government-subsidized film industry. Indeed, in an authoritarian society, he who controls the TV tower holds the power to mold the populace's collectivized mind. What this means, in effect, is that the most vociferous, if completely inconsequential, debate—in some cases, the only debate—on the issues of the day in Russia takes place in a small number of large newspapers, in literary journals and magazines, and in the volumes released by the country's few quality publishers. As such, Russian writing has once again found itself invested with a higher purpose. The writers in today's Russia derive their sense of relevance from having been adjudged irrelevant by the country's rulers (i.e., nonthreatening to the latter's political agenda).

— — —

After reading the work of about fifty young Russian writers, we selected twenty-two to include in *Rasskazy*. Many have been published in distinguished Russian journals and magazines, from *Friendship of Peoples* (*Druzhba Narodov*) to the venerable *New World* (*Novi Mir*) and *Banner* (*Znamya*), to Russian *Esquire*. Several are winners and finalists for Russia's most prestigious literary awards, such as the Debut, the Eureka, the Russian Booker, and the National Bestseller (the bestowing of this last award, incidentally, has nothing whatsoever to do with the selected book's sales). Some have already published several books, while others so far have only a few stories in literary journals to their credit. With only a couple exceptions, this is the first time their work has appeared in English.

We set out to choose stories that show the range of aesthetics and subject matter with which the new generation of Russian writers are working. The post-Soviet Russian authors most Western readers have been exposed to—Victor Pelevin, Vladimir Sorokin, and (to a lesser extent) Tatyana Tolstaya—create work that dwells primarily in the surrealist, absurdist, and dystopic. Conversely, most of the stories in this anthology, presenting the younger face of Russian prose, fall broadly into the category of what can be referred to as New Russian Realism.

Many of the writers explicitly address recent historical events. Arkady Babchenko's and German Sadulaev's highly autobiographical pieces stake opposing points of view in the wars with Chechnya: the former's dutiful Russian soldier voluntarily returns to his military post after a ten-day granted leave only to be inexplicably arrested as a deserter and forced to return to the front; the latter's Chechen narrator inhabits a magical-realist, postapocalyptic wasteland under siege, beset by unspeakable horrors that are made manifest through the transformation of humans into dragons and werewolves.

Roman Senchin's "History" takes place during the April 2007 government opposition rally at which former chess champion Garry Kasparov was arrested. The narrator is a retired professor of German history, the type whose engagement with recent history allows him to avoid the latest developments in the country. He finds himself mistaken for a protestor and arrested, thereby forced suddenly to confront the reality of modern Russia, as well as the tangential fact that a book by a foreign historian that he's carrying may be used to build a case against him as an extremist.

Some stories deploy the postmodernist vocabulary and syntax of heightened semantic displacement as they wrestle with the incongruities of Russian life turning yet again, once more, resolutely against everyone's hopes, however timid.

Olga Zondberg writes about bloggers seeking to communicate to the world at large, through online polls and prompts, their perceptions of life and the unreal quality of their own desires. (Such a context is very familiar to many Russian writers, who have utilized the Internet and see electronic publication as a kind of extension of the *Samizdat* self-publishing tradition. Several of the writers included here made themselves known and several of the pieces herein were first published in electronic venues and blogs.)

Ilya Kochergin's protagonist in "A Potential Customer" returns to Moscow on a temporary stay from a forestry assignment in Siberia. He sits around absentmindedly, talking to his friend's wife while playing Civilization on the computer, "quietly building cities and waging wars with neighboring states." But his civilizations always come out underdeveloped. Natalya Klyucharëva's protagonist, reeling from a failed marriage, impulsively moves to the decrepit village of Paradise, where his shack is wallpapered with a map of the Russian Federation, parts of which peel away and flutter to the floor over the course of a year. Even Paradise is a place where Russia falls short of its promise.

Not all of the stories are explicitly political. There are more than a few that are simply coming-of-age pieces set inside a very specific cultural context. Some are sentimental and some are absurdist and follow in the colloquial and comic tradition of Zoshchenko and Kharms. Maria Kamenetskaya's "Between Summer and Fall" depicts a man in the twilight of his life, coming to terms with the Russian proverb "Every man should build a house, plant a tree, raise a son." In "They Talk," Linor Goralik juxtaposes the stunning veracity of overheard and imagined voices, capturing the true rhythm of the modern-day, big-city Russian vernacular. Vladimir Kozlov's story "Drill and Song Day," one of the few that looks back on the final days of the Soviet Union, gives us the expiration of a childhood alongside the expiration of a country. The understated, quiet explosiveness of Kozlov's prose reveals the sheer morose mundanity of life and how convenient solutions to problems such as keeping troublemakers out of the school chorus can have resounding effects.

At this moment in history, as Russia submerges into crisis, calling into question yet another economic and political model of its development, the work in this anthology reminds us that Russia's greatest commodity—and its greatest contribution to the world—has not been oil and gas and armaments. Rather, it's been the successive generations of Russian writers capable of examining life's emotional and intellectual restlessness, its complexity and intensity.

MIKHAIL IOSSEL
JEFF PARKER
January 2009

INTRODUCTION

"The Russians," we say, "I'm reading the Russians," and instantly we're transported back to the nineteenth century, where we gather around the fire with those melancholy gents exchanging wistful stories of their first romances, or spend a white summer night at the dacha with the faded aristocrats all in serious denial about how far their stars have fallen, or crowd into a dank cell to hear a holy monk preach about why we must love our enemies as if they were our brothers. "The Russians," we say, and if we think a bit harder, we may find ourselves a century closer to our own, riding with the Cossacks in the aftermath of the Revolution, or waiting on line to pass a crust of bread to the political prisoners incarcerated at Lyubyanka, or traveling in a spaceship from which we can see, with painful clarity, the privations and excesses of life in the Soviet Union. "The Russians," we say, and if we think really hard, we may recall a few stories or novels from a time even nearer to ours, stories in which the characters are trying to dig their way out from under decades of terror and lies, or exploring fantastic landscapes populated with shamans, werewolves, and assorted revenants whose antics often seem to have intriguing parallels with everyday life in contemporary Russia.

But what about today? we might ask. What are the Russians writing today? If we think even harder still, and ask around a little, we may come to realize that if we don't know the answer, it's not entirely our fault.

For comfort—if we can possibly call it comfort—we can cite the grim statistics: Pitifully few books are translated each year from other languages—any other languages—into English. The total—including technical books—numbers only in the hundreds. So how can we possibly know if a literary scene is thriving in Moscow or St. Petersburg, or in Grozny, or in the Siberian taiga? In fact, it's far more likely that we will be offered a new translation of *War and Peace* (two were published last year alone) than an opportunity to find out what the former Soviet Union's young novelists and poets are thinking and saying and writing.

How fortunate we are, then, that we now have *Rasskazy: New Fiction from a New Russia*, a freshly translated volume of selections from the freshest voices. Traditional or "experimental," harrowing or comic, reportorial or imagined, these short stories and excerpts from longer works make it clear that the Russians are still doing some, if not all, of the things that their ancestors were doing in Tolstoy's time and, in fact, many things that humans have done at every moment in our collective history.

They gossip; they fall in love and have sex and get pregnant; they fight wars and long for peace. They go to school and sing in the choir. They have nervous breakdowns, lose friends, eat dumplings and drink vodka, find God, debate the merits of life in the country vs. the city. They find end-runs around the painful truth. At moments, their metaphysical and philosophical speculations, such as the following passage from Nikolai Epikhin's "Richeva," sound remarkably like the sort of thing one might find in Turgenev:

> People who love money and a life of luxury and who are ready to deceive anyone for this personal happiness, to insult, to kill, and so on, these people will honestly tell you: *Yes, I am ready to step over people in order to have the good life.* . . . If this is what a person is saying, he of course does not elicit any sympathy from me. But at least I know exactly what to expect from him, and as such he can be forgiven in some ways.

On the other hand, you can't help thinking that Turgenev would have an awfully hard time understanding what most of these characters do all day, especially with their spare time. They talk on their cell phones and send text messages, they work on their laptops and blog and log onto social networks. They not only watch TV but also write TV screenplays. They are, after all, citizens of the twenty-first century.

The shadow of a long and glorious tradition hangs—mostly lightly—over some of this. In one story, "Bregovich's Sixth Journey," the narrator names a dog, kept on a chain, after Ivan Denisovich, one of literature's most celebrated prisoners. Some of the strongest selections in the anthology concern the war in Chechnya, and one can hear echoes of Isaac Babel in the casual brutalities of "The Killer and His Little Friend" and Arkady Babchenko's portrayal of a reluctant soldier. And yet we always feel that we are in the presence of something that is, as the title promises, new.

What's new is the chance to learn how people are living and thinking and feeling in a world that literature describes better than any other source of information. What's new is the opportunity to learn so much more (and in so much greater depth) than anything we have been hearing about what it is like to try to survive on either side of the war in Chechnya. What's new is the rhythm and snap of the hip, modern, contemporary voices that we would expect to hear rattling into a cell phone in the booth next to ours, and the rendering of that voice into an English that's as idiomatic and confident as we imagine these speakers to be. What's new is the window opening on what the new Russian writers are doing with language, and with the perpetual challenge of making people on the page sound like people in life.

So thanks to Mikhial Iossel and Jeff Parker, the editors of Rasskazy. "Spasibo" to the twenty-two writers included here, and to their able translators. Thanks for helping us Anglophones find out that the literature of the former Soviet Union is not only alive and well but also hale and hearty and thriving. "Ah, the Russians," we say. "We're reading the Russians." Yet now what we mean is not only the past—but also the present and the future.

FRANCINE PROSE

THEY TALK

Linor Goralik
Translated by Mikhail Iossel

". . . DO YOU KNOW how I knew spring was here? I found a skull in the garden. I immediately looked for a bullet hole in it. Nope, no hole. Just some stupid fucker croaked in the garden."

— — —

". . . this, you know, sort of middle-aged lady, not really old, the kind of one, like, actually quite beautiful, with this, like, mink boa with little tails on it, well made-up, and with her also a young girl, maybe about twenty or so. And it's such a pleasure for me, you know, to look at them, that they are sitting together in a coffee shop, drinking coffee, during the day, on December 31. I'm sitting there, half listening to them while I'm reading the menu, and I'm thinking this could be, like, for example, an aunt and her niece. They're truly close, and so they've met to congratulate each other with the New Year. There's something very beautiful in this, somehow, and then the girl probably will go to meet friends to celebrate—well, in other words, a pretty clear picture. And the girl is telling the lady, you know, about what's going on in her life and whatnot, and I'm listening, I generally like to listen in on strangers' conversations. And so she's telling her something about some Anya, that this Anya's seeing her boss, and he took her somewhere, and now somebody's been fired, and the lady keeps nodding, and then this girl says: 'And Anya—her mother also abandoned her, but not like you did me . . .'—and then the rest of the sentence. But this I already couldn't make out; at this point my hearing switched off."

———

". . . still, like, shaking all over. And the whole day, you know, I'm like ill, totally turning inside out. And I decide I'm not going home 'cause I've finally fucking had it with her. No, come on, six years I'm living with this woman, six years, and she fucking throws these kinds of tantrums over some fucking powdered detergent? Telling you, she's fucking nuts, sees nothing in the world but her housecleaning. Fucking nuts. And she, like, yells at me: 'I'm fucking tired of this fucking shit, don't want to see you again, get the fuck out of here, you only think about yourself, go fucking die!' I tell her: 'Can you even hear yourself, what kind of words you're using? You're raising a daughter and this is how you carry on?' So she just threw this same sweater at me! And I—what can I say?—well, that's it, I decided that was it. *Get lost*, you say—fine, that's it, I got lost! And so I'm like this all day, you know, walking around and thinking: *Okay, so, I'll spend the night at my mother's, all the most essential things I'll come and get tomorrow, while she's at work, she still has money for now, so I'll leave an extra couple hundred on the table, for my conscience, you know—and that's it, and she can go to . . . I'll talk to Natashka myself . . .* And so at this point, you know, we're already going out for lunch, but I've forgotten my cell, so I say to the guys: 'Guys, I'll catch up with you shortly,' and so I run back in—and the phone rings. And I pick up, thinking, *Whoever you are, you can go fuck yourself*, and suddenly I hear, well, wailing. Real concrete wailing, like a siren, sobbing and sniffling her nose. My heart drops to my gut; immediately I think—*Something with Natashka*. I say: 'Lena, what's with her, what's with her? Lena, tell me, what's with her?' And she goes: 'Wooooo . . . With whooo?' Right away I feel relief. In general I can't take it when she cries, my heart just starts falling out, I forget everything, no anger, no nothing, just this, you know . . . I say: 'Sweetie, honey, tell me, what's wrong?' She just wails. Then says: 'I read in the paaaaper . . .' 'What,' I say, 'what's in the paper, baby?' Thinking—maybe relatives or something, maybe who knows what. And she's like: 'Woohooo . . . in the paper . . . that all men . . . Yyyyhh . . . That in twenty thousand years . . . Well, not twenty, but . . . That you'll all diiie ouuuuut . . . Your chromosome . . . Woohooo . . .' 'Lenochka,' I say, 'what in the world are you talking about?' And she's like: 'Your chromosome's being destroyed . . . oooohhh . . . One hundred thousand years—and you'll all be gone . . . It'll only be uuuuuus . . .' I say: 'Lenka, so what of it?' And she goes: 'Lyesha, Lyeshechka, don't die out, please! Come home, right now, please, pleeease!' So again I didn't buy the powdered detergent. Nuts, I'm telling you, crazy!"

— — —

". . . anyway, fifteen years old. That is, she was still in high school. And this was exactly when they started teaching the upper classes safe sex and sexual health, and she was already in her seventh month. And everyone—both girls and boys—had to carry a doll around the clock, to understand what responsibility for a child means. And so she carried it—in one hand her belly, in the other the doll."

— — —

". . . to talk with someone, I'm human, after all, I also can't go on like this! But with whom can I talk? With dad—he starts crying, well, actually, no, you know, but—I mean, with dad? With dad there's no point. But with who? Alik comes home from work at ten o'clock and plops down on the sofa still in his boots. I once tried to tell him something and he goes, like: 'Just let me die in peace,' as if I was, you know, his . . . his . . . God knows what. But I'm human, you know, I do need to talk with someone! So I was getting off on Lyubanka, Pushechnaya exit, and there's the Children's World right there, and I just thought, you know, *You can all go to hell!* So I went in and there, like, on the first floor, there is some kind of carousel, you know, and I bought myself a plush rabbit. The kind, you know, like, with the long legs, kind of faded-looking? Like, you know, you know the kind I'm talking about, yeah? Six hundred rubles, to be sure, but, after all, I can afford it, can't I? The last time I bought myself a pair of jeans was nine months ago, so I can spend six hundred rubles, can't I? Anyway, I stuffed him into a bag and carried him to my room, and, you know, Alik goes to bed and I lock myself in the bathroom, I sit the rabbit on a board and, like, tell him absolutely everything, you know, pour out my whole soul, until there's not like even a single drop left . . . The first night it was like this until six in the morning. You wouldn't believe, I wailed, took pills, whatever else, what didn't I do? . . . And so, you know, after that there wasn't a single evening that I wouldn't at least find a minute. And I hid him in the cupboard, you know, where the pipes are, we hang a bag in there, with an enema in it, of course nobody ever looks in there, so that's where I kept him. And yesterday dad had his usual, you know, happening again, so I pulled him through with pills, put him to bed, and went right to the rabbit, and once I started telling him—I just couldn't stop, you know, talked and talked, talked and talked, and I, you know, I kind of shook him like, hard, and I said to him: 'Well, why do you always keep quiet?' And here he looked at me and said: 'Listen, did it ever occur to you to ask me, maybe just once, how *I* am doing?'"

— — —

". . . wife comes home, and the cat smells of another woman's perfume."

— — —

". . . during the war. He made it all the way to Berlin and sent her a parcel from the frontline with some kind of children's things for Mother and Pasha, tablecloths, something else, and a luxurious chiffon peignoir. Well, here, you get of course they hadn't ever seen the likes of such, right? She unfolds it—and there's a single vermicelli stuck to it. As if some woman had been eating and accidentally dropped one. She retched for about twenty minutes, you know, then she grabbed the children and that's it. He spent half a year looking for her afterward."

— — —

"... I grabbed Lenka by the hand—and ran up to the neighbors. It's like this now once every week: he gets smashed and heads right for her, his paws digging ahead of himself, you know, like an excavator. So me and her are already trained: jump into our boots—and run. But besides that it'd be a shame to complain. There's Natasha. Everyone told me: there is not a man on earth who will ever love someone else's daughter, but there you have it, wouldn't you know."

— — —

"... and so I'm walking and suddenly feel someone's eyes on me. And I'm wearing this black-and-white checkered coat, you know, total scream of fashion then. Inka got it for me, cost two months' salary. And so I'm walking, down that side, right, you know, where that—well, art salon or artists' house or whatever is, right? Where the Indian restaurant is now. And suddenly I totally, like, feel someone's looking at me, can you imagine? So I turn my head, carefully like, and there, you know, on the other side, walks a young man, get this, looking openly and not even, like, hiding. And there's something, you know, about him . . . something in him . . . maybe looking like some actor or something . . . But I—get this—I just at that exact moment, I knew: *That's it, this is my future husband.* Well, you know, do you believe these things happen? It's like, I only looked at him for a second and already I knew everything. And so I, well, I keep walking, proudly, ignoring him, over toward the Neglinnaya, but my heart is like *thump-thump, thump-thump, thump-thump.* I glance sideways-like—and he, you know, is walking across, diagonally, as if to the sidewalk's edge. And I realize we're going to meet precisely at the corner. And I'm not even thinking what to say, because I already, you know, understand everything, you understand? Like, everything's already clear and understood without words. And I'm walking and just thinking: *I could've gone to pick up those shoes first,* and that's it. And there's nothing else in my head, just this: *I could've been picking up those idiotic shoes now and never would've met my husband!* And I, like, keep glancing over—and he's already stepping off the sidewalk, and even starting to walk faster, so as to intercept me, see. And here— get this—just like that, a car shoots out—and like woooooosh!

And literally—I mean literally—within two centimeters from him. Really, seriously, within two centimeters. I'm standing there, even my heart stopped cold. Just can't move. And he's also standing, like a statue. And then—get this—he turns around—and starts walking right back, like, over to that one, you know, the metro, almost like half running . . . And I'm standing there and thinking: *Those shoes, I bet they aren't even ready yet.*"

— — —

". . . and until the dog kicks the bucket, you're not moving it from that apartment."

— — —

". . . trained myself so that at moments like these my head just switches off. I'm a robot. I already knew within one block, by the smell, that it was a fucking nightmare up there. And indeed— nothing was left of the café, just a wall. And so I just flip this little switch in my head: ticktock. I am robot, I am robot. Well, and then for three hours we do you know what. In fact, we just break into groups of three people: two collect, one zips up the bags. So here, I'm the one zippering—*zzzziip*, and it's like these weren't even people but just, like, different kinds of objects we're putting into those sacks. Four groups of us there were, done within three hours. Tsvi tells me: 'Okay, let's do one last walk-around, just in case.' Fine, what's it to me, I'm a robot. We go around looking into every little corner, debris everywhere, wherever possible we turn things over a little. Seems like we've picked up everything. And then, out of the corner of my eye, I catch some movement. I'm like—'What's this?' Take a look, and right there by the wall, the one that didn't collapse, there's this sort of cupboard, completely intact, and in it are rotating pastries. And that's when I threw up."

— — —

"... and screaming. And the dream is always the same: Mother slaps his face and asks: 'Was it you who ate the chocolate?' He wails and says: 'No!' Mother slaps his face: 'Was it you who ate the chocolate?' He: 'No!' Mother slaps the face: 'Was it you who ate the chocolate?' Here he breaks down and screams: 'YES! YES!' And his mother slaps him across the face, hard, with the back of her hand and shouts: 'Haven't I taught you—never own up to anything!' Terrible, isn't it? For half a year I couldn't get it out of him, what was this nightmare he was having, he'd just say: 'What nightmare, no nightmare, everything's fine.'"

— — —

"... when he loved me, I wasn't jealous, and when he didn't love me—I was. I'd start calling, aggravating both myself and him, until one time an ambulance came for me."

— — —

"... belong to this one rich person, and I have to sing when he tells me to. Because if I keep on doing this for another year, my band and I will get together enough cash to get ahead. But he's a totally wild person, doesn't want to understand anything, it's all the same to him—if you're sick, tired, have personal problems—still, go, sing. Vera went to her sister's wedding, so he fired her. But I know this is necessary, or else we'll never get ahead at all, very difficult. So I bear it. Yeah, and so he and his friends were grilling up some kabobs somewhere, and he called me—come, sing. And this was outdoors, and it was September already. I get there, he gives me this humongous coat, like a barrel, you know. And I felt so disgusted, you know, to be singing in this coat and all, I almost lost it. I explain to him: 'Singing in cold air is bad for you, singing is all about breathing, if I breathe this kind of air normally, tomorrow I'll have no vocal chords, and if I don't breathe, and sing only with my vocal chords alone, I'll still lose them anyway.' And all this is at his dacha, huge dacha, pheasants, peacocks, dogs. And a silent pregnant wife follows behind him everywhere. I'm thinking, you know—it probably is a lucky marriage, she lives well, but her life must be awful, it seems to me. 'No,' he tells me, 'sing.' I would have quit a long time ago, but me and my band won't get ahead without his money, and I want to. Well, no, I still would have quit a long time ago anyway, but he comes to me, after I've sung, sits down, and cries. No, not groping, why do you keep asking these fucking bullshit questions, huh?"

— — —

"...his daughter accidentally slammed the hamster in the door, and he cried afterward. Kept saying: 'Such an amazing dude he was!'"

— — —

"...I ask, 'Mama, what should I get you for New Year's?' And she tells me, the bitch, you know what?—'Don't buy anything, sonny, maybe I won't live that long ...'"

— — —

"...always loved my wife, loved her so much, you can't even imagine. And as for her loving me? Well, at least it seemed to me—maybe not so much. Mother says to me: 'Why don't you get yourself a mistress? Your wife will love you more.' So I found myself a woman. Didn't love her, of course. I loved my wife; I didn't love this one. But I kept going to her. Then I think: *I need my wife to find out*. But I can't tell her. I did all of this for that, but I just can't bring myself to tell her. Mother tells me: 'Why don't you tell the children, they'll pass everything on to her.' And my children, I've told you about them, two sons, one had just entered college back then, and the youngest was fifteen. So I called for them, I came home, got them together, and said: 'Children, listen to me. I'm going to tell you a terrible thing, and you will have to forgive me. I have, children, apart from your mother, I have another woman.' And then I keep silent. They kind of look at each other for a moment, then suddenly burst into laughter! And

the youngest slaps me on the shoulder and says: 'You go, Daddy-o!'
And the oldest says: 'Awesome, man. Don't worry, we won't rat you
out.' And so I still keep going to that woman, even until this day. It's
just hell knows what."

— — —

"...and the Day of Judgment, by the way, already happened, only no
one noticed it. It's just that from that day things went well for some,
and for others they went badly."

— — —

"...saw her yesterday. Well, I'll tell you this—it's not even important
how she looks, or that she's beautiful—well, yes, she's beautiful, I
won't dispute that, what's true is true—but that's not what's important. What's important is what I saw: *nothing* will come of it for them.
No-thing. Eight years of marriage, Marina—quite a haul. I know
him like this, understand, like this, like my own palm, like these here
five fingers. So, believe you me: with this woman, nothing will work
out for him, no-thing. She will suck his blood and throw him out,
and he'll come crawling to me again. You'll see, mark my words.
I've even calmed down. And actually, you know, when I'd only just
learned about all this, I couldn't eat for two weeks, completely, nothing. I lost seven kilos. That was such a joy, such an amazing feeling!"

— — —

"...on that day everyone, of course, showed their true colors. For
example, my best friend, Lepyokha, he called me and started shouting: 'Dude, do you even know what's going down here, over by the
White House?' 'Well,' I say, 'I know, sure, I'm watching the television,
what the ...' 'No!' he shouts. 'Dude, you have no idea! There are such
hot bitches here! One can fuck them right on top of the tanks!' Well,
so I went to my wife—back then we were still married—and I tell
her: 'My dear, I have to go to the White House, to the barricades—

to defend freedom and democracy!' And she, wouldn't you know it, didn't let me go! That bitch, I forgave her everything, but this cruel heartlessness on her part I never forgave, and never will."

— — —

"...she's a weak, timid, needy, completely untalented, a very hard-to-take, very miserable woman. And we should feel sorry for her, instead of saying such nasty things about her."

— — —

"...by the way, the last time your mobile didn't switch off, and I sat for about five minutes, listening to how you were walking through the snow. *Thup-thup, thup-thup*. I almost cried."

— — —

"...little doggie runs, dirty-dirty, its ears rosy-rosy, and see-through. And here I thought: *Devil knows, maybe I should've given birth back then*."

— — —

"...because God will fulfill your every wish if your thoughts are pure. My grandmother taught me—you always have to wish people well, even if something happens to you, you know, anything. It works, seriously. For example, when that bitch said that I was a junkie because I was pale, I decided: *No, I'm not going there*, you know, *I'm just not doing it, I'm not*. I did what instead? I prayed in the evening, real well, I said: 'Dear God! Please deliver good health unto all my friends and acquaintances!' And the very next morning that bitch fell down the stairs to her death."

— — —

". . . haven't been in a supermarket in a long time. Would really like to go there sometime."

— — —

". . . so I bought season tickets to the opera. I'm going to start building the normal life of a single person."

— — —

". . . don't go to class reunions, so as not to indulge my pride. Otherwise you walk out of there with the kind of feeling a decent person is not supposed to have. I mean, look, the majority of them live in such a way that Google can't even find them."

— — —

". . . *don't be distracted by fucking bullshit, Pasha. You're always getting distracted by fucking bullshit.* I also remember one time, I take a look— a woman, kind of unfamiliar-looking, but then I look more—no, familiar, used to work at my research institute, it's just this different angle through the lens, plus she's cut her hair, you know, like a fur hat, sort of, wears it like a hat. I adjusted the lens more into focus, looked again: sure, she's changed, of course, time—no arguing with time. And eating something. I adjusted some more: popcorn. She's eating popcorn. Walking down the street with popcorn. Where'd she get it? For some reason, I suddenly got totally hung up on this: where'd she get it? Then I pictured this thing: seriously, you've got to really want the popcorn, go to the popcorn, I mean, the movie theater, go inside the movie theater, you know, buy the popcorn, and leave, in order to eat it on the go. I, like, pictured it with my own eyes, and she was always like that, a stubborn goat. Walking down the square and eating. I followed her to the corner, adjusted the focus some more, got a ring on her finger. That's how I got distracted, and then they're in my ear: 'Blue, we don't understand the delay. Blue, are you working or what?' My guy, you see, he'd gotten away while I was distracted. Of course, I did get him still, but that's how sometimes you get distracted by some kind of fucking bullshit, and then you walk around all mad for a couple of days."

— — —

"...day. All morning I've tried to write a script, but all I kept turning out was some kind of cheap melodrama. Because this doesn't happen in real life—I mean such sheer intensity of tragedy. One minute everyone dies; next thing you know it's something else. Inexpressible soul-wrenching all the way. Long story short, I went to pick up my suit, and kept thinking in the subway: *No, really, is this normal?* Because art—it is precisely that, this ability to discern big issues in small things. The drama, that is, in the simple things of life. And the more I think about this, you know, the worse I feel. And then, at Lubyanka, I suddenly decide: *Ah, the hell with it, this suit. I'm going to get off now, walk over to Captains, and just have a drink there.* That's right. So I get out, and right at the exit, already upstairs, right away three SMSs come in at once, in a row. From three different people, obviously. As follows: *I'm in psych ward, held here forcibly for now; Anya died yesterday. Not flying in; Dad keeps crying asking I bring him home.* I read once, read twice, read three times, and suddenly I realize I've been staring at my phone for fifteen minutes already, walking in circles around the station pillar."

A POTENTIAL CUSTOMER

ILYA KOCHERGIN
Translated by Anna Gunin

KOLYA AND I WENT on leave from our forestry post. At first we took turns rowing our inflatable boat downstream, then we bypassed the long rapids, and again we rowed. On the fourth day we reached the village and received our money in the sunny and dusty accounts room. The night before the bus, on the fifth day, we began spending our holiday allowance. Kolya and I had long dreamed of drinking— we had spent all winter in the taiga, hadn't visited the village. After a winter like that you certainly need to relieve the boredom.

All our guys from the nature reserve—six people and the director—happened to meet up in the hostel. We crossed the bridge to the store, first we didn't buy much, either the guys couldn't be bothered or they were just playing coy. But then gradually they reddened, started talking a little louder. Kolya came across someone's copy of Omar Khayyam, and what a find this poet was for him. He'd go to the table, take the glass offered to him, drink it, then back to the sofa to stick his nose in the book. At first he called the men, "Hey, just listen to how good this is, it's about wine, it's about all of this!" Then later he called the hostel an "abode of trouble," marked his place with his coarse finger, and lowered his gray, disheveled head onto the book. He fell asleep like that. But I traveled to the other side of the river with the truckers from Belokurikha.

These truckers came in and joined us when our evening was in full swing. And when it fell dark, they set off for more bottles to the all-night store on the other side. It wasn't even a store, it was a café—an ordinary counter with a couple of tables set out and some music playing. Two girls stood at the counter, dancing a little, chatting with the staff. To tell the truth, by then I couldn't see all that well, but one of them—the one nearest me—was very beautiful, and I was drawn to her, or even, you could say, something drew me to her, while the guys from Belokurikha got the vodka.

It's a good thing those truckers drove me away. I tried to fight them off, of course—I would have given anything to stay. But one of them took all the vodka, the other took me, and they carried me off to the truck. "Man, what are you doing?" they said. "If you were that desperate, you should have asked us where to go. Throwing yourself at them girls . . . Do you realize who they are? Man, just one go and you'd have got your rod in one hell of a tangle. We're telling you, whether you like it or not. You'd have had to slog to pay for the medicines later."

So they drove me away. But to be honest, I kept on thinking about that girl for a long time after, maybe because I hadn't really got a good look at her, my vision was already in tunnel mode by then—like looking the wrong way through steamed-up binoculars.

And on the train later I remembered her, while lying around on a bunk for three days on my way to Moscow. Kolya stayed behind in Biysk, at his mother's, and I went to visit mine. I lay on the top bunk and thought: *What if I hadn't caught anything, maybe the truckers lied.* An image, hazy as it was, stood clearly before my eyes, I couldn't forget it—a girl slowly dancing and smiling to herself. The dim vision of her bore a resemblance to my winter dreams in the taiga, where the heavy snowy silence presses on your ears, where fatigue and frost give birth in your lightly sleeping brain to vanishing women with slow movements and loving eyes. These women are blurry and sad.

I remembered them, and also the girls in the café at night, when the lights at the station shone in the dark carriage and I couldn't sleep. In the daytime I forgot about them, looked through the window, looked at the passengers, thought about Moscow and how I'd arrive there. It seemed like Moscow was sighing and waiting for me, that was the feeling I had. I thought about ice cream, oozing its white juice, thought about beer languishing in its bottles, thought about the cracks in the tarmac, about how tense the huge city was. About well-groomed girls frozen before their mirrors in anticipation, about lightbulbs in the street lamps plumping in order to illuminate the nocturnal boulevards for me. I thought of new clothes, American cigarettes, music. And also, of course, of the hunting carbine that I was on my way to get. The purchase of the carbine was the purpose of my trip. And everything I thought about had to be fitted into a month and a half. I needed to make full use of Moscow in that time.

The train arrived in the morning. I had already drawn up a detailed plan for the first two or three days so as not to lose a minute. I reached home humbly, without even looking up, trying to slip past unnoticed. Then I took Mama's dog for a walk (Mama had left a note asking me to take him), scraped my chin with a razor (only leaving my sun-bleached moustache), sat in the hairdresser's (an old woman cut my hair), bought new jeans from a Vietnamese guy at Konkovo market, and only then decided to show myself to the city.

I stood outside our house, opposite Repin Square, smoked a cigarette, expelled the smoke through my nose onto my moustache. A man from the taiga stood there, squinting. I was prepared to be noticed, my plans had allowed for it as an integral part of my vacation, but Moscow sailed past. Sailed in vivid flashes, perfumed scents, the grunt of gear changes, grimy pigeons.

Around fifteen minutes passed. The second cigarette in a row with no special desire to smoke, and the depressing suspicion crept in that this time, as if out of spite, everything would be just as it had been a thousand times before—the very first evening, which had promised so much, would be spent with a book on the sofa. The second, too, and the tenth. My native city would not recognize me, maybe a cop would come up and ask for my papers—nothing more. It happens every time, but I just can't get used to it. From afar it beckons, teases, but as soon as you arrive—you're a distant uninvited relative from the countryside. Cock-tease, damn it, the bitch. And the women here are all like that.

Maybe take five bottles of beer and make my way home. Well, I knew it would turn out this way, so why get upset now? You work yourself up, dream up some fantasy like a teenage girl, and then you're surprised. Examining it logically, what was it I'd wanted? Do I know what it was I'd wanted? Well, seeing as I don't even know, just had some vague dreams, just take yourself home, sit down, and read.

So I stood there, smoked another five minutes, and went home to read a detective novel.

— — —

In the evening Mama came home from work. The first couple of days she would observe me, getting used to me. She probably wouldn't get used to me, just ignore the bits she didn't like.

I read that each of us sits out our whole life in a bubble with walls of mirror and wherever we look, we see only ourselves, in other words, our reflection. You look, for example, at a bear and see not a bear but a wild beast that could kill you, you look at a pretty young girl and think how nice it would be to get between her legs. You don't see them, it's more like you see yourself, on top of the girl or under the bear. So everything gets measured against yourself. Here Mama will once again see not me, but her dear little child, and everything will fall into place.

On the way home from work Mama popped into the shop and bought all sorts of delicious things to eat, her son's favorites. Her son hadn't been home in over a year and now for an entire six weeks he would be with her. I sit and eat these delicious things. Some of them I love, some of them I don't anymore. But I eat them up anyway, with relish. I too have prepared something for her and I anticipate the pleasure of giving it.

Then we go into the living room, and I give her the sable. All women love sable, which means that she too should love it. Mama stands before the mirror and holds the fur to her hair, drapes it around her shoulders imagining a future hat and collar. I show her the sharp claws on the paws, the black springy whiskers and wrinkled noses, and she melts. It brought my winter hunting to completion—it is nice being not just a successful shooter or trapper, it's nice being a breadwinner too. True, there is something intimate in this—a woman stands in furs obtained by you, admiring herself. I even felt rather uncomfortable, and went round to Dima's. He must have got home by now.

In Dima's hallway a bicycle was hanging from the ceiling, like something out of a film. His place has high ceilings, and the corridor is narrow. Dima, his parents, wife, and daughter still live in their communal apartment, waiting for the other tenants to be rehoused. They have been waiting long, because there is an old lady who continues to occupy a room, as though out of spite she doesn't want to abandon her mirror bubble and she hangs on tenaciously to her ninety odd years, while the other tenants are unwilling to move away from the center of town. So towers of boxes grow along Dima's walls, filled with things for their future move into the vacated rooms. What the bottom boxes contain probably no one remembers anymore, they began preparing for the rehousing long ago. The middle layers Dima tried to sort out after his wedding, they found stores put aside during the rationing at the start of the nineties—hardened Zhemchug toothpaste, piles of household soap, toilet paper even.

Dima works, now he has no time for boxes. He works in marketing at an advertising agency and comes home in the evenings. For a man who works in the wilderness and delights in living without family and boxes it feels awkward to tell of the beauty, the pine scent and romance of Siberia. But tell someone he must, someone must hear me. I must tell others of my life, in order to see my reflection in their pupils. So I sit in their kitchen and with a feeling of slight awkwardness and joy watch Dima's plumper physiognomy lighting up and darkening. Toward the end I even hear a little about his office colleagues, about their funny and rather silly boss, and his fellow workers, on the whole all right but rather soulless. That is, they will help you out when you need it, but now and again they can play you such lousy tricks that you'd be amazed.

"And what is it you do in marketing? What, you dream up advertising projects?"

"I put together a profile of the potential customer. Their sex, age, social standing, family status, disposable income—a whole load of stuff. You make up a composite profile of the people who might have a need for some product or other. And then that need gets inflated into the advertisment. Take you, for example, you're a potential customer too. You've worked up your virility, no doubt, with all that fresh meat and open air? Right?"

"Actually I've come to get a carbine."

"It doesn't matter what you came for, you'll end up buying a washing machine, then later you'll be astonished."

Dima showed me the computer that he had acquired recently but that for the most part stands unused—his wife has no need for it, he himself has neither the time nor energy to sit in front of it, and his daughter is still too young. So it only gets used for gaming on the weekends. I touched the monitor while Dima told me all this in a whisper, because his daughter was sleeping in the room. Then we went back to the kitchen, and I went out onto the balcony for a smoke, and he came for company. We leaned our elbows on the iron rails saying nothing. This exchange of news for some reason had drained us.

"Dima, do you get much holiday?"

"Usually twenty-four working days. Well, I can take extra time off."

"Maybe you'll head out with me when I go back? For a month? We can go hunting."

Dima looked, looked down at the street lamp, then spoke:

"Actually that's just what I'd wanted to do, I'd been getting ready since winter, since I got your letter. I even bought a video camera for it. But now things have changed, I'm not sure. I guess I'll have to go to the dacha. Let's talk about it later. To be honest, I'm already dropping off. Let's leave it till the weekend."

"But what's changed? Change it back again."

"Change it back. Well, Natasha is . . . Oh, look, let's talk about it later."

In the kitchen Natasha was clearing away the teacups.

— — —

Before the weekend I decided to do those few things left over from my ruined plan. I submitted the documents for purchasing the carbine, then I went to take a parcel to some distant relatives of Kolya's.

In Biysk Kolya had given me a packet for them with golden root, pine nuts—in short, the usual collection of souvenirs from Siberia. He said, "Phone them up, meet them, and hand it over to them. Tell them I haven't forgotten about them." It was some aunt of his, or was it an aunt of his wife's, to tell the truth I never quite worked it out, because I didn't see this aunt, rather I saw the daughter of the aunt and the daughter's daughter, Olka.

She came to the phone when I rang. Her voice was fresh, I liked it. I said to her, "Maybe we can meet somewhere in the metro?" And she answered, "No, no, come and visit us, tell us all the news." I had to travel to the other side of the world, to Yuzhnoe Butovo.

The door opened, and the first thing I saw was how she flung her hair aside so as to see better. But fling it or not, it bounces back like little springs, into her smile, into her eyes, so again she shakes her head, then holds her hair back with her hand. That was probably the first time in my life I peeped out of my mirror bubble, because I saw nothing but hair and a smile. As they say, nothing personal—just these unruly dark springs and a smile. The door closed, she squatted to find me some slippers, then again flung her hair away to keep it from bothering her—this time not to the side, but straight back, across her forehead, then she broke into laughter, grabbed a clip from the cabinet, and, at last, she clipped it back.

Later, when going over it all again slowly, I realized that with her smile and her sinuous back in that black sweater she reminded me straightaway of a small predator, something like an ermine, if only ermines were dark. The winter before last, I had a little ermine living with me, cleaned out all the mice for me better than a cat—you could hardly keep up with him, even. And here was the same—nothing but movement, Khachaturian's saber dance.

A second ago she had clipped back her hair, now she grabbed a white hair bow, no, not a bow, some kind of hair band, she lifted her arms and made a ponytail, and once again I fell back into my bubble, because her sweater was stretching across her bust. Here the daughter of the aunt came in, I mean the girl's mother, and I began passing on Kolya's greetings and declining coffee. Then we drank coffee with cake.

"Oh, I thought you'd gone there to avoid the army," the mother said.

"No, I just wanted to see the place, I went there and liked it. Almost everyone working there is from the big cities—from . . ."

"Ilyusha, have you been to university? Oh, please go on eating, I'm just curious." She stood behind me chopping meat. "So, your mother lives in the center of Moscow. And do you have a father?"

"My father died in '92."

"What of?"

"Mama, let the man drink his coffee in peace." Olka sat opposite me on the sofa, jerking her leg, showing that her mother's curiosity irritated her.

"Well I'm doing nothing to stop him. Ilyusha, do please drink your coffee, I'm just asking because it's fascinating—a Muscovite, and all of a sudden he ups and leaves for the forest. Are you planning on returning to Moscow soon?"

If you're going to examine me in such depth on all of this, then why go and give me cake and coffee? As soon as I've put my fork in my mouth, you blurt out a new question. And the interesting thing was she asked almost nothing about Kolya, about her own relative— she was only interested in me.

A remarkable mother. She struck me as simply remarkable—she shuffled in her slippers behind my back, she sat down at the table, listened to my answers, staring at my hair or throwing a glance at my shirt and trousers, not looking me in the eye, weighing things up, working them out, remembering about something, nodding, getting up again and rearranging the teacups on the table. She seemed a wonderful lady, because Olka was with me, we were together, while her mother was apart from us. I realized that straightaway, well you can only make faces like that when your mother can't see them, but I could see them, I was privy to them. The mother was simply the backdrop to the event.

Olka and I barely talked, merely shot glances at each other conspiratorially, I went straight for my stupid moustache, began twisting and smoothing it. Then I twiddled the teaspoon in my fingers, turned round to the mother, politely stared at her stiff back, and gave answers as briefly but satisfactorily as possible, turned back, glanced, smiled, then shook the crumbs from my lap, again meeting eyes.

"Olya. Your German."

"Yes, okay, I'll get ready," and Olka left the kitchen.

I finished off the cake and for a good ten minutes fluent answers continuously came out of my mouth. During this time Olka got changed, and we walked to the metro, even traveling two stops together. Then she got out, she needed to go to her German lesson, and I went home.

The next day toward evening I phoned her.

— — —

The sun was bright, it was windy and there was an enormous number of sparrows. We met outside Plekhanov Institute, where she was studying in her third year.

"Well, if you like, we can go to Park Pobedy. I've been there with a friend."

"Okay. To the park."

"No, it has this museum with panoramic models, and it's not cold. There are benches to sit on. Really, it's nice there."

"Yeah, whatever. Oh how funny you looked when you didn't recognize me. First you stuck out your jaw when I jumped out in front of you. Did you get a fright?"

"My jaw? I didn't stick anything out. No, it's just I really didn't recognize you, I certainly wasn't expecting you in a suit. It didn't connect. Why did you shave off your moustache?"

"Oh, it was a stupid moustache. I'd been meaning to shave it off anyway."

"Well you shouldn't have. Let's walk over there, on that side. Over here all those Caucasians are standing about."

"What Caucasians? But it's sunny on this side. Oh, you mean them? What, are you frightened of them? When you're with me? There's no war here."

"Listen, I can't stand them, really. You just have no idea what it's like, you'd understand if you were a girl. The way they look at you—it's disgusting."

"I'd look at you like that too, if I didn't feel shy."

"Yuck! You would never look at me that way. You just have no idea. It's a good thing I'm a brunette, they aren't as interested in brunettes."

"Well, I like it. I mean I like the color of your hair. It looks lovely."

"Ah, but you're not one of them, thank God."

"Olka, come on, let's walk in the sun, really, it's cold over there. But tell me, I didn't quite get it, where did you go on the weekend when you visited your parents, doesn't your mom live with you?"

"No, my parents live in Stupino. Me and my sister are in Moscow, Mama comes over when she's not on call. She cooks for us and all that. And the weekends I spend with them, at the dacha. When you came, my sister was out, you didn't see her."

"You've got a dacha in Stupino as well?"

"Uh huh. It's just Papa doesn't like going into Moscow, so I go out to see him."

"I see. Listen, it's a hell of a way to Stupino, about two hours, I think. I could come with you for company next time, in fact I have nothing to do this weekend. I could plant some potatoes or something for you there."

"No. Don't take offense, but Papa likes the family to be together at the dacha, he misses us. He wants to spend as much time as possible with us. Anyway I usually travel there with my sister Lenka, so there's no need for company."

"Put your arm round mine, it's warmer like that."

"Uh huh."

We traveled on the metro to Kutuzovskaya, walked through a windy area with fountains, and began looking at the battle models. I pretended to be interested, while she didn't even pretend. Soon we found a bench near some kind of ficus tree, or maybe it was a palm—I don't know exactly what it is called. That was where I kissed her.

Her lips were like after a frost—dry and hot, as if a little inflamed. We were still measuring each other up, we were hurrying, and getting in each other's way. We didn't exactly find pleasure, rather we were demonstrating our capabilities, exaggerating and showing off. But we were both lovesick. I in my taiga, and she in her Moscow, apparently. She was constantly following the movements of my hands. She caught her breath, looking into my eyes or gazing somewhere into my hair, remembering about something. For some reason she tried to catch my mouth with hers. Well, that's all right, usually the first time is a bit clumsy.

The ficus was so scraggy that it drew the attention of passersby to our caresses more than it hid us from spectators.

And the next few meetings took place in equally innocuous places. In warm weather it was benches on boulevards, once when it was cold we went to the cinema. She didn't want to come back to my place.

Somehow we didn't manage to meet often.

"Off to your German lesson again?"

"No, I have German on Tuesdays and Thursdays. Tomorrow is body shaping. Well, what's wrong? You want me to be beautiful. Then I need to sweat in a hall."

"Yes . . ."

"But tomorrow you can walk me home from the institute, we'll eat, and then you can take me to body shaping. Don't get upset, chin up. If you want me to be clever and beautiful, you've got to be patient. We both need to be a bit patient. Parting is the fire . . . it's the wind that fans the fires of love. There."

"Have you fallen in love?"

"You've fallen in love yourself."

"I'm in love, I won't deny it."

Here she noticed a little stain on her sleeve, again tangled wires fell onto her face. She softened a little, but then quickly raised her head.

"When? Give the correct answer."

"As soon as I saw you, I fell in love."

"Well done, you're not slow. Only, you know, let's talk about that another time. Not on an empty stomach. Come on, we'll buy some pies at the metro."

— — —

I spent the greater part of my time at Dima's. During the week, while he was at work I sat at his computer and played Civilization. Drank tea with Natasha in the kitchen. On weekends Dima and I took his daughter for walks to the Crimean Embankment or sat in Repin Square with beer, watching his daughter on the swings.

"Natasha won't let you?"

"No, it's not that she won't let me go, it's just she's been ill lately."

"What's wrong?"

"Oh, the works. She'll get a headache, or it'll be some internal problem, or depression. If I go, it would mean leaving her on her own."

"She spends her whole time indoors on her own as it is. And you wouldn't be leaving her alone, she'd have your parents."

"That would be even worse."

"Dima, if you don't come and you smother your great desire, then you've had it. You'll start getting ill yourself, understand?"

"Oh, I've already started. Natasha took me along to be diagnosed. You know what they found? Softening of the spinal column."

"Do people get that?"

"They do. And a whole load of other stuff too."

"But how did they identify it?"

"By the eyes. They examine the retina, is it the retina or . . . well, anyway, the whole eye is looked at on a computer and they diagnose it."

"Was it a lady doctor?"

Dima nodded his head, and we carried on watching the child, listening to the creak of the swing. She had been on the swing for half an hour without a break, another kid was standing nearby, waiting his turn.

"Come off now, love. Let the little boy have a turn too."

The little girl didn't answer and she started to swing even harder.

"Another thing, I'm not meant to drink beer. Oh, I'm just whining."

Dima suddenly set the bottle on the ground, went up to the swing, and stopped it.

"Right, get off," but the girl carried on swinging her head back even harder, and then turning her body downward, squeezing her legs. She was trying to rock the immobile swing, not looking at Papa. "Now you listen to me, get off."

Dima stood and looked at her with a scowl. Then he forcibly removed her, and it all ended in tears.

— — —

Next Tuesday I took Olka to her German lesson. It was warm. We had not been late to a single language class or body shaping session in the entire two weeks. Usually I came to the institute for Olka, then we ate at her place, sat there for a while, went to classes, and then I would leave.

Usually her elder sister, Lenka, was at home, she'd disappear to her room as soon as we arrived, and she'd sit there without a sound. The sisters looked utterly different—Lenka's eyes were prominent, light, and motionless, her head moved somehow in unison with her body, and Lenka had too perfect a posture, which marred her to no end. I secretly named her "homo erectus." With a girl like that you can travel fearlessly to the roughest district, and nobody will harass you.

At first I was put out by the presence of the quiet person on the other side of the wall.

"She won't come in," Olka said to me and drew my head near with her hands. "She's busy reading."

This explanation did little to reassure me, but after a while I got used to it. Our long silence, the creak of the sofa, the broken whispers were so expressive that Lenka could not have failed to notice them. The thought even entered my mind a few times that she enjoyed sitting like that almost next to us, listening to us kissing. I probably didn't get used to it so much as simply resigned myself somewhat. I persuaded myself to be patient.

Oh forget Lenka. We walked to German lessons along a street filled with spring, Olka pressed close to me and told me how in the winter some dumb cop had mistaken her for someone from the Caucasus and demanded her passport. Olka, clearly, had been shaken to the depths of her being.

"No, well, tell me, in what way am I remotely like them?"

"Maybe it was his way of trying to pick you up?"

"Oh what does it matter, I couldn't care less what he had in mind. If they have to deal with gangsters or Caucasians, they should go and deal with them, but they should leave normal people alone."

"Listen, snubby-nose, you're a racist then? What do people from the Caucasus have to do with this?"

"Oh you haven't a clue in your forestry post. Ask any normal person, and he'll tell you what they have to do with it. Anyway, noodle-head, never argue with a beautiful woman."

I would have argued too, but Olka had a way of ending the conversation so that all desire to oppose her fell away. She would go and rub her cheek against my shoulder, and it was all over. Indeed, she had taken a test the day before on personnel management. She was good at that.

Then we stopped and watched a stray dog lying on the lawn gnawing a big bone. We watched it holding the knuckle with its front paws and half closing its eyes as it worked its back teeth. The dog beamed pleasure, the naked bone rolling in the dirt tasted sweet. Nearby on the ground walked a crow and it looked at the dog with one eye, then the other. We gazed long, not thinking of anything, then we turned to each other. Olka lifted her head, stood on her tiptoes, and half closed her eyes. An old lady passing with a trolley bag laughed. We too laughed, I kissed Olka on her happy eyes, and we walked on, very fast, almost running.

"What fools we are, huh?" said Olka happily.

We ran into the sonorous empty building of some secondary school where she had her lessons, walked past the room where her lessons were held, and went one floor higher up the stairs, stopping on the steps. She finally gave up following my hands and sat on my knee. Her skirt rode up. We kissed until we were startled by one of the teachers, and Olka stared at his back with clouded, almost senseless eyes as he walked away.

"Come to my place tomorrow," I said.

"Yes," Olka jolted, turning round as though suddenly remembering me.

— — —

Dima and I fell more and more silent with each other. Sometimes I even left their place, after my game of Civilization, without even waiting for him to come home from work. Natasha had nothing against my visits, she was bored, and we recalled various acquaintances, she told me about how hard it was to get along with their relatives. I kept up the conversation, quietly building cities and waging wars with neighboring states. Only I didn't do too well, my civilizations came out underdeveloped.

That day I didn't go round to their place at all. I just languished the whole day, scarcely lasting till the time when I could go and get Olka, then at last I went for her. I could think of nothing else. We came back to my place. She acted much more calmly than I did, she was just calm and that was it. She looked round the room, glanced through the windows to the yard, she refused some wine and we started to kiss.

"Only I wanted to tell you, you know what? I've firmly decided only to screw when I'm married. Sex is for a husband and wife, do you understand?"

"No. Sex is a relationship between men and women."

"Well, anyway, you've understood me. I want to give my husband a present. We'll get undressed, but there'll be no pants taken off."

"Why?"

"Sweetie, don't argue. A little drop could get on me by accident, and then that would be it."

I didn't bother arguing, we lay on the couch and caressed. The whole time I was trying to remember what you call this kind of dry-style sex. I'd read about it in a magazine, these days the youngsters do it all the time. I looked at her supple back, touched the vertebrae with my fingers. It was some English word, I could only remember that it ended with "ing." *Spinning* and *kidnapping*—that was all I could come up with. This strange pair stubbornly spun in my head, mutating into a chant, like the kind of ditty you get often in the winter, on the long, hard treks in the taiga. You just march across the frozen, snow-covered river, you ski, watching the skis advance one at a time in the snow, and rhythmically repeat to yourself, "Spin-ning-and-kid-nap-ping, spin-ning-and-kid-nap-ping." These chants for some reason help, you focus your entire attention on them, your whole mind tenses in its effort not to lose the rhythm of the non-sensical words, your brain works at full steam, it no longer obeys you, like a child absorbed in its game. You don't notice the miles you've gone, you forget that the straps of the rucksack are digging into your numbed shoulders, that your gullet is parched. At times, beneath your skis, a piece of ice breaks off and is carried away in a black current, the rush of the water becomes clearer, your body petrifies somewhat. You prod a stick out ahead, to the side, cautiously move away from the danger spot, but in your head there continues the steady ticking of words.

Mama rang the doorbell, I put on my jeans, opened the door, and asked her to take the dog for a walk.

"What's going on?" Mama's voice turned somewhat officious.

"Olya's here, give us fifteen minutes, please."

"What for?"

"What do you think? To get dressed," I handed her the lead and closed the door. There's body shaping and peeling too. I have no idea what peeling is. Olka was already doing up the zipper of her skirt, and her face was unhappy.

"Come on, what are you waiting for? I don't want to meet your mother. How excruciatingly shameful, my God."

"What's shameful?"

"You don't realize?"

"She just came home earlier than she should have. How was I to know? She always comes back at six on the dot." I sat on the sofa and began putting on a sock. "Olka, what do you call it when you caress like that but you don't actually put it inside? It's not peeling, is it?"

Olka fell angry.

"If you can't guarantee a safe environment, then why bother inviting me round in the first place?"

Yes, why, indeed? Homo erectus had helped me to restrain myself, sitting in the room next door with her book, in other words, there the situation had restrained me, whereas here I had to restrain myself.

Olka did not stay angry for long. When we walked along the quay in the direction of Novokuznetskaya, she had already forgotten about it and she even gave me a kiss. She didn't come back to my place again, well I didn't insist on it, as there was no point—why bother wasting time on the journey? I was waiting for some point to emerge, and meanwhile we could quite safely torment each other in the kitchen in Yuzhnoe Butovo. Which is what we did.

— — —

The bird cherry blossomed, and probably because of that it became quite warm. I didn't notice at first, but then all of a sudden I noticed. Summer had arrived. I continued to accompany her and meet her as before—her lessons at the institute had finished, but there were still exams, body shaping, German, and she decided to take up driving lessons. She had decided to pass her driving test.

We went to sign her up for lessons. Then we sat on a bench near Chistye Prudy and I said, "Olka, I've been given my carbine permit."

"Congratulations. Don't you feel sorry for those little hares or whatever it is you shoot at? I feel sorry for them, but for some reason I love meat. Shame it's bad for you, though. If you want, I can cook you meat the way I make it for Papa? Do you want some meat, you predator?"

"Well, what I meant was that in a couple of weeks I'll have to go."

We had somehow not spoken about the fact that I would be leaving. Everything had passed quietly in its own way, May had been cold, and my departure had seemed a long way off. Whereas now you could count on one hand the number of meetings we had left. To be honest, I was rather at a loss over this.

"I don't agree." Olka did not look at all lost.

"You don't agree with what?"

"I don't agree that you should go. Because I will miss you." She made herself more comfortable on my lap, carefully studying a passing couple and again she turned to me. "Well, can't you take another two weeks of unpaid leave somehow or other?"

"Oh as it is I've used up my leave, actually the men are clocking me in, they know that you have to wait a long time for a permit."

"Well, all right. But when will you be back?"

What questions she asked. I was frightened of even beginning to think of this. I had got sucked into this so gradually that I hadn't even noticed. When I had gone to their place that first time, it had simply been pleasant to sit and exchange winks with a lively girl. It is nice spending time in an apartment where women live—you go into the bathroom, there are so many bottles of shampoos and gels and whatnot. I had noticed at the time that the toilet seat wouldn't stay in an upright position, it kept falling—clearly there were no men in the place.

Then one thing led to another—we talked, then we kissed, then came flowers, gifts, and somehow things took their own course. If you had asked me when I was traveling to Moscow on the train— well, that was the last thing I'd dreamt of. I had wanted to do things in a fast and modern style, no flowers, no moonlit walks and kisses. And I'd wanted to leave easily and with a clean conscience.

Well at first I didn't even get a proper look at her. Then gradually I began studying her. It was only under the ficus that her dry lips, the color of her eyes—sort of golden—had sunk in. Her coat, her hair. Afterward, I think it was the next time, I saw her nails, so long, manicured, she told me how she paints them even on the inside, I think, with some special pencil. Only you have to spend lots of time on all this beauty, spare no effort. She said, for example, that the best thing for your hair is not a curling iron but curlers, she sleeps in them. But it's really uncomfortable to sleep in them. Nobody does that anymore, but curlers won't damage your hair. In a word, I received a heap of unwanted knowledge, but I saw her hairdo, rather I noticed how her hair had been curled.

Then I observed how small Olka becomes when she curls up and how slender and long she is when she lies on her stomach and, leaning on her elbows, takes a lock of her hair and examines it. Checks to see whether the ends are split. Observed her vertebrae, oh I observed just about everything. I could only remember my ex-wife that well, yes and the bulk of that was already fading from memory.

"Listen, maybe you won't go to Stupino this weekend? You'll have time to go after I leave. You said yourself that Stupino doesn't interest you."

"That's right, I don't like it. The people there are all so simple, I can't bear it."

"Simple?"

"They're as simple as Simon. Criminally simple."

"Meaning you and I are sophisticated?"

"If you were simple, I wouldn't have fallen in love with you. You just find it hard to understand, because you're a Muscovite. Over in your reserve . . . oh never mind. But tell me, do you love me?"

"Yes, I love you."

"Then everything will work itself out. Don't you worry, sweetie, I'm worrying enough as it is. The thing is I know you must never cry in front of men. Never be ill. Men like jolly, healthy women without problems. With big boobs."

"No, I like boobs like yours."

"So mine are small, then?"

"No."

"Sweetie, you're slow. And primitive, because your compliments are uncouth. Okay, let's go."

— — —

Dima sniffed, took a big breath, pursing his lips, he exhaled, then came out with:

"Look, it's definite, I can't come."

"What, you can't boost your health with bracing air, you can't go hunting, eat deer's liver roasted on the campfire to your heart's content, wake up in the morning and lift your head from the saddle serving as your pillow to see the sun rising over the mountains? You can't firm up your backbone, film yourself at the top of the world with your new camera, is that what you're trying to say?"

"Listen, don't rub salt in it. Going out of your way to tempt me— sunrises, my backbone . . . What, you think I don't want to go?" Dima spoke quietly, expressionlessly.

"No you don't, otherwise you'd just up and go. If you really wanted to, you'd go. Because look, what if I leave my job there soon? That'd be it, even if you wanted to, you couldn't come then. Who would invite you, who would give you a horse, a rifle, who'd show you the top of the world?"

"Are you planning on leaving your job?"

"Well, planning or not, what if it happens?"

"Then it would mean I'd never be able to go. Or I could only go after croaking from some incurable disease. Yeah, then I could fly over the top of the world, see how marvelous it is there. Hee hee."

"You're in a jolly mood," I said.

In the evenings, when he came home from work, Dima would sit rather oddly—as if something really had softened in his spine. That's how a drunkard sits—however you sit him, prop him up against the wall, his body will just stay like that, if it doesn't fall. He talks to me, his head barely stirring, only his lips move, and his hand bringing the cup of tea to his mouth. An office worker, in his white shirt and tie.

"Look, after you sent me that letter, I went and chose a video camera, I was still hoping for something. Even decided to buy one of the more expensive models. I thought that you'd come . . . whether I went with you to the mountains or not wasn't even the point. I just thought that you'd come, and *bam!* Something would change. It even became easier to go to work. Really."

I felt uncomfortable when he started telling me this. Sat there in silence, not knowing what to say. And Dima continued:

"Yeah, isn't it interesting—look, soon I'll be turning thirty, in three years I'll be thirty, but here I am waiting about like a teenage girl. What the hell it is I'm waiting for I haven't a clue. I feel like life is stupid, but I can't understand why. Well, when you arrived, at first I was really happy, then suddenly I realized that nothing would change, it would all stay the same. And then I felt bloody awful, when you told me yesterday that you're going back soon."

"Well, of course you got carried away here. I'm not some savior who arrives and—*bam!*"

"Oh there's no need to explain. It's just I'm telling you—I really won't be able to come. It's not even that Natasha is ill or whatever. Of course she could manage without me, and my parents would help.

It's just, you understand, she gets lonesome. At least I've got the other guys at work, I'm off here and there, to someone or other's birthday, I've gone a couple of times on business trips to Serpukhov. It's not that far, but all the same. While she sits there on her own, doesn't see anyone, there's just the child, the cooking, the television. This way I can at least spend my holiday together with her at the dacha. She gets lonesome."

"Look, of course, I don't want to stick my nose into your family problems, but the child could always be sent to kindergarten, and she could get a job."

"Do you think I haven't told her that? You're right, better not to get involved in this. The thing is I just wouldn't enjoy it there. Like you said, I'd lift my head from the saddle, take a look at the beauty, and then I'd remember that she's sitting back home with her in-laws, all lonesome. Then I'd come back and get all excited telling her about it, right? And Natasha would sit there feeling envious. She'd say, 'While you were having a good time, I was ill and suffering.'"

"You're just thinking up excuses, Dima. You need to pull yourself together and everything will change for the better. You just need to make a firm decision."

"Well, I have made my decision. So you go ahead and eat up that fresh liver on my behalf, relish it."

— — —

I bought a carbine, quite cheap, but a good one—a Mosin. Dima and I examined it in the evening in my kitchen, opened the bolt, loaded and unloaded it a few times. Now I had only to register it quickly— and I'd be back on the road. In about ten days.

It was a shame about Dima's decision. If there had been the two of us, it would have made leaving Olka easier, but as it was I couldn't quite imagine how I was going to part from her. I couldn't imagine it at all. Dima and I could have left together, chatted, planned our expedition, got out at the stations and bought beer. Then I'd have introduced him to our guys, to Kolya, celebrated the purchase of the new carbine, boozed it up for a couple of days, and then left for the taiga.

Whereas here could you really call it boozing—we could have a small glass of vodka each in the kitchen, but tomorrow he had to go to work.

The next day Olka and I quarreled slightly for the first time. She had been nervous for the past few days, scrutinizing me, pondering something, stroking my face.

She came with me to the police station to register my weapon, and we sat together in the corridor while I waited my turn. Men stood about, throwing glances now and then at Olka, who sat with her knees tightly shut. They were discussing which type of optics would go best on the Tiger. It turned out that not all sights would stand up to cartridges as powerful as the Tiger's and those for my carbine, in many of the sights something inside would jolt from the recoil. I was listening hard, but couldn't make sense of which was best.

Then I went into the inspector's office, sat there while she stayed in the corridor. Then we left for body shaping.

"Couldn't you have been any quicker, huh, sweetie? There I was, sitting among those hunters. Oh, I ought to drag you along for company to some women's clinic, you'd get an earful there. I read every single poster. Stuff like: 'How to field strip the hunting carbine Wild Boar.' Such a fascinating poster."

"I was as fast as I could."

"You couldn't have gone there on your own, without me? While I was at my lessons, for instance. You didn't think to, right, sweetie?" Olka's voice for some reason was almost breaking.

Then she fell silent and walked with her nose up in the air, my favorite, terribly beautiful little nose. I admired it until she threw me a quick glance and I noticed the tears in her eyes. They spilled out onto her lower eyelids and trembled as she walked, but didn't run down her painted lashes.

"Hey? Hey, you're really upset?"

Olka walked on without answering, and carried her tears so they wouldn't fall in black streams down her face. On her tense neck a sinew quivered. Yes, very independent and proud she is. In a sophisticated manner, just the way she likes. She might have explained just what it was that had distressed her so. I walked too, feeling like a complete idiot. *Can't see that I've done anything wrong, but she won't even talk to me.*

"You don't want to speak? Olka. Hey, what's wrong? We came here so we wouldn't lose any time, so we could be together a little longer. I'll be leaving very soon."

She walks, placing her neat little legs accurately, while I trot after her like Piglet.

"Olka, listen, after all, if it wasn't for all your endless Stupino, body shaping, driving, we could have gone on longer walks, done anything you wanted. You are so awfully busy all the time, but I couldn't go to the cops just once, is that it? Great."

She doesn't answer.

Then I went and told her what I thought about all this. That I was meekly running about after her, that it was exhausting. She never read in her books that we—that is to say, men—don't always enjoy it when women are too businesslike? I bet she hadn't. And here I said something totally unexpected, that I had even decided to leave my forestry job, to marry her, that I had decided on all this, but she couldn't even sit and wait five minutes for me. I said it and was astonished. Well, all that was left was to add that apparently we loved each other rather differently, seeing as I was ready for such sacrifices while she cried over some hunting posters.

There was no sign that she had heard me. But later, while we walked to the metro, somehow everything gradually settled down. Probably we were too surprised—I by what I'd said, she by what she'd heard. And just before body shaping, she managed to tell me that something strange had suddenly come over her simply because in the morning that asshole had offended her. And that I shouldn't be upset.

"What asshole?"

"The driving instructor. Extraordinary jerk, the wretch. If I haven't quite got the hang of the gears, that's no reason to swear at me. Then when my two hours are up, he throws me out right in the middle of the street—'Go on, your time is up!' And it was just beginning to rain. He did it on purpose."

"But why didn't you tell me earlier? I would have understood then."

"Men don't like it when women complain. I'm joking, sweetie, I'm joking. It's just, you know, it makes me mad . . . You find it hard to understand, like . . . Look, you ask me why I need all this—German, body shaping . . . Do you think I enjoy it? Well I don't. But you have to understand, better to spend my time and energy now, then later I'll be able to make my own choices."

"What choices?"

"Where to live, what to do, who can shout at me, who can't, whom to love, whom not to love, everything. What I'm doing now will buy me what I want. If I want to drive a car, then at least all those dark-assed Caucasians won't ogle me so much in the metro. And that wretch won't be able to shout his swear words at me."

"And what will stop him? He'll still swear at you if he wants to."

"No, no. He won't be able to."

"Well, okay. I understand. It's just that I'm a bit offended with you myself, because I thought that for the sake of the one you love, you could miss a few lessons. At least put off your driving lessons for a little while."

"But then it will be too late. I need to do everything before time runs out. You know after all, love comes and goes, but you'll always need food. All right, all right, sweetie, don't be so serious. Kiss me here, and here, right, I'm off. Auf Wiedersehen!"

— — —

I told her that I would return in six months, no more, and that I'd return, of course, for good.

The last few days passed aimlessly. But in the end she didn't go to Stupino. And she didn't accompany me to the station either, because crying in the station, in the middle of all those ladies with their bags, is just stupid. And she couldn't not cry.

After I picked up my ticket, I started getting predeparture fever. This fever is a pleasant feeling, so long as you're not leaving someone behind with sobbed-out eyes and puffy lips. But if you are leaving someone behind, you start getting jerky, then everything just merges into a meaningless jumble—buying the cartridges, the last visits to classes, the bouquet of roses, some little box that I'm not meant to open until I'm back in my forestry reserve, when I'm missing her for real. And all the same you don't have time to get everything done.

On the last evening Mama fried chicken for the road and wrapped up the pieces in foil. Dima watched me packing my things into my rucksack, he sat on a chair and joked. He had a jolly time poking fun at me and my rucksack. But I was already on the road, on my way.

In the morning it was cool, I walked to the metro and we met at a crossroads in the rain, running straight under an arch. Olka was all disheveled, with puffy eyelids, she was saying whatever came into her head, laughing and crying. I thought that departing in the rain was a good omen.

Olka took my hand and put it under her sweater.

"What time did you need to get up to make it here on time?"

"Oh I always get up early. It is barely drizzling, how did I get so wet? Sweetie, tell me, aren't I clever for coming here, huh? Give me some praise. Will you miss me? Only don't lie. Men always get pleasure from deceiving beautiful women, huh? Am I beautiful?"

"Yes. Only you're all cried out. Think of your poor eyes."

She had confessed only two days before that she'd recently had an operation at the Fyodorov clinic. Her vision had apparently improved from minus eight to minus three, but it remained to be seen how things would go. She must have let it slip out by mistake. I was holding out my arms while she stood on the balustrade in some park and said, "Come on, jump over to me." But she said that she couldn't, that something might tear.

As a man I can say for sure that it didn't make me like her less. Although men don't like it when women are ill. On the contrary, I wanted to look after her, so that her wonderful golden eyes—I remembered since that time on the bench under the ficus that they were golden—would not have to suffer anymore. I gazed into them, looking for some scar or trace, but found none. Just golden eyes, Olka's eyes, with their sparkle, with their serious expression, with their coquettishness or tears. Now they were red, and I kissed them again and again.

"Is it time already?" Olka looked awfully unhappy. All her well-groomed, confident, businesslike manner disappeared. There clung to me just a crying woman who was afraid and who felt down. She held my palm to her hardened breast, she was trembling lightly, I think. She was almost ugly.

"Yes, it's time to go. Well, no big deal, we always were short of time. We mustn't be late. I'm joking."

"Are you resentful?" she looked into my eyes as hard as she could. "Why? You know that I only do all this because I have no choice. It's not me, it just needs to be done. But now, darling, listen, now I shall be doing it for the two of us. I shall try my very best. You know, I'm going to start sleeping less. Darling!"

"Yes, Olenyonok."

And then she was left in the arch, while I ran home for my rucksack, then—to the station.

I thought that I had been left on my own, but in the end I was seen off. Dima unexpectedly appeared at the train under a black umbrella, with a briefcase and wearing a tie.

"I managed to take half an hour off—our office isn't far from here, at Krasnye Vorota."

We stood together, I smoked a cigarette, then we shook hands and I went to my place. Dima shaded his eyes with his palm and glanced through the glass into the compartment.

— — —

On the train I remembered Olka, thought about how I would get to the forestry reserve and go shooting with my new carbine, how in the autumn I was sure to catch a stag and I'd bring the antlers to Moscow. When I returned.

I thought about how love forces a person to climb out of his mirror bubble and look at the world without any ulterior motives, just look and see. Otherwise it would be terrible, otherwise we would just hang there in space, in our bubbles, and not even see each other. These bubbles were like balls on a Christmas tree, which are, as it happens, mirrored on the inside, and whoever was sitting inside didn't even realize that outside there was a celebration. I lolled on my bunk, and it felt like I had discovered something new. I liked the analogy with the Christmas tree decorations. I also remembered a line from Kolya's Khayyam: A man is like the world in a mirror—

many-faceted. Although, no, it must be the other way round—the world is in the mirror . . . Well, whatever, the idea of the balls was good, anyway.

I had climbed out of mine and seen Olka. It was so wondrous, it was like Dima said—*bam!*, something's happened. No, of course, the shards of the bubble are still there—when I said I'd marry her, I immediately thought perhaps—seeing as we were nearly man and wife—we could give each other our gifts in advance. But it turned out that advance purchase wasn't allowed.

All the same, what a pity that I would have to leave before the New Year—I couldn't go sable hunting in February. Or maybe I could go and leave straight after? I tried to imagine how I would occupy myself all of a sudden in Moscow. Olka said that we'd sort out a job, it just needed a woman's hand. I decided to think about it later, there was plenty of time ahead: almost half the summer, then the festive Siberian autumn, the bellow of the elk, then the squirrel hunt, the bright sun on the fresh snow.

Three days later I arrived in Gorno-Altaisk, got a ticket for the morning bus to our district and went to stay the night at the elderly couple's in the private sector where I had often stopped on the road. In the evening I paced down the streets of the little Siberian town and looked at the blue foothills rising to the south. I felt strong and renewed.

From the telephone exchange I called Moscow. Then I went out onto the street, had a smoke, and reflected that I had barely known what to say. I heard Olka's voice, and answered something. That's to say I told her what I was expected to, but couldn't adequately explain what I was feeling now. Oh she probably wouldn't really have understood. I decided to try and describe it in a letter. I'd start writing when I arrived.

— — —

That day the elderly couple had heated the bathhouse. I drank tea with them, then took a clean shirt from my rucksack and went to wash off the dirt from the road. I sat in the steam room and sweated. When I came outside, dusk was already falling. I threw a towel over my shoulder, stood and breathed the cool dry air. On the neighboring street a motorcycle rumbled past, and again it was quiet. This silence, especially after Moscow, always gives me a buzz.

On the bench nearby, Irka—the elderly couple's niece—settled herself down and nibbled pine nuts. She looked at me and smiled, then said, "Good bath." A girl of about eighteen, pretty-looking. I saw her last year, but somehow must have failed to notice her. Or she had blossomed.

"Where've you been, then?"

"Oh, just walking."

Why had I not met her on the outward journey? She had time to spare—buckets of it—she could wander about, without lessons, without body shaping, but what a figure. Her frock was breezy and short. She sat and nibbled nuts, staring with brazen eyes.

"How's life? Don't you get bored here?" Ask Olka such a question and she'll straightaway decide you're "simple." While here—it's all right, you need to make small talk about something. What a marvelous dusk, and when you have a girl sitting nearby—everything is perfect. You need to say something, or she'll tire of you and leave.

"Yeah, I get bored," she smiled even more. Then she called Tom over, a huge amiable Newfoundland who dug about in the coal pile in the middle of the yard, hid something, and buried it with his nose. She put her hand on his head. "Tomka, Tomka, are we bored here, huh?"

Irka stroked the dog. I put on my shirt, smoked, and looked at her. Then I too squatted down to stroke Tomka, in order to get closer to Irka's legs.

"Tomka, why do you have such a big head?" I began shaking the dog's ears. He decided that a game had begun, put his front paws on my shoulders, knocked me over, and began licking my face. I somehow extricated myself from under the salivating fool.

"What have you done, you idiot?"

My shirt was all covered in coal. Irka laughed resonantly while Tomka with an expression of readiness on his face spun his head toward her, toward me, and wagged his tail. He was happy that we were paying him attention.

Irka laughed, throwing her face forward. She arched a bit and leaned back on her arms. She glanced at me, then again I saw her neck and white teeth.

"Why are you laughing? Funny, is it? You were bored before, but you've livened up now." I studied her more closely, drew near her, took her by the shoulders, and asked again, this time mechanically:

"Why are you laughing, Irka? Why are you laughing? Come to me."

BREGOVICH'S
SIXTH JOURNEY

OLEG ZOBERN
Translated by Keith Gessen

IT'S FEBRUARY, late at night, in a little village outside Moscow called Lestvino. My headlights are shining on Ivan Denisovich. I've boiled him a pot of *pelmeni*. Sensing the presence of food, he flings himself happily inside his little doghouse, rattles his chain, and jumps back out again. His eyes are lit with a hungry green flame.

I keep the engine running so the battery doesn't die; there's no one around to steal the car anyway. Under the gaze of my headlights I walk toward Ivan Denisovich with my pot of *pelmeni*. Steam rolls off them in the cold and before I reach him I set the pot in the snow—let it cool down a little.

Ivan Denisovich's master, my neighbor Andryukha, doesn't feed him very often. He never lets him inside the house, even when it's cold, even when it's very cold. And he always keeps him on his chain, because Ivan Denisovich might run away.

He's straining toward my pot, snapping his little jaw. The *pelmeni* cool down finally and I bring him the pot. Ivan Denisovich holds it with his paws and gobbles them down. Once in a while he takes a break and looks up gratefully at me.

My neighbor named him Mukhtar, after the famous crime-sniffing dog from the movies, an un-Russian, slant-eyed name. One time I thought I saw barbed wire strung around his doghouse, with little guard towers standing around it. That would make the space between the house and the shed, where Ivan Denisovich's doghouse sits, into a little one-dog prison camp.

And so I started calling Ivan Denisovich Ivan Denisovich, in honor of the famous prisoner. He answers to that now.

This winter I've been feeding him regularly. Almost every weekend I boil him *pelmeni*, macaroni; sometimes I spoil him with fish. Ivan Denisovich has grown fond of me.

I almost never see his owner because I arrive from Moscow late on Friday or Saturday night—times when Andryukha, a drinking man, is sleeping it off.

Andryukha lives here year-round. He's getting on in years and has no family—unless of course you count Ivan Denisovich. But, no: Andryukha couldn't have decided to be both a family member to the prisoner and his warden. That would be too subtle. And he doesn't treat him like family at all.

My dacha is at the edge of the village; the homes here are all privately owned, mostly summer residences—and on the other side of the ravine you can see the center of town with its gray prefab five-stories. I come here to work. It's comfortable, I've gradually brought over a good library, it's quiet. I bring my laptop with me.

I've gotten Ivan Denisovich into music. That is, to a single work of a single artist. He doesn't care for the other songs on the disc, just as he doesn't care for all other music in general.

Now he's finished eating and he expects some entertainment. I open my trunk so he can better hear the rear speakers and subwoofer. I find the Bregovich disc in the glove compartment, slide it into the player. I flip to song number six and turn up the volume.

It opens with a saxophone solo, then the percussion kicks in. A Balkan sadness, magnificently arranged, pours from the trunk of my car. Then Bregovich begins to sing. Ivan Denisovich is ecstatic. He rolls in the snow next to his little hut and, I think, he's singing along. It's just like the first time I played Bregovich for him, back in the fall. What happens in his soul during the performance of song number six—what makes him roll over and howl—I don't know.

The Bregovich disc is a multitrack, which means the recording isn't compressed, it's done right, and each song stands on its own, is its own journey. I borrowed it from a friend—her former roommate was an audio pirate and left her a lot of good stuff.

I have a good sound system in my car: Two amplifiers, a large subwoofer. The rear speakers are on an acoustic shelf, the front ones are on podiums, an expensive Magnitola. The wiring is good. It took me a long time and lots of love to set it up. When I pull up to my house in Moscow, I turn the volume down, so the local hooligans won't decide to have a listen for themselves.

Right now, in this village, when there's no one in the houses around me, I turn it up as loud as it will go.

But then suddenly Andrei's porch lights up and Andrei emerges—pale, in a T-shirt and thermals. He's dead drunk, the way he gets only in winter. I thought Bregovich couldn't wake him.

I turn off the music. Ivan Denisovich stops rolling around in the snow, sits down, and stares at his owner, his tongue hanging out.

It's quiet. You can hear Ivan Denisovich's quick breathing.

"Hey fuckface," Andrei says to him. "Get back in your hut."

Rattling his chain, Ivan Denisovich obeys.

Andryukha turns his crumpled head to me.

"Turn the lights off for chrissake! I'm trying to sleep."

I kill the lights, turn off the engine, lock the door, and go inside.

Tonight I need to study something called "Russian Literature of the Twentieth Century." I'll be administering an exam to that effect to first-years on Wednesday. I find it hard to study this stuff because it's so close to me, it's where I live, in a way. The further back you go in the century, the simpler it is, everything's in its place, whereas here—here you're drinking a beer with some poet who became known at the end of the twentieth century, and it's hard to tell: Is this a genuinely canonical writer, or is it a pathetic asshole who last week took a swing at his young wife and broke her nose?

But with the dead—it's all good. And so, setting myself up in the kitchen under the lamp, turning my laptop on, I divide the writers into the living and the dead and begin with the dead.

From half past one until three I work on the dead poets. I have a good biographical dictionary on CD-ROM. Things are moving along. The dead: they're like family to me already. Take Tarkovsky, take Pasternak. There's no place I'd rather drink a Crimean red with a girl than at Pasternak's grave. And if you walk from his grave, about twenty meters south, the leaves rustling under your feet, there, hidden behind some bushes, is the marble monument to Tarkovsky. You can press yourself against the tile, you can dance around, whatever you like.

Some kind of boundless doggie spiritual gratitude spilled into me during the feeding of Ivan Denisovich, and I sit at my laptop and my books with an especially clear conscience and sturdy will, like a simple soldier just back from the front in 1945, taking a seat at his first university lecture. But for that same reason, Ivan Denisovich keeps circling through my thoughts as I try to learn and memorize texts and dates. He keeps silently arguing with my dead authors, disconcerting them with his presence. I imagine the poet Simonov, for example, buying a fur coat for his wife at the department store in the early 1960s, and there, in the fur, he discovers Ivan Denisovich's staring eyes. They express nothing but the desire to eat cheap chicken *pelmeni*; there's no judgment in those eyes, no anger, but nonetheless everyone feels ashamed—the poet, his wife, the shopgirls. And I, of course, feel terrible.

From three until four in the morning I work on the living poets. It turns out Ivan Denisovich has his paws on the living, too. I've always thought of Benzheev and Kibirov together, like two paragliders working in tandem. There they are, a pair of asocial poets floating above the regime, oblivious that down below, watching and barking at them, are little Ivan Denisoviches in trench coats who ordinarily only give trouble to those walking along the earth. For example, the village poets: the ones whose sons serve in the army, whose daughters get seduced by punk rockers, whose wives try to breed puppies in their homes.

At four in the morning I warm up some bologna in a pan. It's good bologna, "Doctor's Bologna," no fillings. I eat it. Now I need to study the novelists. It's easier with novelists. They don't worry about turning their lives into works of art the way poets do. You can be the biggest lout in the world and it won't affect your novels very much at all.

The best work of the dead novelist Vladimov is filled with the ancient enemies of Ivan Denisovich—dogs who guard prisoners.

The living novelist Senchin has a wandering dog's-eye view of the world. I saw him recently. He's tired of his wife but has nowhere to go.

I finish with the novelists near morning. It's time for a break. I should read something else.

I brought along a new literary almanac that someone gave me as a gift. But I'm not going to read that. It's terrible. I don't even know why I brought it. Maybe out of some indomitable hope for a better life, one in which I read these things. But I don't like the new almanacs. The very word sounds musty and stiff. If it weren't for the inscription from a good friend inside it, I'd have thrown it in the stove by now.

When you come here during the cold months, you need to feed the stove once, after which the electric radiators keep the dacha warm.

It's light out now, time to get back to Moscow. I'll sleep there.

I put my laptop in my bag, gather my books. I flip the switch in the front hall, shutting off the electricity. Close the door. Turn the ignition in my car, warm up the engine. An old lady walks by on the street. Ivan Denisovich barks at her. On the old lady's dark face: a look of boredom and concern.

I begin to wonder about the old lady—about whether she's outlived her old man, what her name is, and then I begin to wonder about a different old man, a writer, the father of the most important Ivan Denisovich in our literature. Not long ago I wanted to meet him, talk to him. But then I learned this is impossible. He lives far from the city, doesn't accept any guests. I considered taking the unofficial route, that is, climbing over his fence and approaching the house to ask for his blessing. But then I learned that his dacha is guarded like a prison camp—that the fence has barbed wire, and in the yard there are guards. In other words, Solzhenitsyn has imprisoned himself voluntarily.

I feel sorry for him, and for all the prisoners of our homeland, and even a little sorry for myself, though I was never in prison. And another wave of pity sweeps over me when I see that old lady. I get out of the car and let Ivan Denisovich off his chain.

Let a new music play the tune of the fate of Ivan Denisovich. Let him study in the corridors of new grassy-halled universities. His sentence is over. And now he roams through the great spaces of our homeland. That is, at first he runs along the fence, past the electric post and the store, and then, when he grows tired, he walks.

HAVE MERCY, YOUR MAJESTY FISH

OLGA ZONDBERG
Translated by Svetlana Ilinskaya and Douglas Robinson

LAST SEPTEMBER, after a long break, Alya blogged again:

> *Today, because the weather was so wonderful, I went for a walk in a nearby park. I was walking slowly in such a peaceful mood that I thought I might sit down on a bench and fall asleep listening to Yann Tiersen on my MP3 player. All of a sudden I saw a tiny mouse dash along the curb toward the trees. Very little, about three centimeters long, not counting its tail.*
>
> *I don't know what happened to me, what instincts were awakened at that moment, but I felt like I really wanted to catch it. Not to kill it, God forbid, and not to take it home—what would I do with it?—but just to catch it.*
>
> *Long story short, I chased this poor little creature among lime trees and poplars until it disappeared. I was absolutely aware that I was doing something wrong.*
>
> *Doctor, is it curable?*

Within an hour three people responded.

Two of them, independently from each other, suggested that in a past life Alya had been a cat, and not, as one specified, some decorative pure-bred but a true hunting kind of cat, one useful in a household.

The third objected, expressing his disbelief in past lives, and suggested that even if we could suppose Alya had had one, there are many reasons a person in this life might want to hunt a mouse without any obvious motivation.

The fourth and last comment came that night when Alya was asleep. She had no time to check in the morning and no Internet connection at work, so she was able to read it only the next evening:

> *What if it has nothing to do with hunting instincts and you simply wanted to watch this little creature gracefully parting the blades of grass that have seen different springs and summers with a swiftness of movement that seemed at first chaotic?*

This was written by one of her seventeen friends, the only one she had never met personally. Alya did not remember where and how she had found him. She had added him out of curiosity.

The next entry she made after New Year's. There was nothing to write about before that.

> *Recently in both Middle Eastern food booths that I pass on my way to and from work there suddenly appeared the sign: "No shawarma."*
>
> *Where did the shawarma go?*
>
> *Do you not read the papers or watch TV? Do you not catch a news feed?*

asked Aleksey, her friend Masha's husband. His new userpic contained a black-and-white road sign that Alya did not understand.

> *I don't read newspapers.*
> *The only TV I watch is horror movies and cooking shows.*
> *What is a news feed?*

The road sign responded with a triple smile as if from under a carnival mask (although Alya hadn't been joking about the TV) and links to the shawarma stories on the most popular news sites.

While Alya was checking the links, her friend Nastya's comment came in: If only she could and loved to cook half as well as Alya did, she would not be at all as worried as she was about the temporary disappearance of some particular street food of questionable quality.

Hey, Alya decided, *I could make homemade shawarma for dinner.* She used to cook with her mother almost every evening, and, truly, she never ate in fast-food places, only at home. Mother could not stand to see "all this junk" from street vendors and diners after work. Over the past few weeks her mother had taken on additional shifts in order to make some extra money for her vacation, and the kitchen had become Alya's domain. For several years her mother had been dreaming not of the usual Turkish beach, but of a country of real pizza and pasta, endless substitutes of which she mass-produced at work daily. Alya's mother works in one of those many chain restaurants that objectively and honestly speaking are too expensive for undemanding eaters and have no gastronomical worth for everybody else, but nonetheless fail to suffer from a lack of customers.

While Alya fried meat and chopped herbs, two more people explained to her the meaning behind the recent changes in the municipal migration law and the coincident shortage of shawarma. She had already read about it on the news sites.

Holding a jar of honey in one hand and the mouse in the other, not without some excitement she clicked on a comment that came in time for evening tea from the only friend she hadn't met personally:

> *There is no God anymore either, but nobody warns us about it in the morning, not with a sign, not by word of mouth, lest people start asking where he disappeared to and why he doesn't exist anymore.*

Picking up on the topic of the local government's recent measures limiting the scope of professional activities for foreigners, Alya came out with a small poll on her blog the next day:

What do you call strangers whose nationality you are unsure of?

For example, suppose you are walking by a construction site, where a group of dark-haired and dark-skinned citizens work and speak a language that you cannot identify. What is the first word that comes to your mind to describe these citizens?

This question was answered by almost all Alya's friends. The majority used the words *immigrants* or *guest workers*. The oldest one chose a slightly archaic expression, "the guests of the capital"—it stuck, he explained, during the era of the forced enthusiasm of monotonous TV and radio voices. Alya's former classmate Nina wrote that subconsciously she honestly could not do anything about her prejudiced attitude toward people of different nationalities. To herself, although she's ashamed of it, she often calls them "darkies" or even "camel jockeys" and believes that without them the city would be a bit cozier. She has never said anything like this out loud.

Alya did not know what to do: Should she delete Nina from her list of friends? Should she reply with something harsh and con-demnatory? It would be a pity to remove her: Nina sometimes told unembellished and yet not at all boring stories about scrapes that she was gifted enough to get herself into. She was also a former class-mate. And not a bad person.

Still wondering what to do with Nina, Alya mechanically reread a few of her own recent posts and immediately decided that someone who had not so long ago been hunting an innocent field mouse had no right to blame others for being xenophobic and aggressive. So she neither shortened the list of her friends nor responded to Nina.

Closer to midnight her only friend whom she hadn't met person-ally (Alya was waiting for his response and partially because of this didn't go to bed) wrote:

I used to call them guest workers too.

But once I accidentally made a slip in speaking and since then I've been calling them nothing but "interbrigades."

But that's probably misleading, because they have nothing in common with real interbrigades. It's like putting criminals and

political dissidents in the same cell.
Both have similar foes.
That's it.

The word *interbrigades* was definitely familiar to Alya, but just then it didn't want to vacate its cozy seat in the first or second row of her long-term memory. Luckily, a modern person has search engines and Wikipedia for just such an occasion. Alya spent another half hour at the monitor and was barely able to wake up in time for work the next morning.

— — —

About a week later Alya posted this entry, and then cross-posted it to a special Web community, where it was suggested that you report cases of parental child abuse:

> *Today I saw a well-groomed and well-dressed young woman slap her child hard and call him "you little bastard," because he was crying and didn't want to go someplace. Bitch. In my mind I wished her a long life in a stinky retirement house for lonely old witches.*
>
> *In connection with this unpleasant story I have a question to those with children: How do you react to their tantrums, disobedience, and other forms of protest?*

The responses poured in for three days at least. Nina the classmate responded that she had never once hit any of her three children and that her older ones usually calm the younger ones in cases like this, sometimes vice versa. Her friend Masha wrote that she would have shot her brat long ago, but was afraid she might miss him and hit an innocent bystander (besides three adults and an extremely mobile five-year-old there were sizable herds of various animal life-forms ranging from stray dogs to exotic insects that lived in and regularly transited through their tiny apartment). Masha's husband, Aleksey, who had changed his userpic from a road sign and now alternated between a koala and a wombat muzzle, cited Kharms: "A plump young mother was rubbing her pretty daughter's face on the brick wall." In the specialized Web community, a discussion was slowly developing and branching out concerning acceptable approaches to comforting crying children (distract them, hug them, talk to them seriously, as a last resort promise them something nice, although this last should not be abused) and on how natural it was to use force for educational purposes and whether it was ever acceptable to hit children for any reason.

The only friend Alya didn't know personally posted one of the last responses to appear in the commentary section:

> *I explained to my daughter early on that a protest is a profanation of dissatisfaction.*

Alya wanted to ask him if those were the exact words he used or what things he did to make this complex concept clear to a child, but didn't dare. She had her own reasons to be afraid of getting closer to people like this, despite the fact that she would have been unable to explain even to herself what lurks beneath the generalization "people like this" and what attributes made her unfamiliar friend resemble those "people like this."

Then Alya took another long break from blogging. Her mother came back from Italy upset, or, to be exact, she liked everything there a lot, but she hadn't anticipated that her return to Russia would spoil her impression of the trip so fast and so irreparably. But they were cooking wonderful dinners with tested or slightly modified recipes together again.

New lines appeared on Alya's blog only at the end of April:

> *Yesterday in the metro two elderly women sitting next to me were talking very loudly and, despite the noise, I heard every word. The strange thing is that although other people's conversations usually switch on my unhealthy curiosity, this time I caught myself not even trying to listen. I was completely uninterested in what they were talking about. I don't even remember what it was about. There was not even anything repellent or*

unpleasant about them. On the contrary, one of them resembled my deceased grandma who brought me up.

It occurred to me: if you are not interested in their real conversation, you should make up your own for them, one that won't bore you or make you feel ashamed for them. So, what would I like to hear around myself?

I've been trying to come up with a suitable dialogue for two days now and failed. I can't do it!

Since then, over the past month, there has only been one comment to this post, from the only friend whom she's never met personally:

Me neither.

HISTORY

ROMAN SENCHIN
Translated by Victoria Mesopir

NIKOLAI DMITRIEVICH put his briefcase on a chair. Sighed. Took
off his raincoat, hung it on a hook on the wall. His cap—above.
Sighed again. Sat down at a small round table with an ashtray and
napkin holder at its center. So as not to smoke, he hid the ashtray
behind the napkin holder. While waiting for the waitress, he gazed
out the window. The glass was tinted, and it seemed that outside it
was already dusk. And indeed, despite the fact that it was eleven in
the morning, the day was overcast, cold—middle of April, yet there
were still snow flurries . . . Oh well, never mind, the winter had been
almost like the ones in Krasnodar, the lawns green until the New
Year, so now one could bear it. It would be over soon . . .

As usual after visiting a bookstore, his head was pleasantly heavy,
he felt as though he'd flown somewhere and had not necessarily seen
but rather grasped something important, and had returned to his real
world a slightly different man.

Nikolai Dmitrievich loved this feeling, probably because of it he
went to the Moskva bookstore often, stood in front of the bookshelves for a long time, picking up first this book, then that one, leafing through the pages, getting lost in the text; then went down into
the used-books section, where, with joy and surprise, he found the
same editions as the ones he had in his home library, like old friends.
Nikolai Dmitrievich rarely bought new books: not that they were
expensive, but he was afraid of being let down. Only that which was

necessary for work, or would reliably be a pleasure to read, found its way into his briefcase. And today could be considered a doubly lucky day—a book both necessary and pleasurable, had made it in. Nikolai Dmitrievich had heard about it a while ago, back in Soviet times, and had from time to time encountered quotations from it—and now, finally, it was out in Russian.

—Menu, sir, the young waitress placed a brown leather folder onto the table and turned to go.

—No, just one second, Nikolai Dmitrievich stopped her.— Double espresso, if you please. That's all.

The girl nodded.

He watched her go. Slim, in a black blouse with short sleeves, blue jeans. Not wearing a uniform—those standard-issue white top–black bottom—yet nevertheless neat-looking, squeaky-clean even. The waitresses in many of the little taverns in Germany were like this, too. Clean, energetic, young. Cozy, somehow . . . At the end of the eighties, beginning of the nineties, Nikolai Dmitrievich had participated in several conferences in Berlin and Köln—the theme of his research had been in vogue then—and that's where he developed this fondness for sitting like this, alone for an hour or so, in these types of little coffee shops. It was very soothing, put one into a working frame of mind. He used to wonder why they didn't have them in Moscow, even contemplated opening one himself. Um, yes, there was the time he'd taken a stab at becoming an entrepreneur . . . But then, not so long ago, the coffee shops materialized. Tens of them, on Tverskaya, on Myasnitskaya, and all over the city, too. Well, thank God. Quiet little nooks in a huge, boisterous city, where one can catch his breath, think in peace, suspend the commotion for a while.

It was in these coffee shops that he felt everything was fine, solidly reliable, he still had strength in him, and there were many full, productive days ahead in his life—and the long life behind also had been full, not a useless, ordinary life. And that life was far, far from being over. Sixty-two, an age of intellectual and physical maturity these days. Now, pushing eighty—that might indeed, probably, be the sunset of life . . . His health, touch wood, was okay—still another fifteen years left, at least. And that's not an insignificant amount of time.

What was it—fifteen years ago? Nineteen ninety-two. April . . .

He recalled—a few animated pictures flashed by—the disheveled, with a crooked tie, Egor Gaidar on a platform; old women, with a look circa the Siege of Leningrad, along the length of Stoleshnikov Lane, with sundry antiques no one was interested in at their feet. Endless manifestations, demonstrations, multicolored food stamps for produce, for soap, for the shriveled, with sickly white coating, smoked sausage at co-op stalls, the long days of anticipation either of a catastrophe or, at long last, a new, happy life . . .

Moscow had become completely different since then, as had the country, also, and the people. He himself, Nikolai Dmitrievich, had become completely different, too. Back then, he'd been forty-seven, yet he had behaved—and, most importantly, had felt—just as he had back in his younger days. He'd done some foolish things, arguing for hours with totally random people, often almost to the point of fighting it out. What had they argued about, and what had been accomplished . . . Well, no, still a lot, in all fairness, although they'd deluded themselves about a lot of things, too.

The girl placed a small tray on the table, with a cup of black coffee and sugar in a glass dispenser.

—Thank you, said Nikolai Dmitrievich.

—You're welcome.

He raised the cup, sipped a little coffee with the tips of his lips. Hot, bitter, but not a nasty bitter, not like the instant or ground coffee at fifty rubles per two hundred grams . . . Ah, the lines back then for coffee of any kind! For anything and everything in general . . . A nightmare. Indeed, more of a nightmarish dream than reality, it seemed now. And yet, it was this period, from '86 to '96, that he remembered most clearly.

Back then, Nikolai Dmitrievich had followed the events happening in his country hypnotically, without a moment's interruption, and even participated in some—how many impromptu meetings he'd attended, he'd lost count—spent whole days in front of the television, listening to delegates' speeches at unending conventions, conferences, Supreme Soviet sessions, applauding the performances of the inter-regionalists, dem-unionists; bought newspapers in bundles, collecting clippings in a fat cardboard binder. Had even kept a diary . . .

The cooling-off began after the presidential elections, in the summer of '96. Or more precisely, during the elections—between the first and second rounds, when from dawn to dusk one endless pro-Yeltsin campaign marathon had been broadcast on television. They sang, danced, cracked jokes, launched fireworks, cursed the Soviet past. And Yeltsin's opponent, the Communist Zyuganov, had appeared for a few minutes from time to time, trying to prove something, to explain, to bring people's attention to something, and not having enough time to do so—and seeing this obvious, but for some reason largely accepted by the majority of people, unfairness, Nikolai Dmitrievich had felt pity and sympathy for the unpleasant, antipathetic Zyuganov, had become afraid of this *pity and sympathy he felt* and, perhaps in order to stay true to his principles—as a historian, he knew more than most about the Communists' crimes—he switched off the television, didn't buy newspapers in the morning, refused to go to another one of those meetings. And very quickly, he just quit following whatever was happening in the country.

At first he was afraid of his indifference, was ashamed of himself, but then had begun to feel a fruitful, work-conducive peace. And he'd realized that during this past decade, he'd completely ceased occupying himself with that which, from early on in his youth, he'd considered his life's calling. Tens of articles in newspapers, three to five lectures per day in various institutions of higher learning, primarily those founded during the perestroika years—those did not count. All that, though pleasurable and useful, was nevertheless merely income supplementing. The serious stuff had become all corked up, and much of what had been accumulated, thought out, and structured in his mind had started to decay over those ten calamitous years . . . But the muses love leisure, as the German proverb says. And so it had required much effort on his part to immerse himself once again into the epoch he studied. Or rather, not merely studied, but attempted to re-create in all its minute details, to find out and bring to light all of its nuances; to lose himself in it.

And gradually, step by step, the present retreated, faded, ceased disturbing him and constantly knocking him off balance. Only the most extreme of its manifestations would get through to him, each time unexpectedly, like a sharp tree branch breaking out of thick fog.

The apartment-building explosions, Yeltsin's voluntary resignation, the Kursk submarine drowning, the Dubrovka hostage crisis, the other crisis in Beslan, the termination of governors' elections, the explosion in the subway, the recent coal mine explosion, with more than one hundred people killed at once ... And yet, his serenity—the serenity of a scholar—was not really disrupted by any or all of this. His book moved ahead, slowly but surely.

Right, well then ... Nikolai Dmitrievich pulled out a cell phone from his jacket pocket. Quarter past eleven. Need to finish the coffee and go home. He would have lunch, then sit down to work. Maybe today he would be able to finish a chapter on the plebiscite of the tenth of April 1938, when ninety-nine percent of Austrians voted for the Anschluss to Germany. Nikolai Dmitrievich had been researching this event since his youth, and he still, to this day, could not fully figure it out. At first, in the airtight Soviet times, he'd only had access to sources that talked about a complete falsification of the plebiscite's results, but now he was prepared to make the deduction that this almost round number was entirely correct—in the spring of 1938 Austrians had wanted to live under Hitler's governance.

And incidentally, the book he had bought today could very well help, too, in supporting his thesis. It was, after all, on that very same subject Nikolai Dmitrievich was researching—the situation in Central Europe in the period between the First and Second World Wars ... Guido Preparato was a serious economist and historian, not given to the sensationalism so many of his fashionable colleagues were prone to these days ... And Nikolai Dmitrievich felt slightly ashamed that he hadn't found this book earlier, at least in English; that he'd only bumped into it today in the bookstore, quite by accident. There could be new details, convincing statistical calculations in it, that might cause him to change his position, open his eyes to something new ... Yes, today had to be dedicated to reading.

Carefully, watching out the corner of his eye how the thickly settled coffee grinds inched toward his lips, he sieved out the rest of his coffee. Put the cup on the saucer. Sighed. Time to go.

—Young lady, he called the waitress, —ring me up.

— — —

Tverskaya Street looked par for the course for the first half of a Saturday—few cars, thin rivulets of pedestrians, the marquee lights of most of the stores switched off . . . Nikolai Dmitrievich remembered the Moscow of his youth, when the streets seemed wider, there was less jostling, and instead there was more space, more air . . . He pulled out a cigarette and with much pleasure, for the second time today, lit up. He made his way slowly to the Pushkinskaya metro station.

His wife didn't like the way he walked, staring at the ground. "It's like you're hiding from someone!" Sometimes she just couldn't contain herself and yanked him by the elbow. He would lift up his head, straighten his shoulders, smile guiltily, but then after a few minutes would again start looking blankly at his feet, lost in thought over what he was reading, or perhaps the topic of an upcoming lecture.

So he walked today, too—immersed in thought—and only lifted his eyes at Kozitsky Lane. Looked left, right—are there any cars?— then forward, and suddenly stopped short. Up ahead, beyond the Yeliseyevsky Gastronom, people were crowding the sidewalk. Ordinary men and women, short skinny guys, and, along the traffic lane, a chain of big-bodied spec-op militiamen, OMON, in bluish-gray camouflage and round helmets.

Nikolai Dmitrievich stood still for a moment, coming to as a result of this sharp, unexpected change in the landscape. Then he remembered—and felt a little better for it—that last night on the television there'd been a warning. The youth of the Young Guard were staging an event at Pushkin Square, and the radicals were planning to disrupt it . . .

In recent years Nikolai Dmitrievich had tried strenuously to give as much of a wide berth as possible to any and all types of meetings, actions, and picket lines—feeling nothing but indifferent disgust toward their participants, the way one might in regard to the cripples sitting in the underground passageways with their ugly mutilations on full display for the world to behold. There had been in the past altogether too many slogans and angry perturbations, too often had he seen on television and in real life the poor and the disfigured, feeling the appropriately deep sympathy for them. Enough already.

His first thought was to turn onto Kozitsky, go around Pushkinskaya, and enter the subway at Chekhovskaya. An extra ten minutes.

True, because of this, instead of one change of trains, he'd have two . . . Escalators, up-down, waiting for the train, the slamming doors of the wagons . . . But the desire to get home quickly, have lunch, and sit down with his book outweighed other considerations—Nikolai Dmitrievich went straight.

At the corner of Tverskaya and Pushkinskaya everything was peaceful. People talked quietly, looking in the direction of Novo-pushkinsky Park, where music blared from speakers and government flags unwound. Nikolai Dmitrievich thought he recognized some who stood at the corner—mostly middle-aged, poorly dressed, with dry, severe faces and expressive eyes, and two or three men, almost old already, sporting thin skipper goatees. These, or those similar to them, had made up the thousands at the meetings and demonstrations in the early nineties . . . By the wall of the Gallery Aktyor, a small row of some sturdy old women, also almost familiar from those past actions and meetings. In their hands—rolled-up papers, most likely homemade banners, something along the lines of the ubiquitous "Down with the Government!"

There were also young people—attractive girls with instant cameras, a dozen or two young men of a decidedly non-warrior-like aspect. But it was mostly journalists who pushed about at the corner; cameramen held their cameras aloft on their shoulders, like weapons. A short, plump, smallish man of about forty, in glasses, with a neat, short beard, shifted from foot to foot at the traffic light. Nikolai Dmitrievich had seen him before, somewhere, too—some kind of politician from the new generation, he seemed to recall . . . Oh well, anyway, there was no time to recall.

—Excuse me. He started to make his way through the crowd to the subway entrance. —Excuse me, please.

He had only a couple of meters or so to the steps of the underground when Ryzhkov, a delegate of the State Duma, wearing a thin gray coat, ran up them. A fold-up umbrella hung from his wrist . . . And immediately, behind his back, emerged the big-bodied OMON men, who stood in a chain.

Here we are, the thought stabbed Nikolai Dmitrievich; he tried to squeeze in between them:

—Excuse me?

The OMON stood like statues, gazing forward blindly; the sidewalk to the right was also already closed, even metal barricades had somehow appeared. People stuck on both sides started getting indignant.

—Hey, let me through, really! Nikolai Dmitrievich pushed lightly on the shoulder of one of the big-bodied ones and received in return not so much a shove, but a sharp jerk, short as an electric shock. He staggered back.

—Hey, what is this? I need the subway!

But looking into the face of one, then another OMON man, he realized—they wouldn't let him through. They simply didn't hear him. He turned around. The crowd at the corner had compacted, Ryzhkov was surrounded tightly by journalists, and, in his soft, quiet voice, was complaining:

—Now you can see for yourselves what's going on. The approaches to Pushkin Square are blocked off, the movement of citizens has been curtailed. The Young Guards of United Russia movement's having a rally at the square, even though as far back as half a month ago, the representatives of Another Russia submitted to the mayor's office a notification of their intent to hold a protesters' march at this same spot. The notification was accepted, but after a few days a spokesperson from the mayor's office informed Another Russia, informally, that specifically on this day and at this very hour, Pushkin Square would be the site of the Young Guards meeting. What we have here is an evident subterfuge . . .

—What are the demands of the protesters' march? asked a yellow-haired journalist—her microphone bore the Channel One sign, although her voice had an accent.

—There is just one main demand: the return of honest, nation-wide elections. This right is guaranteed to all citizens under the constitution . . .

Ryzhkov was replying as he always did in the corridors of the State Duma, with outward calm and reasonableness, yet there was concern in his eyes, his lips quivered. He clearly was trying to restrain himself, so as not to start speaking harshly, directly from his heart . . .

Once upon a time, Nikolai Dmitrievich had felt great sympathy toward this still young and lively, in spite of his considerable term in politics, person. He listened to Ryzhkov's speeches with much interest, keen attention, agreeing with many things the man said. But the years went by, the situation in the country was changing, people's living conditions were changing, too, yet Ryzhkov remained exactly the same, kept saying the exact same things, and was obviously proud of his steadfastness. Well, maybe he was even right, too, to be standing true to his program, with which he became a delegate at the outset of the nineties, but because of this he'd gradually turned into one of those who even back during the times of Nicholas the Second were given an accurate and biting moniker—*Dumets*, the Duma-men. These Duma-men, they always successfully go through every election, never break out of the confines of parliamentary ethics, never lose their parliamentary immunity; dutifully they sit in their seats in the Duma chamber, make appropriate comments about something or other after another law has been passed, sometimes taking exception and expressing their indignation, yet the point of their arguments and comments, the energy of their indignation, fails to reach the people's consciousness, and no one even wants to delve deep into any of those matters—everyone's just fed up . . . Nikolai Dmitrievich knew many such Duma-men in the history of parliaments of many countries—old guards, completely ossified in their legalistic battles, and when something truly historic started happening outside the walls of the parliament, an explosion, a popular revolt, these old guards no longer were capable of understanding what this was, why, what, whatever for. They'd be the first to flee.

And now he was surprised, seeing Ryzhkov here, on this corner, surrounded by old picket-line women, semiold men with the undernourished appearance of unemployed professors, anemic young men in thin old-fashioned "bologna" coats, impotently complaining into the overhanging microphones and dictaphones of random reporters. And again he experienced this pang of an unnerving yet at the same time bracing thought, returning his memory to the turbulent past of fifteen years ago: *If even Ryzhkov is out on the street, it must be something serious* . . . Yes, it was worth it to wait around a while, taking the time to observe. Try to understand.

The questions for the Duma-men ended. The people silently gazed in the direction of Novopushkinsky Park. Fragments of modern music could be heard. From afar drifted in the words: "In the empty field the missile system 'Grad!' Behind us—Putin and Stalingrad!" The old women by the wall, cautiously, stealthily unrolled their scrolls. On them, in magic markers and watercolor, crooked lines were scribbled: "Putin, we don't believe you!" and "There've been worse times before, but never lowlier ones."

—Well, alright, Volodya, a shortish, plump man with the stubble of a beard walked up to Ryzhkov. —I've got to go. All the best.

The Duma-man nodded:

—Yes, Nikita.

—Excuse me, the journalists surrounded the short one, as if only now noticing him. —You're Nikita Belykh? What's your assessment? . . .

He put out his hands:

—I'm here as a private observer, and therefore cannot comment on anything. And with an encouraging, though gentle, careful slap on Ryzhkov's shoulder, he left in the direction of the Kremlin.

—In an hour, the SPS party will be holding a meeting in Slavyanskaya Square, Ryzhkov started to explain. —To us, on the other hand, instead of Pushkin Square, the mayor's office offered the territory of the All-Russian Exhibition Center or Tushinskoye Field—our choice—way outside of the city, wouldn't you know it. Can you imagine where that is?! We cannot interpret this as anything other than pure mockery . . .

—*Unsinn*, the yellow-haired journalist shook her head, and Nikolai Dmitrievich understood where her accent was from, and what that whitish-blue figure one on the microphone signified—German television, the information channel.

And where are the rest of ours? Nikolai started searching with his eyes, but couldn't find anyone. He glanced at his watch. Five minutes to twelve . . . Nothing substantial. It seemed completely nonsensical to stand around, waiting for God knows what. Indeed, what could some fifty people, at best, surrounded by thirty huge young guys—no, men—in helmets and armed with truncheons, be waiting for? And as though heeding Nikolai Dmitrievich's question, one of the nondescript young men suggested to Ryzhkov:

—Vladimir, let's go somewhere. How about to the Teatralnaya . . .

—For now, we stay here, Ryzhkov replied, with uncharacteristic firmness, harshness even. —Our meeting is until 1:00 PM.

At twelve on the dot, on the roof of one of the buildings surrounding the square, the one with the McDonald's in the first floor, a small figure with a flag appeared. The little man unwound the flag and commenced to wave it. Nikolai Dmitrievich took a closer look, scrunched up his eyelids—the flag bore an uncanny resemblance to the Nazi one: red background with a white circle in the center, only instead of a swastika inside the circle, a black sickle and hammer . . . This flag, he knew, was invented by the radical hooligans from Limonov's party; Nikolai Dmitrievich felt sorry for these kids, most of them barely pubescent youths—they were asking for it, throwing eggs, breaking into the presidential administration building, and getting long prison sentences for all those stunts—although, had it been up to him, he'd merely pull them by the ears like nobody's business and belt their asses, if only for this swastika-like symbol alone . . . But now, seeing this repugnant, thoroughly antipathetic flag, Nikolai Dmitrievich felt a burst of renewed energy, joy almost—as if a stream of fresh air had suddenly burst into an airless room with boarded windows and doors.

And all around him, too, the people came to life, started applauding and shouting "Hooray!" Nikolai Dmitrievich glanced at Ryzhkov—even he, the hard-core democrat, had a smile on his face, if a somewhat reserved one. He too had probably felt the fresh air.

In the meantime, at the crossroads all around the square there was the movement of troops from all types of law-enforcement contingents. The OMON, in their bluish-gray pea coats, the lean guys in black uniform, at whom people nodded their heads surreptitiously and uttered quietly, fearfully: "Private guards"; there was also the AF personnel, in green camouflage and ash-colored bulletproof vests; and around Novopushkinsky Park's circumference there stretched rows of newly minted, boyish-looking army conscripts. The militiamen in their ordinary uniforms—blue coats, earmuff hats—could hardly be seen anywhere . . . The massive Ural trucks rumbled by, with their tarped tops and barred windows, walkie-talkies chattered. An atmosphere of army maneuvers. And at the same time, cars moved in their ordinary fashion along Tverskoy and Strastnoy boulevards, traffic lights worked as they always did, and on the giant screen next to the Izvestiya building, advertisement clips were flashing . . . All the while on the sidewalks, groups of people who were guarded by other, helmeted people with truncheons shifted from foot to foot.

— — —

The pointless standing around began to tire Nikolai Dmitrievich, hunger started to bother him. Indeed, he'd only had coffee this morning, while leafing through the new *Issues of History* (he'd been subscribing to the magazine for thirty-six years), and then he'd set out for the bookstore. Bought a book, stopped by the coffee shop. Another cup of coffee . . . Ahead of him was a long, fruitful day, which now was threatening to turn into an empty and nerve-racking one—and, most importantly, this nervousness was apt to carry over into the days ahead. And then he could say good-bye to the working mode, the essential levelheadeness, the measured distance from his immediate surroundings . . . Home, he neded to go home, to his study!

The entrance to the subway was still choked off by the OMON, the sidewalk in the direction of Strastnoy Boulevard—also. The only way to try and get out would be by moving up, along Tverskaya, to the Yeliseyevsky Gastronom.

—Attention! this was Ryzhkov exclaiming. —Members of the media, please come closer to me! Let the journalists through . . . People with microphones, dictaphones, cameras, one even with a step ladder, surrounded the delegate. —I want to make an official statement. Is everyone here? . . . I just got a call from Garry Kasparov. He and a few others have been apprehended on the opposite side of Tverskaya. They're currently being taken to a militia precinct—which one is yet unknown . . .

—They are, confirmed the cameraman on the step ladder. —They've arrested Garry Kimovitch—look!

A PAZ minibus drove slowly along Tverskaya. Nikolai Dmitrievich noticed some faces in the windows. People in the crowd waved at them, flashing victory signs.

—Vladimir Alexandrovich, someone tried to persuade Ryzhkov

again, —let's go somewhere! Why wait here?!

And he replied, in a strangely plaintive, sobbing voice:

—Don't you see what's happening? I won't lead you to the truncheons. We'll stand here until one, and then we'll disperse. We have already accomplished much . . .

Nikolai Dmitrievich smirked: oh yeah, much. A lot. A mute handful of people, without even banners or posters, unless one counted the few homemade banners . . . This is almost how, he'd heard, they now expressed protest in Byelorus—by gathering somewhere on the sidewalk and standing together, or sometimes silently, without banners, walking around town. And in Germany, too, in the year 1935 or thereabouts, the antifascists had shown in this manner that they still existed; and here, also, the Trotskyites, in the late twenties. And who could tell what would happen next . . .

But, at the opposite corner, something started to happen—the dark mass buzzed, swayed, and undulated, pressed tight by the bluish-gray ones in helmets. People on this side shouted:

—Shame! Shame!

Part of the OMON men, circumventing the cars, ran in the direction the shouting was coming from, tightening the chain along the edge of the sidewalk . . . For some reason, the little PAZ minibus with the detainees appeared again, breaking traffic rules while it circled the square . . . Nikolai Dmitrievich, glancing around, sensing an almost clear and present danger, looked up at the roof of the McDonald's. The flag was gone, and some figures walked around up there. However, on the adjacent roof—that of the Izvestiya publishing house—swayed the white-blue-red national flags, and a pull-out banner. Nikolai Dmitrievich squinted to make out the inscription: "Greetings to the march of foreign-currency prostitutes!" And from up there, from that roof, down flew leaflets, torches flared up. Thanks to those, all the rest of the people on the corner noticed the banner, read it, and started whistling, and the cries of "Shame!" grew into a loud, snappy, joint chanting: "Sha-ame! Sha-ame!"

Yes, the atmosphere was getting heated, although Nikolai Dmitrievich could not imagine as to what exactly the few tens of people squeezed by the stone walls of the OMON were capable of doing; and Delegate Ryzhkov kept looking at his watch, as if he were rushing the dials to get to one o'clock, when he could finally announce the meeting over.

But the situation changed abruptly and unexpectedly. From the direction of the Yeliseyevsky Gastronom a wave of dark-clad, short bodies crashed into Nikolai Dmitrievich, and from behind rolled another wave of bluish-gray, tall bodies. And then juicy thumps resounded—*thwack! thwack!*

Not seeing where the thumps were coming from, having swung with the rest of everyone in the direction of the turn onto Strastnoy Lane, Nikolai Dmitrievich remembered this sound at once—this was how rubber batons sounded when they came down on bent backs. There had been a time when he'd heard these thumps often on Moscow's streets . . . And already beyond this short memory flash, running with mincing steps in this tiny but compact human mass along the sidewalk, he, turning around, saw the bent-over, twisted-bodied young men, old women, men, women, men, all covering their heads, pressing into the walls of the Gallery Aktyor, into the pylons and electric poles . . . People were squealing and gasping, and somewhere in the distance the Russian anthem resounded.

Along with everyone else, Nikolai Dmitrievich was climbing into the narrow passage between a house and the closed-off subway entry, his back was covered in sweat and burned in anticipation of a blow, and in his head pulsated: *That's it! That's it!* In one instant, his status, from that of a solid, respectable citizen, a professor, PhD in history, had been reduced to that of a lowly animal being herded somewhere . . . Trying to avoid the truncheons, people were jumping over fallen metallic barriers. An old woman, small and wiry, tripped, fell, gave a helpless *Oy*. Nikolai Dmitrievich stopped momentarily to help lift her up, and immediately received a blow on his left shoulder blade. He didn't feel pain, but his body, disgustingly, jerked as though it wasn't his own, and his visored cap flew off his head.

—Hey, what *is* this?! he started to turn, and got another one right away. And then someone firmly grasped him by the armpits, dragging him away.

People shouted commands from behind: —Squeezing, squeezing out!

—Filling up! Here, bring 'em over here! sounded directions from the front.

Nikolai Dmitrievich was being led to the Urals idling along the sidewalk. The doors of the gray tarp-topped booths in their sides were open, next to them stood men in camouflage, with stone faces and transparent, dead eyes. They looked straight out of some film about robots . . . Talking, trying to explain, arguing with them was pointless.

He glanced along Strastnoy Boulevard. Everywhere the big-bodied men were grabbing the short and dark-clad ones, who tried to weave and duck, run away, break free, trying to stave off the assault with cries of "Shame!" On the asphalt lay scattered the pitiable homemade banners, constitution booklets, and, for some reason, lots of roses. Delegate Ryzhkov, his shoulders hunched, was wandering off slowly . . .

—Move, dispassionately ordered one of the escorts; Nikolai Dmitrievich then was lifted and thrown inside one of the trucks.

— — —

It felt strange and even a little shameful, but the indignation, the rage had disappeared. On the contrary, he became light and peaceful inside . . . Nikolai Dmitrievich knew this about himself—often, in difficult situations, it was as if something inside him switched, shifted, and the calming certainty appeared: all this was not happening to him, but rather to someone else, and he was merely observing someone who looked like him from the side and from slightly above. Observing without any emotion . . . Probably an ability safeguarding him from heart attacks and strokes . . .

He sat down on a bench. Exhaled. Moved his torso—his back tingled. Either from blows or from the evaporated sweat.

Amid the street shouts and piercing whining that could be heard, a sobbing woman's voice kept repeating: —Are you human or not? Are you human? . . . The militia sirens squawked, music boomed like cannon fire from powerful speakers.

Apart from Nikolai Dmitrievich, someone else was in the booth, but he was uninterested; someone else was being tossed in, someone cursed, moaned, tried to break out, someone talked into a cell phone . . .

I've lost my cap, absently thought Nikolai Dmitrievich, and smoothed his hair with his palm. *I should call home . . .*

He pulled out his cell phone, dialed the number. *And what'll I say? That I'm on my way to a militia precinct?* He ran his eyes around the booth's square confines. *Alright, I'll call home when they bring me there.* He put his phone back in his pocket . . . Mmm—yes, this was absurd, of course. And when did it start? And how, with what? Because just five years ago . . . No, he cut himself short, *no need to reminisce and analyze now. Later.*

He sat a while, gazing at the floor. Not thinking wasn't working. About a month ago they'd dispersed a demonstration in Petersburg, two years ago in some town in Bashkiriya they went rampaging, grabbing everybody and their brother in the street, beating them up and dragging them to the precinct, and also the same had happened in Kalmykiya . . . There probably were other such incidents, too, but he hadn't quite followed the news . . . Yet for sure one could pinpoint the moment when it became the norm to chase people around like this, thump them with truncheons, throw them into cop cars. Or maybe it'd never ceased to be like this . . .

He remembered his purchase. *There,* he chuckled to himself, *get some reading done in peace.* He unbuckled his briefcase, pulled out the book. Leafed through the pages for a while, catching with a glance the random lines, noticing the tables and graphs. He always did this in bookstores or at a table, preparing to start reading, warming himself up, getting absorbed. And now the habit didn't fail him, either, and after a few seconds, Nikolai Dmitrievich forgot where he was, what had happened to him. What he was reading he'd known from childhood, yet nevertheless it was interesting, captivating, like a good detective story:

> *On the night of February 27, 1933, the cupola of the Reichstag was lit up with hellish tongues of flame, the building blazed like a giant piece of molten charcoal, drawing around it a crowd of late-night revelers. The Fuhrer was immediately summoned to the scene. Arriving at the smoking remnants of*

that which only the day before had been the Parliament, Hitler exclaimed: "This is a sign from above . . . Now no one will prevent us from crushing Communists with an iron fist." The official version stated that the burning of the Reichstag was an "act of terrorism" committed by the Communists. But in the country at large, there wasn't the slightest sign of a nascent uprising. Everything was quiet. Based on lists put together well in advance, thousands of Communists and Social Democrats were rounded up—Gestapo personnel were the first to appear on the scene, and the concentration camps soon received their first inmates.

Nikolai Dmitrievich rubbed his eyelids—it was dark in the booth—and turned the page.

At the outset of its war against terror, the government made two decrees public—on the 28 of February and the 7 of March, respectively, "for the protection of the citizens and the government,"—which limited the freedom of the press, people's individual freedoms, and the freedom of association. On the 12 of March, the swastika-bearing flag was declared the official national symbol.

—Alright, take these ones to Yakimanka, resounded an order from outside.

—Know the way? Go then.

The door slammed, the lock screeched. The Ural's engine started up.

One of the detained gave a loud, drawn-out sigh, another pulled out a rustling packet of croutons and popped them into his mouth, biting and crunching noisily. Nikolai Dmitrievich closed his eyes— he was very hungry, to the point of feeling nauseated. *Come to think of it, after Beslan something similar started*, came an unwitting comparison. *Not quite so drastically, of course. Yet still—the governors elections were called off, even the presidents are nowadays appointed, and the opposition was squelched definitively. The Duma became engaged in complete rubbish, we'd be better off without it . . . Yes, certainly a resemblance. And . . . and what's next, then?* This scary little question caused Nikolai Dmitrievich to shudder and shake himself, as if trying to awaken, and his back once again felt cold and damp. *Could it possibly happen? . . .*

The truck moved forward. It drove ahead a few meters, and then began to veer leftward slowly. *Going to Maliy Putinkovsky*, Nikolai Dmitrievich determined. *No, to Naryshinsky Lane.*

—Look! a guy sitting at the barred window, with a protuberant burgundy bruise on his forehead, cried out joyously. —They're going! Going!

Nikolai Dmitrievich raised himself a little, glanced outside. Along the sidewalk of Strastnoy moved a short, but dense, solid column. Out of the nearby lanes, archways, and, indeed, as if from the very walls themselves, more and more people poured in. Flags appeared—multicolored and, by and large, unknown to Nikolai Dmitrievich. A black one, with a clenched fist, a blue one, inscribed with the word "Change," the Limonov flags, the light ones, bearing the abbreviations, OGF, RPR, NDS . . .

—Way to go! Onward! the people in the booth rejoiced; and something stirred in Nikolai Dmitrievich's chest, he felt like shouting something.

The column grew rapidly, by the second, and finally, no longer able to fit on the sidewalk, spilled onto the street proper . . . The Ural turned once more, the column disappeared from view. It was replaced by the OMON men, with yellow tags on their sleeves, SARMAT, running somewhere . . . Nikolai Dmitrievich sat back down, opening his book at random.

In May, the Hitlerists began decisively to root out the entire party system of the Weimar Republic: arrested in its entirety was the SDPG party leadership; in one fell swoop, an organization composed of 4 million workers and commanding a capital of 184 billion Reichsmarks was crushed into dust. Not the slightest reaction followed in response from any quarters, to say nothing of any organized resistance. After this it was the turn of the paramilitary nationalistic organizations of the "Steel Helmet" ilk. Then they came after the Catholics . . .

—Excuse me, someone touched Nikolai Dmitrievich on the shoulder; he turned around. Next to him sat a middle-aged man with a wrinkled face. —May I inquire what it is you are reading?

Without any pleasure—he didn't feel like talking to anyone— Nikolai Dmitrievich showed him the cover.

—*Hitler, Inc. How Britain and the USA Created the Third Reich*, read the man.

—And "Inc.," what is this?

—Increase by a factor of one, in English. Is that all?

—Hmm, a dangerous title. Very.

—Why?

—Well, see—in a moment, they'll bring us to the precinct, will search us. They could charge you with extremism, on account of this book.

Nikolai Dmitrievich shrugged his shoulders:

—I bought this book in a state-owned store. I've saved the receipt. Don't be stupid . . .

—Kh-ha, the wrinkled one interrupted with a guffaw. —Nowadays this means nothing. The main thing for them is to find a motive. They'll blow it up, say they detained you with extremist literature and—that's all she wrote. They'll drag you to death in the courts. My friend was raked over the coals because of a book about the Holocaust . . . My advice for you would be somehow to . . . The wrinkled one quickly looked around. —Just throw it away, to be on the safe side . . . You, I can tell, are not someone too experienced in these matters, you have no idea what kinds of stories have started to unfold. Nothing to joke about, nowadays. And what'll they decide to do with us next? That's a good question.

DRILL AND SONG DAY

VLADIMIR KOZLOV
Translated by Andrea Gregovich with Mikhail Iossel

EACH YEAR around the twenty-third of February, to celebrate the anniversary of the Red Army, we had Drill and Song Day at school. Classes from the first through seventh grades made their own "military" uniforms and performed drills in the gym, with rhymed slogans and songs. At two tables in the corner of the gym sat our patrons: our headmistress, school director, military instructor, and the deputy trade-union head from the tire factory. They broke us into groups.

Classes from the first, second, and third grades competed separately. The previous year, our class, then 2-B, had taken second place, and this time we hoped to be first: last year's winners, 3-C, were now 4-C and had to participate in the older-grades' competition. Not only had they taken first place in our school, but at the district level as well, and second in the whole city, and the director always brought them up as an example to other classes.

Our homeroom teacher, Valentina Petrovna—unattractive, prematurely aged (she was no older than thirty at the time, but her face was all wrinkled)—was very worried: What if it didn't come together and we failed to take first place in the school? Even worse, what if we did, but then completely humiliated ourselves at the district level?

We began to prepare for the competition at the end of January. Vera Saprykina's parents, through their theater-club connections, got us red cavalry *budyonovka* cloth helmets and red stripes to sew on our shirts. We learned by heart the song:

> White army, black baron
> Are readying for us again the tsarist throne
> But from the taiga to Britain's far seas . . . etc.

Every day after our lessons, Valentina Petrovna went to find out if there was a class in the gym, and if there wasn't, our whole class went there to sing the song and practice our march with rhymed slogans. Sometimes Valentina Petrovna invited our phys ed teacher, Ksenia Filimonovna, to take a look at how we marched.

Some ten days before the competition, Valentina Petrovna staged a purge, eliminating those who might spoil the class's performance.

"Tsygankov, it'd be dangerous to bring you to the competition: you could show up in a dirty shirt, for crying out loud, or forget to sew your stripes on it. And you, Zhuravin. Same goes for you."

Tsygankov was a small, skinny little guy. He was the youngest of many children in a family that lived in a private house behind the tire factory. His nickname was Piss Boy, because in the morning Tsygankov often reeked of urine, and everyone knew that at night he pissed the bed. Besides that, he often came to school in a dirty shirt. One didn't usually notice this, but when we undressed before phys ed in the cramped, stinky booth and he hung his shirt on a hook, one could see the ring around his collar. I didn't call Tsygankov "Piss Boy" myself, because I had only stopped pissing the bed as recently as second grade.

The other outcast, Zhuravin, spent two years in the first grade and two in the second, and was now on his second year in the third. He was already twelve or thirteen. Zhura was cross-eyed and his mouth was always hanging open, but he was considered the premier hooligan around. He smoked and had a juvenile-offender's record at a local militia precinct.

On Ksenia Filimonovna's prompting, Valentina Petrovna also excluded Korkunova—a fat girl and unremarkable C student who just couldn't march in lockstep with others—and me. I was tall and clumsy and marched unhandsomely. Valentina Petrovna consulted for a long while with Ksenia Filimonovna—I heard them say my last name a few times. Valentina Petrovna was probably hesitant because of my good grades, but in the end, she must have decided that the interests of the whole class—and potentially the entire school, were we to go on to district level—were more important than mine.

I was upset and came home sad. When I told everything to my parents that evening, my mother said, "Maybe I should go to the school and speak to that twit." But Dad convinced her not to go.

"You'll only turn her against Seryozha," he said. "There's no grade given for the competition, after all, and all the grades are in her hands."

Soon I realized I'd lost nothing, while actually gaining something. After class I didn't have to trundle to the gym anymore and march like a moron. Instead I went home, changed clothes, turned on the television or the radio, ate, then sat down to do lessons, and tried to do them as fast as possible so I could play with my construction set or draw in my notebooks.

When the big day was just a week off, even lessons themselves were sacrificed for the sake of preparation. If the gym happened to be free as early as first period, Valentina Petrovna assigned homework and the class went to rehearse. We, the four "rejects," went along, and while the rest marched, we sat on the long, bare, wooden benches by the wall and watched. Valentina Petrovna was always freaking out.

"What is this nonsense?" she would yell. "What kind of marching is this? What kind of singing? A shame and a sin! You want to humiliate me, your own teacher? In front of the whole school? I'd be ashamed to look other teachers in the eye if we didn't take first place."

— — —

"Today we will rehearse for two periods, the second and third. The gym will be free," Valentina Petrovna said right after the bell rang.

The class shouted, "Hooray!"

Almost everyone was happy that instead of doing lessons we were preparing for the competition. To me it made no difference and was even a little upsetting: I did my lessons, fair and square, and now nobody was checking them.

"Let's cut out during second period," Zhura said to Tsygankov and me. "Let them keep hoofing it till they shit themselves."

The three of us sat on a bench. Korkunova was absent—she was sick.

"What if Valentina notices we're not here?" I asked.

"Don't piss yourself, she won't notice."

Tsygankov didn't say anything, but he came with us. Nobody was friends with him or invited him anywhere, so he was probably glad that Zhura had included him.

"First let's see if maybe they brought rolls for the buffet. Then we could fucking cop some," Zhura said.

The buffet was next to the dining room, on the third floor. I hated the dining room because there we were made to eat the gooey, unappetizing mess of semolina gruel or watery potato puree with a flaccid dill pickle. And one time Ivankov from the C class found a cockroach in his beef patty, and all the students came running to see it, and Lenka Vykhina from our class threw up, right on the table.

At the buffet, on the other hand, apart from the withered cheese sandwiches spread out in the glass case, they did sell a few tasty things—pirozhki with jam for five kopecks, for example. True, these pirozhki were delivered rarely, and when they were delivered, an enormous line formed, and there were never enough pirozhki for everyone. But there were also poppy-seed rolls, shortbread, and sugared pretzels. All of it was carried to the third floor from the back entrance, where trucks from the bread factory drove up, right up the stairs, because there wasn't a freight elevator in the school. The buffet lady, Olga Borisovna—a crusty, sinewy old woman—usually enlisted the help of one of the dishwashers, and together they lugged a basket with pirozhki and shortbreads up the stairs, during a class period if possible, so that nobody would try to steal anything.

We were lucky. Down below they had just unloaded the truck, and Borisovna and the dishwasher in her dirty apron were carrying up a basket of rolls.

"Now listen," Zhura commanded. "We run up, snatch two each, then run down."

"Ah, you motherfuckers, I'll kill you!" screamed the dishwasher, but she didn't chase us. We ran down the stairs into the first-floor bathroom and stuffed ourselves with our rolls.

"Wanna smoke?" Zhura asked when we were finished eating.

"Okay," I said.

"And you, Piss Boy?"

"Me too."

Zhura slipped a crumpled pack of Primas from his pocket and gave us each a cigarette, then took out a lighter and lit them all himself. I held the cigarette in my mouth, not knowing what to do with it.

"You, like, drag on it or something, what the fuck's it burning by itself for?" Zhura laughed.

I dragged and began to cough. I looked at Tsygankov—he was smoking like Zhura, inhaling and letting smoke out. I couldn't do it like that.

"Now let's go to the store and cop a fucking loaf," said Zhura.

"You're not full from the rolls?" I asked.

"Nah."

"Maybe we should go get dressed first in the cloakroom."

"Well, you do that if you want, but me, I'm plenty warm."

We skipped the cloakroom. We all three walked down the hall and out into the cold in our uniforms and slippers.

In the store Zhura whispered to us:

"Fucking watch and learn, children."

He inconspicuously shoved a loaf of white bread under his jacket and calmly walked past the cashier and out onto the street. We darted out behind him.

"How often do you do this?" I asked.

"Always," Zhura guffawed. "This ain't pissing the bed for you."

I thought Tsygankov would get offended, but he didn't say anything.

Zhura broke off a piece of bread and passed the rest to us. "Well then, now—let's go ride the elevator."

Tsygankov and I broke off pieces. I noticed that he had dirty hands—not just blue with ink but also covered in some kind of brown crud.

We headed toward the nine-story apartment building, the only building in the whole neighborhood with an elevator. Zhura walked ahead a little, Tsygankov and I following.

"I'll only ride with you," said Tsygankov. "Not with Zhura."

Zhura pushed the red elevator button, and the doors slid apart.

"You go first. We'll come after you," I said.

"All right. I'll wait at the top."

Zhura went into the cabin and pressed the highest button. The doors closed, and the elevator went up with a noise. We heard it stop somewhere high above and the doors open.

I pressed the button and it lit up.

When the elevator came back down, Tsygankov and I stepped into the cabin. The plastic walls were covered in ink doodlings, and the lamp on the ceiling was smeared with soot. I pressed the highest button.

"You're an all right guy," said Tsygankov. "How about you be my friend."

"Okay."

The elevator arrived on the ninth floor, and we got out of the cabin. Zhura was waiting for us by the iron stairs next to a passage leading to the roof.

"Clubhouse is open. Shove on in," he said.

We climbed up the raggedy iron stairs behind him, went into the elevator room, and from there, to the roof, which was covered with snow. Our entire neighborhood was visible: several five-story buildings, the school, whole blocks of wooden houses. The streets were busy with cars, and the tire factory billowed smoke in the distance. Along the edge of the roof ran a banister—it was not very tall, about a meter high or maybe a little less.

Zhura went to the edge, leaned over, and looked down. Then he climbed up onto the banister, sat down, his feet flung over the edge as if it wasn't high up there at all. My legs ached with fear; I was scared of heights.

Zhura turned to us.

"Come on over. Don't be piss-pants. It's awesome up here."

He took out the cigarettes and lit up. Tsygankov went over to him, and Zhura passed him the pack and lighter. Tsygankov took a cigarette and lit up too. I couldn't make myself move.

"Well, what say, you too yellow to sit like me?" Zhura said to Tsygankov. "I understand—you're the Piss Boy."

Tsygankov silently returned the cigarettes and lighter. My legs ached still more, and I thought I might be the one to piss myself.

Tsygankov put his hand on the banister. It was too high for him, and he couldn't just sit on it like Zhura. Tsygankov threw one leg over the banister, pushed off with the other, slipped, and fell.

Zhura looked at me.

"That's fucking it for Piss Boy. But he proved he was no Piss Boy. And you didn't."

Zhura got off the banister and came up to me.

"You're the Piss Boy, Nikonov. A mama's boy."

I was afraid he'd hit me, but he didn't.

"Let's go downstairs. The cops'll come in a minute. They'll ask questions," said Zhura.

"What if we just leave? As if we were never here?"

"What are you, nuts?"

We went back downstairs. A crowd of people surrounded the spot where Tsygankov lay. An ambulance and a militia car showed up. It seemed like I had been dreaming and was just about to wake up.

The cops put us in the car and drove over to the precinct. They interrogated us separately in juvenile-detention rooms.

"Admit it, did you push him off the roof?" the cop asked, grabbing me by the shirt collar and under my throat. "Fess up quick, you little maggot."

I cried quietly. Then my parents arrived, and the cop let me go. The three of us went home. The whole way home we were silent.

— — —

Drill and Song Day was postponed a day because of Tsygankov's funeral. Our whole class went. Tsygankov lay in a coffin, and his mother was keening over him. She was already drunk and from time to time began to swear. Valentina Petrovna cried a lot. Everybody said she was going to jail, because Tsygankov was killed when we were supposed to be in class.

On Drill and Song Day our class took first place. At the district level, we placed only fifth. Valentina Petrovna didn't go to jail, but she left to work at a different school, and Anna Sergeyevna, a teacher trainee, took over for the fourth quarter.

RICHEVA

NIKOLAI EPIKHIN
Translated by Mariya Gusev

1

—I was typing up a text in computer class and all of a sudden the program crashed. I asked one of my classmates to help me. It was my first year of college; I didn't know anyone and didn't understand anything about computers. Well, this girl sat down next to me and began moving the mouse, touching the keys. This was Mashka. Richeva. I think that she also didn't know anything about computers. We never really became friends, just classmates. But even back then I liked her and thought of her as a girl who was kind and cute. I remember there was one time when I cursed really hard, and she didn't talk to me for a week. I followed her around, begging for forgiveness.

Gleb Shelapuha sat on the couch at his friend Sergei Lisichkin's apartment, telling Sergei everything he knew about Richeva. Sergei liked Richeva, and he wanted to know as much as possible about her.

—I don't know, either I've gotten smarter in the last four years, or Richeva has gone bad, but now I don't like her that much, continued Gleb.

—Why? said Sergei. He was calm, and he felt indifferent to anything bad that Gleb might say about Richeva. Sergei was probably in love with her and so paid no attention to her shortcomings but only saw her good qualities, and smiled about them to himself.

—It's not that I don't like her . . . Mashka is cute. Peppy. She's interesting to talk to. She's not crass. I know that she loves children. She herself told me this. And I believe her, and know that it is the truth, but—again, this "but." You know that I divide all people into two categories: people who live for God and people who live for their own pleasure—I call them "weightlifters." Well, there is another category between those two. These people are the most dangerous and, at the same time, I feel very sorry for them. They may seem kind, and well read, and communicative; they will help you when you're in trouble, and may sympathize with you sincerely, offer you help, and so on. But as soon as they are asked to choose between having spirit and having a barbell, these people clamp onto their barbells; they become wild. At that point, you better not try to engage them in conversations about Tolstoi—they will lay such Tolstoi on you, you won't know what happened. And this is the category to which Richeva belongs.

—I don't really understand, Sergei smirked, —why people from this middle category, into which you are unfairly placing Mashka, are worse than the "weightlifters"? And who are these "weightlifters"? I don't understand.

—Let me explain it to you, said Gleb, who somehow seemed happy with this question. —People who love money and a life of luxury and who are ready to deceive anyone for this personal happiness, to insult, to kill, and so on, these people will honestly tell you: *Yes, I am ready to step over people in order to have the good life. I love money, and I am a materialist. I want to live the way that I want to live. There is no God, and the most important thing is me.* If this is what a person is saying, he of course does not elicit any sympathy from me. But at least I know exactly what to expect from him, and as such he can be forgiven in some ways. It is his right to choose how to live. But people in the middle category, to which I, unfortunately, delegate Richeva—even though I care about her dearly and wish her the best and hope that she finally gets her head on straight—while disguising their true nature with the ideas of Christ, continue to live the same way as those in the weightlifters category. And on the outside, everything looks all right. But as soon as you break ground, as soon as you get even half a shovel deep, what you get is pure weightlifting.

Sergei laughed uneasily and went into the kitchen to get some tea.

—Yes, he said, when he returned, —and what am I, in that case? Also, like Richeva, a weightlifter?

—You are not a damn weightlifter! You don't have any barbell, this much is clear. You don't have this internal self-assurance, a belief in your own strength. Because you do not have this strength. You're not rich, not physically well-developed, your social standing is low. You don't have any barbell. And you are not pursuing any—and this is a big plus. But your most important plus is that you virtually never put down people who lift less than you. Although, you shouldn't have upset Misha Veismont.

—And Richeva, supposedly, puts people down?

—On the surface, of course not. She wouldn't scream at a person without a barbell, nor would she laugh at him. But she will not be friends with him. And some of her weightlifting friends have dumped her. Mashka used to be friends with Volkova and Peresekina, and now they barely say hi to each other. And it's all because Richeva's barbell was at around, say, fifty, her freshman year, and has remained about the same. Volkova's is a bit weightier, so that's it, good-bye girl-friend, you are no longer interesting to me. Volkova's and Peresekina's barbells have grown five hundred fold, if not a thousand.

Sergei stared glumly at the floor and said: —I love her. I don't care if she's a weightlifter or not. Richeva is the only one for me. I will love her forever.

Gleb stopped to think about this. He saw that Sergei was being genuine, that he was not just infatuated with Richeva, but that his feelings for her were strong and deep. And he also understood that they could not be together, and that Richeva would eventually dismiss him, even though this was only according to his own theory, and life is stronger and broader than any theories. Gleb wanted to tell Sergei that everything with Richeva would work itself out, and if Sergei tried hard, Richeva would see that he was genuine and not chase him away. But he said something different.

Gleb felt cold. It was getting dark outside, and there were no lights on in the room.

—When we meet twenty years from now, what will you tell me

then? You will have kids, will be married by then.

—Richeva doesn't love me. I'm not going to have any kids, sighed Sergei.

Along with the darkness, a strange and unpleasant feeling descended into the room, and into Sergei's soul. A feeling of melancholy, of doom, as if life has ended, almost without beginning, and there is nothing left to live for. He wanted to live and enjoy life with somebody, but this somebody was not around; this somebody did not need Sergei Lisichkin.

—Don't get upset, it will pass, Gleb noticed that Sergei looked demoralized. They had finished drinking their tea, and he wanted to go home, to sleep. —Why don't you call her by some bad name or something? You may feel better. Do you want me to do it? I'm probably going home soon. Otherwise I won't be able to get out of here.

—Mashka is not like that, said Sergei. —Don't talk about her like that. Understand, she's gathered up and has her hands full with people's hearts. And she's holding them like oranges . . . or, no—like Christmas ornaments. But there are too many of them. One by one they fall out and shatter. She is trying to hold on to them, but she can't. So she keeps picking up more and more. So my heart was broken just like this—accidentally, like a glass ornament dropped on the floor.

2

The next day the first period was a lecture, and the whole class gathered in the large auditorium. Gleb sat in the same row as Sergei. Farther down sat Richeva with her girlfriend Marina Gurova.

The history of religion was being taught by a middle-aged man with glasses and a beard. He served as the pastor in some church but, according to Gleb, he was an atheist, because he didn't seem to believe in what he was saying and talked about Christ like one would about a fairy-tale character, like Baba Yaga or Koshei the Immortal.

Gleb wasn't listening to the lecturer and was looking at Richeva, who was talking with her friend very loudly, as if she were a teacher and was giving a lecture. *She's overdoing it*, thought Gleb, *overplaying it*.

Richeva was being very emotional: she smiled, shrugged her shoulders, took Marina's hand or hugged her. But she was doing it as if she were playing a role in some cheap play. As if she just had to finish playing this boring role and then she could fly off to a banquet with her friends.

Richeva also received and answered notes, winking to her girlfriends, making it look as if each time, having received a note, she had discovered something necessary, such as the meaning of life.

—Look, can't you see? It is impossible not to love her, Sergei said to Gleb.

—She's like the communal mother, nodded Gleb in response.

—Sitting there with Marina, a weightlifter without a barbell. And what's Marina's deal? She broke a leg, damn hedonist, and now has to walk around with a cane. Shouldn't she be settling down, beginning to think about life? Looking around. Asking herself, *How do I live? How should I be living? Maybe I've done something wrong, offended someone—Gleb, for instance?*

—Hush, interrupted Sergei. —Let me hear the lecture.

—He doesn't even know what he's saying, and you're sitting there listening to every word, said Gleb.

—It's interesting. Do you want to watch *Pokrovsky's Gates* tonight?

— My soul can't stand the sight of this weightlifter Marina. It rejects her. And what are these gates? Whom is this movie about? I'm sure it's something gross. I know you.

—The soul. The soul is one and the same.

—One . . . Yes, exactly. You have one soul; I have another. You see soul even in an action flick, even in Mexican soap operas, and you'll also probably find some sort of a grand theory there that is not applicable to real life. In a movie or a novel this invented theory may seem interesting and genius. But as soon as you try, even just in your mind, to apply this theory to life, it falls apart. We are told: *Look, people are killing each other, how great!* This is so you will watch this crap and know what not to do. But people watch it or read about it and become angry, alienated from each other, get dumber, and then die, without understanding why they were born, lived, got old, why they had kids, screamed at them, beat them, and then comforted them.

The lecturer looked toward them, and Gleb stopped talking.

— — —

Marina lived with her younger brother Gerka in a two-bedroom apartment, which their father rented for them. Gerka was out with friends, drinking vodka and beer. Marina was home cooking pasta. The doorbell rang, and Marina went to answer the door. There stood Gleb with a bottle of wine, Sergei with two packages, and Richeva.

—Come on in. I'm glad that you stopped by, she said to Gleb. He got embarrassed and handed her the bottle.

—Here, drink it. It's all for you.

—Thank you. Marina took the wine.

Gleb walked into the entryway and immediately smelled the sharp scent of tobacco and some sort of incense. *She just had a smoke*, he thought.

—Did you cook the pasta? asked Sergei. He took off his jacket and made his way into the kitchen.

Richeva sat down at the table and watched Gleb, who, in slippers, a blue shirt, pants, and a jacket, which he rarely took off indoors, was separating single-serve yogurt containers from each other. He really liked yogurt and ate it when others drank beer and vodka. To anyone who asked, he lied that he was allergic to alcohol and tobacco so he wouldn't be forced to drink and smoke.

—Your napkins are pink, Gleb said to Marina.

On the table, in a small pink bowl with medicines there were pink napkins. An outside observer probably wouldn't have noticed anything unusual about this at first, but if this person took a really good look at the kitchen and the other rooms, he would definitely notice one interesting characteristic of Marina's apartment: everything, starting from the toilet paper and ending with some crutches that were lacquered a blood red, was either pink or close to it. Even some of the prescriptions and vitamins that Marina was taking after the unfortunate fall that broke her leg were pink—but these, Marina pointed out, had been prescribed by her doctor.

Gleb also noticed that Marina had affixed a giant bow onto her bandaged leg. This bow, of course, was pink.

—Your napkins are pink, repeated Gleb, because no one had reacted in any way to his first utterance.

—And why does this surprise you so? You know that I like the color pink. And hate the color yellow.

—Oh come on! exploded Gleb. —What color is your pasta? A year ago you bought multicolored *pelmeni* and when those were cooked, you began picking out the pink ones for yourself, which is why you never got full. And then you hit Misha . . .

—Which Misha?

—Veismont. I'm going to call him right now. What a mess you've made. Do you know why you've got something pink in every hole here? Want me to tell you?

Richeva sat down in Gleb's lap and tried to calm him down.

—What's come over you? Relax.

She was petting his head like a German shepherd's and blowing in his ear.

—Richeva, do you want to know why Marina is surrounded with pink, and why she's a weightlifter?

—No.

—Well then get off me. You're not interested in anything. You all live in your shells, like snails. This one over here is already loaded, he turned to Marina. —Well? Do you like being like this? Listening to crap day after day, stuffing your head with garbage? Marina sat there silently, looking at the bottle of wine and smoking a cigarette. She could barely think.

—But it's so great, continued Gleb, —so great, when your head is clean and light.

—You can only feel that way if you get really drunk, interrupted Sergei. In his red sweater and black jacket, he looked ruddy and tall. —And then in the morning you gradually sober up and begin feeling like a human being.

The pasta was done. Marina began loading up the plates.

— — —

After dinner, Richeva, Sergei, and Marina went into another room to listen to some music. Gleb stayed in the kitchen to wash the dishes.

He put the teapot on the stove and sat down in a chair. From behind the closed door he could hear something scary and incomprehensible. Outside it started raining. Gleb began thinking that it would be great to turn off the room and turn up the cool and damp street.

—What is it? asked Richeva. She had quietly entered the kitchen and sat across from him. —Why are you sad?

—You know, Richeva, said Gleb, looking at the glasses on the table, —I'm not having a good time. I shouldn't have come.

—Why?

—Marina is very much like a stranger to me. It's odd to think that only a year ago, I was in love with her. It's strange how things turn out in life, hmm?

—Yes. Life is like that.

Richeva sighed loudly on purpose, and Gleb was unnerved by this sigh.

She's overplaying, he thought. *I need to go home, before I get angry.*

—Richeva, hey Richeva? Gleb playfully looked into Richeva's eyes, then stopped.

—What?

—Richeva. Why did you do this to Sergei?

—Do what?

—He came to you, bared his soul. And you didn't accept his love . . .

—You don't understand anything about these things, Richeva sounded nervous.

—Of course I don't understand. I can see how you all laugh at me behind my back. And laugh at my weightlifter theory. Unfortunately, I don't have too many more people who will listen to me. I can see that you're all like walls, standing there, your minds set, thinking, *It's okay, we can listen to this fool for a bit.* You are not serious about me, and not serious about anything in general, but I can't stop myself. And stop making that face, as if you understand what I'm talking about.

—I understand, said Richeva quietly, and she tried to compose

her face into innocence and thoughtfulness. But it came out looking
a bit morose, and cunning.

—You're lying.

—I understand, honestly. Well, how can I prove it to you? She
took his hand. —Believe me, it's the truth. I'm interested in what
you have to say. I'm always listening.

Gleb got up and walked over to the sink for a drink. He was
thirsty, but mostly he got up to take his hand away from Richeva's.

—So you never answered me, he said, sitting back down. —What's
with Sergei?

—I don't love him.

—I gladly believe you. And after saying this, how can you say that
you were ever listening to me?

—Well, can you imagine if I came to you with my love? All like
this: *I love you.* What would you say to me? *Go away, Richeva. Where
the heck did you come from?* Wouldn't you say this?

—How do you want me to answer that? said Gleb, then he
stopped to think about it.

No one has yet come to me like that, he thought, *though I have been
rejected. When someone comes to you—to send him away—what kind of a
person does one have to be? A person comes to you, and you can feel that he's
being genuine, that he can't live without you. If you have a soul, how can you
turn him away? You don't send a person away, you empathize with him.*

—Pity degrades a person, said Richeva. —I can't love Sergei. And
I don't want to pity him.

—And so we become so heartless, because we don't comfort
each other, our souls don't ache about others. As far as pity goes, you
can pity someone on the inside and not show it to this person. This
type of pity will not degrade him in any way. How stupid! We can't
even feel sorry for someone where no one sees and hears us—inside
ourselves.

—Don't think about it, it's really nothing.

—You tilt your head the way my dog does, but your smile is pret-
tier. What if I fall in love with you? Then you'll say: *Go away, Gleb.*

—I won't say that.

—And what makes me different from Sergei? What makes me
better than him, that I would deserve this special treatment?

—Don't insult me. Richeva pretended to take offense.

—Don't be mad, Mashka. Everything will be all right. About five years from now, you'll get married to some weightlifter. Make a bunch of babies. You'll remember nothing of me and my dumb theory. You will live a peaceful, quiet life, somewhere in your own little house. Or an apartment.

—You're funny.

—So what? Let's go outside. It's stopped raining.

3

Just after one in the morning they sat down to watch *Pokrovsky's Gates*. Gleb and Richeva sat on one couch, Marina and Sergei on the other. The lights were off. Gleb kept trying to say something, but the others hushed him. Everyone wanted to watch the movie.

Afterward Richeva and Marina went to bed. Sergei was also close to sleep, but Gleb woke him up and said, —Let's go fry some meat.

The freezer was full of beef and pork. The meat was frozen solid, but Gleb didn't want to defrost it: it would take too long. He took a large knife and began preparing it. He sliced the meat into thin slivers, like cheese. Sergei was busy with the potatoes. This uncomplicated process was observed by a small orange kitten with a collar. On this collar there glowed a tiny raspberry-colored paper bow.

—Everything that Marina owns is pink, said Gleb.

—I've noticed, replied Sergei. He didn't like the beginning of this conversation.

—Only her kitten is orange.

—Well, that's because pink cats don't exist in nature.

Gleb laughed loudly. He liked this response.

—You've hit the nail on the head. It's true, pink cats do not exist.

—Why do you dislike her so much? said Sergei.

—Because she's always being contrary, smiles when she should be crying. It's impossible to speak seriously with her. All she wants to do is contradict you. Anything that I say to her is perceived as a put-down or an insult, as if I'm trying to show that I'm better than her. She's not a person, but a boxer. She's assumed a stance and is punching back. She's approached by the coach, the audience, even strangers; they ask her about the weather, about how she's feeling, declare their love. And in return she body punches you. Only once was she ever earnest with me and not on the defensive—when she was drinking homemade wine, which she really liked. She said: *Yes, it tastes good.* I could hear honesty in her voice. She was being genuine—but in what small detail! And even back then, in Petersburg, I was declaring my undying friendship to her and asking her not to send me away. She did not reject me, but not because she got sentimental, I'm sure.

—Why else would she?

—Because of the law of weightlifting: a weightlifter will not attack his opponent. He wants to bite, but he can't. This instinct is gross, but we rely on our instinct, like goblins, and we brag about them. What's so supernatural about that? Try fighting them, try to override them. Marina lives according to relativity theory: it's impossible to prove anything, there is no God, there are no morals, and there is chaos and the universe everywhere. Naturally, she is a cold one.

—Gleb, she's right, said Sergei. —It's not good to be a maximalist.

Gleb quickly washed his hands, walked over to the window, and said to the orange cat, which was perched on the windowsill:

—I'm not a maximalist. Maximalists are people like Marina, like Volkova, people who have pushed their nihilism to the max, their disgust with everything living and sincere, with everything that comes from the heart, from the soul, everything that a human being thinks about happily, and toward which he strives unconditionally.

—Your theory is not right, began Sergei. —In some ways, it is close to life. But in general it has nothing really to do with it.

—I've already heard this somewhere. Could it have been from you? said Gleb with anger.

He looked at Sergei and shuddered internally. In front of Gleb stood a tall, lean person hanging his head low and thinking about something. His hair disheveled, orange, and matted. His gaze heavy, dead.

Why am I telling him all this? thought Gleb. *He's not listening, he's thinking about Richeva. No matter what I say, he stays silent. It may look as if everything is great, but in reality he has one thing on his mind, and I have another. We are very different people. And what should we do now, not talk to each other, not be friends?*

Sergei *was* thinking about something else: that a woman he loved was lying down, asleep, beautiful, beautiful. She was seeing dreams, probably, good ones, ones in which there was no Sergei, and probably never would be. And he was frying potatoes and meat even though he was not hungry. But when you have nothing better to do you might as well eat and try not to think for as long as possible. Not to think about the fact that he, Sergei, was alone, but he wanted another person to be near—a beautiful one or not, it didn't matter—with whom he could talk and share his sadness, for whom he could be glad that this person existed. To smile at, to hold. *It's good*, thought Sergei, *when someone close to you, someone dear, is by your side.* He remembered his grandmother and grandfather.

An exception to the rules, thought Sergei. *They live heart to heart. They don't fight. Only when Granny makes a pot of cabbage soup, Grandpa will try it and say that it's not bad, will pass for dinner. And then, for some reason, he'll smile. And Grandma also seems glad: and it's not clear how they understand each other, what is this law, according to which they live together for so long and never fight, and instead quietly and peacefully love each other.*

Gleb walked across the kitchen, from the window to the refrigerator, opened the cupboard, and took out a box of tea leaves.

Sergei sat at the table moving the potatoes around the pan to make them cool faster. Outside the window it was night, dark and melancholy. The orange kitten was looking out the window; it wanted to run into the street.

Gleb said,—In the third grade, when we were kids, when we were still pure and loved each other, we had to write an essay: "What Do I Want to Be When I Grow Up? What Is Freedom? . . ." and something else in that vein. About three years ago our teacher gave my essay back to me. *Freedom is when you're doing everything that you want to be doing and are not causing harm to others*, I had written. Recently, I read it again and was surprised at what kind of a person I was back then. And what kind of a person I am now. I have become some sort of a half-wit. I've become crass, I swear often. I could scream at someone. I don't respect others' opinions. I only accept my own. I keep arguing with all of you, for some reason, keep criticizing you, don't respect you as proper human beings. But if I really think about it—is this really the way to be? Even if you're not living correctly, in a way that I would like you to, I'm not supposed to be yelling at you, beating you, am I? Something different needs to happen here. And my theory talks about that, as well.

—We also had to write an essay like that. I wanted to be a truck driver, like my father, said Sergei, —and now I no longer care. I need to write a new essay. The old one is obsolete.

—It will do. We are the ones who changed. God is still there, as he always was. He's calling us to him. But we're not going—we think that there is something higher, better.

4

The weekend came and went. On Monday, Sergei and Gleb had the same lecture hall as Richeva. Sergei sat in the auditorium, impatient. He wasn't listening to the lecturer, but was trying to draw something in his notebook, and was waiting for the bell.

Sergei had decided to invite Richeva to go fishing at the end of the week.

Gleb also needed to see Richeva: he had written a poem about what a bad person she was and he wanted to give it to her.

The lecture ended. Gleb and Sergei stepped into the hallway. Almost all of the students had left the auditorium, but Richeva was nowhere to be seen.

Next to Gleb stood Voklova and Peresekina. They were giggling. Gleb thought the girls were laughing at him.

With her jet-black hair, Volkova was not very tall, slightly hunched over, with dark circles shining under her eyes, because of which, from the side, she appeared to be sickly, shy. But as soon as you got closer your opinion of her changed. Her mind was sharp, her personality adaptive, her lack of principles and her regular expressions of self-absorption set her apart from the others. Sometimes, Volkova couldn't be called a person at all. Often, she became a real she-wolf—and not only at midnight. She bared her teeth, she growled and attacked. To tear out another's throat, to put him down, to demonstrate her strength, her hard intellect, is what she liked.

—Woof-woof, said Gleb to himself and stared at Volkova in a friendly way.

Suddenly, the door opened. Richeva walked out of the auditorium. She was laughing and looking back over her shoulder.

—Hi, Mashka, said Volkova in a showy way and came over to Richeva for hugs.

They kissed, then began inquiring about each other's health, praising each other. And everything about the way Richeva, Volkova, and Peresekina looked said that they were not noticing Gleb and Sergei.

Volkova and Peresekina left, and as soon as the girls disappeared around the corner, Richeva approached Gleb:

—What's up?

—Nothing. Everything's great, said Gleb. He had changed his mind about speaking with Richeva. He hid his poem in his pocket and said:

—Tra-la-la.

—What is this *tra-la-la*? Richeva asked with confusion and then got quiet.

—Mashka, said Sergei, —what are you doing on Saturday?

—Why?

—Will you go fishing with us?

Richeva paused.

—No. I'm busy, I have things I need to do.

—I understand, said Gleb, —I understand which things those are. Let's go, he said to Sergei. —We need to buy some glue. The store is going to close soon.

He waved his hand in Richeva's direction and began walking toward the exit:

—I will wait for you outside.

—What's wrong with him? asked Richeva.

—I don't know. So you can't . . . said Sergei.

—No. Richeva shook her head. —There is no way. But you can catch me a big fish and bring it to me, okay?

— — —

—Catch her a fish, grumbled Gleb. He was walking with Sergei to the store. —I'll bring her a fish. The devil knows what's going on in that girl's head!

—Let's sit down, said Sergei.

Up ahead there was an alley with benches. Sergei wasn't feeling well. He felt tired, very slow, and was straining to walk, falling behind Gleb.

—Go ahead, sit down. I don't feel like it, said Gleb.

They were silent for a while.

The heat of May was already full on. The trees had gotten dressed a long time ago; you could see the yellow of dandelions here and there. The sun was shining with glee. Bird song was mixing with the voices of cars—there was a highway nearby.

Gleb was happy, alert. He stood up straight next to the bench where Sergei sat hunched over and sad. Gleb was thinking about something good, light. Sergei, on the contrary, was thinking about his life and couldn't find anything that would make it worthwhile to continue.

—Some weather today, said Gleb.

—Yes, it's quite beautiful. Can I read some poetry to you? asked Sergei.

—Of course, agreed Gleb, and he began walking in circles around the bench.

Sergei read from his notebook, a recently written poem, long and tortured. Gleb tuned in periodically. He was concerned with something else, something that he thought was important, and about which he needed to tell somebody, anybody. If Sergei wouldn't listen to him right then, he would explain everything to his dog at home.

—This poem is genius, lied Gleb. —It's very good, I can hear a good melody. But you know something? You are writing about Richeva . . .

—This poem has a dual meaning.

—Well, okay, let it have a dual meaning. Only you shouldn't be writing poetry for Richeva. You shouldn't be talking to her at all. Do you even understand what just happened?

—No.

—Let me explain it to you. Richeva is coming out of the auditorium. There are two hyper-weightlifters standing next to us, headed by a she-wolf. And what happens? She pays us zero attention. She's too embarrassed to even look in our direction with them there, let alone talk to us. First she approaches them, they lick each other like little animals, and only when the terminators have left the hallway does she come over to us. And what makes us different from Volkova? I'm not factoring God into this equation—it's not for me to judge. But as far as barbells, I have the right to comment, am obligated to. Let's say you and I have barbells weighing ten pounds, and Volkova's weighs a thousand. So who else, if not her, would Richeva be bowing to? Here it is, her highly spirited choice. When barbells are not in the picture everything's great; she's happy with us, playful, friendly. But as soon as a weightlifter whistles—it is as if she doesn't know us at all, and she runs toward him, breaking the waves. When she has to make a choice between the absence of barbells and their presence, she chooses the barbells without thinking. A normal person is not concerned with weightlifting and could care less about the barbells. A normal person pays attention to different things.

—Let me read you some more poetry? said Sergei. He didn't want to listen to Gleb. He sat quietly on the green bench, leafing through his notebook.

—Let's go, that's enough sitting, the store will close. We need to get some glue.

—What do you need it for?

—I'm going to glue together some planes. They're not flying very well.

5

Their path went through a long alley of chestnut trees, which were beginning to bloom. There were no people around. Only a pack of homeless dogs, of different sizes and colors, walked by.

Sergei was silent. Once again his head hung low. Gleb was looking around, looking up, at the balconies, the little edge of the sky. The sky was hidden by the chestnut tree leaves and the uniform houses.

—You know, Lisichkin, began Gleb (he liked calling people by their last names), —I know this one girl. We've known each other for a long time. She's beautiful. Not without a barbell, but she has will power. She has a boyfriend. Most girls would be too scared to look at him, let alone befriend him. He's not that bad, not too creepy. But he's weak, sorry-looking. He's always getting beat up, made fun of. He has no friends. So what? Here, I can say without a "but": *Yes, this is love, without a doubt.* This girl Natashka loves someone without a barbell, and so I say, with pleasure: *Good girl!* Now let's look at a different situation. A girl—say a prime minister's daughter—has fallen in love with a poor young man. Is this it: love?

—Of course, it's love—if he's poor.

—Yes, he's not rich. But he has something else as a barbell, which one could love: he's beautiful, muscular; he has many friends, also just as strong and muscular, and so on. And here I cannot say that this is love. The girl just likes animalistic barbells better. And they are more powerful than the money or the social barbells. But girls are getting smarter these days. It used to be that in order to survive, her husband had to go hunting, kill a mammoth, drag it to the cave. He had to be strong, limber, fearless. And some girls are still living according to those instincts and choose themselves a husband like that—a hunter, a husband-animal. But the female gender is adjusting, getting more intelligent. They've begun to understand that if a husband has money, he'll go and buy a mammoth at the store, and at home a cook will prepare it.

Suddenly Gleb stopped, then said:

—We don't have time to pick up glue. I forgot I need to go see my brother. There is some business . . .

—I don't care either way. I'm going home.

—Bye.

Gleb pretended to be looking for some important object in his bag. Sergei walked away, looking back every once in a while. Gleb waved his hand at him and continued to pointlessly look at his notebooks, touching them periodically.

Gleb waited until Sergei disappeared around a corner and then hurried, walking very fast, back to campus.

Richeva was sitting in the cafeteria, surrounded by a couple of guys unfamiliar to Gleb. —Weightlifters, he whispered.

Gleb bought tea and some pierogies and made himself comfortable at a nearby table. Richeva turned to him and invited him to join them.

Gleb gracefully accepted, although he could see that Richeva had only invited him to be polite.

—You're drinking beer, he said, sitting down.

—Would you like some? offered one of the two guys.

—I don't drink beer. Well, what's your conversation about? asked Gleb.

—Nothing, really. We're just sitting here, resting.

—So you don't have conversations about Tolstoi. I get it. Weightlifters, like yourselves, are always sitting around resting with beer.

Richeva got embarrassed. The guys looked at each other.

—Can I talk to you for a second? said Richeva.

—Sure.

They walked out into the hallway, and Richeva immediately went for the body punch:

—How dare you. Stop saying ridiculous things. How do you know if they are weightlifters or not? You've known them for a long time?

—I could tell by their mugs who they were, right away. Don't you have anything better to do than associate with them?

—Where the heck are you getting these words, *to associate*, *to not associate*? I talk to whomever I want to.

—You don't have the right.

Richeva looked at Gleb and got scared. Gleb had a mean, hateful look, with cynicism and disdain, of which he wasn't ashamed. He wanted to openly tell Richeva what kind of person he thought she was and that he would keep fighting against that kind of person. *You're not letting me live*, could be read in his dark eyes, in his open and fearless face, in his hunched posture.

Gleb was playing with the keys in his pockets, crumpling money. His entire body felt light, free, as if his freedom were contained in this one and only act—to stand there, hating Richeva.

—Don't look at me like that, as if you're going to hit me.

—Don't be scared, your bulls will avenge you, Richeva.

—What is going on with you? Why don't you stop by my place, sometime? Only not today—today I'm busy. We can have some cake, I'll feed you.

—I get a feeling, Richeva, that you talk to me, invite me over, because of pity toward me, or something. Or is this not true? I'm ready to believe that this is not true, but everything around us speaks otherwise. Maybe you yourself don't notice this, but people like myself, like Sergei, are not people of your circle. You want to, maybe, force yourself to believe that this is not true, but there is nothing you can do to help yourself. Understand, nowadays people become friends, get married, and so on, on the basis of barbell equality and not the kinship of spirit. I'm very sorry that you are a person just like all others. You are a common person, with your own particularities, quirks, and so on. But you, like everyone, are living according to the law of the barbell. Over the course of the month, I've observed you very carefully, took note. And I have determined your diagnosis: you are a weightlifter. Go to your Volkova and lift your barbell there. You are not as good at lifting your spirit; your spirit is not a real one. Spirit can never be for show.

Gleb knew that what he was saying wasn't right, that it wasn't the way to talk to people. "Love your enemy," he remembered and thought:

I can't, I don't have the strength to love.

Richeva waited until Gleb stopped talking, turned around, and went back into the cafeteria. She, of course, wanted to say something, but she understood that his mind could not be changed.

And Gleb went home. He didn't bother changing his clothes and just sat on the couch for a long time. Without moving. And even Volchok, his dog, didn't beg to go for a walk in the woods, as he usually did. The dog felt that his owner was upset by something and so laid down nearby, on the rug, and drifted to sleep.

NUCLEAR SPRING

Evgeni Alyokhin
Translated by Victoria Mesopir

TO ME, Elina was undoubtedly a talented person. I admired her. Her independence and wit. For example, she sold tablets against radiation for one hundred twenty roubles a set to dumbfucks— school kids and college freshmen—passing them off as I don't even know what. And she got them for ten. Do the math: one hundred ten roubles, like off a freakin' tree. She also managed to get to classes, write random articles, and party—the last I didn't approve of, although I didn't tell her. Keep in mind, too, she was also a freshman. Like me. Only I wasn't on top of anything. And she was my girl, the very first. The first, not counting the couple of occasions the runner only made it to second base, as they say. But that has nothing to do with anything. I loved Elina; she made me want to cry, laugh, jump, fall, smash to pieces, die like a dog, yet keep on living.

—You want? she asked when it became clear that the beer would soon run out, and we still had highs and lows to reach.

She pulled out some tablets.

Egor and I looked at each other. I'd never considered using wheels, as they say, until the occasion presented itself. I thought for half a second, then decided that I would.

—This is the Toren you've heard of, it's just that I don't have anything better with me. And even this—just a set plus two units— won't be enough."

—Come on, I said. —Not enough! How many of them do you have to take? Twelve for four—not enough?

—Twelve? she asked. —Eight. Six in the set. Six plus two equals eight.

She showed two tablets in her palm. Put them on the table, pulled out a little plastic packing, unscrewed it, poured out another six.

—If we had three each, that'd do it. But we can do this: swallow one and snort the other.

Egor asked:

—Snort the tablets?

—Uh huh. That way they'll work faster and stronger. Gotta crush and snort 'em, just like powder.

—This isn't bad for your health? I asked.

Olya let out a chuckle. Yeah, Elina's friend Olya was also with us. I actually didn't like Olya very much because I suspected Elina was cheating on me with her.

—Give me some kinda paper, Elina said to Egor—because we were at his pad, you see, not because she might find him attractive in any way. That was out of the question.

While Egor found a notebook and tore out a sheet, I, Elina, and Olya (would've been better if she hadn't been with us) each swallowed a tablet, washing it down with the remaining beer. Egor looked at us doubtfully, but then also took a tablet. Then Elina crushed one into a pile on a sheet of paper for me:

—You gonna?

—Yeah, and grease it up, I replied.

I was her guy, and so I immediately snorted that shit. A cold and dry tornado rushed from my nose to my head. But I didn't flinch.

—Nah, I'd better have another drink, said Egor.

—Too bad, I said, and showed him a fist with the thumb up.

In the bathroom, I tuned in to myself. Nothing. The Toren wasn't working so far. That was good: if the others started tripping, I'd have a great time of it. My system was stronger—at least in terms of weed and alcohol—I could take three times as much as Egor. I washed my hands and drank water from the tap. Of course, I know you shouldn't drink tap water, but what could I do, the urge was really strong—and very pressing—and so I drank.

Stepping out into the corridor, I bumped into Egor's mother and smiled at her stupidly. It was better than saying "hi" to her again. And just walking past her like she was empty space also seemed stupid to me. Although, smiling stupidly was probably even more stupid. I walked into stupid Egor's room on rubber legs.

Egor sat at his computer. Elina and Olya sat on his bed, giggling about something. *Your friend Egor is a total bore,* I heard Elina's voice in my head.

—School kids broke into the physics lab with the aim of looting the medicine cabinet, said Elina.

—School kids broke into the physics lab with the aim of looting the medicine cabinet, repeated Olya.

They laughed again. Whether they were putting me on, I couldn't really tell.

— Get that shit the fuck out of here! I said.

—Whoa, said Egor.

—It's a quotation, I said. —From *Jay and Silent Bob Strike Back.*

Egor turned to me and said:

—What they said was also a quotation.

He read to me from some Web site: *School kids broke into the physics lab with the aim of looting the medicine cabinet for Toren. They learned about the effects of the substance during the Basic Life Safety class. After ingesting the tablets, the teens were hospitalized and diagnosed with "poisoning." As per safety regulations, the medicine cabinet should not contain real tablets, but in that district school the tablets were real, for some reason. Now the agents of state narco-control services are leading an investigation throughout regional schools. Medicine cabinets containing Toren are being confiscated.*

Elina and Olya laughed again.

—Yah, and? I asked.

Elina went to the toilet with Olya. They were giggling and holding on to each other. I really didn't like this.

—So, what d'ya think? I asked Egor, meaning his condition.

—I don't know, he replied.

He turned to the computer and switched one song for another.
I said:

—And what d'ya make of Elina?

He jumped up and went to the toilet. After a few seconds he returned and said:

—Fuck, they've locked themselves in and are freakin' neighing it up in there. I got Mother at home.

He left again. And again returned. I didn't care. *Let him walk up and down all he wants*, I thought. I was touching my feet. They had big warm goose bumps running up and down them. I told Egor:

—School kids broke into the physics lab with the aim of looting the medicine cabinet.

He left again, and I lit up. Egor was also seventeen, but as long as we took turns we could smoke at his place. We could smoke, and it was already the middle of the night, and here we were, doing devil knows what.

Egor finally brought Elina and Olya back. Elina said:

—We just couldn't get away from the tap.

—You're too beautiful, I replied, —to be drinking water from the tap.

I looked at Olya. She had a fiery tear rolling down her cheek, like a drop of hot polyethylene, and it left a gray burn on her skin. I decided not to say anything. Let her sort it out for herself. I repeat: this Olya, even though she was a good friend of my beloved, was not someone I liked. She was just a leech. To my mind, she didn't have a single virtue.

Egor switched on the television, only he couldn't decide on a channel: he just kept clicking from one to another, like a half-wit. I watched, not understanding anything from any single show, then my mind slowed down a little and, as a result, I dozed off in the armchair. I came to when I felt hands on my face. It was Elina. At first I couldn't understand what she wanted or who she was. She said:

—Wake up.

And kissed me.

—Why are you sleeping?

I came to, because she never kissed me in front of strangers, as a rule. And when she did kiss me, I immediately got a hard-on.

I looked around—and then understood where I was. Egor and Olya slept on the bed with their backs to each other—and I don't blame them for this: neither one had anything attractive about them.

—What time is it?

Elina looked at her cell and said:

—Already one thirty.

—Let's go to my place? I asked.

—Let's go.

I got up and shook Egor.

—Egor. Egor. We're going.

He got up and walked us to the door. I said:

—Olga will stay with you. Okay?

Egor didn't say a thing. He had a very focused look and a very sleepy one, at the same time.

We went down the staircase. In the driveway I allowed myself to take Elina by the hand. She wasn't against it, and that was nice. I brought her hand to my lips. If not for the dryness in my nose and mouth, everything would've been fine. I remembered that we'd snorted that crap.

—I'm not snorting that stuff anymore. I thought your friend was crying fiery tears.

—Fiery tears? Elina repeated.

We walked out of the courtyard. It wasn't all that far to my place. Walk past the Housing and Maintenance office, beyond the garages, the garage co-op—the co-op head sells moonshine and doesn't give credit—and that's where the private sector begins. That's where I live.

My girl and I were leaving the zone of nuclear pollution.

We walked under the streetlights, and everything was somehow not right. But you couldn't tell whether it was good or bad. Just— not right. Like looking at life through thick glass. I imagined how someone would react if he ate a whole set of Toren: his heart slows down, his senses start working differently, his mind shuts down, and that man, on rubber legs, attempts to scramble the hell out of the lethal level of the radiation zone. The man hallucinates. He sees bright acidic blotches of radiation fall on his clothes and body.

We walked up to my house. I quietly opened the gate, let Elina in, closed it. Seen from above, we must have resembled a couple desperados on the run from pursuers chasing after us in a helicopter and shouting into a megaphone: —Stop, stop, you've got nowhere to run! The window to my room was the nearest to the porch. I walked up to it while Elina stood on the porch. She and I, we worked in such good harmony; our bodies were part of a difficult puzzle that needed to be assembled as quickly as possible to connect all the necessary elements. Hot clots of energy circulated through the veins.

I said:

—I'll have to climb in. Stay.

Elina said nothing; she'd already been witness to this situation twice. I climbed onto the ledge, then grabbed the ventilation window. Carefully, this had to be done carefully, because the pane from the ventilation window had already fallen off once. I stuck my hand through the ventilation window, grabbed the frame on the inside. That's it, the rest was easy. Before this point, a fall was possible. I stretched out my hands and leaned against the windowsill. Next I tensed up and squeezed my torso inside. It was like traveling between two worlds. I found myself inside my room. I got down from the windowsill, pulled off my shoes, opened and shut my eyes several times. Having adjusted to the dark, I quietly went into the corridor. I didn't switch on the light. It was dark in the corridor, but you could see everything if you focused.

The door to my room was opposite the one to my parents' room. My father and stepmother's room. My father wasn't there; he, thank God, was away on business. But my stepmother was home. And, unfortunately, the door to their room was open. I listened. Stepmother was wheezing in the dark—asleep. I stood for some five seconds. Wheezing, sleeping. I walked to the door to the anteroom and pulled it up and toward me so that it wouldn't creak too loudly. I listened again. Among the other sounds—from the running fridge and the ticking clock in the kitchen to the water pressure in the radiator—I isolated stepmother's wheezing. All okay. Then I stepped into the anteroom and opened the door to the outside.

I had to do all this because we only had one key, which opened the door from both sides. If everyone left the house, the key was left in the bath cabin. I don't know why we never made a duplicate for everybody. Such important things, like cutting an extra key, always get forgotten. Sometimes I'm out at night, and my father and step-mother think that I'm sleeping. So it's been with us always, what can you do? It's much simpler in Egor's case. With me, it's more compli-cated. Once, I brought Elina home with me, wanting her to spend the night, but my father wouldn't allow it.

Elina and I quietly tiptoed back to my room. She took her shoes off in the dark and said quietly:

—I need to drink. And pee.

—Hold on, I replied, just as quietly.

I also had to drink, urgently. I stepped out into the corridor, went into the kitchen. Now I didn't try to act quite so undercover. Maybe I just went to the kitchen to get some water at night, what of it? I switched on the kitchen light and drank water out of the three-liter jar. A silver coin jangled against the bottom. They say silver purifies water; that's why it was put there. Only then did I think of closing the door to my parents' room. It must've opened up by itself, this sometimes happened. It was doubtful stepmother was sleeping with the door open on purpose. I switched off the light, stepped out into the corridor, and closed my parents' door. I brought the water to Elina. The whole jar. I too would need more, and more than once. The Sahara desert had spread in my mouth and nose. Elina drank some water, and I took her to the toilet. Everything had to be done with extreme caution. While she peed, I stood in the corridor, listen-ing. Sound of the fridge, sounds in the pipes, the quiet murmur of Elina peeing. All okay. She came out; we returned to the room.

I quickly undressed her, we kissed, I took my clothes off, and there we were, completely naked. The dryness persisted, though. Two thirsts. We had two thirsts; we were in two worlds at once. Each completely unlike the other—like heaven and hell. First I kissed her breasts, I kissed her stomach, I kissed her between her legs, I hugged her tightly in my arms. Got down on her. Elina tried to guide me, but I had already found my own way in. This is the most important moment, there is nothing better, and there never will be. It's like I look at a drop and see the ocean, this eternity that cannot be con-tained. We came, drank some water, then started over. And then one more time. And then we had to leave, because it was already almost seven o'clock. Morning was lightening the room, and we had to leave before stepmother woke up.

We did everything we had done earlier, only in reverse. We dressed quickly. I took Elina out into the corridor, then into the anteroom. Let her out, closed the door with the key. All just as quietly and seriously. Like special-ops commandos. I returned to my room. Climbed out of the ventilation window onto the porch. It had snowed outside. This was impossible, because it was the month of May. But I wanted it this way, and the snow fell.

—Nuclear winter, I said.

And kissed Elina.

—Spring, she corrected.

We quietly walked out of the fenced area; I closed the gate. We walked to the bus stop. The snow crunched under our feet, and our soles left small nuclear-explosion craters in it. We needed to ride downtown and walk around a little. At 8:30 Elina's parents would leave for work. We would go to her place and sleep a little. Then wake up.

At the bus stop, Elina suddenly remembered:

—We forgot Olga.

I didn't like Olga. I was jealous of her. One time, Elina suggested we have a threesome. I didn't want to, but I agreed. And it didn't work for me. I couldn't. I was too embarrassed that there were three of us. With just two—this was never the case. When it was the two of us, I was Elina's cyborg, model Fucker 2003.

Now I said:

—Maybe, Olya will make it home on her own?

I thought Elina would disagree, but she replied:

—Okay.

And a nuclear snowflake fell on her eyelash.

THE DIESEL STOP

Arkady Babchenko
Translated by Nick Allen

THE INVESTIGATOR'S flaming ginger hair almost outshone the feeble, dust-covered lightbulb hanging in the corner of the gloomy cell. Dark green, flaking walls deepened the murk, while the space within them seemed to emanate from the sheet of cheap yellow paper that he placed on the table.

"Right, this is the form about your detention by the militia. Sign it," he said, his triangular face dwarfed by the shock of hair on his head. He reminded me of Klepa the Clown from our ABC kids' show.

"I wasn't detained, Comrade Captain, I came here of my own accord."

"What do you mean you weren't detained? Are you being funny? See here: 'Detained by the militia at Belorussky Station.'"

"I didn't even go to Belorussky," I replied, pulling the paper over to read. It contained the name of some Private Denezhkin.

"That's not me, my name's Babchenko, and I'm a staff sergeant.

"Really?"

He took the sheet and peered at it. "Yes, you're right . . . it's not yours."

— — —

They held me at the commandant's office the morning I returned to get my leave papers stamped. The senior duty officer at my unit had processed my leave and, since my father had died, gave me ten days. I went straight from the airport to the crematorium in my uniform and long boots, arriving just as they sent the coffin into the furnace. The heat made the lice stir beneath my tunic.

That evening my dysentery got worse. Everyone in the regiment got the squirts badly but the constant tension of life at the front kept your metabolism from breaking down completely. But once back home I started to bleed heavily. When I sprayed the bathroom from toilet bowl to ceiling yet another time my mother called an ambulance. I was diagnosed as being in the final stages of acute infectious dysentery, protruding ulcers had appeared in my intestines, and I was to be hospitalized immediately, flushed through with chlorine, and allowed no visitors.

I spent only one day in the hospital. It was more like a detention center, with bars on the windows, metal doors, guards, a separate toilet for each ward, and absolutely no going out into the city. But I was able to escape using a fake pass given to me by of one of the convalescent cases, got past the guard posts, slipped through the fence, and scooted out of there.

I had only ten days and it would have been idiocy to spend them in a hospital bed. You don't think about your health at these moments and simply ignore the need to care for it in the interests of your future. Your immediate future is already determined and holds nothing else apart from the war. Compared to this, bleeding dysentery seems a minor irritation.

And to worry about getting cured is to guess at the future and that's a dangerous pursuit. War is very closely bound to the laws of metaphysics—you can't win continually. It's better to lose continually so that when you really need to you score that big win, you do, just once but when the stakes are highest. Which all means that the worse things are now, the better.

That said, I still took the tablets they gave me in the hospital, so that I didn't give up the ghost completely.

I overstayed my leave, of course, by about ten days. In 1996 they never let anyone out of Mozdok, the main garrison town by Chechnya, because no one ever came back, and if they did it was in no sooner than four months. I only played truant for ten days, hardly worth mentioning.

But they saw things differently in the commandant's office. Instead of just stamping my leave papers, the captain I gave them to through the little window asked me why I was late. I gave him a certificate confirming my sickness that I had gotten from my local doctor. The captain took all the papers and disappeared somewhere.

He came back twenty minutes later.

"Follow me."

We went deep inside the building and then crossed a little court-yard and went out the back door and into another building with long corridors and lots of cabinets. We stopped in a large hall with a giant red carpet and oak paneling, all very grand and fit for a general. There was just one door off the hall that bore a sign saying COM-MANDANT.

"Wait here," the officer said, knocked and went in. He came out shortly after.

"Is everything okay, Comrade Captain?"

"Yes, everything's okay. Let's go."

— — —

Once again we passed through long corridors, only instead of going outside, we descended into a brightly lit basement.

Behind a wide desk sat an athletic-looking officer in dress uni-form. A soldier stood behind him writing something in an exercise book.

The captain handed my papers to the officer.

"Here, we caught another AWOL," he said, using the abbreviation for "absent without leave."

I still had no idea what was going on and waited for them to finish their red tape and finally set me free so I could go straight to the station and buy my ticket to Prokhladny. There I'd change to the branch line and go on to Mozdok and travel from there by convoy to Chechnya.

The officer glanced at my service book, leave papers, and

medical certificate and then barked, "Laces, belt, and dog tags on the table."

The tags hung from my tunic on a long, sturdy cord—*So I don't hang myself in my cell*, the thought flashed through my mind. The reality of what was happening started to dawn on me.

"Comrade Captain, I'm not AWOL, I came of my own accord, you saw for yourself . . . I'm on my way back to my unit!" I protested as the captain strode back down the long corridor.

"Comrade Captain, here's my doctor's note, I'm going back, what are you doing?"

He reached the turn in the corridor, his rapid steps echoing crisply off the walls.

"Comrade Captain!"

He didn't look back.

"Is something not clear, Sergeant? Put your belt, laces, and dog tags on the table!" the officer roared over the desk. His face contorted with fury and the soldier behind him stooped even lower over his exercise book. At any moment he would start to smack me about—his kind doesn't stand on ceremony.

Thoughts cascaded through my head: I had to explain that my dad had died, that I had dysentery and spurted blood from my butt, that it was all there in the doctor's note, that I had no intention of going absent without leave and was on my way back to my unit even though I wasn't fully recovered.

But I was still lagging behind events and said none of this.

Looking the officer in the eyes I took off my dog tags and put them on the table.

"Laces!"

I sat down and removed my laces.

They stood me facing the wall, my hands behind my back, opened a cell that adjoined the room, and led me in.

— — —

You could say that this was the first time during my entire military service that I genuinely felt humiliation. I had been beaten up plenty of times but that's all it was, a beating, not some dreadful moral indignity. That's just the way it was, how people conversed with each other, and the blows were merely a catalyst for some further action, nothing more. No one ground me down per se. The people who hit me had been through more than I had and this gave them the right to give someone else a hiding, or so it seemed at the time.

— — —

The only person who really tormented me was Said, one of the older recruits who would boost his own self-esteem by abusing others. But not even Said took away my freedom of choice: he always left me in a position to influence my life—I could end it at any moment.

Here, their "laces, belt, and dog tags on the table" deprived me of the right to even hang myself. And what was the sense of it all anyway? I was on my way back to the front, all they had to do was let me go and two days later I'd be back in the trenches. Why drag it out, that's all they wanted of me anyway, wasn't it? And what had these people been through themselves to accuse me of anything? Had any of them even seen active service, worked wonders through sheer willpower, spilled blood by the bucket like Red Cavalrymen?

No they hadn't, but still they labelled me AWOL, a scumbag or filthy coward: *You're a deserter and we're going to put you against the wall.*

— — —

The cell was tiny, big enough for a couple of people at a squeeze. No bunk bed, table, or slop bucket, nothing but four walls, floor, and ceiling. It was evidently a basement storage room but it also struck me as the kind of room they take you from for your execution by firing squad.

The barred window was set at the level of the sidewalk and looked out on Basmannaya Street. Sunlight streamed in with glimpses of summer, elegant heels and tanned feet in sandals, hems of skirts and dresses, cigarette butts lying in the dust.

I probably felt like the troops who escaped encirclement in 1941 must have felt as they were still put before a tribunal for desertion, racked with confusion and a realization of the irrevocability of events as they were branded a disgrace to the Red Army and traitors to the motherland.

Nope, no one here gives a damn about your dysentery.

— — —

I stood on my toes, grabbed the bars, and hung there staring out, pondering the irony: if you don't want to go back they lock you up, if you do, they lock you up.

A person who has had his laces and belt taken away soon starts to feel like a creature of a lower order; it's basic psychology. I was actually still wearing my sneakers and with no laces they did look pretty hobo. This street I had just walked down was suddenly so far away, it was still only two inches away from me, but I'd lost any chance of getting back there.

Dammit, how did it all go off the rails like this so fast?

— — —

My two escorts were sitting in the back of a UAZ jeep. They stuck me between them, cramped into a space so small that I could barely move my arms, like some villain in a detective movie. They didn't handcuff me, though, not that I had any intention of trying to escape.

We waited for the escort officer.

"What are you going to the brig for?" one of them asked.

"Overstayed my leave."

"By much?"

"Just ten days."

"Oh boy, you're in for it now, buddy, we've had guys here who were just ten minutes late and landed in the shit, but you . . ."

"So what'll happen to me now?"

"Disciplinary battalion."

"For how long?"

"Three years."

The lieutenant appeared a few minutes later, jumped in the front passenger seat, and turned round.

"Is that your mother standing there by the gate?" he asked me.

"I can't see, probably."

"Hide him," he told the escorts. "Stick him on the floor so his mom doesn't see him, or the hysterics and phone calls will start . . ."

All this was said in front of me without the least awkwardness, as if they were just stating the obvious. And it certainly didn't occur to anyone to tell my mother that they were taking me away.

"How long will you let her stand there?"

The question went unanswered.

"Will someone tell her that I've been moved?"

Again silence.

I climbed over the backseat and sat in the baggage space on the floor. The last thing I needed now was to be crammed down by someone's feet and if they didn't like it they'd have to move me again by force.

The escort officer looked at me but said nothing.

"Let's go."

The driver pulled out and stepped on the gas as we went through the gates. Through the plastic window in the jeep's soft roof I caught a glimpse of my mother's bewildered face. Her son had gone into the commandant's office and vanished.

— — —

The brig they took me to was at Lefortovo Prison, in the basement of the Tsar Peter Barracks. It was a large casemate with vaulted ceilings that dated to tsarist times, windowless, with two rows of cells down a gray, U-shaped corridor and fitted with bars and closed-circuit TV cameras.

The air in prisons is always distinctive. Musty, of course, but not the same mustiness you get in the outside world. It's more the combined smell of cellars, unwashed bodies, boots, chlorine, slop buckets, and something else, something subtle and hard to describe—maybe incarceration itself, a biting smell that pervades your uniform so that even in the barracks you can tell who just did guard duty in the brig.

They took me and a few other newcomers through the exercise yard, a caged ten-square-yard monkey pen in the open air, and admitted us one by one into the next block: "Face the wall, hands behind your back!" We were led to a barber and a disinfector in the sanitizing area, where we were stripped, sat on stools, and shorn bald within five minutes. They gave us one disposable razor among us and drove us like a bunch of monkeys into the shower block, a large ceramic tiled room with a few nozzles and wooden duckboards on the filthy, soapy floor.

We were made to shave everything—armpits, crotches, and even our chests. Already blunt when we got it, the razor mercilessly ripped out the hairs and spots of blood rose around our privates. For some reason I was bothered most of all by my bald crotch, which immediately became . . . I don't even know what—childlike, un-soldierly. I could have cried.

They gave us a couple of wash mittens and even though the escorts stood at the entrance, we took our time, washed happily for about twenty minutes, knowing there would be no such indulgence for a long time to come. Then they gave us our convict uniforms— old tunics and pants with no insignia or belt, foot bindings, and boots—and took us to our cells.

— — —

The body shaving was not the herd treatment we had endured in Mozdok, when we had to form up by the barracks, crouch, and defecate on a piece of paper that we then handed to a young and pretty female doctor for dysentery analysis. Slabs of meat, as the army viewed us, are incapable of feeling embarrassment.

But in this place I didn't feel like a soldier at all anymore, not even like a person in the full sense of the word. To have to stand in front of your escorts and shave your crotch is naturally degrading too, only here the humiliation was not unthinking, as it was in Mozdok, but intentional. It was part of the process of crushing us, part of the game of "investigators and detainees." You have to reduce a person immediately, while he's still susceptible and hasn't taken control of himself and adapted to the here and now.

A detainee is in a constant state of stress, unable to properly gauge his situation. Things that are trifling matters in the free world can assume huge and tragic proportions in a cell. That's why they start to scare you and grind down your will to resist from the get-go: "You've gone and done it now, kid, here it comes. Do you even understand what you've done? It's prison for you now, for a long time. I wouldn't like to be in your shoes," and so on.

And it works. They call you a deserter, a traitor, a walking scumbag, and you start to doubt yourself—what if they're right? There are constant suicide attempts in the brig. Those three years of disciplinary battalion hanging over the soldiers' heads aren't really such a big deal but at the age of eighteen it's a lot, one sixth of your time on this earth, practically your entire adult life so far. And not everyone can handle that thought.

Ideally they would like to erase your personality completely, transform the detainee into just another wet, hairless monkey in the group. I've seen it happen, usually when a guy has been in solitary confinement for a couple of months. His fear of being given extra time in there renders him so pliable and obedient that it's pathetic, even loathsome to see.

And I saw others who were not broken at all because they simply didn't give a damn about anything. These were the ones who slit their wrists more often than anyone, but only for show, so they got taken to the hospital. In the army there is a whole arsenal of practical methods of self-mutilation, from slicing the skin on your belly (you get a horrendous open wound but it's quite harmless) up to and including inhalation of ground glass (you start to cough up blood as if you've got tuberculosis) and self-induced kidney failure (drink a glass of salt and drop from a height straight onto your ass, or, at least, that's what they say).

Here they saw us not only as slabs of meat but also as adversaries. They didn't break us just for the hell of it but with a specific goal in mind. And as we know, for every action there is an opposite reaction; the question is how strong will it be?

— — —

I landed in the sergeants' cell, which I came to realize was considered a privileged one in this highly regulated facility. As sergeants we were indeed treated a little better than the rest.

There were already four others in the cell. One guy, a lanky, dim-witted youngster, was a thief who had smashed a passerby on the head with a metal pipe while he was out on leave with some friends.

The militia sergeant was in for rape and told us how it had happened as we lay in our bunks that first night. He'd met a girl while he'd been out drinking, they danced a bit, kissed, and then later when she changed her mind he had her anyway. The next morning in the cell he tried to take his words back, saying we'd misunderstood him. His prospects were unenviable, a long prison term and not in a disciplinary battalion but in a regular penal colony, and then a life in the gutter. The other two were in for some minor mischief; I think they must have gone AWOL.

This was the best brig I'd ever been in, a showpiece with renovated cells, cameras, and rigidly enforced rules. I don't think there are any more like it in the army. Later I was sent to do my last weeks of army service in Tver, and since I was the only sergeant in the division they immediately made me assistant to the guard commander at the brig. I spent forty-one days there and that place was a different story altogether.

The main difference here was that no one seriously tormented us. It's also probably the only brig in Russia where there was none of the brutal hazing of recruits that we call *dedovshchina*. Everything is done by the book. They didn't do the "gas chamber" here, although this was a widespread practice everywhere else: a bowl of chlorine is put on the floor and a bucket of water is thrown over it, causing the inmate to damned near cough up his lungs in pieces. I'd seen people who'd been through that.

Reveille was at 5:00 AM—you got one hour less sleep in the brig, from 10:00 PM until 5:00. Immediately after reveille you moved fast, as you had just one minute to clear away the fold-down bunk, a large platform for five people that you opened for the night and that occupied almost the entire cell. You would lift it and fasten it with a handle to the wall, and if you weren't quick enough the senior man in the cell instantly got ten more days.

After reveille the brig echoed with metal clanging as bunk frames crashed into the wall, deliberately loudly to show that the cell inmates were up.

I was never the senior man in the cell. When I arrived it was a marine sergeant who was in for some minor offense or other. I overlapped with him for a couple of days before he was released and they made a sharp little guy cell boss. All I really remember about him was that a papilloma popped out on his arm, and every morning the medical orderly brought him tablets and during the day they took him to the infirmary for heat treatment. This guy was still in charge when I left, having landed himself an extra ten days when his morning report struck the brig commander as lacking in respect.

After the bunk is put away the cell boss lines you up by the wall and you wait half an hour to be checked. Guards walk along the corridor the whole time and you stand motionless, waiting for the door to fly open and the guard commander to come in with two men while an armed sentry stands at the entrance.

"Comrade Lieutenant! Cell number three ready for inspection! No violations to report sir!" rings the senior sergeant's report before the officer does roll call.

"Babchenko!"

"Arkady Arkadyevich. Staff sergeant. Ten days."

I shout it out and turn to face the wall, hands behind my back, all fast, loud, and clear—if it's not, then ten more days.

"Cell ready for inspection, sir!"

The guards start the shakedown, slide metal prodders into the ventilation grills, poke around all the corners and gaps, under the light. It doesn't last long, two or three minutes at the most, but this is the tensest time of day. God forbid they find something that contravenes regulations, especially cigarettes. Then the whole cell gets ten more days.

They dished out extra time left and right in this place. If you didn't stand to attention in time when the commander came, ten days; report not fast enough or incorrect, ten days; wrong answer to a question, ten days. It doesn't seem much but if you constantly screwed up they would accrue faster than you could cross them off.

Starting from their original three to five days, people could spend up to three months in this place. They had a list in the guardhouse on which they would enter offenders' names and mark ten days and ten more after that if they were unlucky. These ones would be moved into solitary, where they would start to go crazy and climb the walls, poor bastards. At least one person would slash his veins every week.

So you came to realize very quickly that your term is extremely variable. When you got out depended not on you but on the watch or brig commander, who would dole out extra days like confetti every morning. But we always got through the shakedown without any trouble. They never found our two little hiding places, which were our treasure and were passed on from one set of occupants to the next.

The watch commanders and guards here were generally okay and didn't split hairs about stuff too much, except for one guy who occasionally liked to slap people. But he didn't give out extra time and that's all we cared about.

After the inspection we did morning ablutions.

"Hands behind your back! Face the wall! Follow me!"

Pee, splash water on your face, shave, and brush your teeth, all under close scrutiny, all hurriedly and very uncivilized. "You, you long streak of piss, move it, I've got thirty cells to get through!" shouts the guard, standing beside you and watching to make sure you don't throw any contraband down the drain.

And if you were badly shaven because you had to use an ancient razor that ripped off your skin along with your stubble, that didn't bother anyone—ten days.

Then we got a breakfast of porridge, tea, and bread. They fed us well enough and no one complained of starvation, not that we had anywhere to burn off calories.

After that we had to see the medical orderly, an important moment in the life of a detainee. People always complained about everything and anything, secretly hoping to snag a bed in the infirmary for a few days but mainly just for a change, to talk to someone, get some tablets, provide some sort of diversion.

The medical orderly here was called Funt, a big, fat, amiable guy doing one-year service after finishing medical school. He was good-natured and attentive, never refused anyone anything if he could help it, and never forgot about anybody. I liked Funt a lot so I didn't bother him with fictitious ailments.

After the medical inspection came the hardest bit of all: lots of free time. Six hours of doing nothing at all, an incredible drag. The cell held nothing except two small metal benches that were bolted to the floor on either side of a metal table and the mounting for the bunk. The whole cell measured five paces by four and there really was nothing to do in it.

During the day we weren't allowed to open up the bunk, which the watch commander would sometimes lock to the wall in case we were tempted. It was also categorically forbidden to lie down, let alone sleep—the brig is not a holiday camp but a means of influencing us for the better, as the commander liked to remind us, and we were supposed to spend the whole day reflecting on our misdeeds.

Sleeping and smoking were also prohibited, as was going to the toilet. Basically, nothing was allowed; you could only stand, sit, walk around, and talk quietly. And if you broke any of the rules, you got ten more days.

What saved us was playing charades, or "hippopotamus," as we call it in Russian. You split into two teams, one chooses a word, picks someone from the other team, and whispers it in his ear, and he then has to act it out to his team using only gestures and no words. The toughest ones to do are words like *industrialization*.

We played charades for two weeks, apart from the days when we got a new guy. We didn't give him a hard time but rather made him feel welcome—a new face is always entertaining, who is he, where's he from, where did he serve, who does he knows, what he did in civilian life, what does he like to drink and how drunk had he got on it? All this injected new life into conversations in the cell, enough for a whole day. Then it was back to charades. It must have been an amusing sight, five fools sitting silently in a cell, posturing and gesturing to one another and periodically lapsing into stifled belly laughs.

If you needed the toilet, that was your problem. A guy in the next cell was in agony with diarrhea, held it and held it, knocked for ages, and begged the guards in vain and then finally let the lot go in the spittoon bowl, each cell had one. There was no ventilation and the stink was unbearable. The sentries ran in and rushed him and his bowl into the crapper, gave him a rag, and brought chlorine and water. But they didn't give him a gas chamber, it seemed it was just for disinfection. The stench of the chlorine was strong but not overwhelming, so we were racked with coughing but at least our lungs stayed in our chests and our eyes in their sockets.

Then lunch, the highpoint in our day. It starts at the mouth of the corridor when you hear the clanging of pots being opened and bowls being passed into the cells, and you try to guess what they are serving from the smell. While they wheel the trolley to your cell at the end of the U-shaped corridor by the latrines (also a privilege—you spend less time running to the crapper and save precious seconds for yourself), you sit for an hour and listen to them serving the food, sniffing at the air, which sets your stomach moving. You peer from the corner of your eye through the peephole to catch a glance of the trolley and finally it comes into view, just two more cells and then you. You sit on the floor like good little kids with the cell boss at the front, poised like a runner on the starting blocks before he takes the bowl and dishes out the food. Everything has to be done in a flash, without a second's delay.

Then you chew, slowly, thoughtfully, and listen to the trolley as it turns the corner and starts the journey back down the other length of the corridor. All of this lasts about an hour and a half—nothing kills time as effectively as the lunch ritual.

After you eat the day stretches out in reverse order, with another three-hour block of free time. The urge to doze after lunch is unbearable; you don't get enough sleep in this place and that is a torment in itself. You aren't even allowed to close your eyes for a moment. If they catch you nodding off, even while sitting bolt upright, it's a violation, and all the worse for you if you prop your head on your elbow. You just have to get through it and there's no easy way, so you somehow pull yourself through this thick, cloying expanse of inactivity, your body reeling to the point of nausea, your head swimming, your eyes all bloodshot in the hot, sticky, stuffy cell as you try not to succumb to slumber's lure.

Then comes suppertime followed by the evening roll call and shakedown.

"Babchenko!"

"Arkady Arkadyevich. Staff sergeant. Ten days!"

"Hands behind your back! Face the wall! Follow me!"

And finally evening ablutions. This time round you get more time so you can go to the can in peace, and then you turn in.

It's bliss when you can finally lie down. The watch commander unlocks the bunks during the evening shakedown, but you can only open them when given the order. He shouts "Turn in!" and thirty handles are instantly unhooked and thirty frames crash down onto their mountings with the speed of a bullet, and at long last you throw yourself down. Your ribs press onto bare boards and despite your bindings your feet freeze—they still haven't switched on the heating and the nights are damned cold. The ceiling bulb remains on but nothing keeps you from sleep and more sleep. And in the morning it begins all over again.

"Babchenko!"

"Arkady Arkadyevich. Staff sergeant. Ten days!"

"Hands behind your back! Face the wall! Follow me!"

— — —

In fact I spent a total of thirteen days in that cell, barely leaving its four walls. Waiting to complete the time was so psychologically grueling that these thirteen days constitute a separate chapter of my life, greater than school or institute put together. And we're not talking about five years or even one, but barely two weeks.

I couldn't escape the thought that when the time was up they would pack me off to a real jail. The sentence constantly hung over me, bore down on me physically, I wracked myself every second and the burden seemed to eat away at my very core. Three years. Three more whole years!

And yet it was still like a vacation of sorts. No one put me in an armored personnel carrier and drove me out on missions and the future was at least clear for those two weeks. If you live two weeks hour for hour, it's a long time. I had a roof over my head and food, what more could I want?

The only problem we had was getting smokes. There were cameras in the corridors, which is why no one beat us up, but that also made it hard to come to an arrangement with the guards. Although of course we always managed—it was made easier by the location of the sergeants' cell on the bend at the far end of the corridor. I got fifteen cigarettes for my fifty-dollar Zippo lighter (kept in the depositary where no one dared to steal anything) and the guys in the cell were over the moon. Once, after another negotiation with the guards, I even brought back bananas and two apples—in my underpants.

Despite the strict regime we made sure we always had something to smoke. We took turns to light up, one of us would inhale and the others would work like helicopters, whirling tunics above our heads with all our might to ventilate the cell. We only smoked at night, when the guards weren't on the prowl. The brig commander was gone and the watch commander was asleep, and when it came down to it, the guards really couldn't care less whether we smoked or not. Because any one of them could also wind up in a cell straight from his post, and then he'd have to smoke in secret as well, just like I did at the brig in Tver.

I did forty-one watches in eight months there, either as a member of the guard or a cell inmate—it varied. The commander, Captain Zheleznyakov, was a terrible man, always finding some ten-year-old cigarette butt under the skirting board and giving me time for it. I'd promptly have to hand in my rifle, belt, and laces to the lieutenant, watch him load it onto the truck with the cheerfully departing guard members, and then get locked in a cell myself.

But Zheleznyakov couldn't put me in for more than a day because I was the only sergeant in the division. So when the lieutenant returned two days later for fresh duty with the now downcast guard, they led me out of the cell, gave me back my rifle, belt, and laces, and I rejoined the team. I'd rattle off my duties to the captain and go on guard again and "ensure cleanliness and order."

And that's how we passed our army service, either sitting in a cell or standing on guard. That's also why it's always possible to work out something with the guards—both "detainee" and "guard" are concepts as interchangeable as "incarceration" and "release." Today you are on one side of the bars, tomorrow the other.

We even felt a kind of inner superiority over the guards at the Moscow brig. They had power but no spirit about them, whereas after two or three days we started to develop both spirit and a measure of healthy indifference. Arrest in the army always boosts the unofficial status of a soldier. Russia is a country of former inmates and our army lives by the same laws as a prison colony, so any brush with the law garners you a bit of street credibility. The person with the authority is not the one who observes the law, but he who breaks it.

Those who sweated it out in solitary were practically regarded as hard-baked jailbirds. The system gave those guys the hardest time of all, not really to break them, but to see how much they could take and, odd as it may sound, to confirm that they could take anything. All of which only went to reinforce their authority as a result.

Whether in solitary or not, most of us were far from angels and were in for a reason. We also knew how to provoke or psychologically reduce a person, and many of us had been through things that the boys in the refined Moscow district army had never dreamed of.

But in this regulated environment there was one big minus— they didn't take sergeants out to work. For a detainee, work was not a punishment as one might think, but a privilege, freedom. People would bend over backwards to get assigned to work anywhere, even carrying dirty dishes in the kitchen. Because there you could smoke, drink tea, chat, simply be without supervision, walk without having to hold your hands behind your back or stand nose to the wall every time someone came by. After a four-by-five cell the kitchen seems like a divisional parade square.

Actually, they did take us out to the monkey pen a couple of times. In this life, everything is relative. On the first day the cage in the yard seemed like a concentration camp to me. When they took us out a week later it was heaven, first days of fall and a blue sky, even if it was partly obscured by metal grids with an armed sentry pacing on top of them. But we didn't look at the studs on his boots and in fact barely noticed him—all we saw was the sky and the clouds as we walked round in a circle, our hands behind our backs, inhaling and exhaling both the fresh air and this apparition of freedom.

— — —

"Right." The investigator put the errant document about my supposed arrest back in his briefcase, a crude leather thing dating back to Soviet times with two ugly locks on chunky straps.

My father had owned exactly the same briefcase and would take it to work with him every day, although he never seemed to have much to put in it. He was an engineer who built rocket gantries at a secret factory and simply would not have been allowed to carry any documents with him outside work. Not long before his death he was promoted to chief engineer and his last project was the gantry for the *Buran* space shuttle.

The whole project fell apart. *Buran* made one flight into space and then they took it to the Gorky Park in Moscow and built a beer bar inside it. After the Soviet Union broke up the Baikonur space center was left in another country, independent Kazakhstan, and everyone who worked in the space program was instantly reduced to poverty with no prospects of reemployment. My father didn't have it in him to trade or steal and never even tried, he simply had zero aptitude for the country's new ways. He hit the bottle and soon became a slave to drink, and ultimately died of it.

And all that remains of him is a photograph of Baikonur showing a huge field of red poppies in front of the launch pad, a medal and certificate for his work bearing the personal signature of Soviet leader Mikhail Gorbachev, and the faint scent of those small Kazakh melons he used to bring back with him from his work trips.

"So what will happen to me now?"

"Prison will happen to you. For a long time."

— — —

You could feel the military machine working more than ever here, in this cell where they did the interrogations. In the army your fate is decided by dozens and even hundreds of people. You no longer belong to yourself—others determine where you live, what you wear and eat, and basically how you exist. And in my case, the machine was geared toward breaking me.

First starvation in the Ural marshes, where in minus twenty-two Fahrenheit there was one hundred percent humidity and everyone was rotting, pus and blood running in clots down their legs and into their boots. Then the camp in Mozdok, with its nightly beatings, wire tightened round your fingers, stars branded on your hands, smashed teeth, heroin, theft and sale of weapons, insanity.

And the meat grinder of Chechnya with its endless treachery and slaughter, the death of my father, my dysentery, and the death of my grandmother, who outlived her son by just two months. The paralysis of my other grandmother, who to earn money to buy her grandson out of the war would peddle chocolates on suburban trains. All she earned from that was a stroke. Then my mother's desperation at my absence, which grew so bad she actually came to Chechnya to see me. And now prison.

Thank you, Mother Russia.

There were, of course, exceptions. That pretty young doctor at the military commissar's office who sent me for examination genuinely wanted me to get out of doing service. She shifted my induction into the army by half a year and that's a long time in war. I didn't go into the army with the rest of my draft and as a result I was spared the slaughter of Bamut.

Then there was the major who placed my file in a separate folder on the runway in Mozdok. He wasn't trying to do me a favor and had pulled out my file from a pile of 1,500 without looking. So I stayed in Mozdok with ten others while my buddies Vovka and Kisel flew to Chechnya that very day. I wanted to be with them, begged the major to send me too, but he was immovable and so I escaped the horrors of May 1996. Then the senior NCO gave me two periods of leave, and finally my father got sick and passed away, which kept me out of the slaughter of August and the Russian withdrawal from Chechnya.

These people steered me through life like through a minefield and I stayed alive, although this wasn't how it was supposed to be. As God is my witness, I never once played hooky or fiddled things; they gave orders, I went, they gave orders, I did my service. It was fate that always led me out of the war.

But the system doggedly countered fate's intervention. I'd got through the minefield in one piece but there at the edge stood the commandant and the investigator with a boat hook that they used to drag me right back in there so they didn't have to brave the mines themselves: "Go on, son, go and be a hero, it's your duty. You're not allowed to live, that's not yours for the taking, so go and do your service and get killed in the process if you can."

And that captain in the little window at the commandant's office—what difference did it make to him if I was a bit overdue? He could just stamp my papers and forget about me and that's that, I'm already back at the front. No, instead he had to catch a deserter.

Come to that, what difference did one more snot-nosed eighteen-year-old make to the commandant? It's not as if this boy is asking to be moved closer to home or wants to jump ship altogether, he's trying to get back to Chechnya. Was the army really any worse off for my ten days and was that really worth locking me up for? But regardless, that's what he did, to cover his own ass.

And the investigator, Klepa the Clown, didn't he just restore justice, enforce the law, and punish a criminal by throwing a boy into the brig?

Now I have three years of disciplinary battalion ahead of me and then I still have a year to serve after that—your time in detention doesn't affect the length of your service, so I'm now looking at four years.

And the million-dollar question is what for? For allowing myself ten extra days of life?

— — —

The investigator delved into his briefcase again and passed me a blank sheet of paper.

"Write."

"Write what?"

"An admission of guilt."

"But I'm not guilty, I wasn't trying to flee the army. Can't you just let me go, Comrade Captain, and I'll be back at my unit before the day is over?"

"Go on, get writing, it's for the best. Write 'I, Babchenko Arkady Arkardyevich, Staff Sergeant, date of birth, accept the full terms of my service in the army and agree to continue my service in any part of Russia' . . . in *any* part of Russia," he repeated

I wrote what he said, signed and dated it, and handed the sheet back to him. All I had left to work with were words and promises, and this investigator already looked less like a captain with a lousy salary and more like the very Lord of Fate.

He carefully returned the paper to his briefcase.

I was already starting to feel stupefied and indifferent toward all of this and even my own life, exhausted by constantly having to claw my way out of the shit. If it's jail it's jail, just lock me up and balls to the lot of you. If it's Kamchatka, then Kamchatka it is, get on with it and take me there. If it's a dishonorable discharge, fine, I really couldn't give a damn anymore.

I now realize that this captain, commandant, and investigator were merely the latest turns of fate's wheel, taking me farther and farther from the war, although unlike the pretty doctor they didn't wish me the slightest bit of good fortune. But nor did they wish me bad fortune. I simply wasn't a human being in their eyes but a sheet of paper, a number on a file, an expired document, and this all had to be put through the motions. I seriously doubt they gave a thought to the fact that there were real living people behind all these documents and that they held their fate in the balance. They simply couldn't care less whether I went to jail, died, or survived, and that's all there was to it.

But that's how my fate was decided nonetheless. If the captain hadn't followed his instructions to the letter I would have been back in the trenches within a day. The war ended during the three months I spent under investigation and I never went back to Mozdok. What can I possibly say about that except thank you, Comrade Captain?

— — —

I was either just quick on my feet or something else came into play here, but they didn't give me extra time in the brig. Two weeks later they took me to a transfer substation in the regiment called the Serviceman's Assembly Point, or the SAP, where they would gather all the flotsam and jetsam, AWOL cases, deserters, cripples, and the like and decide whether to throw them in jail, demobilize them, or just send them back where they came from.

They created a SAP especially for Chechnya since people fled from there in droves. The high command announced something like an amnesty after devising a loophole just for this purpose: if you had run away not from the army as such but from the brutality of *dedovshchina* and still had no objection to serving, they didn't jail you but transferred you to another unit. Theoretically, any soldier could come here and turn himself in.

The Chechnya SAP was generally referred to as the Diesel Stop, because everyone who was kept there was potentially lined up for the disciplinary battalion, or the "Diesel" as we called it.

Of those who fought in the first Chechen war from 1994–96, a huge number passed through the Diesel Stop, each with his own story to tell. There was a guy who after serving his two years earned himself four more for smashing some kid's back. He did two of them in jail and they swapped the other two for army service, so his overall military service appeared to span from 1994–2000, as he scrawled in pen on the wall of the commandant's office.

He was a funny guy, seemed barely four feet tall with his cap on, and was toothless, the result of a bullet in the mouth. He used to laugh too hard and dislocate his jaw.

There was another guy who got shot and lay on his own in the foothills for a day before they picked him up and took him unconscious to the hospital. During the month he spent there the defense ministry sent his mother the funeral payment and a coffin that she was told contained her son's remains.

Then he came round, went home, and wound up at the Diesel Stop. Now the command had to decide what to do with him: send him back to Chechnya to get finished off for real or to demobilize this picture of life who was officially deceased.

There was also Pshenichnikov, a feeble, broken spirit who hadn't even managed to do any fighting worth mentioning. They were driving him up to the front on a carrier when it hit a mine and he escaped with a severe concussion.

And this guy Andrianenko had both his kneecaps shot through and could hardly bend his legs, leaving him to walk like he was on stilts. But he still had a year of service to go.

The Stop is where I ran into my old friend Kolya Belyaev, who was drafted straight into the army from an orphanage. We got to know each other at the draft station after our call-up and were packed off to the training school in the same truck. I was later assigned to a signals regiment in Mozdok while he went to the 166th Infantry Brigade. Later we both got sent to Chechnya. Then my father died and two days after that a sniper shot Kolya through the shin in Grozny. A nurse had tried to reach a wounded man and the shooter killed her; Kolya was hit as he went to pull her out.

— — —

Many of them I no longer remember. It wasn't easy to dig out these names and faces from my mental archives because all I'd done for years was try to forget them. Now I have a family, a wife, and kids, have become a different person. The past lies in the recesses of my memory, thrust into some far corner of my brain, and it's an ordeal to retrieve it. The only way is through drinking vodka, although I'm wary about digging it all back up because I don't want to revert to the person I was then and have to go through it all again. That's a sure slide into the abyss and once you're down there it gets harder to haul yourself out with every passing year.

But once you start, more of the faces return. There was also

Tim—I don't remember if that was his name or a nickname. Tim was a quiet, diligent boy who went through training with me and Kolya and also came through Chechnya. Later we finished our service together in Tver.

Five guys who served with me in Mozdok also passed through the Stop. They stole the fuel pump from a carrier and sold it to a local contractor we called the Greek and went AWOL using the proceeds. They took local trains all the way to Moscow, where three of them even spent the night at my home, which they then robbed. I was most bothered by the loss of two new suits from America that someone had sent to my mom for me. I never even got to wear them.

While I was in Tver I ran into one of them, Shiryaev, who was finishing his service in the unit next to mine. They came over to use our sauna and I recognized him immediately and I'm sure vice versa, but he pretended he hadn't noticed me and walked away.

Also waiting at the Stop for a decision on his fate was this kid who had been taken prisoner, escaped, and lived with a Chechen family for several weeks. They hid him from the rebels and later drove him to Moscow in the trunk of a car. In the meantime his unit was dissolved and re-formed elsewhere and he simply had nowhere to go back to. The effects of his captivity remained with him for the rest of his days, and, to make matters worse, the nephew of his host family later came to Moscow and kidnapped his sister.

Stories, stories, and more stories, a never-ending stream of separate fates. People ran away from tormentors, from the fighting, got left behind by their units, escaped from captivity, vanished without trace, woke up in hospitals.

Many didn't return from leave, just didn't have the strength to go back. If a person was ready to die while he was down in Chechnya it didn't mean he felt the same back in Moscow. In the dark days of 1941 people didn't spare a thought for their lives, but when it got to 1945 no one wanted to die. The same applied here. To go to war is much more terrifying the second time round.

Our proud ranks were sent to Chechnya to the beat of a marching band, decked out with golden chevrons and gleaming parade boots. Within six months those who had managed to get out met up at the Diesel Stop, clad in lice-infested rags, their bodies charred, mangled, and full of bullet holes, eyes empty and souls barren. And then they tried us for desertion.

Many of my draft came this way and met up here like shadows, recounted what they had been through and who had been killed and injured. They lived together for a while, hugged each other, and parted ways for good this time, never to meet again.

It was a human river that never stopped flowing, the Via Dolorosa, the Way of Suffering. People came and went, would be sent to jail, demobilized, or sent back to the war. Some would go to a new unit and others to the disciplinary battalion, and their places were promptly filled by new people. But the numbers never varied too much, there were always about two hundred fifty soldiers at the Diesel Stop, two hundred of which invariably came from Chechnya. It's so typically Russian, to herd people into a meat grinder and then sentence them for desertion.

Those who didn't come from Chechnya had generally fled the army because of starvation and brutality. There were several guys from units on Sakhalin Island in the Far East. I remember one of them had reached Moscow in forty-five days traveling on goods trains. He lived like a tramp, ate from the garbage, slept in station toilets, and hid in storage lockers under the carriages.

But there were also those individuals who never fit into any community, slippery small-fries who always try to find a more comfortable bolt-hole and care only about their own skins, secretly scoffing their mother's pies in the visiting room and leaving behind only a gray, faceless memory when they finally move on. They didn't fit in here any more than they did in other places and usually just found their way out and kept running. No one really had much to do with them.

Although there was one guy I still remember well, a devious Muscovite who'd been through the Stop twice, run away, and then later got moved to Nizhny Novgorod and vanished from there too. He found his way to Tver, where we met, spun me a load of bullshit about his supposed war exploits like some Chechen Rambo, and then got beaten half to death by a mob in the toilet a few days later for screwing someone over. He really got it bad, they slashed up his face and by the time they finished with him the whole place was daubed in his blood. Russia's army is a tough place and people will be savagely taken down in a moment if need be.

The next day he took off yet again, and this time they probably won't even take him back at the SAP, not even they had any stomach for his type.

The pecking order there and at the Stop was basically the same as in the country's penal colonies, which we call "the zone." But the top dogs in the army system were always the "Chechens," the ones who had come from the war.

You name it, you'd have probably found them at the Stop—crooks, bandits, escaped or released prisoners, and cripples of all descriptions, which made for a dismal turnout at times:

"Ivanov, take sentry duty!"—"I can't, sir, I've got no fingers."

"Damn . . . Petrov, take sentry duty!"—"Can't sir, my knees are shot through."

"Sidorov! All present and correct, nothing torn off? Right, take sentry duty!"

"I can't sir, I'm shell-shocked."

"Dammit, when will they finally demob you cripples?"

"Never sir, we still have to serve in the disciplinary battalion."

But regardless of what they did to us and what some of us had done ourselves—I'll say again, we weren't angels either—I have fond memories of most of the people around me in those days.

Through some twist of fate or possibly a sick joke, the Diesel Stop was located within the First Command Regiment, the country's most privileged military formation, a showpiece that is practically impossible to get into unless you have connections or plenty of money, and even then you still have to be at least six feet tall.

This regiment also comprises the Guard of Honor. Whenever you see handsome, granite-jawed soldiers greeting foreign presidents at the airport, flanking a red carpet in razor-edged uniforms, sashes, and white gloves and wearing mirrored, four-hundred-dollar boots, remember that these guys lived in the same barracks as us.

We lived at the Diesel Stop and they lived in the Elephant Pen. The Guard of Honor soldiers were called the elephants because they stomped up and down the parade ground for eight hours a day. Their entire military training consisted of nothing but marching drill and they would quick march and goose-step and toss their carbines from port to shoulder from breakfast until supper. The soles of their feet should crash down on the asphalt in perfect time, the whole company in unison. They'd do fifty minutes of stomping, then fifty minutes of stretching, and then more stomping. As a rule, by the time they finished their service their knees were done for, but still, their training was a ballet to behold and what they did with their rifles was pure art, very beautiful and a fitting decoration for any parade.

Meanwhile, we would smoke in the latrines on the second floor and watch them through the window. We didn't envy them and harbored no dreams of joining their ranks. It was impossible anyway, the Stop and the Pen might be located in the same barracks but they existed as parallel worlds. For some reason they coincided in the same time and space but there was no direct transition from the one world to the other—they were too different.

They had white gloves, sashes, the admiration of presidents, and a place by the eternal flame at the Kremlin wall. We had maimed hands, shell-shock, trenches, starvation, prison, and lice. Despite our separate existences, there was, however, one slight point of connection. We were a useful visual aid to them, a reminder of what not to be, and their officers would tell the men: "If you do your service badly you'll be sent to Chechnya. Your punishment stands up there, smoking behind the window on the second floor."

This was no threat but a reality in some units. In training, one of our sergeants got sent to the front for drinking cleaning fluid. The threat of Chechnya made the others do better, including these honor guards, who after peering up at our window would stretch their legs like never before. I don't know what they were to us, alien beings perhaps.

We Diesel Stoppers led separate lives in the regiment and didn't really belong to the army; we were merely waiting for our fates to be decided. Instead of some set dress we wore whatever we had arrived in, camouflage fatigues, parade uniform, smocks, tunics, long boots, short boots, sneakers. Some guys had medals and awards for battle injuries, others had no decorations and no fingers.

We didn't do any drill, fat chance of getting us to march after the fighting we'd done and the jail time we were facing. People just spat on the whole business—there would be only one outcome whether you did drill or not, so why exert yourself unnecessarily? So instead of trying to march us smartly to the canteen, the officers would just shove us around by the back of the head like a dumb herd.

The Stop commander was one Colonel Zimin, a loud, round, cheerful Winnie the Pooh type who was always in excellent spirits, always joking and liked to pat the soldiers affectionately on the cheek when talking to them. He would tell us over and again that everything would be just fine, and he treated us well. Whenever possible he would allow us visitors and on occasions even grant short spells of home leave.

But he didn't show his face that often in the barracks and was far removed from our daily problems. I always got the impression that if we told him about the war, he'd exclaim, "Really, you were in Chechnya? There's a war going on there? Well I never. So why did you run from there? Oh well, never mind, everything will be just fine."

So the place was run by the lieutenant colonel; I forget his name but I can still see his face and don't exactly have fond memories of him. He was the one who decided how soldiers were assigned from here, who would go back to Chechnya and who wouldn't. For money he'd make sure you were moved closer to home and he was also open to offers to keep you out of jail. For a sizable sum he'd demobilize you altogether, he hinted that much to my mom but got nothing from her.

There was also a lieutenant we nicknamed Sting—that's army slang for "face"—which fitted his ugly mug perfectly. It was long like a horse's, pointy, with crooked features as if it had been carved by a drunken carpenter. The picture was completed by a big drooping nose that almost touched a heavily protruding jaw, plus a low forehead, a receding hairline, and eyes that were set too close together.

Clumsy and vindictive, Sting did everything by the book, with no initiative whatsoever and even less regard for us as human beings. Most of all we hated him for being a conscript himself—he was serving two years after graduating from college.

The rest of the officers had little to do with us and did not regard us as soldiers but rather as scum that should have been skimmed off and disposed of in jail long ago. But what else could you expect from the pampered ranks of the prestigious "Arbat Military District"?

We had the effect of a red rag to a bull on these polished officers. Every second man among them felt obliged to give us a hard time for everything, right down to our appearance, berating us for mismatched clothing, undone buttons, or failure to salute.

One day, some major passed Andrianenko without receiving the slightest acknowledgment from him—in Chechnya no one wore rank insignia and or ever saluted, that could earn you a smack in the mouth for revealing the identity of an officer to snipers. The major went crazy and tried to force Andrianenko to do a parade march, an impossibility given his crippled, stiltlike gait.

Of course the major had no way of knowing about the shattered knees, but to us that was just one more example of our betrayal by the system. And as for a matching uniform, where were we supposed to get that from?

— — —

The senior NCO at the Stop was Igor Makeyev, or Mak, a sergeant from Kaluga. Mak was a huge hulk of a man, about six foot six inches tall with a chest that barely fit through the door frame. He had fists the size of heads and size fourteen feet, and his hat perched on a bull's head set on a bull's haunches rising from a bull's torso. To match his physique, he had a murderous face that seemed capable of breaking boards with a glance.

Yet at the same time his vast build was proportionate and even elegant. Despite his mass he was incredibly agile, with amazing reactions that enabled his loglike arms to deal lightning blows. When Mak wasn't weightlifting he was kickboxing, flitting around the training hall on his toes, God only knows how they didn't break under his weight. I was forever baffled that he hadn't been snapped up by the Special Forces.

His favorite pastime was to chase young punks around Kaluga, and every time he came back from leave he'd have some new tale about brawls with packs of adversaries—I seem to recall his optimum number was six, any less wasn't much of a challenge.

One day Mak got Pshenichnikov to stand on a stool, put a cigarette in his mouth, and told him not to move a muscle. He squared up to him a couple of times, jumped and did a roundhouse kick, swiping the cigarette from his lips. I was standing to one side and it seemed like a truck had passed half an inch from Pshenichnikov's nose.

Yes, Mak had winning ways all right, and was further enhanced by a slight speech defect that made him hiss the letter *s*. The only thing he lacked was a scar across his cheek, which would have completed the ensemble.

But I don't remember him ever hitting anyone. He had no need to, all he had to do was give the word and people would jump, and happily so because we revered him. He ran the place right and never humiliated the weaker ones or took anything from them. There was something almost noble about him and we instinctively knew he was the best boss we could hope for.

Rather than keeping his distance like the rest of the regiment, Mak lived alongside us and never looked down on us. He regarded us as *his* company and himself as a part of the whole. He had great affection for his men and, unlike Sting and his ilk, saw us as people and not dregs.

He would readily go to the headquarters and lock horns with Sting over some issue affecting us, and was extremely adept at conveying to the higher-ups that it wasn't worth bothering his guys unreasonably.

Through his own strength of will and belief in life, Mak would not allow us to give up on ourselves and would always key us up when the going got tough. Sure we were a hard bunch of drinkers, fighters, villains, and veterans, but at the same time, the experience of war, trauma and injury, incarceration, investigation, and looming lengthy prison terms combined to trip us up. And many of us might have fallen and not risen again if we had not had Mak to steady us and help us back on our feet.

He gave us the strength to fight the system and fight for ourselves. And when people were transferred from the Stop to jail, they left the barracks with grins and balled fists as if to say "Lock me up then, I'll get out some day, you can count on it."

The only thing he would not tolerate was lowlife behavior, some-one showing himself no respect, an absence of inner dignity, which is basically why all the shit happens to a person in the first place.

To screw Mak over was regarded as a serious transgression. If anyone gave him the finger or failed to come back from leave he would lose his cool and flip into a rage. The company would lose all of its leave rights, and to screw over the company as a whole was in his eyes the absolutely worst crime of all.

But not even in these extreme cases do I ever remember him beating anyone up. Generally the guys who let him and all of us down mended their ways or just somehow faded from view for the duration and the problem would resolve itself.

And so life at the Stop steadily ticked on.

No one ever entrusted us with weapons so we were never given any guard duty in the regiment. We were basically used as cheap labor, peeling potatoes in the kitchen, carrying vats full of leftovers, and other menial tasks.

Those who didn't have regular jobs were forever vanishing into the defense ministry hospital, which was located two blocks down from the regiment. To get in there you had to convince a medical commission that you weren't right in the head, and if you played your cards right you could spend a month between clean sheets in a civilian institution on mental health grounds.

Everyone at the Stop tried to get some sort of mental diagnosis; it was regarded as legitimate leave and bore no stigma whatsoever. And since we weren't doing any useful service, why indeed shouldn't we get a decent rest once in a while? So the guys went in for examina-tion, took it easy, came out a month later, and happily did the rest of their time.

One day, Pyotr, our registrar, asked me if everything was okay with my head. I said yes and he was taken aback: "So no nightmares or noises in your ears?"

"No," I answered truthfully.

Then he asked me bluntly, "Are you stupid or what? Don't you want a nice break in the nuthouse?" And sure enough, I suddenly remembered these bad dreams and unbearable giddy spells I'd been having, and that confounded rushing noise in my head.

For their part, the doctors were well aware of what was going on. When I saw the psychiatrist, a venomous old dear in glasses, I spun her such a mountain of crap about drug addiction and post-combat stress disorder that she was at first rendered speechless by my brazen performance. Then she told me she'd never met such a blatant faker in all her years and packed me off to the Kashenko Hospital for three weeks of observation.

I was placed in a ward with the addicts and alcoholics, people wracked by cold turkey withdrawal or shaking with delirium tremens, walking zombies pumped full of sedatives who drooled on the floor and left pools of pee behind them, prison convicts who'd slit their veins, junkies covered in heroin tracks, tramps who'd managed to get a bed and escape the wintry streets, and a host of other interesting sights.

There was one other malingerer like me in the ward. We understood everything well and were grateful for our beds. We were soon given jobs in the kitchen and for our efforts they allowed us to drink vodka in the evenings.

When my time in the ward was up the head doctor didn't even bother calling me before a medical commission and just sent me back—you had your rest, now let others get a turn.

— — —

There was, however, one kind of guard duty at the Diesel Stop called "Special Cargo" that we would be given to spare the delicate members of the Honor Guard from doing it. Our job was to deliver coffins.

On average two or three coffins would pass through Moscow every day, usually arriving from Chechnya but not always—in this army plenty of people also got killed far away from the war.

We had to collect the coffins at one of the Moscow railway stations, load them into a truck, and drive them to another station or the airport. Sometimes there was an escort with them, sometimes the parents would travel with the coffin. They might be heavy or very light, in which case you'd know that there wasn't a whole person inside but just what they could find, maybe an arm or a leg.

Occasionally they would bring us Muscovites, which was particularly bad because then you'd have to take the cargo directly to the family home and give it to the mother.

It was a task that I came to do often and at my own request, which was facilitated by my special place in Mak's unofficial staff.

Mak always gave the Diesel sergeants a boost when he could, and in turn demanded of them that they behave like sergeants. And from the privates he would demand that they in turn grow into sergeants. By this time I had served ten months, and having stepped in a few times as the senior NCO when he was away and done everything right, I gradually became his deputy. There were plenty of other sergeants in the company but Mak only chose two deputies, me and Volchok.

I think Volchok had served in Nizhny Novgorod, I know he hadn't been in Chechnya. He was quick and cheerful and able to stand up for himself, and a bit of a dandy with it—he always rolled up the sleeves of his four-tone camouflage smock and tucked matching pants into a fine pair of gleaming boots. It was all part of the act; Volchok was a cunning devil and calculating. He had served more than a year before he took off from his unit for some reason, I don't know why, but it definitely wasn't because of bullying. Maybe he just wanted to be closer to home.

We didn't particularly get on with each other; there was no hostility between us, but nor was there any discernible friendship. We existed at a measured distance from one another, and like two planets we circled the same sun, Mak.

When the company fell in, we didn't stand in the ranks but in front of them, next to Mak, who, while expecting us to be dutiful sergeants, gave us a free hand to do as we wished. We could smoke, drink vodka in the store room, or wash in the shower room when we liked, a privilege the rest were not allowed.

Basically Mak divided up the chores and saw to the overall management of the company, and we would take care of daily business while he went to work out in the sports hall.

I wasn't a senior soldier in terms of the length of my service, yet I was in charge of guys who were close to demobilization. No one seemed to resent this though; Mak had made the company into one unified organism and people just got on with their assigned tasks, regardless of the usual army pecking order. There was no *dedovshchina* or even preferential treatment of soldiers by others who came from the same part of Russia, both of which are usually present in our army units. I still find their absence at the Stop remarkable.

I had certain perks, but I didn't particularly use my deputy's status to show off. Mak didn't encourage it at all, but I chose to work with the others, up to a point, that is; it didn't mean I would crawl around on the barracks floor with a cleaning rag. I had my own duties to attend to but still liked to grab a shovel and join in with digging work at the regiment gatehouse, for example. I thrived on this physical work in the fresh winter air, it was enjoyable and had some sense of purpose to it. And most importantly, it provided a distraction from the thought of jail. But Volchok never worked with the rest of the company.

Whatever the differences between us, we never let Mak down. I remember something he once said: "I have two good sergeants, Babchenko and Volchok, and that's why I don't need any more."

I have accomplished a lot in the twelve years since then, but to this day it's still some of the best praise I ever received.

— — —

What I did use my elevated status for was to ensure I got work as often as possible with the Special Cargo. If Mak didn't need me for something more important he would always let me go.

I moved a lot of coffins, I don't know how many, probably several dozen in total. I did it because it gave me a connection to the life I had known as a soldier on active duty, a life that had started to slip away from me here. The boys lying in those zinc caskets were my brothers in arms and I wanted to be with them again, even if it had to be like this.

I'd come back from Chechnya once already and hadn't wanted to come back on this second spell of leave. That's why I overstayed those ten lousy days: I attached no meaning to them and mentally I had already gone beyond them and was back down in Chechnya. I actually wanted to go back to the front, not because I longed to fight but simply because the world that I was most connected to was there and I was tired of losing it.

Every time people intervened to change the circumstances around me I lost everyone I cared about at the moment. *Everyone.* All the people I was friends with, loved, hated, or barely knew had gone as if obliterated by a nuclear bomb. There had been a place where I once lived and people who inhabited it, but now there were just ruins and erased memories in my head, nothing more. All of the people closest to me had ceased to exist, been killed or shunted off to different units, leaving no trace behind them, no addresses or photographs, often not even surnames. Sometimes not even their faces remained. Everyone who had been a part of that past life had disappeared.

During my years of service my life changed completely on five occasions, or rather didn't change but ceased and started all over again. And every time I myself would start from scratch too.

First I lost my school friends, family, institute, and peacetime life when I was called up. Then in the Urals I lost Belyaev, Yakushev, Mistakidi, Tyurin, Vorobya, and a load of others when I was sent to the Caucasus. Later, at the landing strip in Mozdok, I was to lose Vova Tatarintsev, Kisel, Anisimov, Sanya Lyubinski, and another 1,500 guys.

Later in Mozdok I also had to leave behind Loop, Bondar, Rybakov, Snegur, Aunty Lucy, and a bunch of other people. And Zyuzik, Osipov, Tatarin, Pan, Berezhnoi, Smiler, and Romashka remained in Chechnya when I left again.

I had only just threaded together some strands of my life, begun to establish some kind of continuity, and then they were abruptly severed again, and everything was torn apart once more. Now it's back to the beginning and I have to start building new surrounds with people, friends, enemies, fellow travelers, surround myself with them, just to lose them again at some point.

In the end you grow weary of this and become a loner and stop allowing people to get near to you. People no longer stir emotions in you and indifference toward others starts to set in. In losing those close to you, you also betray them in a way, and that's tough to deal with.

I looked for a lot of them, like Zyuzik, Osipov, and Aunty Lucy, the kind old lady who used to feed me in Mozdok. But I only found a few, fragments of the past that no longer even evoke melancholy. A total feeling of emptiness—that was my payment for coming back.

— — —

Twelve years later a friend of mine brought me a DVD with footage of the fighting in Grozny. It was shot on August 11, 1996; there's a sniper on the roof and a Chechen with a grenade launcher in the next window, a burning tank with the mechanic still stuck inside because the hatch jammed. They blow it open with plastic explosives and drag the guy out with hooks. His head is all charred. The next scene is at the medical battalion of the 166th Infantry Brigade. A familiar contract soldier is telling how he got shot and how a nurse crawled over to help him and got shot in the arm and was finally killed by the shooter.

Sometimes you can't believe all this really happened in your life, that you went to war in Chechnya. Can it really be true? Did that nurse and Belyaev really exist, or was it just a dream, your memory playing tricks on you? Was there ever a Diesel Stop? There couldn't have been, surely, that can't have been me.

And then they bring you a DVD and there it is, and you watch this past life of yours that never came to fruition. Twelve years later I find out that the nurse was called Yulia.

Kolya Belyaev has a crooked homemade tattoo on his shoulder of a dog's head and the words "Moriturus te salutant"—We who are about to die salute you. The old composition of the 166th called themselves the Rabid Dogs and were based in Tver, where I served out my time.

The circle closed itself one way or another, just like the war became my fate, one way or another, for the rest of my days.

I met Kolya Belyaev a couple of times after the army. He was doing well, his leg had healed, and he was making good money building wardrobes in some private firm. I was single at the time; he and his wife came to stay and we drank ourselves stupid. He gave me a silk tie, which I still have, and I gave him my one and only smart shirt as I didn't have anything else to give him.

Then I went off to the second Chechen war as a contract soldier and never called him again, although he only lives in the Moscow suburb of Izmailovo.

— — —

Most often we would go to Kursk Station to pick up Special Cargo, because that was where trains from the Caucasus arrived in the capital. The district around the station is close to my apartment in Taganka; I was born and raised here, went to school here, and spent my childhood on these streets.

Now I was driving along the same streets I roamed as a kid, but in the back of an army truck, with dead people lying in zinc coffins on the floor. I could see my past life flashing by through the tarpaulin window like a film and I knew there would never be any way back. That was all gone and now I was transporting dead people past casinos with Mercedes-Benzes parked outside them. I couldn't get my head round any of it.

— — —

Klepa the Clown didn't summon me for questioning again. Evidently he couldn't pin anything else on me apart from the overstay on my leave, although I know for a fact that they sent inquiries to Mozdok. But my company didn't exist anymore; it was dissolved while I was at the Stop, so no one answered the inquiries. I doubt I even figured anymore in the regiment's records—at any rate, I didn't receive any written proof of having participated in combat operations.

Nor did Klepa get wind of the case of the two missing fly rockets that could still come back to haunt me—some of the older soldiers took the rockets when I was once on armory duty in the company and swapped them in Mozdok for a bunch of heroin and food. I wrote them off in the log as battle losses; it was risky, but I got away with it and the case was closed. It wouldn't have done him any good

ARKADY BABCHENKO

even if he had nosed around, who cared anymore about those two rockets anyway?

So I was elated when they summoned me and said that was an end to the matter, that I had done my time and was now due to go back to the army. No prison after all!

The Diesel Stop was located in the Moscow military district and that's automatically where I should have been assigned to serve next. So my fate was practically decided: I'd be posted no more than two hundred fifty miles from home, which, in a country the size of Russia, is just down the road.

They assembled a few of us by the headquarters and told us to wait for our escort. Autumn had now arrived and it was rainy and cold.

My mom and grandmother had visited me earlier that day. Evidently they seemed to sense something was up.

Parents were often admitted to the barracks to hand over documents and certificates, talk to the commanders, or whatever. It was they who did most of the work in your investigation. If you need a certificate saying your son isn't a deserter, then go to Chechnya yourself and get one. The prosecutor's office simply didn't handle these matters so it fell to the parents.

They met with the lieutenant colonel in his office and were told that I was being sent back to Chechnya.

That piece of paper the investigator pushed over to me in the cell—"Go on, get writing, it's for the best"—and which I had signed took a very different course. "Any part of Russia" turned out to be far from what I had naïvely imagined—Kamchatka or the Lake Baikal region—and meant Chechnya and only Chechnya, nothing else.

You died in vain, Dad, they will have their way with me whatever.

— — —

A person's condition in life is in a constant state of change. Several personalities pass through our bodies over the years and at different times we may be completely different people.

In order to survive you have to be a good soldier, and to be a good soldier you have to treat your life and death equally, with equal indifference. There comes a point when you no longer give a damn and, more importantly, understand that you will probably die in the end, because all you have left inside you is hatred and a fierce longing to rip everyone around you to pieces. So you accept your own death as the only outcome, and then and only then do you become a good soldier. And as paradoxical as it sounds, your readiness to die actually improves your chances of living. It's hard to explain this interrelation, back to metaphysics again, I suppose.

My father passed away just as I was starting to become a good soldier. There, at the front, I had no other choice; I understood that this was the only possibility and duly accepted it. But now everything had changed. During the time I spent under investigation the war in Chechnya finished, the sides signed the Khasavyurt truce, and Moscow ordered the withdrawal of its forces from the rebel republic. We had lost the war.

There was no one left from my company in Mozdok. Minayev, the company commander, had succumbed to full-blown alcoholism, Senior Warrant Officer Savchenko was transferred to the infantry and sent to Grozny, and Shiryaev, Yakunin, and Ginger had all run away to Moscow and robbed my family's apartment. Loop's mom came to get him and he went on leave and didn't come back, got transferred to Vladikavkaz.

Anton Vedernikov quit the army. Snegur managed to stay in the hospital and had no intention of returning, even if they threatened to put him against the wall. Fixa, Tolik, and Dimas, our senior recruits, became contract soldiers and were also transferred elsewhere. Zyuzik and Osipov went to Chechnya and I don't know what became of them. And that's it, there was no more company as I knew it and nowhere to go back to.

But the main thing was that I myself had changed. During this time I had lost most of my family in one way or another. My father died, as his mother, my grandmother, did two months later. My other grandmother, who had sold chocolates on trains, was now paralyzed after her stroke.

Now only my mother came to visit me, but she had been reduced to a grieving shadow by now, a half person with lifeless eyes. During my year of army service she had withered from a woman in bloom to an old lady with a crooked mouth. She seemed to have already buried me in her mind, spoke to me distractedly, evasively. She had even been to Chechnya to look for me and had seen the place with her own eyes, and for her I remained there at a block post where she had once spent the night. It was like going to a cemetery when I came home—all that was left of the family was photographs. Hell, even my dog had died.

I was practically alone now and was not even whole myself at this stage, whole in body, perhaps, but crippled within. The war didn't just take away my personality and change me, erasing that romantically minded, long-haired eighteen-year-old; it took away my life as I knew it. Everyone who had once filled it was dead or as good as.

You could not assemble a complete person from my mother and me at that point. Of all the many attributes of the human spirit, we had only managed to retain the half that no longer believes in anything, wants nothing, and hopes for nothing. We each had the same half person.

He was some son of a bitch, that investigator.

— — —

Voices were being raised in the headquarters.

"You swines, I don't see you doing much service for your country but you send the boys down there easily enough!" my mother shrieked.

"But he signed the documents himself," countered the lieutenant colonel. "See here . . . 'I agree to serve in any part of Russia.'"

"What kind of people are you, he's already done his bit and more. His father died, I'm sick, and he's now the only breadwinner left in the family!"

She was crying, her face black with rage. I remember her at that moment; she had just started to believe that her son had finally got out and what did she get: *any part of Russia.*

I was beyond caring at this stage. What seemed to be the only exit out of all of this had slammed shut and everything had gone right back to where it was—there was no escaping this whirlpool and if you got sucked in they'd finish you off. Only the pretty boys with money escaped.

It was just a shame they went through all this rigmarole, better to just finish you off immediately, not drag it out and put you on the torture rack. Still, these people were only doing their job; they didn't start the war and they didn't create such an army. They were part of the system and the system demanded that they herd boys off to the slaughter, and so they herded them dutifully.

But they did it in a shitty way, through trickery and deceit, fake documents and papers—anything but do it directly and openly.

Why couldn't they have just let me go straightaway? When I first appealed to them, when there was still a chance for me to keep hold of my people and not break life's continuity? Why the hell did they have to lock me up, brand me a deserter, and start a case against me? Just so they could make a convict of me, send me into oblivion to atone with blood when everything had already crumbled about me and all that is dear to me was gone?

Now what was left of my world had converged on this place, now hinged on the Diesel Stop. I'd already gone to Chechnya twice, voluntarily, and I had no wish to go back there a third time when the end of the war was in sight.

In August, when I had sat with the commanding officer on the runway waiting to board the helicopters to the front, I was prepared to die. Now I didn't want to die. And nor did just going back to the camp in Mozdok so someone could smash out my remaining teeth appeal too much. I was kind of tired of all that now.

I spent three months at the Stop, during which time they tried to send me back three times, each time quietly. Every time my new family there defended me, simply wouldn't let them take me. Our departure to fight in Chechnya was regarded as voluntary, and if nothing else, this account serves to show just how voluntary this act really was.

— — —

Late last autumn, toward the end of November, I wheedled a more or less serviceable tunic and boots out of our quarter master, Kazulya,

packed my kit bag, and collected my new orders. I then said good-
bye to all these guys I'd grown attached to, hugged each one, raised
my fist in the air, and walked out the gate.

I crossed the snow-covered parade ground, showed the sentry at
the gatehouse my orders, and went out into the street. Moscow was
slipping into winter, the bright sunlight cut my eyes, the air was crisp
and clean in my lungs, and I was surrounded by space. Volchok was
in the park with a team from the Stop, chipping sheet ice from the
paths. I went over to them, and we stood together and lit up.

"So are you out of here now?"

"Yep."

"Go on then, good luck to you."

"You too."

We hugged and I shook hands with all of the guys in turn, said
farewell and headed toward Leningrad Station—I had to reach my
unit this same day, I hadn't been given any leave.

Behind me a group of ten men led by Sergeant Volkov shoveled
snow and ice. In the barracks, Whale, Taksa, Belyaev, Andrianenko,
and Tim smoked in the second-floor latrines while Pshenichnikov
kept them company—he never did learn how to smoke. I knew they
would be up there on the windowsill discussing my departure, or
more likely just sitting in silence.

Mak, Kazulya, and Pyotr the registrar were all going about their
business, Sting was starting his duty shift about now, and the lieutenant colonel was doing paperwork in the headquarters.

I never saw any of these people again—they and the Stop are
gone forever.

— — —

It was getting dark when I reached Tver. My orders contained only
the number of the unit and I had no idea how to find it. I checked
where the commandant's office was located, got on a local bus, and
went there.

In the Tver Command Headquarters they were surprised that I'd
come alone, without an officer leading me by the hand. That wasn't
something they were used to here, where they lived rather by the

principle that "Wherever you kiss a soldier, your lips will always find an ass."

They directed me to the tram stop and told me to go to the end, so off I went. It was strangely fun to go back to the army on a tram, and there was no need to drag me there in handcuffs. So much for me being a scumbag, I was going of my own accord, all on my own, scarcely the behavior of a deserter.

We at the Diesel Stop were many things, but I can say that we weren't deserters, we'd all had countless opportunities to run away. We wanted one thing and one thing only: to serve out our time with some human dignity and not like beasts going to the slaughter, and then draw a line under all this. Is that really such a criminal desire?

— — —

When I reported for duty at the headquarters of my new unit they too were surprised that I had made my way there without an escort. They assigned me to the control battery of their antiaircraft division, and that's where I served out the remainder of my service, in the 166th Brigade in Tver.

By now there was no one left who had been to Chechnya and they didn't even know that they had once been known as the Rabid Dogs. Apart from my tags, I no longer carried any hint of Chechnya about me, not my Caucasus Cross, no entry in my service book or my personal file. There wasn't even anyone who could confirm I had ever been there. It was as if the company had never existed.

A few months later during spring, the deputy supply officer saw my dog tags in the sauna and asked why I had not been decommissioned yet—your two-year term was always shortened to eighteen months for serving in Chechnya. I told him that I had come from the Diesel Stop.

"Aaah," he intoned solemnly. "And you haven't got any documents? Oh well, what can you do, serve out your time I guess."

He was a good guy and later he went to the headquarters to find out more about me. But there wasn't anything he could do to help because there was no proof to support my case. There was no one left from my previous worlds. The war had seen to that.

WHY THE SKY DOESN'T FALL

GERMAN SADULAEV
Translated by Anna Gunin

I

EVERY EVENING after eight I'm left here alone. The long chains of rooms are filled with old furniture and archives, in the office are computers, in the apartment there's a sofa, a cupboard and television. I work here, and this is where I live. I live here because it's very convenient—the journey home from work takes less than a minute. Because someone has to live here, anyway, to answer the after-hours phone calls. To turn the lights on and off in the windows, to keep people with bad intentions away. That's what I explain to the few people who ask. That's what I explain to myself. It isn't true.

In reality I live here because I have nowhere else to live. Because I have no home. Everyone has a home. Where he lived, where his parents lived. A little log house in the country, a room in a communal apartment. Birds have their nests, wild animals their dens. I have nowhere to lay my head. Although I'm an ordinary ghost, one of billions of ghosts.

And I do have a house. Now it stands dark and empty. The autumn is heavy, cold. The windows haven't been glazed since the commandant's headquarters were blown up. There it is, the commandant's headquarters; you can see it if you stand on the veranda. Only, now there is no veranda. And no glass in the windows. Nobody glazes the windows anymore. There is no point glazing the windows. The panes shatter during the explosions. The house is empty. Whatever could be sold or swapped for a bag of marijuana was taken by the Russian soldiers who entered my yard in armored personnel carriers. What the soldiers left went on booze for my alcoholic uncle, whom my father had entrusted to live in and look after the house. Yesterday I had a dream. The garden: right in its center is the large, spreading cherry tree. Flanked by little cherry tree sisters. I remember planting them with Father. Remember them growing, donning their bridal blossoms each spring. This was only a dream. The cherry trees have been chopped down, and their gnarled stumps jut above the gray earth.

I walk down the long corridor. From room to room. We often had guests, and almost without fail they'd say that in our house you could lose your way. I didn't understand them at the time. But later I understood. When living in cramped flats, rooms, corners of rooms. Where no one could lose his way. In our house you really could lose your way. Each child had a room of his own; our parents had their own room; in the main room we would gather to watch television and read the newspaper aloud; in a separate room was the library, where we received guests; besides the kitchen there was also a dining room, although in the summer we loved to take lunch on the spacious glass-covered veranda. And to read books, lying on the saggy couch in a heap of old quilts.

Books. The books went as kindling the winter my sister and her husband tried to warm a single room. Here, on the woodstove, is where they cooked, where they heated up water for washing. And here are the scraps of glossy paper, singed at the edges. The *Large Soviet Encyclopaedia*—that lasted well. Its thick sheets and cardboard cover ignited poorly but burned long, almost as long as logs of willow.

The lane had three large cottages, each divided into two halves: six families in all. We lived without street name or house number. One day we decided to write a collective request to the executive committee. Opinion over a name was divided. Father suggested "Willow Lane." In our yard grew huge weeping willows, visible from afar, flooding the view of the lane with emerald green from wherever you looked. How my sisters disliked them! Whatever the time of year, they shed leaves and branches, and Mama would issue orders to sweep the spacious yard. I too swept, though more often I carried the rubbish out on my good old homemade cart, which my uncle the alcoholic had built. And then I'd run to the library, to the books.

Perhaps something had survived that winter? Impressive folios of academic translations of the Rig Veda and Mahābhārata. Collected works with gilt lettering bound in green: Tolstoy, Bunin, Turgenev, Chekhov. Bound in blue: John Steinbeck. Various editions of Sergey Yesenin. Most loved of all were a small volume of the selected poems of Nikolay Gumilev and a slim red hardback book bearing a trefoil: Jorge Luis Borges.

The lane never did receive a name. The penultimate stamp in my Soviet passport reads "State Farm Jalka Estate." That's what they called our state farm. It was given this name in Soviet times. Named after the river running through the village. Through our village runs the river Bass. Whereas the Jalka flows near Gudermes. But the powers above got into a muddle. They named the state farm in the village near Gudermes "Bass," and ours "Jalka." In the village Bass, on the bank of the Jalka, lived our relatives. My first cousin.

They were betrayed. The youths from the sabotage team, mere kids, were sent on ahead—to mine the roads in front of the advancing Federal troops. He was very gifted. At home he made all sorts of cunning contraptions and he also grew flowers in the greenhouse. He always had flowers in his greenhouse—even in winter. They made a good demolition man of him. They were sent on ahead. But at that very moment the commander was selling their corpses to the Russian generals. They were still alive when the commander sold their corpses to the Russian generals. Gudermes was surrendered without a fight. The sabotage team was encircled. They were killed from a safe distance, slowly and merrily. Victory had been paid for. The corpses were brought to town on a truck and dumped in the central square. Mothers, howling, dug their children out from the heap of bodies and carried them home. How could they carry them, weighted down with death, in their thin, wrinkled arms? Well, that's nothing. That's another question. Empty, frantic eyes, hearts frozen with grief—how could they now carry their hearts, so large, heavy, useless?

Beyond my window is a late white St. Petersburg autumn. The quiet of an old lane. The quiet of an imperial building. And memories. Like explosions. Once my memory was a strawberry field. Now my memory is a minefield.

When I was fifteen or sixteen, I wrote two novellas. They were terrible. The first, a long one in gothic style, recounted a tale about werewolves: a wolf and a vixen who came to a carnival in the town of Alraune. Their masks were the best in the carnival. Genuine beasts' heads on human shoulders! And in every inn they visited, when they left, the wooden floors became sodden with blood, red as young wine. They found themselves in a castle and sat down at the long table of a knight—the castle's owner. The son of a great Crusader, who in one of his heroic campaigns for the glory of Christ had killed, among hundreds of innocent village dwellers, the father and mother of two infants. Heathens. Who had remained true to the customs of their forefathers and didn't want to accept the Savior. He had christened them with the sword. He ordered that the children be tossed into a wagon. During the night, wild beasts attacked the camp where they had stopped in the forest. The next morning many knights lay with their throats sliced from ear to ear. And the children—a boy and a girl—had disappeared. The young owner of the castle seated at the long table recalled this family legend and asked all the guests to take their masks off. Only two masqueraders—wearing the wolf and fox heads—would not remove their masks. The knight fought and defeated the werewolves. With his sharp sword he struck the bestial heads from their shoulders and, impaling them with a long spear, cast them into the hearth. A flame shot out of the fireplace in a furious whirlwind. That night the town of Alraune burnt to the ground. The people from the neighboring villages claimed to see in the flames and smoke over the town the silhouettes of monstrous beasts—a wolf and a vixen—running across the sky.

The second novella was short. It told how early one morning a Pioneer detachment walked out of a secret cave and marched to the beat of a drum through a provincial Soviet town. The detachment sang: "Raise our bonfires higher, navy nights!" When they left, a flame came crashing down from the skies. The novella was called "Alraunsk, Burnt Again."

Each in his own way, we all saw it, we felt it in our skin, in our memory of the future we foresaw the flame from the skies. It already streamed over us, invisibly but palpably, when the fields were still filled with strawberries. Delicious, large strawberries grew in the forest glades near Serzhen-Yurt. Serzhen-Yurt was destroyed twice. In the first war it was wiped from the face of the earth by carpet bombing, multiple rocket launchers, heavy artillery. People are amazing. In the brief interim between the wars they built houses again—beautiful stone-and-brick houses, the kind you can live in for centuries. On this wonderful land where large strawberries grow, where the water in the rivers is clear as crystal, where the freshness of the submountain air dizzies you. On this accursed land, crossed by the road to Vedeno. The road to the mountain stronghold of the Resistance. A road that one group wants to seize, and another group wants to hold on to at any cost. On this road stood Serzhen-Yurt. Before, when such a village existed. In the second war it was again wiped from the face of the earth by carpet bombing, multiple rocket launchers, heavy artillery.

Alraune is the Arabic name for the mandrake plant. In medieval times magical powers were attributed to mandrake; a powder made from its root was an ingredient in magic potions. The mandrake root resembles a human figure. According to legend, it grows on the site of a murder. When you pick mandrake from the earth, it emits a human moan. Anyone who picks mandrake will die without fail. Therefore, the plant is drawn out of the earth by tying it to the tail of a dog. Who is then doomed to death.

Now strawberries grow in these fields. Even more, it seems, than before. Sweet, intoxicating strawberries. Nobody picks them. The mines. Everyone laid mines. The Federals and the rebels. Nobody knows the patterns, the maps. Legs ripped off young soldiers. Children torn to pieces. Strawberries grow well in fields watered with thick, rich human blood. But perhaps they are no longer strawberries. Perhaps it is mandrake growing in the forest fields near Serzhen-Yurt. Mandrake brings death, mandrake moans and explodes in mines under the feet of anyone who steps across this paradisaic earth, across this hellish earth.

When I finish writing this story, I too can die calmly. Everyone has already died. What am I doing here, alone in this void, in this quiet? I knew that I must compose one book. I waited for wisdom, which comes with the passing of years, waited for gray temples and composure of mind. Now I have begun. It feels like I don't have long left. And what about the gray head? My temples have already turned gray. I'm not yet thirty. But our generation fell into the zone of fire. Everyone has already died. When I finish this tale, I too can calmly die.

II

Our families were friends. We had a lot in common. Their mama had the same name as mine. Our fathers bought identical cars. Weekends and holidays, picnics in the countryside, New Year's eves and birthdays we spent together. In the cold, empty house we still have the photo album; there are many photographs of us in the forest, on the bank of the river—our parents playing cards, we're running through the fields, chasing a ball, bandying a badminton shuttlecock. Their only son was roughly my age. And we both had two sisters. I have never met another driver like Valid. It was quite terrifying to sit in the car as he chased down the road at night. Though he never had a single accident. Valid was very tall and beautiful. Women loved him. He was desperately brave. After serving in the army, he stayed in Moscow. He used to send money to his parents. He sent cars to be resold. The day came, and he returned himself. For good. His lofty, bare forehead had been shot clean through. The war was beginning there. The only good Chechen is a dead Chechen. Valid became a good Chechen and returned home. His lofty, bare forehead had been shot clean through. Since then, I often see him in dreams and talk with him. We talk about everything. And he always smiles. I no longer notice the hole caked with red blood in the middle of his forehead. All the same, these are difficult dreams.

III

I have never been in the mountains. None of us has ever been in the mountains. We lived in Shali. This name translates as "place of the plain." Shali is an ancient settlement in the heart of Ichkeria. In Soviet times it was a village, but one of the largest in the world. With more than thirty thousand inhabitants. The only one larger was somewhere in Africa. We took pride in this. Then Shali became a town. An ordinary, small provincial town, like many along Russia's fringes.

But I've never been in the mountains. It's true, sometimes we saw the mountains. In fine, cloudless weather, the Greater Caucasian range soared up like a wondrous vision over the southern brink of the horizon. And it was strange to see the snowy caps of the summits on hot southern days. The gorges, glaciers—all was clear to see, in detail. In the morning we would go out to school, and the road led straight to the horizon, to the fairy-tale blue mountains with shimmering white peaks.

There were hills, too. Wooded hills at the foot of the mountains, at Serzhen-Yurt. And strange forestless heights in the fields. In India they say that mountains once knew how to fly. But the tsar of the skies, the god of war Indra severed their wings with lightning. And they fell to the ground. I saw those mountains when traveling by train through the country around Kurukshetra. The landscape looks truly bizarre—no ridges, no foothills. Just a field with a hill in it, as though it had fallen from the sky. I believe it. Now I believe it. I know that plenty can fall when nobody holds up the sky. Even mountains. Mountains too can fall from the sky.

Such a hill stands west of Shali. In the flat, bare field is a high, woodless hill. The Bald Mountain. It is thought that such mountains are an assembly point for evil spirits. In reality, these are the memories of the heathen shrines set upon the summits of such hills. Our ancestors carried out sacrifices here, kindled the sacred fire. For here it is closer to the sky, the abode of the gods. I think in olden times that mountain too had a shrine. Near the ancient settlement, it is the site closest to the sky.

We were drawn to the hill. As kids, we saw it while playing. Then one day we gathered for an expedition. We trudged long, on the trails through the forest belt, through the overgrown thicket, along the edge of the golden wheat fields, across the bare plain with the abandoned oil-pumping units. Long we scrambled up the steep slope. And we made it. On the level summit of the hill stood two huge oil containers, empty and rusty. We scrambled to the very top. The entire village spread out before our eyes. The silver ribbon of the Bass snaked. The groves shone green beyond the village, the state farm fields glowed yellow. And the sky. The sky was so close.

On the rusty sides of the tank in huge letters we—my best friend, Dinka, and I—scratched out the names of our sweethearts. I wrote the name Larisa. Larisa had studied with me in Class 7C, School No. 8. She was the daughter of the chairman of the district KGB. Ginger-haired, with a sweet, freckly face and a light, joyous character. I think she's still alive. Because they left, long ago. At the end of Class 8, Larisa said good-bye to us. Her father had been transferred to another location, and they were leaving. She looked at me sadly on our last day, a warm, sunny day in May. Later I received a letter, one letter. I think she's still alive. Because they left long ago, long before the sky fell. And because I've never seen her in dreams. Not once seen her in the city of the dead.

You could check your watch by him. Every day, after lunch, he would appear in the sky. Every day the dragon came for new victims. He would drop a full bomb load onto the village, onto the quiet, peaceful homes. And the homes blazed; there burst cluster bombs banned by international conventions and dart bombs unknown to international conventions. And each time he'd finished his bombing, the dragon would start to mock. He knew there was no air defense. Oh, he knew there were no serious armed formations at all. Just a defense squad—guerrillas with a hotchpotch of small arms bought at the market and some double-barrelled hunting guns. He would come at low altitude, skimming the treetops, and, at full thrust, just for fun, he'd shoot from his machine guns at the people fleeing through the streets—the women, children, and the elderly escaping from the burning buildings. Until his ammunition ran out. Then the dragon flew off. But the next day the dragon would be back.

The dragon flew in from the west, where in the evening the setting sun flares like a funeral pyre. Passing over the village, he would turn around and come back. He would turn around above the bald hill.

He was brought down by a single shot, an incendiary charge from an ordinary Kalashnikov, while the dragon maneuvered for another run. Flying low, afraid of nobody, skimming the treetops. He knew there was no air defense. And no Stingers. If only there had been Stingers! But there were no Stingers. So they brought him down with an ordinary Kalashnikov. Two guerrillas squatted on the Bald Mountain, under the empty tanks, on the flat summit of the Bald Mountain, where once stood the ancient shrines of our ancestors. For it is closer to the sky, where the gods live. Where the dragons live.

The bullet hit the fuel tank, the airplane caught fire. The pilot tried to pull the burning machine out of its dive. But an explosion boomed. The plane fell into the vast flat field where earlier, when there were no dragons, wheat had grown. The ejection seat worked, expelling the pilot into the sky; the parachute's white canopy opened. Two guerrillas were waiting for him where he landed. I don't know if he was dead already or merely unconscious when he reached the ground. One of the guerrillas pulled from his boot a long knife and—in a wide slice from ear to ear—cut the pilot's throat.

They carried him through the streets on a homemade cart, a sturdy homemade cart, used earlier for carrying refuse. He had an Asiatic face, no longer expressing anything. His head—hanging from his neck bone—was dragged through the dusty road. Out of each house came women who spat in his face, delivering the most ancient, the most terrible curses upon the dragon's soul and his entire clan, in all its offshoots and generations. There wasn't a street—wasn't a family—to which he had not brought death. Now he rode through the village on the refuse cart, and women spat in his face. The blood no longer poured from his sliced throat. But did he have blood, like the blood a human has? Perhaps he had blood, but of another kind: the dark green blood of a dragon, and a cold snake's heart.

IV

Why am I writing this book? For whom? Why have I left my bed, thrown off two blankets? It is cold. This winter in St. Petersburg is very cold. The old building has large windows and no amount of radiators could heat the room. But I feel warm under two blankets. I lie and look at the white tiles of the lowered ceiling. A few tiles are missing. I look up for hours and mechanically rearrange the tiles in my mind, imagining what geometric shapes could be made from the combinations of the voids. And I think. Well, no, I don't think. Thinking involves something dynamic. My consciousness is static. I simply remember. I remember it all.

For whom am I writing this book? Nobody will read it, nobody could understand it. Nobody will accept it. On either side of the line of fire. Nobody needs a book like this, it's not limited to either system of propaganda. Not one of its heroes' names is sensationally famous, oh nobody knew of them while they were alive, they were ordinary people. This book can't even offer the sophisticated youth any postmodernism.

Why have I left my bed, thrown off two blankets? For whom am I writing this book?

For them. Nobody knew them while they were alive; they were ordinary people. Now nothing is left, and it's as though they never existed. But they did exist. This is my town—the town of the dead—and I should engrave a memorial plaque for each home. This is the book of the dead and it should have a line about each of them. This is my duty. For this I was left among the living. Left for a while.

The living don't need my book. The dead do. I know this. I remember this while I imagine the geometric shapes emerging from the compositions of voids.

"A crown of sonnets is a complex poetic form. Together, the first lines from each sonnet create a final key sonnet. In Russian poetry, only one such work exists, composed by an obscure poet at the turn of the century. His crown of sonnets is named 'To the Dead of the First World War.'"

V

On that visit, in the tall, slender girl with large eyes I didn't immediately recognize Mariam. Which was hardly surprising. When I'd last seen her, she had still been a child of seven or eight. She had looked funny, flap-eared. Glancing at her now, the last thing you'd do was laugh. Taller than me, and I'm certainly not short when standing up straight. A beautiful, fine-featured face. Lustrous, piercingly blue eyes. A bride. Mariam herself laughed, said there wasn't a guy here whom she couldn't look down upon, meaning her height. But that was out of maidenly modesty. In reality she was engaged.

Mariam was Valid's younger sister. Some years earlier Valid had returned to the homeland, and the eyes of the parents who'd lost their only son were devoured with grief. Mariam was the youngest child. Bereaved by loss, her parents now devoted all their desperate love to her.

Spirits of evil, demons of dark caves, descendants of dragons and snakes, bloodless monsters tormenting in ancient times the earth and its inhabitants. Now they have returned. They are garbed in green clothes like the skin of giant bog toads, epaulettes like barbs. The one with the biggest barbs, the one who has more of these barbs, is revered by these monsters as the boss, the rest of the monsters obeying his commands.

They calculated everything with precision. After the strike of the surface-to-surface rocket on the very heart of Shali, on the crowd of people who'd arrived—some on their own business, some because they'd believed the rumors that the authorities were finally issuing pensions and child benefits—they waited for two hours. That would be time enough for the relatives to carry the hundreds of dead bodies, the hundreds of wounded, into the houses, to try to save those still living. They calculated with precision that the wounded would be carried to the nearest houses, not far from the center: you cannot carry people losing blood all the way to the village outskirts. Two hours after the strike with the terrible might of a surface-to-surface war missile on a peaceful village and unarmed people, the town center and adjoining streets were showered with mortar fire.

In the house of Mariam's relatives, not far from the center, they were bandaging my sister, found among the wounded.

Shells rained down on the house and yard. From under the rubble they dug out my sister, unconscious but alive. Mariam and her cousin were in the car. A shell fell straight onto the vehicle. Tattered clothes, spattered in blood. As before, when we children climbed in the garden—spattered with ripe cherry juice.

Two people remain on this earth as living ghosts. First their only son, then their daughter. Early in the morning they came here again, to the cemetery. Where else do they have left to go? Ah, how sweet for them the thought that they too will soon be able to lie down in this earth. Right here, nearby . . . We'll all be close, our little son, our little daughter . . . We'll be together . . . As we used to be, remember, when we lived in Serzhen-Yurt, the village that is no more, in the house of which only ashes remain. Remember, we used to gather berries in the forest glades? Where are you now? In which glades do you gather berries? Who will smooth your messy hair, who'll kiss your little white hands, who will cuddle you in the land of the dead, in the place where the sun never rises? Are you cold in the earth, do you long for the sun, for the sky? Don't long for them, because the sun has burnt out, and the sky is no more; it fell and smashed and killed us all. And it only seems that you are there and we are here. We too are there, we're already there, in the place where there is no sun or sky.

They came in the morning—early in the morning, very early. But they were not first. By the fresh grave, by the mound of earth lay a boy. His thin shoulders were shaking, and one name burst out endlessly along with his sobs. Happiness had escaped—happiness had been so close; the first and only love of his entire life now lay in this earth. The lilac will never flower, there will be no light-filled spring joy. Life has ended, no hope is left. She was sixteen. What did they kill her for? For the blue, piercing blue of her eyes? For her smile, filling my heart with warmth? What did they kill her for? Earth, take me, I am young and strong, take my blood, my flesh: let her go, let her walk upon the grasses, let her plait flowers into her glorious hair . . . don't stay silent, earth! He gets up. He should feel ashamed; he's a man, he should not cry, he knows how to suffer pain. He should feel ashamed, but he doesn't. He no longer feels anything. He is seventeen. No, he is seventeen thousand, he is already old, knows how to feel nothing but pain. He walks away, through the fragments of sky, to the place where he'll now live, to a world in which spring never comes, where the sun never rises.

VI

Narts, *narts*, ancient *bogatyrs*, tear the rock asunder, come out from the mountains, look—the sky has fallen, no one is holding the sky up!

See what has happened to your earth, your people!

Evil dragons fly over the houses, gardens, and cornfields, burning everything with their foul-smelling breath, pelting down incandescent steel from the skies. Horrific monsters crawl over the earth, spewing out death. Hordes of cannibals scour the villages, killing and devouring your children.

Narts, arise from the thousands of centuries, save the world, as you saved it at the dawn of time! Slay the dragons, the monsters, chase the cannibals away to the faraway, cold, snowy lands, to the place where they ought to live, devouring each other.

They were a tribe of earthly gods, warriors without equal. But the era of heroes passed, ominous signs of decline arose everywhere. And the earth could no longer support them. They took a step and sank up to their knees from the weight of their bodies, from their own might. They took another—and sank up to their hips. They left for the mountains, but there, too, the age-old stone slabs cracked from their tread. They realized that their time had passed. No one could kill them, there wasn't a warrior or weapon that could strike them dead. So the *narts* boiled up seething copper in a huge cauldron and drank it. Yet even then, the *narts* didn't die straightaway. Long they lay in the cave, tormented by thirst. A rock pigeon brought the *narts* water in its beak. As they died, the *narts* stroked the pigeon. Ever since, on the head and neck of the pigeon there has remained a stripe of molten copper.

VII

It became a ritual. Every day after class Ruslanbek and I would fight, after goading each other with hurtful words. The entire class would gather to watch. The boys would stand in a circle, accompanying each successful blow or throw with loud hollers. The fighting went on with varying success. That day, I kicked Ruslanbek in the stomach, but my opponent stepped back just in time and grabbed my leg. In another instant he'd have jerked the leg to himself; not having expected such a turn of events, I bent my leg at the knee and with all my weight laid into my duellist. He fell on his back straight onto some large cobbles of burnt coal scattered over the school yard.

Finding myself on top, I began to strangle him. Ruslanbek resisted. Suddenly I saw tears welling up in his eyes from wild, unvoiced pain. Something flipped in me. Somehow all these spectators seemed vile, yelling enthusiastically at the sight of our tussle. *Found yourself some gladiators*, I thought angrily, relaxed my grip, and got up. Ruslanbek leapt up, overcoming his pain, and got ready to throw himself at me. I stretched out my hand to him. "No hard feelings," I said in Chechen.

We became friends. Sat at the same desk, skipped lessons together. Rode after school on passing military trucks to the soldiers' lake to bathe. The lake was dug specially for tanks and infantry combat vehicles, as a water obstacle for crossing during training exercises. Our mountain brooks are brisk and shallow, whereas in these artificial lakes you could swim long in the calm water.

I remember how we swam in the autumn, how we climbed out onto the bank and—shivering from the cold—smoked a packet of Kosmos cigarettes. For us it seemed a terribly forbidden but grown-up and manly deed. I remember how we returned, once again in a truck a short distance from the military unit. Ruslanbek had an open, easygoing character; cheerfully and simply he asked the soldiers, and they laughed and gave us a lift.

Ruslanbek had a nickname, a word that translates from Chechen as "holes." He was awarded this name by our classmate—and his neighbor—Rasul. Rasul's parents were rich, they bought their son expensive tape recorders and brand-name clothes. Rasul's papa worked as the head of the warehouse. Ruslanbek's mama was a teacher, his father a bus driver. And there were two sisters as well, who also had to be clothed. So Ruslanbek had few clothes. A navy school uniform and not much else, by the looks of it. Arriving home from school, he'd go off to play outdoors in the same clothes. Ruslanbek was a lively boy, and it is hardly surprising that his clothes would become worn to holes depressingly fast.

One day Ruslanbek's mother heard the neighborhood children teasing him. She chased her son home, made him take off his navy jacket, trousers, and shirt. She sewed up all the holes, crying quietly, spilling tears onto the dusty garments. From that day on, Ruslanbek, even when playing on the streets, would wear a suit that, though it was the same old threadbare one, had always been washed and darned by his mother's hand.

The name stuck regardless. But not for his mother. His mother called him Rusik. He had light blond hair and blue eyes. Among Chechens you will often see people with "Slavic" looks. Some explain this as the influence of mixed marriages. But the elders say that a real Chechen is fair-haired or red-headed, with blue or green eyes, with gentle facial features. Whereas dark hair, large noses— these are in fact the consequences of many centuries of crossing with our neighboring peoples.

Everyone still remembers Ruslanbek's extraordinary eagerness for socially useful work. Without being asked, he'd be the first to run up and push a stuck car; for days on end he would drive about with his neighbors if he noticed them planning some building job or maintenance; no old lady could go past him carrying bags. Ruslanbek would take the bags and walk the woman home, diverting her with polite conversation along the way. Rasul always laughed at him for this unsolicited kindness, which at times seemed meddling.

Probably because of this personality trait, he was one of the first to join the defense squad. The guerrillas were setting up watches at the edge of the village. The purpose of such patrolling was altogether prosaic. There was no combat action, but the Russian soldiers, driven to a half-animal state, would run off with weapons from the units stationed at the peacefully surrendered village, plunder everything in sight, and kill everyone they met on the way.

Lord, what was there to take from Ruslanbek's house? Now, Rasul's house offered easy pickings. But Rasul had not volunteered for the watches. Most likely he had left, long ago, and was living in Russia.

Besides the ever-hungry and drunken soldiers, there were snipers too. The snipers sat in hiding and got bored. To relieve the tedium, the snipers would shoot at people. Rather, at Chechens. Ruslanbek died swiftly, easily. He probably didn't even have time to feel anything. The sniper's bullet went straight into his heart, and he fell on his back as though he'd choked. His wide-open, surprised eyes reflected for the last time the sky—so clear and blue.

Ruslanbek's body was taken home; they began preparing his

ablutions and burial. His mother, aged and crazy from grief, stood over her son. To her it seemed he'd merely fallen asleep. Only, here on his shirt, on his chest was a tiny little hole. But that's no big deal. She'll sew up the hole. She always sewed up the holes in his clothes, so that the mean neighborhood kids wouldn't tease her sweet fair-haired treasure. Let me sew up the hole! Why are you holding my arms, why are you crying on my shoulders, where are you taking me? Let me go, I have to sew up the hole while my son is asleep; see, he'll wake up and go out onto the streets to play, and I can't let him out in rags, the boys will laugh at him, let me sew up this small hole, let me go, let me go to him . . .

VIII

Long ago it began, from the first days of the war. "Mama, I had a strange dream. It was our neighborhood, and I'm walking, as usual, along the path through the field, to the state farm canteen where we used to buy fresh warm bread. But the field is covered in bomb craters, smoke and ruins are all that's left of the canteen and the warehouse opposite it, smoke drifts over the land, over the heaps of charred bricks . . ."

"Yes, my son. That's what it's like. The field is full of craters, the canteen and the warehouse opposite it were destroyed. Lots of buildings have been destroyed, my son. Lots of people have died . . ."

Since then I often dream of our town. Only now I don't dream of it like that—no, I see it calm and at peace. The way I knew it and saw it in childhood. All the buildings are intact, there are no craters in the fields, no craters in the streets, no traces of shrapnel on the fences and the walls of the houses.

And in this town live people. Plenty of people! I meet them everywhere along my way, on every street, on the pavement alongside the road. I know each of them. We greet each other, we chat. And I walk on farther. I meet plenty of people on the way.

Only all these people are dead.

I have never seen in the town of my dreams, in the town of the dead, anyone who is still alive. And if I see someone there for the first time, then I'll soon hear of his death.

When these dreams start, I feel bad. I feel like I'm ill. The whole day I walk about as though in a dream, but as soon as I fall asleep, I find myself in the place where yesterday's dream ended. I feel good there, with them. And I feel bad here, with you. I tell them this; they nod their heads in sympathy, and say, "Yes, we know. There, no one will understand you. Stay here with us. See, we're all already here. Only you are still there. Come over to us and stay."

IX

For some reason, my neighbors used to recall Ibragim most often of all. Ibrashka. That's how he was known after my mama successfully nicknamed him. Ibrashka was our village idiot. He suffered from oligophrenia, and, at his advanced age, he was at the developmental level of a child. We grew up, became adult, but Ibrashka remained in eternal childhood. He was very funny and kind; we would often abuse this and poke fun at him. He played football with us, went out to tend the cows. And he was big and strong. It is known that nature compensates in strength for any shortfall of brains. And he was stubborn. When he made up his mind to do something, no one could stop him.

The Fascists were carrying out a reprisal. People hid in the cellars from the blind rounds, from the grenades hurling down everywhere, from the mortar fire. The retaliators would not leave for a long time. The children in the cellars cried. They pleaded for water. Ibrashka stood up, took a bucket, and moved toward the door. They tried not to let him go . . . But how could they not let him go?

"Ibrashka is good . . . the children want to drink . . . Ibrashka's going to go and get them water . . . everyone will say: 'Thanks, Ibrashka!' The children will drink . . . Ibrashka knows where there's water . . . Ibrashka goes and gets water every day, it's not far! . . . Everyone will be happy, everyone will say: 'Good Ibrashka!'"

The Fascists saw him, in his daft clothing, with the grimace of feeblemindedness on his face. From Ibrashka's looks one could not help but realize he was ill . . . They drove after him in their armored personnel carriers and, laughing heartily, hurried him along with bursts from their submachine guns . . . Ibrashka quickened his pace . . .

It's nothing . . . Ibrashka will get some water . . . Ibrashka is good . . .

One of the first rounds, it seems, hit his leg . . . Ibrashka fell . . . With a clatter the empty bucket rolled over the cobblestone . . .

Why does it hurt so much? . . . Why are they laughing? . . . Ibrashka is good . . . Ibrashka's gone to get water . . . The children want to drink . . .

The retaliators drove closer to the person writhing on the road. A few breezy rounds from the submachine gun finished him off.

That was how they found him. That was how they buried him. Eternally stamped on Ibragim's face are pain and childish bewilderment.

x

I remember what a cheerful lass Lakshmi was. She was younger than me and lived in the neighboring house, with her father, mother, and brother. I remember well how terribly cheerful she was. I recall this because now she has become quite different.

She is just as friendly, just as hardworking. Probably even more hardworking than before. As if trying to become oblivious in her everyday chores. But it is as though she has forgotten how to laugh. In her large dark-brown eyes the spark has dampened forever. In its place are uncried tears.

They were travelling to their relatives, trying to get out of the bombing zone. A Russian driver was taking them. The car was stopped at a checkpoint. The soldiers dragged the driver out and started to beat him. "What's this," they said, "sold out to the wogs? Transporting combatants, are you?" And they laid into him.

In the car sat the combatants. Fat, rather funny, and kind—as chubby people often are—Mansur, Lakshmi's father; combatant Lakshmi—a girl of fifteen; twelve-year-old combatant Issa; and the chief combatant of all—their mama, Tamara.

Mansur got out of the car. He started pleading: "Guys, don't beat up our driver. He hasn't done anything. We've got our documents on us. We're going to our relatives. You can search the car. And look, here, take this . . ." Mansur reached into his inner pocket and brought out a worn note, from the last of his cash, saved for an emergency.

"Ah, a wog's got out." The soldiers began laughing malevolently. One cocked his submachine gun . . .

There's a burst of fire . . . Lakshmi sees her father—his hands flapping ridiculously—sink to the ground . . . She doesn't hear her own scream . . . Doesn't hear her brother and mother's screams . . . She sees her father . . . No . . . Don't . . . In the stomach . . . a burst of fire . . . From right up close . . . But the blood for some reason comes out of his mouth . . . He hasn't died all at once . . . In the stomach . . . He still hasn't died . . . For some reason he's even tried to get up . . . With his stomach torn apart . . . And he's fallen . . . He was alive when the soldier walked up, calmly took from his spasmodically trembling hand the worn banknote, and, kicking the dying man, said:

"I hate those wogs."

XI

To the north of our lane was a large field of the state farm. Usually it was planted with maize. Or left to lie fallow. When the field was left fallow, it ran wild with thistle, tall as a person.

During autumn in Ichkeria the sky turns gray, the earth dark brown. Low clouds carry cold, interminable showers. Returning from school, I headed for the yard to tend to the animals. I had to feed the inhabitants of our farm . . . Change the water, clean out the barn. A lot of work for a boy at an age when many of his peers know nothing but play. Our family had it hard, and we all worked without stint.

But I had my games, too. When I finished my chores in the yard, I went out into the field. I played at war. In my hand I held a wooden sword. I walked up to the edge of the field. The wind swayed the tops of the dead thistle. I challenged the field to battle.

Wedged among the tight rows of dry sticks jutting from the earth, I began to hack, left and right, with my wooden sword. In my mind, the field of dead thistle was a horde of enemy forces, and I an ancient *bogatyr*. I hacked, hacked and moved ever farther, ever deeper into the enemy formation. Until, wearied, I fell on the dark-brown earth. On my clothes, like bleeding wounds, clusters of prickles glowed red. I lay and looked at the gray sky. The wind swayed the dead branches.

And I seemed to hear. The patter of horses, the din of an enormous force. Alien, unintelligible speech. They've come once more, the hordes. And I seemed to remember. Once more I took my sword and went out into the field, one against a thousand.

And once more I was killed.

XII

Spring has come to St. Petersburg . . .

There are puddles and mud outside. But in the sky the sun is warm. Yes, the world still has a sun, and not just a white stain above us, as it was in the winter. It gives off heat like a country stove.

Probably I need to wander through the lanes and courtyards, breathe in the smells of thawing refuse, listen to the loud, springtime cawing of the crows. I did all this in my previous lives and perhaps I'll do it in the next.

In this one, I sit in the old building. I look into the flickering glow of the monitor. Sometimes I read books, books on history, books about times long since past. It is absurd. Now things are different. Everything is entirely different. Now things are utterly different.

. . . And there was the land of Sim Sim to the north of the Great Mountains. It was settled by people who cultivated the earth and worked metal. The large city in the heart of the land of Sim Sim had ornate walls and tall towers. The people of Sim Sim never attacked anyone, never started wars.

But others attacked them. The land of Sim Sim occupied a site at the gateway between north and south, and conquerors from each side strove to break through. Alexander the Two-Horned, Timur the Lame, Khan Baty . . . The proud people of Sim Sim would not swear allegiance to the empires, they went out to battle against the enormous armies. And they fell in battle.

Sim Sim became deserted . . . The remnants of its people hid in the mountains. Centuries passed, and they returned to their native land, but a new conqueror once more eliminated the rebellious.

There is an ancient song about Bird's Wing Tower . . . Timur the Lame, the great conqueror, was so embittered at the resistance of the little nation that he sent a reprisal expedition to the mountains. Timur's warriors threw from the tall cliffs everyone they found in the mountains. Thus had Timur commanded, for the only good Chechen is a peaceful Chechen, and the only peaceful Chechen is a dead Chechen.

Three times the warriors of Sim Sim went out to battle with the army of the Golden Horde. They were betrayed by all their allies, who had been bought by the Tatar khans. Yet only when not a single warrior was left living could the Horde break through the gateway to the north and attack the kingdom of Rus. The years passed. Mothers nursed their children, and ere their beards were grown, they had raised a revolt against the khan's rule.

To quell the uprising of the rebellious Chechens the khan appointed his faithful vassals—the Russian princes. The princes and their retinues hurried to help the Tatars deal with the people who had stood till their last breath on the frontline, shielding Rus and Europe from the Horde. Thus Russians first came to the land of Sim Sim. They burned the villages and killed the people—men, women, children, and the elderly. The only good Chechen is a dead Chechen. They helped the Tatars; the khan was pleased with them. He expressed his gratitude in his own peculiar manner. Shortly, one of the Russian princes arriving in Sim Sim, site of the summer head-quarters of the Horde, to pay tribute was dishonored and killed.

After the fall of the Golden Horde, several new khanates formed on its ruins, continuing the tradition of this cruelest, wildest, and most barbarous empire in the whole of mankind's history. One of them, under its slant-eyed leaders, has endured to this day. The Moscow Khaganate—the Oil Horde.

XIII

When will this book end? I am tired—why, whatever for, who writes all these new pages, more and more of them? They said the war is over. So why does this book write itself, on and on?

Early one morning above the fields of Ichkeria stood a dense, milky fog. The lowing of the cows echoed softly, as though wrapped in felt. And the shot of a sniper thudded, like cotton against a carpet from which a bride diligently beats out dust.

Toyita had been a diligent bride. She'd had no shortage of chores. Four children, two still suckling. Her mother-in-law was already old, not her former self. When her husband—in whose arms the beloved wife had died—buried her, he buried his desire for life itself. So the neighbors said: "Poor children, what'll happen to them now? People die—we've all grown used to that. People are killed by the Russians. Here, we're used to that. But the children—they haven't been killed. If they were, it wouldn't surprise us. The Russians kill everyone. But so far no one has killed them—well, how are they to live, without a mama?"

She simply went out to herd the cows to pasture. She did this every morning. But that morning the sniper's ganja had run out. Or perhaps he'd grazed his leg. Well, he was in a bad mood. And he decided to kill someone.

And all Chechens are werewolves. Sure, by day they pretend to be innocent people. But at night each Chechen turns into a wolf and goes out to kill Russians. He cuts the Russian's head off and drinks his blood. That's why all the Chechens have to be killed, the peaceful ones too. The only peaceful Chechen is a dead Chechen.

It was they, the werewolves, who blew up a truck full of soldiers driving from the unit based just outside the village, at the pasture field. Well, the soldiers had already finished their war and were driving to pick up their combat pay—666 roubles for each day of war. Such a round figure. They were driving, these good, sweet Russian guys. Snipers, submachine gunners. To get their money and go home. To their sweet brides, to their mothers. But their truck was blown up by bad Chechen wolves. Who gunned them down, right here on the road. And scratched out with a knife on the side of the blown-up truck: "Welcome to hell. Admission: 666 roubles."

XIV

If I were a writer, I'd write a book about this. Or a short story. But I am merely a fragment of somebody's life. And in my heart's mirror are reflected eyes—but I don't remember who that person was.

At school I was the best in class at writing compositions. The teachers would pass them around. One was published in the local newspaper. It was called "We Need Peace." The epigraph was a quote from Jonathan Swift: "War! That mad game the world so loves to play."

I probably wanted to become a writer. Now I don't know, cannot remember, I'm not sure whether that was me. If I were a writer, I'd write a book, a short story at least.

But I'm merely a schoolboy, back at my desk, these thirteen years have not passed, and I'm writing a composition. Free choice. My composition is called "Why the Sky Doesn't Fall." It's about a pilot. Perhaps I am that pilot.

I have fair hair and blue eyes; I have flown from a faraway snowy land. This mighty bird of prey obeys my hands. I am a warrior, carrying out my assignment. To destroy the objective marked on the map. Beneath the wings of the plane lies unknown land. I make for the target. In the optics I see a peaceful village, residents absorbed in their daily chores, children playing on the lawn by their houses.

This is the objective.

And I hear an inner voice. No, not quite inner, rather, it comes from behind, a little to the left. A whisper works its way through the crackle of the headset:

> *It's what you have to do. And it's what you've always wanted to do. Kill. You're tired of living at peace, bound by thousands of restrictions and rules. By morality and law. But you've always wanted to kill. Back home you'd be tried and sent to prison for it. Here, for doing the same, you'll be selected for an award. Just do it. Kill. Now you've been given might and power. Take control of the lives and deaths of these unknown people, who mean nothing to you. Feel yourself a god . . .*

And I drop lower, take aim at the house. My hand lies on the target-bombing button . . . But . . . perhaps, could it be . . . there's a sharp fall in altitude, my head is humming . . . I see the skin of my hand turn green, covering with bumps, my fingers lengthen, growing sharp claws, dragon's claws. I lift my head and look at the sky. The sky fills with cracks, more and more; I hear a ringing; the sky is ready to shatter like a glass dome.

And I understand. Understand why the sky doesn't fall. The sky doesn't fall while we remain human. And it shatters when we choose to take the place of God and turn into dragons.

I lift my airplane, fly it away from the village. Landing on the wide wheat field, at the woodless hill . . . I climb out from the cockpit, tinker at the fuel tanks, and move off to a safe distance.

The iron bird with the full load of bombs explodes, deafening the world with a bang. I take off the helmet with the incessant radio calls and toss it far aside.

The weather is clear and cloudless: on the horizon, like a miraculous vision, appears an unknown mountain range. I've never been in the mountains. So strange to see the snowy caps of the summits on this sultry day. And I go, go through the field of wheat, heading straight for the horizon, to the fairy-tale blue mountains with shimmering white peaks.

MORE ELDERLY PERSON

DMITRY DANILOV
Translated by Douglas Robinson

YOU'VE GOT YOUR PASSPORT.

Yes.

And your discharge.

Yes, yes.

And your certificate.

Of course.

The simultaneous appearance in the entry hall of a more elderly person and a younger person.

The unbearable yellow morning winter light of the lamp on the ceiling.

Dirty light-blue wallpaper.

A bag (the string kind Russians call an *avoska*) set by the more elderly person against the wall. The bag's loss of form and firmness, the bag's sliding down the wall, the rolling out of the bag of a formless object, carelessly wrapped, god knows in what. The restoration by the more elderly person of the bag's form and firmness, the cramming back into the bag of the carelessly wrapped object.

The shifting from one foot to the other of the younger person. The bloating of the face, the general, fuzzy, unfocused appearance of the younger person.

What, let's go already.

Sure.

The simultaneous attempts to put on shoes and coats in the narrow entry hall, the sluggish pushing, the attempts to tie shoelaces, to shrug arms into sleeves. The old woolen winter coat of an indeterminate dark color with innumerable hairs and pieces of lint and fuzz stuck to it. The greasy jacket of an indeterminate dark color with feathers working their way to the surface here and there. They call jackets like this "parkas" probably; they're filled with down or some such. The sullen hat with earflaps, saturated with heavy years and thoughts. The woolen cap, black, so impossible to tell how dirty it is, but still visibly dirty, yes, very dirty.

The *avoska* in hand, the bag on shoulder.

You've got everything.

Yes.

Let's go then.

— — —

The sleepiness, the dryness of mouth, the trembling of hands while working the keys.

It is not a fact that this is father and son, not a fact at all. And they don't look like grandfather and grandson. Even less like brother and brother. The exact degree of their relatedness is hard to establish.

The cold, the blackness, the blueness, the snow, the streetlights. Perovo station.

These buildings were built in the sixties for the workers at the Hammer and Sickle factory. It was an easy commute: take the 24 tram to Third Vladimirsky Street, then turn left and go down the Enthusiasts Road to the factory. And back: up the Enthusiasts Road, take a right on Vladimirsky, and keep going till you get to the buildings that were built in the sixties for the workers at the Hammer and Sickle factory.

Workers at the Hammer and Sickle factory live here to this day, but nowadays they mostly ride the metro, from the Perovo station to the Ilich Square station, and then back.

Many of the workers at the Hammer and Sickle factory became alcoholics and died of alcoholism or other circumstances. Others did not become alcoholics and did not die. Still others did not become alcoholics, but died. And there are those who became alcoholics but have not yet died. They still live in these buildings that were built in the sixties for the workers at the Hammer and Sickle factory, those who drank heavily, those who died, and those who kept on living.

It may be that they are uncle and nephew. It may also be that they are not.

The clackety-clack of the 24 tram, turning off Third Vladimirsky onto Green Prospect.

It is not entirely clear why the prospect was called Green. Most likely the creators of the prospect thought that it might someday become a boulevard, lush with plantings, and that the residents of the buildings built in the sixties for the workers at the Hammer and Sickle factory would walk down it of an evening or on weekends through green trees and bushes and would fall in love with this place, and it would become, as the travel guides might put it, a garden spot, a favorite of the local residents. But somehow nothing ever came of this idea. There are trees, yes, but not the kind that create an atmosphere, nothing like what you'd expect on a street called Green Prospect. They're weak, puny, embittered, these trees and bushes, and as a result the prospect is more gray than green, but you can't call it Gray—it would be impossible even to imagine the maps or the street signs on the buildings saying Gray Prospect—but, on the other hand, whyever not, if there's a Red Square, a Green Prospect, and a Lilac Boulevard, there should also be a Black Street, a Brown Boulevard, and a Gray Prospect. But for some reason it isn't done to name streets and prospects that way.

But maybe it should be.

The progress down Green Prospect to the Perovo metro station through the crystal-clear cold air and the snow and the light of the orange street lamps. The not entirely successful attempts not to fall while navigating the iced-over steps.

How far to ride. On the metro with a transfer, then a long way on the commuter train.

Damn.

The unsuccessful attempt to squeeze into the train car quickly and find a seat. The thickness of the passenger mass, the howl and thunder of the train. The rising nausea, the steadfast hopeless stoicism.

The crowd on the escalator up to the Marxistsky metro station, the crowd on the escalator down to the Tagansky-Radial.

The younger person made exactly this trip yesterday, in the throngs, feeling nauseous, only going in the other direction and with other purposes, or, actually with no particular purpose at all.

The more elderly person didn't make this trip yesterday but sat in the kitchen staring fixedly out the window at the Perovo trees, buildings, and darkening sky.

The traveling along the purple line, Begovaya-Polezhaevskaya-October Field. After October Field the thinning of the crowds.

The route could have been different: first to Tretyakovskaya, transfer to the orange line, then to the Riga station, there board a practically empty commuter train. That way would have been far better, less time on the metro, more on the commuter train, better to travel on the commuter train than on the metro, but for some reason everyone does it this way, or almost everyone, travel to a distant station that is linked to a railway platform, to Tushinskaya or Vyzhno or the Warsaw station, strange, somehow.

The Tushinskaya metro station, the Tushino railway station. The darkness, the dawn, the wind, the steel and the asphalt of the Tushino station.

On one of the tracks stands a freight train with fourteen cars.

The commuter trains from Volokolamsk, New Jerusalem, Dedovsk, Nakhabino, bringing to the Tushino station a huge collection of passengers.

Practically empty commuter trains to Nakhabino, Dedovsk, New Jerusalem, Volokolamsk.

The commuter train to Shakhovskaya, practically empty.

Step free of the closing doors, next stop, Pavshino.

The train will pass the platform at the Trikotazhnaya station without stopping. Please be attentive.

Be attentive. Be attentive. Be attentive.

The need to sleep, but the lack of desire to sleep. On the metro the desire to sleep was strong, but now it is no longer.

Sitting facing each other, riding.

The more elderly person hardly ever wants to sleep; he usually stares fixedly at something, not out the window and not at the younger person sitting across from him, just somewhere off to one side; his gaze follows along the edge of the seat, the window frame, a piece of the train car's wall; his peripheral vision picks up, outside the window, the lightening of the sky and fleeting glimpses of things rushing by.

Conversation between them does nevertheless take place, consisting of seventy percent vocalizations, sighs, and silence. A careful analysis of their remarks might suggest that the more elderly person lodges more claims and complaints against the younger person and that the younger person rejects these claims and complaints and lodges his own claims and complaints against the more elderly person, basically the same ones, but the more elderly person emits emotionally tinged grunts like "eh" or "ah" and waves his hand, and the younger person stretches and yawns, and the more elderly person looks away again, over at the window frame and the wall, and the younger person does fall asleep after all, though at first he didn't want to sleep, and he dreams that he is riding the commuter train from Tushino to Shakhovskaya, and across from him sits the more elderly person looking off somewhere.

The reaching into the bag for the thermos, the screwing off of its cap, which simultaneously fulfills the function of a cup, the movements methodical, measured, precise—what's the hurry?—the pulling out of the cork, the pouring into the cap/cup of the liquid contained in the thermos, to all appearances hot or at least warm, the recorking of the thermos, the slow sipping of the hot liquid, which has the smell and aftertaste of plastic and cork, the drinking of the liquid, the screwing of the cap back onto the thermos, the stowing of the thermos back in the bag.

And again the glance somewhere away, to the place where the window frame is visible, the edge of the seat opposite, and a piece of the train car's wall.

The dreaming that the commuter train proceeded, then abruptly stopped.

The commuter train abruptly stops. He wakes. The commuter train starts moving again.

Across the aisle, obliquely, sits a young woman. People like the younger person are inclined to characterize young women like this with the word *attractive*, although, to be honest, it would be difficult to say anything positive about the outward appearance of this young woman.

The stops less frequent, the distance between them longer. The names denser. Lesodolgorukovo. Dubosekovo.

The yawning, the vague expression, the inability to decide what to look at.

The immobility, the looking at the window frame and the piece of the wall.

To travel from Tushino to Shakhovskaya takes just under three hours; it's a long way, a distant corner of Moscow Province. In Shakhovskaya it seems that Moscow is far away, thousands of kilometers from there, or as if it didn't even exist at all, green Moscow commuter trains and license plates from the Moscow suburbs the only reminders of the city.

At the far end of the train car sits a stooped person who from a distance seems old, but may in fact not be old, may be middle-aged, in his prime, as they say, mature, so to speak, a husband, or possibly a young person with his whole life in front of him, a hundred roads open before him, living an interesting and affluent life, or uninteresting and unaffluent, quiet, monotonous, and wretched; things go differently for different people, don't they, so why can't a young man at a certain point in his biography be sitting stooped and even bent over in a cold light-filled empty commuter train thundering into Shakhovskaya station?

At Volokolamsk the young woman and the stooped person get off the train; the stooped person walks past their window and turns out to be a woman of middle years, quite elegant, and in the younger person's head there flits the single abrupt word *attractive*.

The opening of the thermos. Drink. No. Go ahead, drink, it's hot. No, don't want to. As you wish. The sipping of the dark, hot liquid, smelling of cork and plastic.

The platform of the 133 Kilometer station. The closing of the thermos, the stuffing of the thermos into the *avoska*. The platform of the 149 Kilometer station.

Shakhovskaya station.

The *avoska* in hand, the bag on shoulder. The dreaminess, the yawn, the light return of intoxication from the frosty fresh air. The stoic not-quite-there silence, the squeezing in hand of the *avoska* handles.

In the square in front of the station two gigantic K-701 tractors plow snow. They are called "Kirovets tractors." They are made in St. Petersburg in the Kirovsky factory. This is why they are called Kirovets tractors.

The tractors with their enormous size completely dominate the surrounding landscape, houses, little trees, sheds. They appear taller than any object, any building in the area. Although, of course, this is not true, nothing more than an optical illusion.

Nothing need to be bought? No, later. Maybe. Shall we go in? I tell you we don't need to, we have everything. We'll go in later.

The square, the marketplace, the road, the road between houses, the courtyard, the five-story building, the entrance, the stairs to the fifth floor, the door, the apartment.

The smell of long hard monotonous agonizing lonely life. The shortness of breath and the absence of that shortness. The sorrowful sobbing furniture. The teakettle on the stove. The refrigerator, sign of humility and submission.

The simultaneous shedding of coats and boots in the crowded entry hall, the attempt to hang the coat and jacket on the hanger, the falling of the jacket off the hanger, the renewed attempt to hang the jacket on the hanger.

The *avoska*, set against the wall, loses form and firmness, slides down the wall. Out of the *avoska* rolls a formless, carelessly wrapped, shapeless object. The more elderly person takes the object, carries it into the kitchen, and lays it on the table.

If these people had belonged to another social class, if they had had another level of education, different conceptions of the good and the required, the younger person would have begun bustling about brightly, would have said something along the lines of *I'll put the tea on, you rest, don't worry, I'll do everything*, and the more elderly person would have stretched out on the sofa, thrown his hands behind his head, sighed heavily, and said something on the order of *man, I'm tired* or *man, what an exhausting trip* or *man, that wore me out*, but in this case everything goes differently. The younger person stretches out on the sofa, turns away, and instantly falls asleep, and the more elderly person fills the teakettle with water, lights the gas range, puts the kettle on the fire, and sits in a chair by the window.

The younger person sleeps, the teakettle gradually heats up, and the more elderly person sits in the kitchen, staring fixedly out the window at the trees, the houses, and the still light sky.

THE PLESHCHEYEV LAKE MONSTER

MARIANNA GEIDE
Translated by Anna Gunin

IT'S NOT A PLACE. It's the name of a city. A city-state: a rider could easily gallop from one end to the other long before the sun sets, in a mere fifty-ruble set-fare ride—that's what the cab prices are like round here. It's no place for anyone, but there are good places here. It's a good place for not being—that's what sort of a place it is.

Here communications are difficult. Not absent, but difficult. Here any gust of wind in your head will subside in the fifteen minutes it takes to walk to the post office. Here you have nothing left but to run your fingers over the buttons of the remote control, over the keyboard, over the tabletop. Here you can drum your fingers for hours, until you are brought a mug of pale beer, which you have no love of but accept for lack of an alternative.

Cause-and-effect relations do not thrive here. Nor do friendly relations. The very change of the seasons seems an idiotic annual coincidence, and not the natural order of things. Because all of nature is contained in apple trees, which bear fruit or don't, depending on whether there was frost in May or there wasn't, and everything else grows too feebly, is sold too feebly to build your world upon. This year, I don't think there was any frost, and I look at the apple blossom, look fleetingly, so as not to go out of my mind.

You have only to stand still before the cherry trees when they are
on the threshold. Little spheres and blossoms, the pupil narrows and
widens to make a sphere into a blossom and a blossom into a sphere
again. Until the young ones burst open and the older ones begin to
fall. You can still forget that they are destined to shed their petals, set,
swell, enlarge, blacken, burst, rot, having dropped their stones onto
the earth. All will be rough and dark from stones, because they are
wildlings. But at this moment they turn from spheres into blossoms
and from blossoms into spheres for no purpose. It has no meaning.

We wanted to look at the Japanese cherry but we didn't go. *Any
moment now the Japanese cherry will blossom*, we said to each other, and
sometimes to others. None of us knew quite where to find the Japanese cherry in the large and overgrown arboretum. We wanted to go,
rather, I wanted to, remembering how last autumn A. had buried a
green branch of a nut tree in the yellowing pine needles. Around us
even rows of an unknown variety of pine parted, trunks bare to the
level of our heads, we fitted beneath them, like under a ceiling, with
all our possessions—a bottle of screwdriver and a green branch from
a nut tree. A. had broken it off, as was her wont to break off beautiful
things and then bury them without waiting for them to wither. I see
the still-living clusters of bird cherry, well and truly torn from the
body by someone who apparently passed by not long before, and I
remember A. I think: *Perhaps it's not too late to look at the Japanese cherry,
perhaps we could call someone over who will later be buried under the fallen
petals of the Japanese cherry, which we won't be able to tell from any other
type of cherry tree.* Because here you stop knowing of Japan's existence,
all you can do is imagine some Japan instead of this nonplace and
hand out names. Just hand out names, greet everyone who comes
with a name, as the best thing that is left of humanity in this place.

Where each time I ask: *What kind of herb is this?*—and hear the
answer: *I don't know.* But each time you ask: *Ah, what kind of herb is
this?*—and hear the answer: *It's borage.*

It hasn't yet iced over. Yes, there's still hope that everything can be
resolved naturally, because, well, there still remain the simplest, most
fertile and stillborn of possible cause-and-effect relations—those that
connect the year. Well, neither of us ever had any deep knowledge

of astronomy, perhaps because we were born in cities that were too brightly illuminated.

On the day of the beheading of John the Baptist, Herodias's daughter paced out the yearly ritual dance around an empty dish named Pleshcheyev Lake. She danced and danced, and cracked the bone protruding from the side of her foot, the daughter of Herodias crumpled in a tiny load onto her moaning leg. And there was no one around to help her, because there was no one around at all. Herodias's daughter danced thus on each of those days for no one, like the wind that will blow even if the grass has long ago died and lies beneath snow. *All this has happened before,* so spoke the silence, but Herodias's daughter did not understand the language of silence—all this has happened long ago, St. John the Baptist died and was raised, everyone died and was raised, while she's left to lie on her cracked bone, and the mirror—or the lake—lies smooth or rustles with shells from which everything living or dead was long ago washed, now there is only the rustling of the wind, which is neither living nor dead.

When I first saw her. Later I can stare long at my childhood desire to give names and bewail it, well, that alone makes me alive. Perhaps from that same warped savageness that makes people turn words from a foreign language inside out, instead of turning inside out and mutilating their own throats and pronouncing by heart someone else's sounds, unfamiliar half-closed sounds produced by a musical instrument that once arrived from foreign lands. On Sunday, instead of being raised, they did the reverse.

"She lived on a good plot, though the house was built awfully long ago and very poorly, we both had our eye on it, to tell the truth, through a doubtful right—some ancestor of ours supposedly lived there once, and then sold it, or maybe rented it—we weren't very interested in it at the time, because we were young and didn't take up much space in our rooms, half the time we didn't occupy them at all, chasing about on bicycles, earning some laughable pittance through gathering empty bottles, or a-tenner-a-kilo strawberries, or just random information. Then we stopped having enough space under our roof, and outside the frost set in, made our teeth chatter. We never met her of our own will, it's just that her devil-knows-what kind of home was right opposite the rapids, we often dug for worms beyond her fence, and she let us. Back then one of us pinched and marveled at the fine black soil, how could it have got on the bank, he even tried it with his teeth. I've never had any great love of earth, that's to say I enjoy touching it but not eating it. My brother had an eye for earth, worms, everything that rots and wriggles, and he understood this earth immediately, he said, 'It's barren, just sand.' And it did look like sand, you could give it any number of years at all, it spoke with effort, joylessly, and it hardly understood what it was saying and to whom. I straightaway enjoyed echoing its 'hoi, hoi,' it didn't come out quite the same, but it was fun, and my brother was blunt, he jabbed his finger into it and repeated: 'Sand, it's barren,' then jabbed it again, confirming that it was sand and barren. Then he jabbed into the emptiness beyond the lake, where the shore could be guessed, probably more by the lights beginning than by the land, and he said: 'Shoo.' Then he stamped his feet heavily and sat down."

The fisherman narrated this not to us, as we passed, rather he stood on the bridge and told another fisherman, we had nothing at all to do with it and understood nothing—we took to fantasizing in our idiotic fashion about what it all meant. The fisherman was most likely talking about his own world, about fish, and we about ours, about worms and black earth.

In the "Ocean" shop there were carp in the aquarium, their mouths opened, closed, opened, and on the road in the dust a little fish jumped about, it had been caught from the lake, a small one caught by a nimble boy. The flapping contents of the lake, plucked into an entirely alien, hostile world, whose last thought would have been, "Well, how do they breathe this stuff, those, what do you call them, people, how do they breathe this stuff they call air, rather than biting the oxygen out of the soft H_2O, must be like drinking pure spirits by mistake, burn your throat," and his last thought will be: "I am a fish." But in the "Ocean" shop, like on the screen during an omphaloscopy, the living contents of the ocean swim, opening their mouths, at eighty-five rubles per kilo. Well, not contents of the ocean, mirror carp are hardly likely to live in the ocean. Scallops' muscles press up to one another in little jars. Before bottling them, they were told to relax so they'd take up more space. I wasn't sick, but it became rather disgusting to live.

"And when we went in, it turned out that the whole house was filled with little freaky kiddies, sitting and watching, whose placenta hadn't been washed off, yes, with short undeveloped fingers, that was perhaps the most unhuman thing about them—their short undeveloped fingers. For a long time we couldn't decide whether they were, in fact, children, then we had to call in the neighbors and drag them out from under the bench, from under the table, there was some kind of furniture too, apparently left by the former occupants. It wasn't clear where they had sprung from. Because she almost never went out and didn't mix with anyone."

We dug out old newspaper files in the hope of discovering at least something about the monsters on the shores of Pleshcheyev Lake. For some reason we wanted monsters to live on the shore, perhaps they would be us.

We discovered only a maniac, but he was meek, completely crazy, and he attacked only the goats grazing beneath the steep slope, who saved themselves by a lethal kick of their hind legs: we felt more sorry for the meek maniac who passed away from peritonitis resulting from the disturbance to his appendix than for the goats. We decided that the monster would definitely be us, because there was no one else.

The many-legged, bare-legged street on the weekends, smooth-handed, pale-skinned, had not had time to roast in the still young sun, had not had time to complain of the heat: the predicted wind swooped and upset all the apple carts, the dry biscuits and cotton dressing gowns on the stalls, they gathered up their things, they packed them away and that was it. But we walked a long time searching for good shoes, which have disappeared, in the nature of things, by reason of the daft fashion for pointy toes. We walked and walked, stamped our left foot, our right on the boxes, then bought them and calmed down. Turned into normal friendly monsters.

There remained one question, purely rhetorical: What is "Turkish leather" made from?

I abandoned myself to my favorite pastime: making up what happened next to the short-fingered subchildren from the devil-knows-where house. Were they taken in to help around the house by tender-hearted neighbors or did they scatter across the gullies and now caught the stupider birds for their subsistence? About the monster, which we were in the habit of referring to as "her" or "Herodias's daughter," we established that one fine day it crumbled into sand, touched by big brother's shout of "shoo." I am a monster, I'm off hunting. You want to take a look at the monster? But did you ask the monster whether it wanted to look at you?

In the evening, do you know, they dance, our fellow citizens dance too, after the sun's head has flopped down, and the street lamps, the wicked creatures, just won't light up. To go in under the sign, no farther, to freeze and watch the hall quake, you need only gaze at the mirror ball, they probably have one of those, and everything there is shoddy, like the music in a bus, like shoes made from Turkish leather, but if you reach out and touch their skin, it will be just like the kind all good people have—warm, soft, and sweaty. We didn't go to look, we went to bed. We feared that they would fear the monsters and beat them with their clubs or empty beer bottles.

That is to say, nothing of the sort, we were planning nothing of the sort, we leave them alone, they leave us alone, we touch intelligible and friendly objects, we deal with unintelligible and friendly people, go to the post office and ring up A.:

"Never would have thought that pauses could cost so much, I mean, that I could make so many pauses, in all that time you could have said, say, something like this:

'One of those subchildren suddenly turned up at the market selling sunflower seeds, it had grown and had turned from a subchild into an ordinary child, its fingers had lengthened and turned out quite nimble, because it was forever shelling seeds with them, you see, all of them had rotten teeth, they just sprang out rotten, replacing the milk teeth, which were rotten too. It has a nice-colored face, a few freckles, thin long hair of a freckly shade, but take note: it cannot speak at all, only knows how to count to seven—the price of a glassful of seeds. But you won't be able to pull a fast one on it: it will count up to seven in any coins, and if there aren't seven it won't give you the seeds. In this place everyone loves sunflower seeds, they even have signs up in the buses: Kindly eat your seeds with the shell on. He's called Katya.'"

"M., you are lying," A. will say to this. "You are lying without blushing, what a monster you are."

"And so what," I will say to this, "so I lie, why shouldn't I lie, I doctor you because I feel you are deficient in lies, this life is insufficient in lies."

But there's no point in us lying to each other, how can one monster lie to another, it can only collect different truths and mix them together. Move around the city in different directions fibbing about something each time:

"And the oldest of them, can you imagine, became deputy rector of the agricultural academy. That's to say they taught him to speak, they even taught him to sign his name, not with a cross, but in handwriting, as if his surname was Sheberstov. Only he stayed like that—made of sand, every time the cleaning woman comes to sweep and wash the floor, he ever so politely disappears, waits in the storeroom till they switch off the electricity, then sneaks into his office and disintegrates on the floor. The wind flies in through the cracks and rustles the sand. In the morning he reassembles and carries out his official duties, shrinking little by little. But sometimes he will look at the cleaning woman and say nothing, only swishes his foot, like, *Where's that sand from, won't you tell me?* But when did this all happen? Long ago, probably. If indeed it happened at all, then it was long, long ago."

Assistant Professor Mushinsky came to stay, he harrumphed:

"This would be a good place for a conference, if you could get a grant . . ."

He arrived, he parked, he let me press my foot on his Volga's accelerator, I said: "In my hands this is a weapon," and wouldn't press it. Assistant Professor Mushinsky harrumphed:

"Everything is a weapon in your hands, you don't know how to handle hard objects."

Maybe I don't, well what of it? And what need have I of hard objects? I love soft objects, warm objects, cats. Whatever else, there are certainly enough cats here, all of them different. Some have four legs, others don't have four legs. Assistant Professor Mushinsky amused us with barefaced fantasy:

"You could open a store here, selling you know what? Vacuum cleaners. Oh, you'd rake in the money."

"Ah, dearest one, here you could open a store selling air, water, words, sleep—here they need so little that if you could imagine a total absence of air, water, words, all the same you wouldn't rake it in. Dust is dust, plain and simple, everyone knows where it comes from, but no one grieves over it, usually they sweep it up, they put it out with the rubbish, but the fact that this is our pulverized skin and bones, who cares about that?"

Assistant Professor Mushinsky mocked that we were ashes and ashes we'd remain, he drank his coffee and left for Rostov. We felt sad, and not because we didn't think we were ashes, but simply because Assistant Professor Mushinsky had told us of the death of another former friend, that is to say he'd become irrevocably former. I suspected all my former friends of dying, who, presumably, had not thought to die nor thought of my death. We reflected on the death of Herodias's daughter:

Did Herodias's daughter have any sort of brain? Could you possibly dance like that if you had a brain?

We imagined the dance: undoubtedly heels falling heavily against the earth. Small dents left, by which it was possible to work out roughly the path of the feet.

But other than the feet there was nothing. Everything else was pushed away from the foot by free dizziness—indeed, each hollow, marrow-filled bone experienced dizziness, and we don't know, we can only guess that the muscles clenched and relaxed, slightly opening the folds of skin, indeed Herodias's daughter was entirely coated in tiny shells that breathed pure oxygen, such as is found in the air, and when a speck fell between the folds, a pearl grew on her forehead, was Herodias's daughter twelve years old?

She echoed the movements of the earth that struck into her foot, the movements of the air that struck into her eardrums, the movements of the voice that demanded to demand: Herodias's daughter, to be honest, was a complete fool. She echoed everything she was told. Sometimes they scolded her for this: *Don't repeat any old nastiness, you fool.*

Oh, Assistant Professor Mushinsky, an expert on the synoptic gospels, said on such cases that all this was merely plucked out of the air, you stare at the ceiling too much, go study something more concrete.

We sit and stare at the ceiling. We gaze as Herodias's daughter's dance blossoms on the ceiling in some mysterious choreograms. You speak:

"Every movement is performed by the entire body, Meyerhold says."

I speak:

"May the right hand not know what the left hand is doing."

You speak:

"Perhaps, if we were brainless. But we aren't brainless."

Or:

"Only in very special cases. Like the knee-jerk reflex, for example."

I watch and watch. If you watch long enough, then you'll start feeling your gaze on the other person.

I watch and watch, this is how I'll discover a wormhole in you and I'll start to crawl inside it with my vision, folding up, relaxing, folding up, relaxing, like a caterpillar, or rather like a second heart, which, without asking, pumps your blood out through invisible veins, a little heart that you won't notice until . . .

This is nonsense, but just as well it's my vision, and not that of a complete stranger, somewhere not in Australia but certainly on the other side of the lake.

Evelina Georgievna, come and visit to drink some screwdriver, otherwise repulsion will outweigh all other parts of the world. Come and visit, do visit, this house hasn't seen a human soul for a long time.

Otherwise repulsion will twist all other parts of the body, and someone will have to come and cut the knot with his piercing *dddring* on our doorbell. You approach the door, and beyond it—*dddring*, a shard, some fragile object shattered against too sharp a sound.

We were monsters. We went to the store could you give us some screwdriver please? In the entrance we brushed against the Chinese bell with the part of the soul towering above the cranium, or perhaps it was the wind. Come here, wind, make this happen. Objects collapse, fall out of hands, then fall out of sight, the roll of toilet paper unwound down the whole corridor into the kitchen and came to a standstill at the half-crossed threshold, we reflect: if you whop a head hard, then it will roll, yards and yards and yards will be left behind, and it will all be sheer hatred. We read aloud:

"Hatred is when you gaze without gazing your fill, you watch without watching your fill, you see without seeing your fill. You can gaze or watch something of your own free will, whereas you see only what you see, for instance, beyond the window I always see a sky of various sorts, and there's the same old thing: the stadium, the lake, the registry office, all upside down, and beneath them, again: the stadium, the lake, the registry office, like in a mirror, I watch and cannot watch my fill, because I am waiting for something to change in the view, like a gust of wind, but I see always the same old thing: the registry office, the lake, the stadium, I hate it. I feel like going out into the street and hurting this view with my body, but it's all liquid as milk, it drips down your skin and cannot be smashed, and your skin remains firm, did you know that from the milk's point of view, the glass is totally round, firm, and it is located in the very middle of the milk? 'What rubbish,' said Professor Mushinsky, who hadn't shifted his Gestalt for fifteen frigging years, 'milk cannot think, because it is in suspension, it contains no internal unity, better to say water.' But I say that is precisely the point—milk is in suspension, because water is an inorganic compound that couldn't give a fuck, whereas milk consists of suspended organic compounds that can already think, and they can curdle, they can expel from themselves all that is inorganic, that is to say, water, and rise to the surface as butter, or shit, which in my personal point of view is one and the same thing. 'You shouldn't say that,' said Professor Mushinsky fifteen frigging years later, 'butter is a nutritious and calorific product, if used intelligently and for its intended purpose.' Shit, I objected fifteen years later, can also be used intelligently. In some regions it is dried and used for fuel and building material."

Mmm yes, you said, *what you'll have in your head in fifteen years' time I'd be ashamed to say, ah, what a monster you are.* By the way, this is all wrong, because in fifteen years' time Assistant Professor Mushinsky will already be hopelessly dead six years. But this means merely that fifteen years later I too was dead and spoke to the professor in the language of those who were already dead. There's no doubt about it, the whole point was cholesterol, but even in fifteen years he'll refuse to admit that the point was cholesterol plaque. People who eat a lot of butter will eventually get cholesterol plaque, which impedes the normal flow of blood. Well, and if you eat no butter at all, then you get the opposite, cholesterol holes, that is to say ulcers, and they don't help the flow of blood either. In the kingdom of the dead, Professor Mushinsky and I will find each other through the principle of complementarity and we will be resurrected, the inner surfaces of our veins brushing against one another.

"Nonsense—is resurrection really governed by such imbecilic principles? I reckon I'll become part of a completely different person, no, not part of you, and not part of an assistant professor, in fact not part of anyone whom we know personally, I had quite different plans for the future . . ."

"You feel you are in mittens, but you know for sure that you want gloves. That's to say, back when you were little it seemed that it would not last forever, this stupid elastic across your back and inside your sleeves so you wouldn't lose your mittens, that later you'd grow up and when you were big, you'd wear gloves, you grew up, but your mittens remained, and you'd have shed them, but all around there's frost, such a frost that you only feel warm inside and you know that if you take the mittens off, you'll get frozen stiff and die. Mittens have their merits: your fingers are all together and they warm each other up, the very slenderest part of the human body, but in gloves you can wriggle your fingers about ever so quickly, and make various movements that you can't do in mittens, hold a cigarette, show passing people a victory sign, for a few seconds I allow these mittens to hang from their stupid elastic and I see my hands, they look almost blue despite the mittens, they'll wither if I look at them too long, I look at them briefly and put those damned mittens on again, is it always so cold here? 'Yes, here it's always this cold, perhaps, if the worst comes to the worst, you can lock yourself up in some warm place for a while and cut yourself some gloves from those mittens, it'll be hit or miss, well, they might not fit, no, right from the start the size was too small, if only they'd been two sizes bigger, then you could have cut something out, well, something at least, because here it's still terribly cold and so it will be to the end.'"

"Lord, who exists not, because you exist not, lord, take this away from me, lord, change my hands for some that are the same only in gloves, I have never felt so blooming lousy, lord, I have almost ceased to exist, that's why I can speak to you, who doesn't exist at all, take me and change me so that the emptiness where my heart should be could be fit for at least something, because it is crooked and snaking, other than shrews nothing feels at home in it, but I am frightened of shrews, lord who exists not, I feel I am your slave, with nowhere to go, because I am free, utterly free, to the extent that only a shrew would understand. I know that if I were someone imagined, for example, by the great Goethe, I would be imagined by him for one thing alone, to hang myself in the end, only I know that I wasn't imagined by the great Goethe, because, however great, all the same he died long ago, I wasn't imagined by anyone, lord, that's why my 'why' doesn't matter to me, my shrews, my death, what's happening to me now, my emptiness, what I get from you, I love you, my emptiness, because other than you I have nothing . . .'"

"You're talking drivel, utter drivel," you say.

"No, I'm not talking drivel, it's like in the riddle of Heraclitus, until you grasp it, you have it, when you grasp it, you don't, and this was very correctly remarked upon by I don't remember who—that I am a louse, only you can't catch me and squash me, I'm much faster than you and I can jump to seven times my height, whereas you can't even jump half your height again, and which of us is the lesser evil remains to be seen . . .'"

The irises by the store, flat, monotone, budding, sticking out of the flower bed in the rain for two days, filled up with water and attained the third dimension, until the heat evaporated this borrowed water out of them and made them flat again. There are these children's books with cardboard cities inside that pop up and tuck away, you just need to bend the folds. Lord, make the emptiness within me erect a city inside me, which the inhabitants will walk about, to and fro, with feet of fingers. It was just like that in our house: the whole winter long, and a significant part of the spring, it wasn't possible to walk in it, because the windows were locked and the air ran out, and we open the windows now, we wash the windows, there is wind in our heads, we can move and fall. Now I'll tell you a fairy tale about a man who fell out of love with god.

"Once there lived a man who was loved by god, and he succeeded in everything in this life, in seeing, and hearing, and being married to another person, to a woman, and they had, I don't remember exactly, twelve, I think, children, or was it nine, when you have so many you stop being able to tell them apart, but he could tell them apart, because he loved them, he knew them all by name, and then—no, here they didn't all go and drop dead, and his face didn't break out in leprosy, it's just god fell out of love with him and everything ended, ended, ended, the children grew up, the wife colored her hair with peroxide, they gained a couple of spare rooms in the house, but the man continued living with clear skin, only god no longer loved him and this was unbearable, the man turned to drink but the wife tried to stop him and the children shouted: 'Daddy, Daddy, let's go watch the hockey championship,' 'Look, I don't want to!' one terrible day Daddy exploded, 'I don't want to watch the hockey championship, because—how can I tell you this, my dear ones—because were I sober now, I would chop you all up with a fucking axe, but I am drunk and acknowledge people's right to life, labor, rest, private property, and I won't chop you up with an axe, I'll simply tell you something: god fell out of love with me and today I finally understood this, now let me die.'"

"Is it a Nietzschean fairy tale?" asks Evelina Georgievna, putting down her cup.

"No, Evelina Georgievna, it's not a Nietzschean fairy tale, look, if man got wind that god had died, then that would be a Nietzschean fairy tale, but god stayed the same as before in the fairy tale, only he no longer loved that man. God stopped existing for the man, started existing in his own right."

"Can god really change state, doesn't he exist as immutable good? Maybe it was the man who changed and stopped loving god?" asks Evelina Georgievna, putting down her cup.

"No, Evelina Georgievna, this man stayed the same as before, turned toward god, it's just, it's just—how can I say this to you—it's not easy to say, let's say it like this: movement caught in the motionless is beautiful. While the man was striving towards god, they were beautiful: god was motionless, and the man was in motion. When man saw god in himself, he froze, enthralled by him. But god loves the beautiful no less than man does, much more in fact. Therefore, from purely aesthetic considerations, he darted aside and disappeared from man's sight, leaving him in motionlessness to catch the trail of elusive good."

A sad story, however.

Evelina Georgievna put down her thrice emptied cup. All three of us, including Evelina Georgievna, were already so fucking fed up that we experienced a hotter desire to kiss Evelina Georgievna and to execute against her some kind of gentle violence, but in the depths of our souls we doubted that she would understand us. We put on a CD and began talking Evelina Georgievna into dancing something from her life for us.

"No, no, don't try to talk me into it, I never did have an ear for music or a good voice. Though I've heard that you can develop a voice even if you have absolutely none at all. You can develop it just like that, out of nothing. But did you ever read about Ellen Kelly…"

About Ellen Kelly:

Once upon a time there lived a girl called Ellen Kelly, and she had neither eyes, nor ears, nor tongue. Rather, she had all of these, but she could neither see, nor hear, nor speak, she could only moo revoltingly, so we could say that she had none of these. In the land where Ellen Kelly lived, people treated handicapped children with respect, so Ellen wanted for nothing, she was fed, washed, dressed, undressed, they didn't let her stumble against hard objects. Ellen Kelly was perfectly happy. Then suddenly one fine day she felt someone touch her hand. She thought that they wanted to feed her, and despite the fact that she did not feel like eating, she opened her mouth, but nothing came. That is to say they did not begin feeding her. Then her hand was touched a second time. If Ellen Kelly had known how to think in words, this is what she would have thought: *What the devil are you touching me for, if you're not going to feed me? Stop it at once!* However she knew no words, therefore she simply thought. But her hand was touched a third time. Ellen Kelly began to moo menacingly. Her hand was touched again. Ellen Kelly became hysterical, she began pounding with her fists against nearby hard objects, not-so-hard objects, and empty space in an effort to reach and destroy the source of irritation, but it eluded her. Once more her hand was touched. Finally Ellen had to accept this meaningless phenomenon, and later she even learnt to find in it a certain logic. Her initial loathing gave way to curiosity, then to interest. Ellen Kelly understood that things have names. In time she learned to pronounce these names and even to give names to things of her own accord. Then she died, of course.

But someone taps your cerebral cortex from the inside, and you don't see him, don't hear him, you don't know his name, at first you experience loathing, then you get used to it, then you become per-fectly happy and cannot live without this tapping. But then it stops, and you wait and wait, you start to get tired of waiting, but you carry on waiting all the same.

"But you promised, lightning of our lord, that you'd always be in my brain, so where are you, lightning of our lord, why do I feel like thinking about potato peelings and reading newspapers? Where are you, lightning of our lord, I don't want to live without you in my brain, I don't see the point in living without you in my brain."

"Go on living, slowly, with dignity, walk to work, buy cherries, they're in season now. Work, rest, live, leave people alone, and they will leave you alone, well you know that I exist, and I know that you exist," replies the lightning of our Lord before disappearing altogether.

We'll take a trip to Königsberg, we'll go for sure, let's go this autumn, we'll extract the stones from the cherries with our tongues and spit them out, we'll memorize words in German, French, and Greek, and when the summer ends, we'll go to Königsberg, we'll take a plane, because indeed the thing is—by land you need a visa, but in the sky no one will ask you for one. Ideally you need to break right out of orbit, wait till the earth has rotated the necessary number of degrees, and land boldly in any place you like, because beyond orbit certainly no one will ask you for a visa. You just freeze, freeze for a long, long moment, close your eyes, and when you open them—the lightning of our lord will return, because that's what always happens to those suffering from manic-depressive psychosis . . .

"Evelina Georgievna, do try and sing, you said yourself: 'You can develop a voice . . . '"

If Evelina Georgievna had known how to speak, that is, to speak her thoughts, then she would have said: "I don't want you, I don't want to sing to you, I don't want to tell you about my first love, nor my second, I don't want to drink screwdrivers with you, I don't want to do anything with you, I sit here with you only because I have nothing to do, but my thoughts are far away in Warsaw, at the entomologists' conference . . ."

Evelina Georgievna says: "Why don't you have any chairs in your house?"

I was sick of answering this question to the point that I felt like just buying some damned chairs so as to be left in peace. But you answer with a different explanation each time, because repeating the same old thing is tedious:

"Because sitting on chairs is bad for you, it spoils your posture, unless you hold your back straight the whole time, which is a pain";

"Because when I was little, a chair collapsed under me, and now I'm scared of chairs, I sit only on the floor or in armchairs";

"Because he was forever crudely amusing himself by pulling the chair from under me whenever I tried to sit down";

"Because sitting is a half measure, we should either lie down altogether or walk."

In the end I got fed up of hearing all these answers about chairs, and I felt like calling A., which I did, as soon as I'd taken Evelina Georgievna to the hairdresser's:

"Good evening, what on earth is happening in the world?"

And each time you start dreaming up some dignified solution to this unearthly bliss in the noncity, it turns out that it has already taken place in some New Wave film. For all that, each night with absurd regularity something scratches behind the fridge, you start dreaming up what it might be, the cleverest thing that springs to mind is a gremlin.

"Gremlins haven't existed since World War II. I know what it is. Our unborn daughter, that's what."

"Judging by the sounds, more likely our unbought dog."

I close my eyes and start thinking about A. It's quite simple: you can boldly think whatever you like, because from your conversation with A. you can never grasp what has happened to her, or you grasp that nothing happened. The only certain thing is the branch, buried in the arboretum almost a year ago now. There is no lightning of our lord, there is silence and the unbought dog scratching behind the fridge.

When I go to sleep, I dream of a city like this one: there too you walk down an entirely urban-style built-up street and suddenly, glancing into an archway, you discover that everything through this archway is different, only in our city this difference is always the same: a neglected yard, two people, perhaps more, perhaps no one, frozen in unpremeditated poses, and a cat washing its hind leg, while in the dream this arch has some familiar but very faraway object, for example, the sea, or a church erecting its tented roof higher than you can see from this miserable two-meter arch, which you left behind without the use of your feet, or the Nikitsky Botanical Gardens with some anonymous plant, its lilac innards turned inside out, or A. in that dress that she wore long ago in Sokolniki Park, with round buttons right up to the collarbone, in terribly soft, terribly fluid pools of light. Or I find myself in Königsberg, which I've never set eyes on except on the television. You and I walk by night down the same streets, it's a fact, but in the view through the archways we see completely different things. Sometimes we walk down this street together (Rostovskaya Street, it's also Moskovskaya Street, it's also the Moscow-Yaroslavl highway) and at some point we walk into the arch, but only I find myself inside, while you are whacked into your own dream, where in the pools of sunlight someone meets you, someone whom I've never seen and probably never will see, I desperately want to know how your dream continues, but the desire to see the continuation of my own always wins out.

You tell me the next morning some nonsense, you disappeared into the archway on Bolshaya Nikitskaya (*hmm*, I think) in the evening coming out of the Rakhmaninov Hall conservatory, you silently joined or you were silently joined by someone of the *keanureeves* genre, you walked through places that were indiscernible due to the unbelievably poor for Moscow but quite ordinary for our nonplace illumination and said nothing, because in dreams it's quite normal to say nothing and yet understand: *she (or he) was the one*, in reality, there is also, to the left, the outline of some Roman building (well, let's say), at the end of the dream he knifed you with your silent agreement (well, let's say). I do not tell you nonsense one degree more nonsensical and far less gripping: I dreamed of an enormous Newfoundland, whom a very distant relative sent me from Canada for riding on, you have to feed the Newfoundland on ten-kilogram bags of dog food twice a day, which I don't like at all, I want to get rid of this monster, but I can't climb off him, for I don't know how to stop him, and when I try to coax him he attempts to bite me. I do not tell you, but I sadly note to myself that the newly acquired country that I'd dreamed of seeing appeared in the dream not at all as it should have.

Then we split up in the same direction but different distances: you, to teach English at the children's home, I, to write fairy tales about analytic philosophy for postgraduates. I too am fed up of saying the same old thing for over three years, and as a result each time something makes me embellish with words of my own. Luckily the postgraduate exams are also my responsibility, so no one and nothing suffers from these extravagances, except my conscience, which cannot suffer, for it does not exist. But your experiments with the English language in around ten years will advance:

"When I first saw Larisa Dmitrievna, I immediately realized—she is something. She wasn't like the other children's home teachers, she had style. It sounds funny, but I realized this as soon as I looked at her feet: all the teachers that summer were walking about in such pointy sandals with spiky heels, while Larisa Dmitrievna was in square-toed thick platforms. In other respects Larisa Dmitrievna's clothing was quite the same as that which all the teachers wore that summer, but her hair, it was dyed a color not entirely respectable for our location.

That year we began to study English, we had no textbooks, so Larisa Dmitrievna had to bring printouts, she said that as far as she was concerned they were the best textbook for beginners. As soon as I heard Larisa Dmitrievna's pronunciation, I understood: she was a real specialist in her field. She spoke in just the same incomprehensible way as they did in the songs on the music channel that they let us watch on Sundays after our walk. For seven years Larisa Dmitrievna taught us, I was considered one of the best students, and not only in English. I was one of the few who, when I got a room after leaving the home, didn't find a job in my hometown, but decided to apply to study law at the capital's university. During the preparation for the entrance exams it transpired that Larisa Dmitrievna, through her levity of character and her innate perfectionism, had invented for the English language two extra past tenses, one future one, and a middle voice. After getting a C in my language tests and failing my entrance exams, for a while I tried to find Larisa Dmitrievna and maim her, but by then she'd already left the city."

You say: "That's not quite true, I do, of course, allow myself liberties, but certainly not to that extent. I'm sure that it really happened just the way your former pupil will tell me in ten years' time."

Professor Mushinsky on his way from Rostov to Moscow set me a riddle: A certain X, whose mother after the death of his father entered into an illegal marriage with his father's brother, arranges a terribly theatrical act in order to push the mother's spouse to a step that he does not wish to take. I said: "Hamlet," Professor Mushinsky said: "Herodias's daughter," he chuckled and left for Moscow. I thought: *You can doubt, you can dance, but not the two together.* I've always preferred doubting. And you dancing. But in any case it will all end badly. And if it were possible to unite these two actions—what would happen then, huh?

We read the future on the map of the region, this is not the very distant future, in order to read your entire life from beginning to end, you would require a map of the former Soviet Union, very large and detailed, it would be good to stick such a map on the ceiling (it'll take up the whole ceiling) and pelt it with blobs of plasticine like in school (and, I'm ashamed to say, at the institute too). It doesn't always work out, for instance:

MARIANNA GEIDE

Assistant Professor Mushinsky promised to take us to Rostov, and in a month's time the weather will be just the kind for the windshield to hold crooked droplets in two arches, for us to chase the smoke out through the narrow crack, though he didn't want us to, for us first to change our minds, then feel ashamed before the assistant professor and go all the same, for a rainbow to appear over Nero when we arrive, and a lopsided and no longer dangerous pillar of cloudburst to stand at the smidge of earth and sky, and we'll pass through the absent gates of the monastery and realize that here, despite the wandering rooster, the sheets that are soaked instead of drying, and the two old men of worldly appearance and gender, we are already in the grounds of the convent, and then, passing straight through, we won't notice that we can already smoke and laugh loudly, and to the homeless begging for "coins and crumbs" we will stay as silent as partisans . . .

"Though in reality everything will be quite the reverse, the weather when we depart will be gentle and sunny, only toward midday it will begin to grow dark, yes, that's right, dark, and when entering the city the weather will break into tears, only the faint hotel lights will crack unfunny jokes in our faces in order to cheer us up, while in the window there is only rain, road, rain, and the dregs of an electric bulb, and Assistant Professor Mushinsky will grow bored at the provincial conference and want to drain with us the fifty-gram instant-coffee jar with the old-as-the-bible cognac Former White Stork, true, we won't go with him, because that day we'll be too lazy to wake up."

We read the future on the map, which should have been thrown away as an element too disarming before the burden of the future. From this point our future is almost as visible as our past, it's important not to mix them up. I recall vividly our meeting with A. upon returning from Königsberg. It will be winter, that is to say not entirely winter, around November, let's say, but all the puddles will already be frozen over with cracks, all the indoor markets will be busy selling persimmons, also frozen over with cracks of unbearable tartness, but the open-air markets will temporarily disappear from the nature of things, we will, I know, drink beer right in front of the ugly WHEEL BALANCING sign and come out with everything we know and don't know about events that have happened to us, and

THE PLESHCHEYEV LAKE MONSTER

suddenly A. will say something completely unexpected, let's say—
that she's getting married, it won't be unpleasant to us, although it
won't be pleasant either, see, by this time we will be occupied with
something else entirely, but the fact that one and a half years ago
A. buried a nut branch in the pine needles, this, I expect, we won't
forget for a long time.

"My god, my god, brrr! How hopelessly close to us all of this is,
yes, how hopelessly far away everything distant is. We ply open the
pistachio shells, extract from them the pearl and firm mollusc at the
same time, the cases fall onto the saucer and rustle like seashells.
Here is one form of the distant, picked, packed, exported, sold from
afar for killing our spirit. They say: 'Die, fall asleep, calm down,' in a
subsiding and with a subsiding volume of voice, 'just calm down here
for good, because no matter where you go after, no matter where
you will be after, you'll attain your immortality here, without explanation, through your own desire, and toward the end of your life no
other desire will remain save the desire to come here.'"

I think about A., about our unborn daughter, thrown out through
the door down the steps into her, not our, present time, one hundred
twenty kilometers away, think about A., whom I remember as yet
another lost opportunity. Sometimes I want to write her a letter with
"Come straightaway," but I realize that the lightning of our lord who
exists not never strikes the same tree twice, and I am a tree, and my
timber innards are scorched, my branches open out above the rough
charcoal emptiness and also dare to turn green and break out in diseased growth, and nothing will ever visit for long the emptiness that
I love and sometimes hate to death. Because I love my emptiness,
and I hate my emptiness to death, and it will never yield its place to
anything else.

Monster, monster of Pleshcheyev Lake, one day you will lick
your cracked leg and stand at full height. We went to look at the
blue stone, it's not blue at all and, to tell the truth, not a stone, it
is approximately a meteorite. I wanted to be like them, like those
from whom the blue stone has not been removed, and it continues
to tease with its invisible and perhaps indeed blue underside. And to
tie a strip from my clothes to the scraggy twig protruding nearby. I
didn't do this. You said:

"'Blue' in those times signified 'sacred,' the color blue was the darkest color they could get."

If they were now to take it into their heads to pick the most vivid color, the stone would phosphoresce orange or loud-pink, but were they to ask me to choose the symbol of the divine, I would ponder briefly and select as god the father, the son, and the holy ghost the illuminated highway that moves forth, back, and nowhere, standing on the spot. From a distance it emits a divine *hum, hum*, without which I probably couldn't fall asleep, were I not accustomed, in five years of existence here, to imagine it before sleep in order to become oblivious of the day, a hum in complete harmony with the music of the spheres: I love this hum as much as I hated it many years ago, when I first entered the university hostel, like I hated the enormous window without blinds at a devilish height, on I know which story but I won't say, but then I got used to it.

I love this hum, as I love the white noise before the beginning of music, or the white noise of flour (it's always the same, no matter what follows), and lightning, whiter than which there is nothing, which never—or almost never—strikes twice, though everything is possible. I love you for the fact that sometimes you are far from me, very sometimes, but very far. In my dream, in my death, which—and this is easy to work out by the map—will come later. I love myself too—in my dreams and my death.

"Live, work, don't think about me," says the lightning of our lord.

"But I am destroyed, scorched, eviscerated by you, lightning of our lord, how can I carry on living?"

Evelina Georgievna comes, she doesn't look at us, she is sad. Evelina Georgievna, I know, feels profound sympathy for you and she wants to talk with you in her language, in a language unknown to me, but also unknown to you, because only five people on earth know it, and, as I found out by chance, Evelina Georgievna is one of them. I don't need to be present, and I leave for the post office, because, as has been noted, here you can only call people from the post office.

I walk out and think about what I will say to A. I'm in the most pathetic mood ever:

"A., please do pay us a visit, oh this politeness between us is ridiculous, look come right away, to 20–22, it's a number that's sure to bring you luck, come, because I've dreamed of you already for the third week in a row and it's always in the same context, which is already something, because you—yes, yes—you've dreamed of me for the third week too, yes simply because I don't know who to give all this to other than you, but the cherry tree isn't in blossom anymore, though the yellow irises, dark yellow irises are blooming, come and look at them, like they come to look at an exhibition of one (or two) pictures, at the crumpled petals of the full-blown roses, at the tight lips of the unblown rosehips, at me, for goodness sake, at you, for goodness sake, I haven't looked at you in ages, haven't seen you silent, speaking, walking, shrinking from the cold, I haven't . . ."

Of course I have only to reach the post office, pay for a booth, wait for it to become free, dial the number, wait for A. to answer, everything immediately stops, and we are as courteous as before, aided by dementedly polite phrases, I reckon this is normal. I buy a bottle of beer, I mean two, and continue:

Let's talk rather about Minou Drouet, a character no less and no more remarkable than Ellen Kelly. When I get home I'll tell Evelina Georgievna this, of course, if she would like me to:

"Once upon a time there was a girl called Minou Drouet. And one day she was struck by the lightning of our lord. That is to say Minou Drouet simply walked down the street suspecting nothing other than some grit in her shoe and she was suddenly struck by the lightning of our lord. It would be wrong to think that the lightning of our lord suddenly whacked her and her soul was carried to heaven, only those who have never been whacked by the lightning of our lord think so, but it was nothing fucking like that, Minou Drouet simply walked and walked, and suddenly she felt someone tapping her head with a finger: one—one-one—one, well, it taps and taps regardless, Minou Drouet wasn't just walking along for the sake of it, she was going to some *l'école* where she had three lessons of *lettres* a week, in which they were learning about M. Corneille, M. Racine, M. Voltaire, or something of the kind. She walked and walked, and in her head there was a tapping: one—one-one—one, well it tapped and tapped, and in the lesson she suddenly

SPIT

KIRILL RYABOV
Translated by Victoria Mesopir

HIS NAME WAS Vitya Abrosimov, but everyone, even the doctors and nurses, not to mention his fellow patients, called him Spit. This sorry sobriquet was due to one, not exactly pleasant, particularity. At moments of extreme mental agitation, Vitya would start screaming hysterically, rip at the collar of his shirt, and contort his face wildly. Something happened to his articulation, his speech became incoherent, and out of his lips, twisted in frenzied spasms, flew copious amounts of saliva. The people around him would recoil in disgust, wiping their spattered faces.

However, after seven years in the hospital, his illness had been contained, his condition stabilized. Vitya no longer posed any threat to those around him, and he was transferred from the violent section to a normal ward. He had long stopped yelling in a deranged voice at the top of his lungs, but the sobriquet had stuck for life. Few among his comrades-in-misfortune remembered his real name.

That morning Vitya Abrosimov was brought to the head of the clinic to be released. The doctor was a young, affable man with the beautiful given name Ernest and the none-too-lovely patronymic Adolfovich. He had only worked at the hospital for a few months, hadn't yet had time to pick up any crazy shit from his charges, and did not in the least fit in with the routinely banal image of a half-mad sadist-psychiatrist. His good nature relaxed the patients, to an extent, but also caused an unpleasant disquiet. His friendliness appeared to be a mask concealing something truly frightening.

When Vitya walked into his office, Ernest Adolfovich was standing by a window lit up by spring sunlight and was letting clouds of cigarette smoke out through the ventilation transom. Vitya kept waiting for Ernest all of a sudden to scream, grab the ashtray off the table, and fling it into his face. This, of course, didn't happen, but Vitya was still on edge. He started to suspect the doctor was a homo. There was no basis whatsoever for this suspicion, but it was just as improbable that absolutely nothing was wrong with him . . . For some reason, the thought of some abnormality lurking below the surface of the doctor's calmness and affability pleased Vitya.

—Well, what say, Victor, shall we say farewell? Ernest said, turning around.

—I guess so, replied Vitya, sitting down at the table.

—Seven years—it's a long time, pronounced Ernest after he paused to stub out his smoke, close the transom, and sit down opposite Vitya. —It's not so easy to return to normal life. But what's one to do? One has to try. You are now well, you're a rightful member of society. There's nothing left for you to do here.

Vitya was silent.

—But it's also not so difficult. You still have your room in the communal apartment. You'll receive a disability pension. Maybe a bit of work will come along, what have you. You're still a pretty young fellow . . .

—Uh-huh, said Vitya indifferently.

—You still writing poems?

—Quit long time ago.

—Why?

—It's all rubbish . . .

—Why rubbish? They even published you in *The Neva* . . .

—Rubbish, repeated Vitya.

Ernest was silent for a while, gazing out the window.

—You should reestablish contact with your relatives, that's what. No matter how you slice it, it'll be difficult for you on your own, at first.

—Mother died, Vitya said in a deadpan voice.

—Try to sort things out with your brother, Ernest said.

—That probably won't work, Vitya replied quietly.

—Time passes. Who knows?

—He never even visited once, said Vitya.

—You should try to understand him. What's going on in his soul, only God knows that. You should try . . .

—I'll try.

Vitya walked through the hospital yard to the gates. An old bag hung from his shoulder. In the pockets of his jacket were the communal apartment keys, a packet of cigarettes, and a medical certificate.

Suddenly someone called out of a window on the top floor:

—Hey, Spit, where're you going?

Vitya didn't look back.

— — —

The old cavernous courtyard hadn't changed at all over the years, just like it hadn't changed at all in the past half century. The same flock of pigeons by the garbage dumpsters under the dark gateway, the same murky windows and old entrance doors. Even the rusty hull of the hunchbacked Zaporozhetz, which hadn't been driven for a good quarter of a century, hadn't gone anywhere.

Vitya sat down on a bench in the children's playground and lit up a cigarette. Inhaling the pungent smoke of the cheap Nord-Star, he noticed that his hands were shaking. When he'd passed through the hospital gates, he'd felt nothing but his usual drowsiness. If Ernest had suddenly come running out after him, shouting: —Wait, Abrosimov, stop, don't move, I signed you out by mistake, you still have another five years here, Vitya would have turned around and gone back to his ward without a word of argument. But then he'd felt anxious while ascending the metro escalator. And when he'd seen his old building, with its dilapidated façade, worn out by more than a century of life, he experienced the acute sensation of having swallowed a giant chunk of ice. Everything started to feel like a dream, and he became afraid he might wake up to find himself tied to his iron cot with towels.

Vitya finished his cigarette in four powerful drags, got up, and walked through the front door. The same semidarkness, replete with the smell of fried potatoes and dampness from the basement enveloped him. The same busted-up mailboxes. The same out-of-order elevator with the same warning sign that had hung there for years.

Unhurriedly, Vitya climbed the staircase to the third floor, saw his door, still with the same, time-faded leatherette padding on it, and pulled the keys out from his pocket. Two keys hung on the metallic ring—one for the communal-apartment door, tone for his room. But Vitya, with an unpleasant feeling, suddenly realized that the key to the apartment would be of no use to him now: a new, shiny lock had been cut into the door, and the old key didn't fit in the grooves. It was, he thought, as though someone had found out beforehand about his release and rushed to put in an obstacle.

Vitya put the keys back in his pocket and looked at the row of buzzers with tenants' names written next to them. The neighbors were still the same, only the surname Abrasimovs had been carelessly smeared over with green paint. Of course, his brother had moved in with his wife some eleven years ago, and Mother . . . and Vitya himself was no more, either. His brother had probably figured he wasn't coming back and, so as not to upset visitors, had wiped off the surname. It was to be expected, although this singular differentiation against the backdrop of everything else, frozen solid in time, was indeed unpleasant.

Vitya stopped on the name Yashchenko and pressed three short rings in a quick succession. The door opened surprisingly fast. On the threshold stood a short, elderly woman in an old terry-cloth bathrobe and funny glasses straight from the early sixties. In old Soviet movies school directors and research physicists wore glasses like that.

The woman looked quizzically at Vitya and said nothing.

—Zoya Ivanovna, said Vitya. —So much time has passed, and you still open the door, without asking "Who is it?"

—I . . . she said. —You . . . My God!

—Vitya Abrosimov, he said. —Have I changed much?

—Goodness, goodness, Victor . . . I thought you'd died . . .

—You weren't all that mistaken, said Vitya.

—Can I smoke? asked Vitya, walking into the kitchen.

—Of course, replied Zoya Ivanovna. —I'm home alone . . . Everyone's at work . . . And my Ivan Sergeyevich has gone to walk Glashka.

—Who's Glashka? asked Vitya, then remembered the gray, fat pug.

—Oh Vitya, I don't even know . . . This, I wasn't expecting. You just fell out of the blue.

—Don't worry, I'm not violent . . .

—What're you talking about, it's not about that. You maybe want to eat something? They probably didn't feed you well there?

Vitya shrugged his shoulders and remembered that he wanted to smoke.

—I don't know, whatever . . . Soup, from seven . . . ummm . . . grains . . . Something else . . . I could have some tea.

She lit the gas burner on the stove and put the kettle on. Vitya noticed how tense her back was, as if she expected to be stabbed.

—How's it been here anyway? he asked, so as not to be silent.

—Well, how . . . You know. Everything the same . . . replied Zoya Ivanovna uncertainly. —Everyone's alive, it seems . . .

—You seen Lyosha? asked Vitya.

—Lyosha? She turned, and her voice sounded terribly, disgustingly fake, like a drunk person's trying to pass for a sober one. —He stopped by . . . ummm . . . at the beginning of the month . . .

Vitya stayed silent for a while, then shoved his still-unlit cigarette into a crumpled packet, and got up.

—Alright, I'll go to my room . . .

The neighbor blinked fearfully.

—Don't be afraid, Zoya Ivanovna, I didn't run away. I was released this morning. If you want, I can show you the certificate . . .

He reached into his pocket, but the woman hastily took him by the hand.

—Hold on, Vitya . . . I'm not about that . . . There's something else here, understand?

—What?

The kettle let out a muffled whistle.

—Hold on . . .

She removed the kettle.

—Let me pour you some. Do you want a cookie? Or jam? I rolled the jam into jars this fall.

And again her voice sounded false, while she herself, her whole body tensed up.

—What happened? said Vitya tiredly.

—Lyosha, you see, Lyosha . . .

—What, Lyosha?

—He rented your room out to Azerbaijanis. They've lived there half a year already. He came recently and took another half year in advance from them. They even changed the locks.

Vitya was silent, slightly concussed by what he'd heard.

—I don't know what to do, Vitya. Lyosha threw out all your things a long time ago, and these Azerbaijanis put in a new door to the room. You can't get in there.

—But aren't I registered there? said Vitya uncertainly.

—Lyosha was planning to take your name off a long time ago . . . I don't know if he did, after all, or not . . .

Vitya pulled out a cigarette, lit it, and started puffing, focusing only on smoking.

—And these, where are they? he asked.

—Who?

—Azerbaijanis.

—They're at the market. They go to trade every day. But it's unlikely you'll come to terms with them. They've already paid for the room, so they won't even let you on the threshold. Impudent bastards. They told me: "We'll make shish kebab out of your cur." You better not tangle with them.

—So what do I do now, live at the train station? asked Vitya.

—Oy, Vitya . . . Wait, maybe, you'll drink some tea?

He didn't reply.

—You need to meet with Lyosha.

—I can't, replied Vitya.

— There's no other way. He's your brother after all.

—He won't even let me near him. You know that.

—Who knows?! So much time has passed.

Vitya suddenly realized that the neighbor was talking to him exactly like Ernest Adolfovich had, and he smiled stupidly.

—No other way out, you understand? Surely you can't go to the train station . . . or return to the hospital?

Vitya opened the ventilation transom and threw out his cigarette.

—He still lives in the same place?

—I don't know, replied Zoya Ivanovna. —But, probably, he's still there . . . Wait, he left me a number, didn't he, asked me to call him, if those Azers started doing something sketchy . . . Hold on there . . .

She went to her room and returned with a small sheet, torn out of a notebook. Vitya looked for a long time at the unusual number, which resembled a bank safe code.

—What's this? I don't understand...

—That's his cell phone, replied Zoya Ivanovna.

—What?

—Cell phone, she repeated quietly. —Vitya, don't you know what a cell phone is?

He returned the sheet to her.

—I'll go to him myself. That'll be better. Probably. I don't know. I don't know anything.

—Go meet with him, of course, it's better than by phone . . .

Vitya took his bag.

—I'll go . . . May I, though . . . May I have some tea?

— — —

He left the building, which had suddenly, in an instant, become a stranger to him, and lit up a cigarette. His smokes were running out. His money was running out. The same could be said about his life. True, though, he had felt exactly the same way seven years ago, when two big guys in uniform were twisting his hands behind his back to snap on the handcuffs.

Near the front door he crossed paths with Ivan Sergeyevich. The man was leading a fat pug on a leash. The animal moved its short crooked legs with difficulty, wheezing spasmodically.

—Need to lose weight, that's what, the neighbor was admonishing it. —Soon you won't even be able to walk . . . Go on a diet, you know? And you'll shit less, too . . .

The neighbor walked by, not recognizing Vitya. Vitya thought, *Now he will go home and his wife will tell him everything right there, in the doorway. He'll likely even run to the window at once, without so much as removing his shoes.*

Vitya hastily left the yard and walked in the direction of the metro.

— — —

There was a steel door and an intercom. Vitya stood for some time, waiting for someone to come out so that he could go in. He did not want to start a conversation with his brother over the intercom. What do you say? *Hi, Lyosha, it's me, your brother Victor. I got released today. Open the door, please.* And in reply—what? *Victor? Get the fuck out of here, Victor!*

He wanted to meet face to face. Although, truth be told, he really didn't want to meet with his brother at all. But since there was no other choice, then better do it face to face.

However, nobody was coming out the front door. Nobody was going in, either.

Vitya pressed the intercom button. He heard the call buzzing. A woman's voice answered.

—Is Alexei home? asked Vitya, feeling a cold rivulet of sweat run between his shoulder blades.

—He went out, the woman answered curtly.

—To work? asked Vitya.

—Just out. Come back later.

—Are you his wife?

She didn't reply.

Vitya walked across the courtyard and sat down on a bench. There was no one in sight. Sleeping neighborhoods always looked like this, as if a plague had rolled through them. Especially in the courtyards. Rarely, a person would emerge, flash by like a shadow, and disappear as if he never was. Vitya lit up his last cigarette, let out a cloud of

smoke into the clear sky, and saw a person coming out the front door.
Vitya bolted up, then immediately sat down. It would be stupid to
run. The door had already slammed shut. And the man, most likely,
had no connection to his brother.

The cigarette smoldered away quickly, but the time stretched like
a piece of toffee.

An hour passed. The sun had shifted in the sky inconspicuously,
and now it shone in Vitya's face. He got up and walked to the front
door. An old woman with a poodle came out, but Vitya did not
go in.

Then Lyosha appeared. He came out from behind the chestnut
bushes with two heavy shopping bags in his hands. He had barely
changed in seven years. Gained a little weight, cut his hair short. But
in every other regard, he was the same.

He walked to the door, set the bags down, and reached into his
pocket for the keys.

—Lyosha, Vitya called quietly.

His brother turned quickly, looked in all directions, then stopped
his glance on Vitya.

—You're back?

—I was released this morning, replied Vitya. —I didn't want to
come to you . . .

—Who released you? Lyosha interrupted.

—Well, the doctor . . . replied Vitya, puzzled.

—The doctor? repeated Lyosha, taking a step.

—The doctor.

—And is the doctor as fucked up as you are? Or they're all like
that there? Who could have let you out? You were supposed to kick
off there. You've no business being around people! yelled Lyosha.
—Scum! You're a fucking psychopath! You've no business around
people! You were supposed to die in your nuthouse! What are you
doing here? Bitch! Who released you? Who? You've got nothing
here!

—I am well, replied Vitya loudly.

—You, bitch, are sick through your whole skull! You're not
allowed to be released . . .

—I'm well.

—. . . among normal people. You're supposed to sit behind bars! Bitch! Filthy swine!

—I am better now, replied Vitya in a shaky voice. —I am better now, you hear?

—Beast! Lyosha shouted. —Why did you come here? Who invited you?

He suddenly bent down, quickly pulled something out of a bag, and flung it at Vitya. A glass beer bottle whizzed by, centimeters away from his left temple, and smashed loudly behind his back, fizzing.

—I am better now! Vitya cried out in a constricted voice.

A packet of dumplings hit him painlessly in the chest and thumped to the ground.

—I'm well!

—Die, louse!

A tin of canned food hit Vitya in the teeth. A sharp pain shot through his head. His mouth immediately filled with thick, salty blood.

—I'm well! gurgled Vitya.

—You must die!

Vitya slowly retreated under the bombardment of processed foods flying through the air with machine-gun-like frequency.

—I'm better now. I'm better now. Better now. he repeated in a whisper. —I'm well. I'm well. I was released! I'm well.

—Scum! Lyosha howled in a deranged voice. —You killed her! Filth! Filth! You were supposed to die.

He wailed, grabbed his head, and fell to the ground.

A light breeze rustled the empty bags.

—I'm well. Well. Vitya repeated.

Blood trickled down his chin. His face contorted and his speech suddenly became incoherent.

—I'm 'ell . . . im 'ell . . . im 'ell . . . Vitya shouted, pulling his shirt collar away from his neck as if it were choking him.

And out of his mouth sprays of saliva mixed with blood.

THE UNBELIEVABLE AND TRAGIC HISTORY OF MISHA SHTRIKOV AND HIS CRUEL WIFE

VADIM KALININ
Translated by Mariya Gusev

PLEASE LET'S DO THIS without too much cynicism! Back in the snot-nosed days of youth I, same as everyone, was also selling pocket aircraft bombs and mustard gas, but then I heard the song about a thousand paper cranes, and ever since that time I stick exclusively to children's toy design.

Misha Shtrikov was making love with his one and only boyfriend when his wife came home directly from the podium, flooding the room with the scent of perfume and women's stockings. She squealed loudly at the sight of unscrubbed frying pans, dirty laundry, and her copulating spouse, and upon hearing this sound Misha's boyfriend, a person with an exquisitely delicate nervous system, immediately jumped out the window, breaking the glass and two of his own ribs, landing directly onto the prized bushes of nightmarish roses, purple with tan polka dots, which grew underneath. Misha, stunned by this sudden stage change, committed the unforgivable: he turned around and, using his whole body, as he was taught as a youth in kickboxing school, drove his fist into his wife's right eye socket. Twelve seconds later he repented, but it was already too late.

Masha Shtrikov's job as a motivational speaker was to demonstrate her woman's dignity on the podium, and it was precisely this dignity that had now sustained damage. This dignified woman made 4,200 conventional monetary units a day (in the future—CMU), 4,000 of which went toward maintenance of her appearance at the appropriate level, and two hundred toward supporting her husband. In this way it follows that a podium devoid of her presence the next day would result in the further deterioration of her appearance level the day after that. However, Masha was a woman who was not used to losing her position, and so it took her less than a second to think through the next move:

—My husband, starting tomorrow you'll be the one feeding this family!

—And how is that? Misha's surprise was sincere.

—With your *ass*! Once uttered, this word fell directly through the earth's crust, through its mantle, through the entire geological mess into the center of the planet—it carried that much weight.

Masha grabbed two phones and, pressing both receivers with her shoulders to her porcelain-pale aural cavities, dialed two numbers at the same time with both her hands. Having received a response from each recipient, she articulated some text with an even, calm voice, then hung up the phones.

Misha, red as a lobster, was sitting on one corner of the couch, immense as the Ukranian steppe, wrapping himself in a sorry little robe with a design depicting two copulating swans when the room was invaded by two calm and businesslike men. One of them was wearing a white robe, the other a blue bulletproof vest. The men undressed and immediately, without any extra words, established an intimate relationship with Misha, first together, then one at a time. Then they re-dressed, carefully and with dignity, paid the bill, and left.

Three weeks have passed, and now we see Misha Shtrikov in a completely different position. We see an expensive suite of some hotel, where this young man is lying prostrate on a sheet, wet from love sweat; there are posters on the walls depicting his buttocks, and also the buttocks of other handsome young men. From the corner of our right eye we notice a man getting dressed behind a screen.

And now this man walks out from behind the screen, passes through the room right in front of us, and departs through the open door, through which we can hear the approaching tapping of high heels and the velvet little voice of Masha Shtrikov: "Break! Break!" she announces. On the bed Misha sighs with relief and turns over onto his back. Masha bursts into the room, glowing and sweet, dropping mysterious bundles onto the floor. Immediately following her is an elderly woman with a silver cross in her wrinkled décolleté and a tray of tasty and aromatic food.

—I'm not going to eat, says Misha.

—Why, my love? There is confusion on Masha's face, sincere as one's very first disappointment.

—If I eat, then later I'll have to shit, and I can't, my behind hurts.

—Look what I bought for you. Masha opens the bundles and finds, finally, a tiny vial with the Statue of Liberty on the label. —This is a miracle salve from Hollywood, bring your little bum here. Masha rubs the salve into Misha's anus. —Well, does it hurt a little less, I can see, it doesn't hurt at all, very soon your bum will become strong as steel, and delicate as down. Be patient, my dear, just six more officers of the queen's fleet and eight young movie producers from the Emirates left . . .

— — —

Masha throws the sheet she pulls out from under Misha into the wastebasket and lays down a new one, saying:

—"Antincontinence," amazing sheets—diapers—that absorb any excretion of the human body without losing their dryness and freshness for decades. I'm writing down another 1,000 CMU. Into your account, my dear.

Misha is crying small dumb tears, while Masha feeds him black caviar with a spoon and pets his curly, blue-black hair with her narrow white palm.

How much time has passed since—Misha has no idea. Everything has been swallowed, ground into a fine mud by the whirlpool of male bodies, tan and white, tight and flabby, with rippled, hanging guts; a

whirlpool of curly, shaved, tattooed crotches, crowned with members
of all colors, shapes, and sizes. Misha is sitting, dressed in a mesh tennis
top and poplin jeans, in the backseat of a semi-empty Ikarus, which
is flying through the red Van Gogh's steppe directly toward the post-
Aksenov island of Crimea. He's on a tour. His very first.

The bus stops near a well. The troupe makes a bonfire, wine and
baskets of snacks appear. The party lasts until 2:00 AM. The bus driver,
a clean-cut blond with coarse fingers wearing mirrored glasses, is
whispering about something with Masha.

—I've saved money for a long time. I trained for two months,
to pass the contest to become the driver for your troupe. And now
that we've had a bit to drink, I can speak about my thirst without
reservation . . .

—I can't say no to a beauty like yourself, replies Masha and snaps
her fingers.

Misha gets up from his seat, and he and the driver, their arms
around each other and him holding a bottle of red wine between his
fingers, depart into the fields, toward a huge collective farm haystack,
shrouded in lemon fog. Directly into the sunset.

Misha gifted the driver with an unbelievable night, and now a
moist, trembling morning has arrived. The driver kisses into the
bloody rivulet on Misha's cracked lip and very quietly whispers into
his right ear:

—I will make some money and will buy you out, so I can set you
free. I will give this monster as much money as she wants, and you'll
be able to buy yourself a little house in the countryside, get yourself
a kind little wife and five or six kids, and I will spend the night with
you once a week, on my way from Kharkov to Simferopol.

Misha's silence is complex and piercingly sad, and in his eyes
shines the irreproducible morning humidity of the steppe.

The troupe disembarks in Yalta. The bus turns, like a steamboat,
and dissolves into the melting smog. Misha sees, in its rear window,
a huge poster of low print quality. *I will return for you, Shtrikov!* the
poster says. Misha looks around, perplexed.

This scene is observed by Yura Cherniy, through the window of
his villa. His parents have a summer home on Foros, and on their land
is located a unique well. If you throw a stone into this well, it will

reach the surface of the water only after four hours. At the bottom
of this well live tiny glowing crabs. If you place a crab like this under
the microscope, you will see that it has a human face and, additionally, an amazingly beautiful one. All the hot people of this world can
be divided into two groups: hot people with a crab, and hot people
without one. The first group includes the real hot items, and the
second—you can figure it out for yourself. Yura walks through the
heated yard toward a bunker made of blindingly white steel, dials a
code consisting of eight hundred numbers on the concrete door, and
it slides away to the left. When Yura climbs back out of the bunker,
he is holding, in his right hand, a vial made from rock crystal, with a
permanently fused stopper. At the bottom of the vial glows a magical greenish eight-legged speck of grain. *I will return for you, Shtrikov!*
hisses Yura through his teeth. Then he goes upstairs into the memorial room and takes a revolver off the wall, which was given to his
heroic grandfather by the famed Soviet general Budenny.

Masha Shtrikov's room. She comes home with Yura, holding
hands with him. He stays at the door, she sits down on a very wide
bed with a canopy. Yura, standing at the door, pulls out the revolver
and shoots her in the chest.

—This is Budenny's revolver! he announces into the rumbling
of the shot.

—This is the bulletproof vest of Marilyn Monroe! Masha unbut-
tons her blouse and displays bulletproof transparent lacy lingerie.
Then she gets up, approaches the boy, takes away the revolver and
the vial, and passionately kisses him on the lips.

An early Saturday morning. In the window frame there is a matte
green sea, worthy of glassblowers and steel smiths. Misha is lying on
his stomach, Masha, wearing glasses, is entering the last four hundred orders into the database, Yura, with a short automatic under his
jacket, is studying a diaper ad in *Without Words* magazine. A wind
enters the room, saturated with the aroma of the morning dew, red
wine, and grape-wood logs, and following it is a huge young man
with a red face, wearing Bermuda shorts.

—The Union of Society for Preservation of the Sexual Majority, he utters in singsong, —demands the immediate and permanent
liberation of Mikhail Shtrikov.

Yura pulls out the automatic; the young man pulls out a document signed by the mayor of the city, president of the motherland, and various other worthy individuals.

—The house is surrounded, states Masha. —Let them all go fuck themselves.

A crowd of busty chicks and young men with shaved heads bursts into the rooms. They pick Misha up and carry him out into God's light, his face registering surprise and a funny twilight happiness. Misha is carried down the streets, as his liberators chant and dance, directly into the restaurant Yesterday's Argonaut. The crowd disappears into the building, and a poster is hung on its door on the exterior side: "Reserved for an indefinite period of time."

From this second on, it seems that Misha's life is changed forever. At six in the morning, he must wake up and clean the restaurant, liberating it from the consequences of the previous day's drinking bash, then follows a cold shower, a change of clothes, and a reception of delegations and private individuals, up to eight banquets in a row on average, where each toast Misha misses is perceived by anyone present as evidence of his unhappiness with his liberation. Which is why, each time, Misha drinks two portions instead of one, so he can demonstrate to everybody how happy he is with his freedom. After this, Misha goes fishing with his newly acquired friends, then to a wushu class, to soccer, to the tennis court, to skydive, and to rock climb. In the evening, a modest supper in the company of three hundred of his closest friends and four hundred and fifty tender girlfriends with wine and dancing. By three in the morning, it's time to get into a little healthy sex, since each of his half-a-thousand brand-new girlfriends desires to make sure with her own eyes that Misha indeed is a fully fledged representative of the sexual majority and that five or six ladies a night is not a burden for him. This is not easy for Misha, but he does not grumble or complain, anything to never return to the hell that his marriage bed had become for him.

This whole time, meaning the last sixteen full days and nights, Masha sits across from the restaurant on a wooden bench, and, notwithstanding the terrible heat, has not a moist drop on her well-shaped, pale face. She, without a second's interruption, is talking on her cell phone, only pausing to apply more lipstick or to light a new cigarette. At the conclusion of the sixteen days and nights, a Bacchus-rosy, tan, and muscularly toned Misha emerges on the restaurant steps, in the company of the formerly mentioned modest young man.

—Forgive me, friend! says the young man to Misha. —The parliament has signed a decree about your return to your family. Since the time when Shtrikov Company paused its operations, the influx of foreign tourists to Yalta has dropped by fourteen percent, and this is equivalent to economic death for the entire district.

By this time, Misha's eyes have gathered so much surprise, that even I, observing this scene from aboard the *Guernica* cruise ship, have lost my cool and dialed the number of Shtrikov Company, to place an order on mutually beneficial conditions.

Masha and Misha, looking at each other with surprise and fear, like Shakespeare's lovers after their very first tryst, are entering the bedroom. Masha puts on Misha's neck a nonrestraining collar with a digital lock, and ties a leash made from the fibers of hibiscus to the metal ring she's thoughtfully built into the wall. Misha sits on his haunches and begins to sing the old student song about Natashka. Masha falls asleep to the sounds of this uncomplicated melody and sleeps for two weeks, during which I am able to enjoy Misha's company for free, so that by the time of Masha's awakening I can prepare a series of posters that, without any open propaganda of gay prostitution, must convey, with high print quality, the unique qualities of Misha's ass.

September. Simferopol. The velvet season. Shtrikov Company is closed down for nonpayment of taxes. Misha, Yura, and myself are sitting in a cozy bar on the first floor of the summer office of Shtrikov Company. From here, a wonderful view unfolds, onto the tent settlement that has grown right on the beach. Several tan youths are pitching a ball over a net. The ball distorts into an oval because of the smog and dry wine. On the roof of one of the tents is written, in black marker, *The Presence of Women Is Undesirable.* I am well informed that each youth living in tent town has a number tattooed on his inner thigh, which signifies his place in line, and I am also aware of the sad fact that during this season Shtrikov Company will only be able to satisfy the first sixteen thousand, and from those only the ones who hold the diploma of "Official Friend of the Shtrikovs." The rest will have to wait, no matter how hard they jump all over this beach in hopes of catching Misha's attention.

—Tell him . . . whispers Yura to Misha.

—You tell him . . . replies Misha, in a whisper.

—All right, I'll tell him, but for that you will dedicate your next day off to me.

—For Misha's next day off, I retort, —we are going to the aquarium to swim with the crocodiles. So what were you trying to tell me, young man?

—I'm sorry, Vadim, whispers Yura slowly. —I know that you don't want to pick up the old trade, but we can no longer wait.

—So you're bending your line again, I answer. —I've already told you that I can't stand nonverbal extremism. You know that everything in this life begins as a healthy pastime and ends with the latrine hole. Why do you need to upset a person? If each steamboat eventually will fall apart and sink all by itself . . .

—In that case, remarks Misha, —on my next day off, Yura and I will go to the Museum of the Execution of the Twenty-six Kommunars of Baku. It will be sensitive and educational at the same time.

I sigh with resignation and open my leather bag. I reach into the bag and pull out a ladies' diamond pin.

—No! Yura, with the movement of a professional fighter, moves my hand aside. —It needs to be foolproof. Not anything less than ten kilograms of crystalline TNT equivalent.

Such charming people . . . — my surprise is genuine—*and they're talking about some sort of kilograms of TNT equivalent . . .* and again, to my great shame, I dive into the bag and give something to Yura— something I've been saving for myself—a garnet medallion, executed in the shape of an aircraft bomb with President Kennedy's portrait on it, remotely controlled by a snap of your fingers from a distance of up to four hundred kilometers.

Yura hides what he just received in his pocket when he hears Masha's gentle voice announcing through the speakers: "Let's get to work, boys!" And Misha returns to bed, Yura returns to the monitors of the coast patrol, and I to the goddamned Mac, throwing together the next prospect, advertising the magic salve from Hollywood and bedsheets "Antincontinence," by the official distributor in Russia, Shtrikov Company.

On the evening of the next day, the four of us, meaning Misha, Masha, Yura, and I are resting at a remote beach, where even the most enraptured fans of Misha's talent are not able to find us. Masha insisted that we spend this next Misha's day off all together. Masha, on whose neck the medallion is already shining, enters the warm multilayered water and quickly, skillfully swims toward the very real horizon. As soon as her head is no longer visible even through a pair of binoculars, Yura snaps his fingers, and the breeze carries to us a light scent of smoke and the rumbling of a distant explosion. —The echo of the great war! whispers Misha through his teeth. —Yes, probably it was one of the fascist's mines, I agree. We gather the remains of our supper into the baskets and ride home. There are tears in our eyes.

In place of our dear office we find a crater twenty meters deep, a triple convoy, and criminology experts.

—What does this mean? Misha asks the logical question.

—Oh, I reply. —I forgot to tell you, this morning I gave Masha a replica of the medallion with glass pieces instead of garnets, as she shouldn't be wearing such expensive jewelry to the beach.

—How dare you! Misha's face registers genuine jealousy.

From the smoke, chaos, and flames emerges Masha, to the right of her is a man in uniform, to the left—also a man, and also in uniform, but of a different color.

—Dear Yuri, she whispers in the most erotic way, —as chief of security, you must understand that this case will not remain without consequences for you. And you, Vadim, will have to avoid, against your preferences, any sadomasochistic notes in the marketing materials that you are producing. And my Mishenka will have to work some overtime, as our company will be entering rough days . . .

Any sentient human being who has managed to read everything of the above undoubtedly understands that the described situation could in no way continue for an indefinitely long time, and, undoubtedly, my curious reader—and a smart reader is always a curious reader, as opposed to a smart regular person—would want to know how all of this ridiculousness ended. And it ended like this.

Once, when the four of us were lounging in armchairs after a busy workday, I got up, walked over to the stereo, and turned off the already stale My Bloody Valentine, in place of which I inserted a cassette, which I have been listening to the last couple of days:

> . . . The very last of the
> paper cranes had fallen from a child's hands,
> And the little girl did not survive,
> As many of the others around.

Can you imagine that Masha, up until this day, had never heard this song? Not even in the Young Pioneers camps! Before the last chords had ended she began weeping, and her predatory makeup began to flow in black streams over the white powder of her aging face. Misha, who had never before seen Masha in such a position, stood up to his full height and slammed his fist on the table. Then silently packed his things, silently opened the safe and took his half of the family budget belonging to him by law, went outside, caught a cab, and sped inside it toward the airport with the firm intention to fly to Arcadia, to the Adriatic, to Lesbos, to Madagascar, to the polar station Mir—anywhere where he could give himself away for free.

And Yura tried to catch him, slipped and fell, hit his head on the tiled floor, sustained brain trauma, and five months later got into military school.

BETWEEN SUMMER AND FALL

MARIA KAMENETSKAYA
Translated by Julia Mikhailova

"OH, WHAT TO GET YOU for your birthday? You should think about it, after all, it's a landmark birthday. Otherwise we'll come up with something on our own, and who knows what we'll come up with."

Georgi Ivanovich had been threatened with this landmark birthday for several weeks, but he didn't know how to answer the question.

He couldn't just say, "I don't want anything."

The birthday of Georgi Ivanovich fell neither in fall nor summer but somewhere in between. In terms of weather, such a birth date was unclear and approximate. Georgi Ivanovich was used to the fact that, on the eve of his birthday, everybody scattered with frowns on their faces because they were burdened by the transition between seasons, the debts of summer and the ever-earlier darkness. They were lazily getting used to thick fabrics, so reluctantly, as if they'd spent half the year running around in T-shirts.

Georgi Ivanovich liked to slip quietly into the next year without toasting each achievement with a shot of vodka.

"It has to be something special—maybe a restaurant? Or a theater? Or maybe the best option is just to celebrate at home. Who do you want to invite?" His son thought out loud into the receiver.

"I don't want anything special. Don't yell." Georgi Ivanovich felt confused and ill at ease. "I've already had landmark birthdays in my life. And I'll probably live to have another."

"Complaints are the last thing we need from you. We haven't seen each other for a hundred years, and we won't see each other for another hundred if you keep talking nonsense!" shouted his son.

"The fall will settle all scores." Georgi Ivanovich answered with one of his sayings. He loved sayings, variegated little bits of makeshift wisdom. He had spoken in them his whole life, and he wasn't bad at it.

"Harmony enlarges the home," Georgi Ivanovich used to tell his wife when she complained about their cramped apartment.

"Seek out new joys, but don't abandon the old joy," he begged of his son when he left for another city.

Yes, now his son, Valera, lived in another city, his daughter, Vika, in another part of town. His wife, Varya, slept a lot. Whether they were yelling at each other or not yelling at each other, they all got together seldom. Georgi Ivanovich sometimes missed them, but he was satisfied.

His life went along smoothly, as if it were a made-up story. Georgi Ivanovich built a house, brought up his son. It was now this very son he had brought up who was shouting—how else?—at him. Valera was constantly stressed out, but when he was a child he cried all the time.

Once, when Georgi Ivanovich was building his dacha, he and Valera went to the plot together. Valera was just about eleven, and it was his dream to someday sleep in a sleeping bag in a construction shelter. He was a city boy. They worked the whole day and ate potatoes and eggs. Valera went outside to count stars and pee. He came back and started to cry. The son cried half of the night for no reason and asked his father not to tell anyone about it. Georgi Ivanovich even became a bit mad. He didn't know what to do, hug Valera or pour vodka for him or blaspheme him with wisdom.

In the morning Valera felt better. He carried boards and kept asking whether they might hunt for mushrooms. It was the end of September, Georgi Ivanovich had smoothly entered his next year.

No, there weren't any mushrooms at all, he answered his son, look at how cold it was, snow already in the forest.

Then the sky grew overcast, in preparation to cloak the earth in winter.

On Monday they returned to the city, Valera went to school and straightaway got into a fight.

Since then they didn't go to dacha together. Georgi Ivanovich sometimes fantasized: Here he was sitting with his son, neither of them saying much, drinking a little . . . Valera had grown into a complete city boy. He chased vodka with little pickles, which he stabbed with a toothpick and popped into his mouth. Georgi Ivanovich couldn't tolerate these pickles. To make a long story short, they didn't go to dacha together anymore.

His daughter, Vika, in compliance with masculine logic, grew up to rely on herself. Now Vika waited for when she would have children, and she kept waiting impatiently.

"Listen, it just came to me. You know we haven't gone to dacha at all this year," Georgi Ivanovich said in the evening to his wife. "On my birthday, let's swing by there."

Varya answered that she was most certainly not going to lug food there, and let Valerik drive them in one of his cars, one that has enough space for all of them, including the dishes.

"You know what I just remembered," he later confessed to his son. "Do you remember our dacha? Well, think back. Not a single decent tree there, all of them old and hardly bearing any fruit. Pruny apples, I won't even mention what passes for plums. This is what I remembered—when we took the plot, all the trees were already there. They matured, blossomed, gave fruit. Remember? I didn't plant a single tree myself."

"So what?" asked Valera.

"Let's buy saplings," said Georgi Ivanovich in a whisper. "And I will plant a tree. Then it will be the way I like. You know how?"

Vova was silent.

"I built a house . . ." Georgi Ivanovich prompted him.

"I got it, I got it," his son said. "You built a house, you brought up a son, you plant a tree. No problem."

Three little apple saplings were put into bags. Georgi Ivanovich decided to plant two himself and one could be Valera's if he wanted. One must start with something. Vika promised that her husband would join them later, when he was done with his own business.

Valera said that his wife had augmented her lips and temporarily couldn't speak.

"Her face is swollen. It's scary to look at her," complained Valera to his mother. "A saint couldn't bear to lay eyes on her."

A saint couldn't bear to lay eyes on her. Georgi Ivanovich quietly smiled.

"You can't talk that way about your spouse," Varya said, standing up for her son's wife. "I hope you didn't disclose this opinion of yours to her. And where do women get strange ideas like this?"

"Any chance it's too late by now to start planting?" asked Vika, rubbing her very flat stomach. "Won't the saplings fall? Look how strong the wind is."

"If we plant them right they won't fall." Georgi Ivanovich impatiently jingled his keys and paced by the shed.

The day was cold and sunny. Under the green trees golden leaves curled like bagels. The neighbors chopped logs and steam roared from their chimney as if from a locomotive.

The window frame on the veranda was split, in the kitchen— traces of mice. In loneliness the house stood gloomily such that the first thing any guest noticed about it was its incongruities, and holes.

They grabbed the rags, brought some water. They dusted, washed—and the house started to come to life. Varya brought out some garden gloves, two pairs, and clothing that resembled aprons. Varya said it was all part of his birthday gift, and the second half of the gift she didn't have time to buy because no one helps her around the kitchen.

"Had I known you needed it, I'd have helped," Georgi Ivanovich said, surprised.

"Right, get out of here." His wife waved him away.

"Well, okay, let's go," he announced.

They dug the holes. They smelled dampness and the stink of rotten fur in the soil. Valera began to cough.

"Do you smoke a lot?" asked Georgi Ivanovich.

"I smoke when I want to," answered the son. "If people annoy me a lot, I smoke a lot. At home, I blow the smoke through the air vent."

"Everyone gives it up eventually," noted Georgi Ivanovich.

"Exchange lives with me, and I'll give up everything in a second," said Valera.

The son held the saplings by the neck, Georgi Ivanovich made neat holes and ordered everyone around.

"Should I take a picture of you?" offered Valera.

"All right," Georgi Ivanovich permitted and leaned on the spade.

One put the sapling into the hole and the other covered the roots with a small hill of soil.

The saplings—crab apples—trembled, straightened up, and promised to survive.

But things didn't turn out the way Georgi Ivanovich had imagined them. For starters, they planted all three trees too close to one another.

"In those aprons you look like crazy surgeons," announced Vika, leaning for a moment out of the house. The daughter had on two sweaters that made her look fatter than she was. "Let's eat, because mama's already yawning."

The four of them ate salads, meat jelly, smoked fish. The wife and children made toasts—how very good it was to be at dacha, and how cool that he had thought of it, and they must, of course, come more often.

"Priceless is, that which is accomplished in time," said a thankful Georgi Ivanovich.

"Gera, you'll have to trudge over here every week now," warned Varvara. "Or do you think now that they're planted they'll grow on their own? Like with every living thing, you have to take care of them. Such a pity, such a pity if they perish."

"Both Valera and I will come here," Georgi Ivanovich promised.

The son chewed the meat jelly.

Georgi Ivanovich often had pain in his back, a spot jumped in front of his eyes, and in his chest something pinched. That's why

Valera, businesslike and kind, he would put the house in order, would buy a new dining table and repaint the walls. The veranda would become bright and noisy with the sound of guests. And also, he dreamt, there would be lots of photos in the house, Vika is crazy about photos, let her bring them.

The beds don't squeak. The rooms are decorated with flowers. Yes, we still need to plant flowers, but this will not be his, not Georgi Ivanovich's, concern.

These trees need about ten more years to grow and give apples, he found out. Someday the veranda floor will be covered with apples. Especially if it's a good harvest year, then all the baskets will be full, and boxes, and the new dining table covered in apples. Georgi Ivanovich liked still lifes with apples a lot; he hoped that in real life it would look the same as in paintings.

"You take care of the house and the garden," he said to his son.

"What do you mean—take care? When?" Valera asked, looking up from a crossword. "Damn, I already forgot how to solve crosswords."

"And plant new trees, to liven things up," suggested Georgi Ivanovich. "Just imagine, an apple orchard behind the window. Just imagine—this very veranda, all covered in apples. You love apples? Well of course you love them. Everyone loves apples, right?"

Yellow apples are good for preserves. Red—for children; children think if apples are bright, they're tasty. Though indeed the most tasty apples—they're white-green, with veins. The trees go ballistic—hurling their fruit. Wherever you go, everywhere it smells like stewing sugar. Harvest year.

Colorful apples dropped on the veranda, right on the floor. Where else could they go, the whole place is covered in them. The apples started rolling and stopped.

RUSSIAN HALLOWEEN

ALEKSANDER BEZZUBTSEV-KONDAKOV
Translated by Victoria Mesopir

—I ENVY YOU! said Anton with assurance. —Yes, I envy you. Your
new apartment—it's like starting life on a new page, it's as if you were
born again today.

—It's unlikely that a person is born into the world quite so tired,
replied Igor, standing motionless by the window. He was studying
the landscape outside with a bored look, shifting his glance from
the low and heavy sky to the neighboring concrete-block box of a
Khrushchevka apartment building. Every building in the surrounding area was yellow. The landscape of Petersburg's deep interior.

—Eh, all this will pass . . . Anton feigned optimism. —It's old,
brother, as old as the earth. People meet, fall in love, get married, and
a little later divorced. You can't escape it. It's the law of life . . .

—The law of life, you say? . . . Somehow I don't remember you
and your Svetka getting divorced.

—In regards to Svetka and I, a different law of life is at play.

Igor didn't bother questioning his friend further as to what this
strange law of life was, or why Anton had ten happy—or at least,
outwardly happy—years of married life, while Igor's family life
had started splitting at the seams in the very first month after the
wedding, culminating in the unavoidable, as it turned out, finale
. . . After his divorce from Dashka, who, three years ago, as if sensing the short-lived nature of their marriage, had decided to keep
her maiden name, there followed the sale of the apartment, all sorts

of technicalities involving property, and Igor now found himself in this two-room apartment on the outskirts of town. This law of life worked in strange ways.

—By the way, Igoryukha, happy holidays to you . . . Anton took the half-drained bottle of vodka, poured himself some more. —And I don't mean the housewarming!

—What're you talking about?

—I know what I'm talking about. Today's Halloween, see? Svetka told me this morning. It's a holiday, she says, a Celtic one, when the dead return to earth to bid farewell to their loved ones. Well, let's go: to Halloween! and he raised his shot glass.

Igor came back to the table, silently toasted his friend, and downed his shot. To his surprise, today he was drinking and not getting drunk . . . *Maybe the shit's fake*, he thought indifferently, some kind of unusual chemical taste in his mouth.

—We're Russian people, yet we're drinking to American holidays, Igor remarked. —There you have it, the crisis of national identity, in full view . . .

Then they stood outside for a long time, trying to hitch a ride for Anton . . . But it turned out cars rarely passed down this street.

Somewhere not far off, a freight car thundered, and a suburban train gave a short cry. The air was cold and damp.

—Ech, shit, should've called for a cab! Anton grumbled. —No damn way to get out of here . . . And it's too far to the metro.

—Now you understand what a goddamn hole I've landed myself in, said Igor with a look of gloomy triumph.

—Nah, it's alright—it's alright! Anton stomped his feet. —Think about it: you have fresh air, enough space for a morning jog. I can just imagine how good it'll be here in the spring, when everything turns green, birds start singing. Over there, behind the bushes, seems to be some kind of stream. Possibly snowdrops bloom here.

—But I've spent my whole life in midtown. First on Pazyezzhaya, then on Marat. Never thought I'd end my days in the sticks . . .

—I don't like your pessimism. This is not the attitude to start a new life with . . .

Naked branches above their heads sliced through the wind.

A green Zhiguli six, which sped indifferently along the street toward the two of them, squealed its brakes and flew into a puddle covered in thin, caramel crustlike ice, almost splashing Anton with a murky wave. Anton pulled open the rusty door.

—Prospekt Kultury . . . Paying three hundred. Okay? Deal . . . and turning to Igor, he waved a hand, —Good luck! Once again, happy housewarming, happy Halloween!

The first snow began to fall on the city. The sky immediately lost its height. In an instant the snow poured, abundantly, hurriedly. The snow rushed to powder the city up, although there was still one month to go before the arrival of the real, calendar-approved winter. The descent of the heavy tufts gave the impression of frozen time: only the snow moved, ethereally, while everything else was plunged into a winter reverie—the caravan of woolen clouds above the city was motionless, the sounds of trains grew quieter, people hid in unlit apartments, and even the smoke from the thick stout chimney of the local heating plant could no longer be seen. The city was emptying, and the entire earth—all of life—merged with the close, snowy sky. Igor walked slower and looked up: a large cellular net of snowflakes flew down at breakneck speed, covering houses and trees, quickly whitening the yards with their newly dead grass. The wind pushed a creaking swing on the children's playground.

At the spot where he had parked his car, next to the corner entryway, Igor discovered a drift of fluffy snow. The snow seemed to change when it hit the ground—it was no longer so light, and each crystalline particle became terrestrial rather than heavenly. For some reason, it seemed that if you touched it, the snow would be warm . . . Igor cleared the windshield of his Ford with a hand. The snow melted in his palm, and the remaining water was indeed warm.

Trampled snow was melting by the elevator. Igor stopped by the metal mailboxes, painted a caustic green color with apartment numbers carelessly scribbled in red paint . . . He located box ninety-eight and opened it with a small key. It turned out that the box was stuffed with junk mail, flyers and free newspapers. Igor scooped them out. He noticed a bunch of keys dangling from box number fifty-three. After contemplating it for a few moments, Igor decided to do a good deed and pulled out the forgotten keys. He started climbing the staircase, studying the apartment numbers . . .

He stopped in front of a peeling, leather-upholstered door and touched the caved-in doorbell. Warm kitchen smells floated on the staircase. But it also smelt of poverty and that hospital scent of unhappiness and suffering. Igor thought dismally that these smells would soon saturate him, and all his friends would think him a loser. Behind the door no footsteps could be heard, but suddenly a bright light shined in Igor's face.

Igor gasped, recoiling.

Out of the slightly open door peered a grotesque mug. Not an animal one, nor human either. Yellow skin, all grooves and wrinkles, a humongous nose with wide, hairy nostrils, and an agile lipless mouth revealing momentarily a glistening row of teeth. Suddenly the leather face compressed, crumpled, and out from underneath it peeked a laughing girl. Goodness, it was only a mask . . . Igor had never seen such lifelike horror.

—Scaaared? asked the girl in delight. —Getting ready for Halloween.

—I gathered, replied Igor with a stutter.

Like a magician, she held the mask in her hand, gently stroking it. The girl was an indeterminable age. A white T-shirt tightly hugged her large breasts with nipples pushing through the fabric, but on the whole her figure seemed adolescent, with thin arms and frail shoulders. And something not just childish but downright infantile was imprinted on her face: huge gray eyes with a fixed stare, slightly parted small lips, round sumptuous cheeks. Orange-colored hair hung in a fringe down to her eyebrows. Igor couldn't quite figure out whether it was a child in front of him, or a grown woman. And even though it was quiet in the apartment, it seemed as though the girl had just stepped out of a boisterous party of some kind, abundant in alcohol, laughter, and masquerade. It seemed, too, that even the present carefree expression on her face would come off, much like that horrendous mask, and underneath it would emerge yet another, third face.

—Are these your keys? Igor showed her the bunch of keys. He fixed his brow to hide his embarrassment about his initial fright.

—Ours! exclaimed the girl. —Where did you find them?

—You left them in the mailbox.

—No, really! . . . That's Vera, she's such a scatterbrain. Thank you! And who are you?

—A neighbor, from ninety-eight.

—What do you mean, from ninety-eight? That's where the Rash-kins live.

—Not anymore. I bought that apartment.

—What? And Petka left, too? the girl asked in surprise, and the amazed expression made her face look completely childish . . . *Fifteen, at most*, decided Igor. *Pretty little thing, goddamn it.*

—Well, yes, and Petka also, Igor assured her, although he had no idea who Petka might be.

—Didn't even say good-bye, or leave an address, the swine, said the girl sadly.

—Where would I even look for him now?

—I'm afraid I don't know! Igor shrugged his shoulders. —Well, good-bye.

He hurried to leave, sensing that a prolonged contemplation of her breasts in the thin clinging material and her full doughy cheeks wouldn't bring anything but a bout of neurosis. *You've taken the keys, now roll the hell along, as far away as possible, with your Petka-the-swine and scatterbrained Vera . . . From what genetic material,* he wondered, *does nature mold these types of creatures—not of complete forms or perfect proportions, absolutely not, but possessed with some kind of hypnotic, hallucinogenic appearance, with child's arms and the breasts of a nursing woman, and with eyes as though imprinted with the question*: So, how do you like me? "The law of life," Anton would have said, and he probably would've been right. Igor looked back, catching a glimpse of the not-yet-closed door to the apartment. The girl, once again wearing the ugly wrinkly mask, stood in the soft-honey light in the doorway, making wild gestures, her whole body jerking to the beat of inaudible music . . . Her spastic movements, the flashing of her skinny legs, caused Igor to recall an eerie ancient etching called "The Dance of Death." —La-la-la . . . Tum-tum-tum, carried over to Igor. The girl was imagining herself onstage, in the glare of Klieg lights, and she thirsted for attention. A strange peculiarity of female psychology, it seemed to Igor, was that women were shy to admit their desire to be appealing to men, and not just to one man (husband, lover, boss . . .), but to all—or at least the majority—of men. Dariya always argued with Igor, declaring that she was only dressing up and putting on makeup so that she would be pleased with herself, feel good about herself—and the very persistence with which she tried to convey these thoughts to her husband made Igor realize to what degree she was being insincere: if you're making yourself up just for yourself, then maybe you can make out with yourself in bed, too? This girl from apartment fifty-three was not like that; she didn't even think to hide her natural instinct to lure men.

Igor stopped at his floor . . . Next to his apartment door on the dirty tiled floor was some kind of oblong object, a tiny coffin in which lay a rag doll in a dark jacket and tie. Attached to the coffin was a note written in big red letters: *Wassup, Petka! Dead Joe has come to you.* Cursing loudly, Igor kicked the coffin away. *They all seem to have gone mad here!* Igor was full of hate toward this unknown Petka, to whose apartment had come not Dead Joe at all but its absolutely live and rightful new occupant, Igor Selyeznov. He recalled his own recent phrase: "Crisis of national identity." *Crisis . . . Crisis . . . Fall aggravation . . . Yellow house, a whole street of yellow houses. In a black-black city a yellow-yellow house . . .*

In the hall Igor looked dismally over the boxes and bundles of his belongings. He didn't feel like unpacking, but he at least had to take out some dishes, find his bedding somewhere in the bags. In the empty apartment each noise resounded, booming down the giant halls and off the arched ceilings—the echo lent Igor's new dwelling a slight romantic flavor, but on the whole this two-roomer evoked dull sadness in his soul. The recent metamorphosis of his life seemed unfair to him. At least, thankfully, the car remained his, since it had been bought a few months before the wedding and therefore, during the divorce, didn't count as "jointly accumulated property," unlike the apartment on Marat Street, into whose repairs and improvement Igor had been sinking almost all of his recent earnings. His soul was already gloomy even before the stupid joke with Dead Joe . . . Indeed, it was a sad event—housewarming.

Igor sat on a crate in which books were packed, like the evil skeleton Koshei on his magic chest. Now all that remained was to wither away from boredom.

Suddenly he heard the wailing of a car alarm . . . Igor walked into the kitchen and looked out the window. Wouldn't you know it, it was his Ford, screaming and flashing its yellow indicator lights. Grabbing the alarm remote, Igor leapt out of the apartment, tugging his coat on along the way. The lift was occupied, so Igor ran down the stairs. By the time he reached the first floor, the alarm was silent. The car, intact and unharmed, stood there, still covered in snow. Nobody had attempted to break into it; there weren't even any visible tracks in the fresh snow. It was unclear why the Ford had called for him, what had so scared it. Possibly, it wasn't used to the new place and had felt lonely . . .

While running, Igor had almost tripped over a man sitting on the steps. Returning to his apartment, he found the man still there with a decrepit woman leaning over him. He was a smallish man in a black knit hat and stained quilt jacket slept, his shoulder against the bent railing. Snow melted on his sleeves. Locks of long gray hair fell onto his tattered collar. The fellow was curled up against the cold, knees pressed against his chest and head pulled into his shoulders. His worn-out boots resembled hoofs. A cigarette smoldered on the ground next to him. The woman had completely white hair and wore a faded leather jacket thrown over a dressing gown and felt boots with no stockings.

—Young man . . . the woman turned to Igor with hope in her eyes. —Please help me haul him. It's not far, we live on the second floor.

—He was what, celebrating Halloween? asked Igor.

—What? . . . Huween what? the woman repeated.

—It's Halloween today, some sort of holiday.

—What's it in honor of?

—Heck knows . . . sighed Igor, thrusting his arm under the elbow of his unmoving neighbor. —Get up, dude! Igor shouted in his ear.

Waking up, the man started to move, snapping his joints, smacking his lips. He tensed his legs, but they stretched out pointlessly, like poles. He reeked of tobacco, vodka, and, it seemed, acetone. From one side he was lifted by Igor, from the other by the gasping spouse. Something inside the man gurgled, splashed around mightily, like liquid in a barrel.

—At least he made it home . . . else he'd have fallen somewhere and frozen.

—Yes, that's good, agreed Igor, standing the alkie on his feet.

Strangely enough, the man didn't fall—and, finding himself in a vertical position, even unglued his swollen lids, though, it seemed, without seeing anything whatsoever in front of him. While the old woman opened the door of the apartment, Igor supported the wino, who, swaying as though the floor were disappearing from under his feet, kept grabbing spasmodically at Igor's sleeve. On his broad, flat hand with jutting-out veins a blue tattoo stood out: *Venya*.

—Here we are now. Home. Be well, dude. You're safe now, Igor bid farewell, nudging the man into the opened door.

This time there were no talismans at his door . . . *Such fun people live in these apartments!* Igor was now determined to unpack the boxes and crates immediately. Time to make the apartment lived in. Walking into the living room, he clapped his hands and looked around. Where to begin?

Although the previous owners had done renovations before the sale, Igor did not like the garish flowery wallpaper or the dirt-gray-colored carpeting, and even less so the ceilings with thin cracks snaking across them. But Igor did not want to invest any time or money into his new apartment, and he caught himself on this thought—realizing that, for some reason, he perceived the apartment as just a temporary dwelling. Earlier that morning, walking into the entry-way, he had experienced a feeling similar to that of going to visit someone at a house where one can't stand to be—visiting himself, it turned out . . . He couldn't quite believe he was really registered at this two-roomer on the outskirts of the city. He still had to get used to this idea, and it was, strangely enough, much harder than coming to terms with his status as a bachelor. In any event, he needed to chase away these digressive thoughts quickly . . . And the windows in the apartment would have to be replaced—the wooden frames with metal handles did not shut tightly and snow gathered in the cracks; the windowsill edges were jagged and their finish split.

The silence was broken by the shrill doorbell. Without looking through the peephole, Igor flung open the door. He saw the girl from apartment fifty-three. For a second, Igor thought she must have rung him by mistake. The girl was looking up at him with keen gray eyes.

—Excuse me . . . she said and, wrinkling the bridge of her nose, broke out in scattered laughter. —I realized I'd played an unfortunate joke. You must have found that coffin of ours! My sister and I left it there, we didn't know the Rashkins had moved . . . Sorry . . . This little present was meant for Petka, for Halloween! Pretty rad dude lived here, Petka. Forgive us!

—Yeah, it's alright . . . replied Igor.

—My name's Ksenia, by the way, she introduced herself, continuing to irradiate him with her childlike eyes, —or simply Ksu.

—I'm Igor. Strange present.

—Halloween is that kind of holiday. Horrific! Tonight is the night of vampires and fallen women, giggled Ksenia, and her lips formed a pink circle.

—I don't like it, it reminds me of the cemetery. Why're you standing there, Ksu? Come in . . . Although I don't have anything to sit on, the furniture arrives tomorrow, so for now, crates instead of chairs. Ksenia flashed sidelong past Igor, just like an Egyptian bas-relief, quickly and determinedly, as if afraid Igor might revoke the invitation. The girl was wearing a black sweater and blue jeans, and her belt was pulled so tight, it was unclear how she could breathe . . . The apartment instantly filled with the smell of her perfume. Stretching out her neck, she peeked into the living room, where a computer screen flickered on the floor, then walked with bouncing steps into the kitchen, where a kitchen table, gas stove, microwave, and fridge stood. Remembering his actions down on the staircase next to apartment fifty-three, the short and empty conversation with the girl, Igor couldn't understand how exactly he had intimated that they could meet again and, moreover, in his apartment. Maybe he had looked at her in a kind of way that left no doubt . . . Must have been some sign on his part. Or else the girl had thought something up herself.

—Maybe I can help you around the house? she asked, looking around the kitchen.

—But there's nothing in the house yet to help around with . . .

—Are you from Peter or someplace else?

—Native Peterburger . . .

—And where's your family?

—No family, Igor replied simply.

—I seeee, Ksenia dragged out, and all of a sudden asked innocently: —Do you have roaches here?

—Don't think so . . .

—Us, we got lots of 'em. She sat on a crate that was pulled up to the table, putting her arms around sharp angular knees. —They crawl from everywhere, from the ventilation, from behind the wallpaper. We've already poured all sorts of powders and poisons with some kind of chemicals and whatnot, but they could care less. Put the light on at night, and the whole wall is covered. Those huge, sluggish, whiskered bastards breed by the thousands . . . We're used to them.

—So disgusting . . . Igor cringed.

With every second he had less and less doubt as to why the girl had come. Igor started to feel intoxicated, either from the delayed effects of the vodka or from the closeness of a woman's body— probably from both. It was no longer possible to resist the delirium that had suddenly overtaken him . . . Strange, only five minutes ago Igor had been completely sober. The intoxication concentrated within him with unusual quickness. Igor felt that in another minute or two, an attack of nausea would turn him inside out, and it seemed to him the kitchen was spinning. His stomach felt painfully squeezed. In an effort not to lose his balance, Igor stared fixedly at Ksenia, and as long as he didn't shift his gaze, the "seasickness" ceased to torment him, all the surrounding objects appeared to be in their places, and nothing spun or swayed.

Ksenia smirked knowingly, with a snapping in her knees she jumped off the crate and, unbuckling her belt, quickly freed herself first of her jeans, and then of her underwear. Her legs were skinny, covered in tiny white hairs. The toes on her feet were minuscule, rounded with little toenails painted red.

—I'm not taking off my sweater, it's cold in here, at your place, she said sensibly, flicking her orange fringe away from her forehead.

Ksenia folded the removed clothing on the kitchen table. She had on the black sweater, with a high fluffy collar, and below the sweater was a pale, sunken stomach. Now her figure, with its full bust, narrow hips, and skinny little legs, seemed even more out of proportion. Naked below the waist, she was particularly arousing to Igor; this was an insane, totally crazy contrast: a serious, large-eyed face, thick black sweater and, below, a shamelessly naked body, with bare feet that left quickly evaporating footprints on the linoleum floor. Not taking her eyes off Igor, Ksu stroked her pulled-in stomach, on which bluish veins showed through the skin, with the palm of her hand. Igor was shocked by her calm.

Feeling the quick misfires of his heartbeat, he walked right up to her, looked down into her unblinking eyes, took her trim buttocks in both hands, easily lifted and sat her on the table. The empty vodka bottle rolled, fell to the floor, but didn't break. Ksenia noisily sucked in air, and a spasmodic grimace flashed over her face. She was rolling her head, as if continuing the bizarre pantomime started back on the stairs.

—Yes . . . Yes . . . More . . . Don't stop . . . she uttered through clenched teeth, jerking her head in rhythm with Igor's movements. Her fingers resolutely squeezed his arms above the elbow.

Igor's hand, having slipped under her sweater, encountered protruding ribs.

The "seasickness" abated. Igor's body, benumbed but a moment ago, once again came under his control. Exhaling loudly, he freed his larynx of the air stuck in it.

—So cold in here, said Ksu, with a shivering sigh. —It's blowing from the window . . . I just froze on this table—just feel, my ass is totally icy. Brrr . . . Can you feel? Yes, yes, touch it right here, I like it. Oh . . . she lifted a knee-bent leg.

Igor took her panties off the table, touching the silky fabric.

—I'll take them as a keepsake. Will you let me?

—Take them. Ksenia shrugged a shoulder. —By the way, from the start you gave the impression of an intelligent man.

—Yeah? And how did this express itself?

—You didn't give me any bullshit, like, you know, at my tender age and such . . . I'm not a fool, I understood that you and I just wanted the same thing. I hate those soul-saving discussions. Can't it simply happen that two people just want to have sex? That simple, I mean! Why overcomplicate things, right?

—And when did you learn to understand what a man wants?

—At birth, she replied, pulling the narrow jeans over her naked buttocks, and then, suddenly, added: —Only you shouldn't think that I'm like that, you know . . . putting out for everyone at once . . .

—I don't think anything like that, said Igor.

—That's right! It's just that you're really cool. One can immediately tell a successful man.

—You're exaggerating. But thank you . . . This really helped me. Listen, Ksu, I have beer. Let's have a drink?

—No way. My parents'll kill me if they smell it.

Igor laughed:

—You're really something . . . And if they find out what we've been up to here?

—They won't. Looking around again, she said, —You should get drapes for the windows . . . Or everyone can see everything when the light's on . . .

He couldn't get up the nerve to ask her the tactless question about her age. *What's the difference, anyway . . .* thought Igor. *Not a little girl anymore, that much is clear. Grown woman, no matter what her age.* And among those questions he could have, and probably should have, asked her, the one of age, somehow, didn't seem to be the most important . . . After all, he knew nothing about her, except her name.

—Well, I'm off! They're probably looking for me already, Ksu said, businesslike, smoothing out her sweater with her palms. —Bye! Happy holiday to you! . . . she cracked up, already at the threshold. Her orange hair flashed in the doorway.

Igor closed the door behind her. *This,* he thought, *is probably how a suddenly resuscitated person feels, seeing the paramedics leave . . .*

A shimmering snowy darkness was behind the window. The silvery dust outside stuck to it.

In the bedroom, Igor lay down on the mattress on the floor and covered his face with Ksu's underwear. Now her bodily smell, akin to the sharp scent of pine, no longer aroused him, but, on the contrary, it submerged him into a weightless oblivion, and he hovered between sleep and wakefulness, not seeing anything, yet tuning keenly into the muffled sounds of the city outside. It was as if Ksenia hadn't left, but rather had melted away, spilled into the air, phantomlike, and become accessible not by sight, but by smell alone. Igor slowly inhaled the air, and felt it filling his lungs warmly and viscously, penetrating every cell of his relaxed body.

In the hall his cell phone buzzed and chirped. No peace for him this evening! Igor bolted up. Grabbing the phone, he saw Svetlana, Anton's wife's, number lit up on the display. What could this mean?

—Igor, Igor! Svetlana chattered into the phone, agitated. —Is Anton with you? Did he come back to your place?

—No. What happened?

Igor pictured Svetlana's face, always pale and pensive, with narrow eyes resembling fluttering dragonfly wings. Svetka had graduated from the conservatory and worked in a musical school; music for her was the reason for living . . . Practical, business-minded Anton loved his wife, but, it seemed, didn't understand what she lived for. Svetka had something in her that didn't fit in with one's traditional concept of life. Their marriage was a union of opposites. Sometimes Svetlana closed her eyes, as if shielding herself from those surrounding her, and Igor thought that probably, in those moments, music was born inside of her. Now poor Svetka was on the verge of hysterics, sobbing into the receiver.

—He called me after he left you, and he's not here yet! It's been three hours already. And he doesn't answer the phone. Igor, something's happened to him! she almost shouted.

—Oh shoot . . . Igor breathed out.

—We need to look for him, Igor!

—But where? . . . Igor thought out loud. —Sveta, are you listening? Don't be hysterical. Things happen. I'm getting dressed now and going . . . Going! he repeated, trying to sounds confident.

—Thank you, Igoryosha. I'm very worried, she said in an unexpectedly quiet voice.

Igor whirled around the apartment, looked for a sweater in his bag, then, not finding it, put on a jean jacket. He was hurrying, while not knowing where exactly he should drive . . . Probably to Svetka and Anton's home. There wasn't really anywhere else to go, where else would one look? . . . He looked at his watch: indeed, Anton had left three hours ago. The drive to Prospekt Kultury was about forty minutes. Anton had always been a predictable kind of person, he'd never strayed or gone on unplanned binges, he was almost never late. And today he hadn't been drunk to such a degree that would cause him to get lost and not make it home. Perhaps he'd had a heart attack and the driver took him to the hospital? But Anton had never once complained about his health, he was a sturdy guy. Igor tried to remember the green Zhiguli Anton had left in. The windows had been tinted pitch-black (a starless night reigned inside the green Zhiguli), and Igor hadn't seen the driver. And he obviously hadn't paid any attention to the number on the license plate. A regular old Zhiguli six, one among thousands of others. But wait! Had Anton actually gone home? They'd spent half the day sitting in the kitchen of the new apartment, reflecting on how today life would start on a new page, mark a new birth. What if, getting inside the green Zhiguli, he had already known he wouldn't be going home in it? What if Anton had decided also to be born again? Today, on the day of the first snow. The snowy shroud in its impermanent "cultural layer" probably still retained traces of the parted friends—at the place where the old green Zhiguli had broken the caramel ice of the puddle.

Beyond the white grove resembling an architectural structure, a brightly lit-up suburban train rushed by with a clattering sound. And the snow kept falling; the sky was lit up from below by city lights, which pierced it, like spokes, and from the chimney of the heating plant, in a straight pink column rose smoke, like an unmoving axis around which the heavenly sphere rotated. *It may be*, thought Igor, *that the trajectories of planets break just as frequently as people's destinies* . . . On the ground the clean snow was void of markings of any kind, as if all things material melted cleanly into it. In which direction the metro station was, Igor could not establish. He stood looking around, perplexed. The creaking children's swing in the yard reminded him of a gallows with a body swaying under the cross beam . . . There was no wind, but the swing still creaked. Igor walked erratically, hearing his own crunching footsteps as he passed the dark garages.

IT ALL DEPENDS ON WHO YOU BELIEVE

MARIA BOTEVA

Translated by Victoria Mesopir

1

AS A RESULT everyone decided it was as if she had died more precisely not quite died but it was simply easier for everyone to think and look at her photographs in that light easier to explain it all like this to yourself and so everyone thought this. As a result. It seemed to everyone as a result that if you thought like this life would go on as it had before just roll along and it went like it went as usual only it didn't really roll there no where it was supposed to and for some it went completely down the drain but what can you do, you can't predict everything in advance, and the same here, the same way someone simply got lost in all this and moved somewhere to another city and nothing else was ever heard of him, that kind of story. At least it's known about her she is under the protection of many people there and everyone is around her so there's someone to look out for her one way or another, everything is all right with her but those who disappeared somewhere for good well with them it's still unclear how their lives are unfolding. As a result.

It was easier for everyone to think it was as if she had died well not quite died of course, but left this world, this familiar life, although in actual fact she simply went through another door, if one can express oneself figuratively, meaning she simply found herself another place only you can't drag everyone there and not everyone will go that's what the deal is and this is the situation that occurred. That is everything was just only beginning with her and now all that's happening as soon as every day begins so it begins with her, always the same one or more accurately one and the same woman walks under the window beats a board a ringing wooden wake-up call at the same time as we wake up who knows where and not always at home not too much loved we could easily lose this house for example the owners could raise the rent or simply chase you out you always have to carry your toothbrush with you. You've got to be on your guard. Save up the butter if one is to talk like they do.

More exactly you can actually get in and see her if you make arrangements they can even let you in you only need a long skirt that is not so complicated of course you have to tear yourself away from the usual flow that is your everyday life and go there, and make arrangements in addition more discussions lie ahead while you live there discussions in the library or like that in the corridor outside depending on the time of year maybe they'll not even let you near her. They'll think that now it's bad for her how bad for her? Getting there it's not that it's far but while you're going you see not only the city but you see the fields also and then again houses but before these were fields and they still remain in your eyes and the smells of the earth also every time you look at the fields your eyes become sad that is, your glance sort of brightens but if you go often and see a lot all the others suddenly after some time say: *you're a good person only your eyes are so sad* that's all they tell you, and how are you to know if it's good or bad this kind of eyes and so she had eyes like these. Not always.

These eyes. Reminds me of a story when we were sitting in the kitchen and talking about many things there that is, most all she spoke and we looked and thought, *what a person.* In front of us sits a person who is also in love but is scared to death of admitting it and taking some kind of steps so we sat all night and listened, we had one bottle of champagne which of course we drank very quickly and what's there to talk about of course immediately there were five of us that's probably about all and what is a bottle of champagne for five people it's not even serious. That's it no need for excuses everyone

there was an adult at least if not twenty-one then older than eighteen that's for sure. With no nothing. Drank and talked. And that's
how we discovered she was in love and not just with anyone but
a teacher yes teacher of a noble profession for men but good God
where on earth did she find him, and by the morning we'd talked to
a point where her eyes started to shine that is, shone became shiny
and her face reddened pleasantly and we said: *right now go to him and
quickly* the trams had just started running and people were going to
work it was already getting late that is, now not only the factories
but other people were already working or at least would soon start
and she believed us. Then we took her under the elbows and led her
to the bus and didn't once hit ourselves not on the step or stone or
handrail and we rode laughing everyone else around us also became
jovial even in this throng, in the morning always this kind of throng
in the morning rush hour always even in the summer it can be bad
and yet everyone has vacation so what's there to say about spring
when we took her. To school. Like a small child. In the hall we saw
she was climbing to the second floor to the teachers' lounge this was
a typical school so we weren't mistaken that the teachers' lounge was
on the second floor and immediately started shouting even though
the second lesson had already started and we shouted in truth not for
very long but still because we were happy. For her.

It could be said that we ourselves pushed her there and he said
to wait when he saw her *I still have a lesson and then I'm free* but
they didn't have anything if of course you don't count the bottle
of cognac and she hadn't slept all night or drank cognac before this
so it happened that she got drunk they drank in the park warming
themselves spring April he had to bid her farewell kissed her on the
cheek and afterward there was nothing else.

It's still surprising how short the road became after that as a result
we had recently been looking at photographs she was such a beauty,
God.

2

It's clear obviously that if I were writing my story about how everyone decided it would be easier to think of her as not being there that

is, among us no longer in this world but at first we didn't understand anything not to mention couldn't imagine anything at all hadn't the foggiest what this was about and why it happened like this and now where could we go further, there just was no going further so it turns out what to do for us—see we, old war horses, we didn't have words to explain this although we know everything about love. It's been clear for a long time about love and that you need to pound and fluff up pillows otherwise sleep won't be good and in the same vein and including also love. And so she fell in love with a teacher God knows only where he came from and drank cognac with him but didn't become a drunk already a good thing because she only drank one little time. God knows what would have happened further but it didn't continue because there was no continuation of this love, this love of hers because as everyone understood as they were supposed to as it was made clear that morning that he didn't love her. And subsequently either. He didn't even think of loving her. Well that's solid. Only this added sadness to her eyes these eyes can be like this when you go along a mixed landscape when this landscape then mixes up with a forest and then again houses houses houses. If I had written about each of her days then I would have already reached the end but that's just the thing that a person is so busy with work self family I don't make excuses. I'm like everyone else, a person forgets that there are things that need to be told to others and they so that they can stop and think and continue living because they have nothing left to do here there's still nothing you can do. Here there are no choices.

3

It's so hard to find words not enough to know the alphabet there's something else here as if someone looking into your eyes wants to say something but keeps quiet and let them be quiet, that's because you don't know what to say here, at first you want to tell others but even they cry too because everyone who knew everyone who knows her says: *why didn't she say good-bye so precious beautiful clever she's our birthmark above the lip*. From the right. Or from the left it's always so hard to understand where's left or right especially when you're looking at a photograph you see from the left and the person you see is on the right so go figure, and the signature says: to the left. To the left for the one who's looking or the one who'd been snapped you want to ask immediately but who are you going to ask here everyone has already written and gone and you just read and sort it out.

Besides which a wonderful figure tiny waist wide hips everything she wears looks good curly hair light brown from birth, and hands, thin fingers played the piano in childhood then stopped, eyes the only thing that let her down was her voice which was too low but you could get used to it all the same, with age or with something else it became better especially over the telephone. You could hear a gentle creature was talking her mother had given her pills in child-hood put salve in her nostrils before going on walks knitted scarves and mittens she too learnt to knit she did it for free not taking money sometimes taking it but only from strangers. Everyone was happy. It was done well, what else?

4

And generally speaking she was protected from deadly disease hun-ger because even when they divorced, her brother she had an older brother became the main provider for all three, he quickly under-stood that one could live without butter yes butter cream there was again some kind of default, otherwise they didn't know her mother didn't know and never thought about it. And then there was humanitarian aid too America sent four kilograms of salted butter cream so for some time again with butter and then already without it although once a week nice chicken teacher's salary + child support. Lived like this until grew up amen.

And even if someone had told somebody back then that she would be gone after several years then nobody would have believed it because first there was no one to tell other than her mother her brother her divorced father gave child support and she didn't have friends back then girlfriends appeared later. Not as a result of but before she was baptized and went along that path so it can be said that her friends were her own big reward. Her own personal accomplishment solely because her mother did everything she could she wouldn't be friends with anyone, and said specifically: *you have epilepsy do not leave the house for long* and she didn't and only read books television board games monopoly with herself but she always did well for herself, talent always finds a way, always went to citywide competition finals placed at the top in Russian language always correctly putting in the commas everywhere.

5

Back then as she later confessed to us she was also in love wouldn't you know it this womanly love even when you're only fifteen or sixteen not to mention going forward but as was always the case with her this love of hers ended in nothing that is, it ended with nothing just all went out and all everything remained the way it was up until the teacher we took her on the bus to see all of us together but there too it ended in nothing so that's it just cognac on a bench. Such a beautiful one he let slip by.

Already during that time she then started dyeing her hair had wavy hair began dyeing it and it suited her very much she straightened her overbite and you'll ask where was the money from, her father had become some big cheese and even though he already didn't need to pay child support but he voluntarily gave her money so that she could straighten the overbite so she straightened it. Became totally beautiful, she did, although it's true the voice was still not quite right or not really like not quite right but just at first one's not used to it this happens but then you get used to it and then she just suddenly didn't have any flaws anymore as though she never had them everybody asked why guys didn't circle around her chase her and that's because it's hard to explain why that's why. Because one has to catch people guys it was possible to catch guys she just didn't know how but finally even she managed also. As a result of the teeth.

6

But it was not the teacher who was then long forgotten she simply calmed down and kept wanting to start drinking she started, she simply began buying herself wine every day but then she got scared three days passed and she was scared, *I'm a smart person*, she told herself—*I have bad family history* and she never drank again not wine not cognac. Lips sweeter than honey wine sweeter than grape skins it was then she calmed down strangely but her mother reacted calmly to her sin and even asked about the details but these she already didn't tell she only told her that a young scholar always she goes out and does something crazy. He came to see her so bedraggled happy-looking skinny in glasses hair so light you could say it was white albino pants falling off. How could you love someone like that?

7

The thing is she believed him. Much of it has to do with who you believe you think at first it may not be so much but then it turns out much of it has to do with who you believe or don't believe you start believing and there goes your life rolling smoothly along or conversely stumbling all the way. As a result. Maybe later it can turn back but that turn also will be as a result of who you believe or don't believe somebody anybody. Now she believed him maybe because he was a young scholar and kept struggling to get a government grant but what would you expect from the government although it's true it was a little bit easier back then with this and so he struggled and better still it was to go abroad and live and work and think and breathe science there and as for where she would go if this came to pass nobody thought about that. In the same way nobody thought about what she would do when she found out he was married and there was such a sin here his body was sweeter to her than anything more so than her own home. We also didn't know back then but it's hard to tell if we'd have even told her or not she was so very happy overjoyed with her towheaded one it would have been a pity to tell and this continued two or three years not more and she was on the pill all that time so as not to get pregnant she personally wanted a child but kept quiet as though feeling there was life everywhere but being forced to bear it childless.

8

Then once she had a dream she had not yet left him her scholar and she had a dream like she was dying from inflammation of the lungs the illness pneumonia so then she dies suddenly catching it because of drenching her feet in the winter and there you have it she's lying and thinking, *I'm going to die soon and I haven't even had communion been baptized* and she woke up and you know where these thoughts were from? And it's true back then she wasn't that is, still not baptized and where did the communion come from here she asked him he didn't know only hugged her tighter. She almost got under a tram then slept badly nightmares and here suddenly wouldn't you know it communion and she went to church to witness communion trod upon water all those signs symbols of some kind one might think if one were to analyze this logically, so next day she went to the monastery about work selling fabric there worked at a company selling fabric she'd been there before the monastery but here they suddenly told her the nuns they said: *look at you you should put on a skirt you look so your eyes so beautiful and sad.* I've mentioned her eyes if you look and think much you'll have such eyes and so that didn't escape them and they invited her to live with them as a pilgrim and so she went.

And there they told her what sin was upon her and she needed to get baptized and married otherwise she would die like that in sin needed to hurry because time is precious and one can die at any moment and so she remembered that tram she'd almost gotten under but it stopped short within an inch, remembered her mother's pills all those aspirin polyvitamins ambroxol nospa and so on, remembered everything yes you want to live you'll remember all that and more and how it gets hot in your throat and in your eyes that's tears boiling from fear keep rolling down and down even down the chin. And there she went with all that all those new fears of hers thoughts tears she went to him her beloved and here then it was revealed he was married and had a child so she broke up with him on the spot yes and how immediately and it's true he kept calling insisting persisting coming over was even preparing to get divorced but that never went beyond words didn't reach the deeds stage she was unyielding and he stopped insisting in the end he did have a wife already after all. Her mother also wasn't supportive. Better with someone like him even than all alone that was her opinion having herself lived without a husband for God knows how many years she's sick now.

She decided well decided not really decided but it just happened that way she started going there you know confession communion so many new terms and meanings one can't even remember them all but the point is people stopped recognizing her yes girlfriends she had girlfriends sure had found them for herself after school after her childhood but you know they all of us her friends we wouldn't similarly get hooked on that all that despite baptized all sure but as for going to church no not too often there was more than enough on our plate as is all other business, and here how would you like it Lent, abstinence it's time to get married and who needs you with your abstinence and so we sinned and not only this one sin but also evil dark thoughts bad gluttony and the main thing—hurt and anger she too used to be like us at first but then became almost saintly putting out the fire in her loins not shaving her legs praying day and night.

9

Here he was given the final turnaround and he left without a trace he swallowed it his family didn't fall apart yes she cried at first but then calmed down had to fulfill the penance this is what they call the punishment forty bows in the morning and forty in the evening all with prayers. You'd come to visit her sit down she feeds you without meat herself in a skirt headscarf, prays only in it, calls to come with her on Sundays but who's getting up so early it's enough that you don't get enough sleep during the week so nobody went she went alone to church incidentally it was in the same park where she drank cognac with that teacher such a small world you'd think there were no other places left to go on earth. All hope for the sky.

1 0

That's where we were and spoke the same language and between us was one bottle of wine for everyone several of us there were talking and crying looking and thinking what a person God how beautiful God help her but it was too late or rather back then it wasn't too late yet simply we should have done things taken upon ourselves to take action but then who knew it'd all turn out like this that she'd fall for that scholar and he'd turn out to be married and with a son had we known we wouldn't have turned off the lights as it were. You've already taken this path what can you do there's no way back what can we do now it's not about us there's no turning left or right only straight ahead and even that path is narrow nothing to do that's it yes there was still some hope left that at least well like she always said: *I want a child husband family I was born for childbirth* so that's what she'd say now too. The priest her religious mentor spiritual father he said he'd find her a suitor and almost his words came to pass except she didn't like him that man the suitor was a hairdresser something she didn't like about him well how do you like that. And then she took this path even further it took her and met some man along the way good thing at least she didn't fall into some kind of sect this would have been a disgrace yes pure disgrace for her to get up in the morning leave the house knock on doors talk about God in ordinary words like we talk about work so maybe it was all for the better or maybe not you go and try to figure it out now it's all so complicated like right and left and even more so yes they wrote the Bible so now go read what it says: *seek and ye shall find* so she sought and found became saved found like hundreds and hundreds and millions after this book, but my story is only about but one such found one and even then it's easier to think of her as not alive that is, simply not being with us which is easier less painful.

She said nothing to us about the child just went to work at another place and said quoted from memory: *who do you serve God or mammon,* and replied to herself: *I don't want to serve mammon* and went to work selling candles at a temple and there she also received a shady salary by the way gray money called that is, the money was split in two parts and one was written officially on a document the other was not entered anywhere and just given out directly so that people could live at least somehow and so there they paid her like that and we used to ask: *how's that* and *does this mean the church also cheats?* She said: *well, so, I shouldn't have told you now you won't like the church* and she asked us to go to confession and we even went some-times but not to her priest spiritual father that is, she only tells him everything him only and doesn't tell us now never did a single thing about what's on her soul that is, what is really on her soul literally and not what she says about loving thy neighbor. She said she loved us as usual.

11

There they told her that the child might be born in a bad way that is, not bad but sick would need treatment suffer and this means money nerves time and it's not clear either what the end result would be. Spit on all this to be sure what difference does it make anyway whether sick or not and why suddenly sick she after all didn't smoke or drink was not an alcoholic she herself was healthy wasn't she and so would also give birth to a healthy normal child too for crying out loud what does an innocent child have to do with this? The thing is she believed them.

It's as if we didn't speak the same language talked in different tongues like tears by the rivers of Babylon because it got difficult to understand her even for her mother who also called asked for advice just even one word of advice on how to lure her out of there see she'd come home and the house the candles, the house would start to smell of candles she'd immediately say it's stuffy hard to breathe these buses smell of people. They smell sure we too smell the people but what do you say to her mother at this point her brother got married and disappeared silence is golden nothing from him her father gave money so she could dress fashionably find a good man get married everyone had this task to marry her off she herself used to say: *if I'm not married by thirty I'll join a monastery what else is left nothing* she felt sad so sad were her eyes as if she saw too much emptiness.

Some machinery of no return had been set in motion if one were to speak scientifically about it an irreversible process kind of pitiful lonely sad water hurts the throat drinking cold water is more fun than talking crying grieving with tears she says from the heart:

I believe. And so what now we what we shouldn't like eat delicious candy or something sure we also believe yet we look at life happily optimistically okay look here's a person come love him but she can't God first.

1 2

It wouldn't seem like such a big deal well so a person decided to join a monastery and did went to that monastery of hers and went away yes went away amen what's it to us and we should be happy happily full of happiness she's happy she went away it's all good she did as she pleased what's it to us all the more so this is your close friend and Simon caught Peter by promise became a fisher of men and so he caught as promised but that's the point the thing is you weren't caught or maybe you will you will be caught somewhere you can see the nets you yourself are walking the depths and you know God exists but somewhere far away and that means everything's permitted you can do anything, every breath sings hosanna what else is there, yes but to her he became close and she got caught and then it seemed to everyone as though she'd died well not died died, just simply left this world for another. And that is where she is now among others her beauty hidden she became Christ's bride and only says prayers aloud doesn't see us she left the world the bothersome the dismaying but we wouldn't bother her we'd only come to see her sometimes visit think talk in one tongue would not look into her shining eyes what's the point now.

And as a result that's where she's alive now and where her soul lives and prays also aggrieved also among everyone and she too prays resists petrification turning into stone leads a healthy life spiritually and every day thinks about that which is the most important and the same cannot be said about us ignorant sinners but what are we to her now also as if not even there. The thing is she believes I don't know how to end this story pity what a pity so sad.

RULES

Anna Starobinets
Translated by Ellen Litman

THE BLACK CRACKS in the Asphalt Rules were imposing their conditions. They were a threat. They turned up too often and disturbed all the rhythm. Sasha skittered rapidly down the street, his sweaty palms shoved into the pockets of his jeans; he had to walk like this: four short steps—fifth across the crack, step on the right foot—again four steps—and another black, gnawed-around-the-edges stripe, step on the left foot. Except the cracks kept coming up on the third and second steps, and Sasha would brake abruptly, stumble, fitfully shift his feet, but often he still stepped with the wrong foot and, terrified, hurried forward, trying to merely glance at the cracks out of the corner of his eye, but under no circumstance look into them, not to spot the stuck-inside candy wrappers, shards, coins, and the shoots of dusty grass splattered with engine oil. To see only the black stripes, sharp borders, which he wasn't allowed to touch.

Inside the subway station the Rules suddenly changed. The steady squares of apricot tiles covering the platform played a different game. Now, vice versa, their edges had to be stepped on, and in such a way that they fit exactly across the center of the foot. It got easier to move: the stripes came up more often, but at regular intervals, and it was possible to adapt. Somewhere along the way, the squares unexpectedly released Sasha from their strong geometrical grip. And the silent voice that directed the game and never made mistakes, this voice, almost tenderly, confirmed: it's a break, absolute freedom,

you can walk any way you want. Sasha trustingly lifted his foot from
a stripe and walked on, skipping along, trying to look only up or
from side to side. Father took hold of Sasha's hand, they stepped over
the narrow darkness between the platform and the train door and
entered the car.

— — —

For dinner they had sour cabbage soup and potatoes with sturgeon.
The heavy fish smell, accompanied by a violin concerto on the radio,
normally elicited in Mother a sense of home comfort. In Father—a
surge of inexplicable anguish (whereas potatoes with mushrooms,
on the contrary, improved his mood) and an acute urge to make a
phone call. Sasha didn't like fish. But since it contained phosphorus,
fish was included on the list of mandatory dinner tortures. With his
tongue, Sasha carefully explored the fishy mush behind his cheeks,
searching for errant bones that could accidentally perforate his
esophagus and then, through the blood vessels, reach his heart. Next
he divided each chomped-through lump into small portions and
hesitantly swallowed.

"Sanya, don't rock on the stool! That's why its legs get loosened,"
Mother snapped, irritated, and then immediately turned on her
husband: "What are you doing? You know perfectly well we put fish
bones into the trash pile on the left. We only put into the right one
what can be given to the neighbors' dogs."

With a resigned smile, Father shoved his paw into the cropped
kefir carton—used for minor food scraps—and raked out the fish
bones. The placid expression rarely left his face. For one thing, the
face itself—the round, smoothly shaven pancake with kindly plump
lips—invited it. And for another thing, the ten years of practice.
From the first day of his married life, Father steadfastly followed the
teachings of Dale Carnegie: Smile. He had a charming smile.

The phone rang during tea.

"Sasha, pick it up, you're the nearest."

Sasha waited exactly four rings and said, "Speaking"—just like
Father did.

"Hello? Hello?" An unfamiliar female voice chirped sweetly through the weak crackling. "Could you please get your dad?"

Still crunching on a bit of waffle torte with nuts, Father rested his content face against the receiver.

"Speaking. No, you've got the wrong number. Yep, try another one."

Five minutes later "Für Elise" whined dolefully from the pocket of Father's pants.

"What's going on, not a minute's rest . . . Yes, speaking. *Hel-llo*, Viktor Alekseich! Yes, all the documents are ready . . . Well, if it's very urgent, I guess I could get them in today . . ."

Father's voice hushed behind the tightly closed kitchen door. Mother slammed the lid onto the pot of soup and stashed it on the low shelf of the fridge.

— — —

Sasha was lying on his back with his eyes closed. He could never fall asleep on his back, but the Rules forbade him from turning onto his side right away. First he had to stay on his back. Besides, he'd still have to get up. And turn the light on—after his parents had retreated into their room and would not be able to notice the criminal yellow stripe beneath his bedroom door. It was already past eleven, and according to the rules strictly observed by the whole family, Sasha was supposed to be asleep. But according to the other Rules, he had to get up. To check if the vase on the windowsill was placed correctly. It hadn't used to be like this—at night, the Game would always stop. But lately, it happened more and more often. Under the electric light, some of the objects would manage to slip from Sasha's focus. Then, after everything grew dark, unexpectedly—in a wave of sticky cold sweat, in a rapid heartbeat—they announced themselves. They *could have been placed incorrectly*. What's more, a while ago. Sometimes he remembered the objects he hadn't adjusted in days. If they were left like that—something would happen. Something terrible and *final*, something that would turn his life into a nightmare and completely disturb the order of things. If he was late adjusting the objects—

regular mishaps would follow. If he did it on time—nothing would happen at all. Incentives weren't stipulated in the Rules. Only punishments. Only the constant fear of the big Violation.

The vase was really worrying him now. Just before bed, Sasha had checked how it was placed, but now he felt he should've shifted it to the left just a little. A tiny bit. He got up and turned on the light. The vase was almost all right. But he absolutely had to touch it. To shift it to the left some one thousandth degree of a millimeter. Sasha quickly tapped the vase on the right and returned to bed.

Almost asleep, already on his side, he suddenly felt that something else in his room would remain incorrect and irretrievable if he allowed himself to doze off just now.

He got up and switched the light on again. Turned around and almost screamed in horror. His books, his notebooks, textbooks, photographs, the painting on the wall, the porcelain ballerina, the calendar, the pens, the paper clips, the computer keyboard, the tapes, the blanket on his bed, still repeating the contours of his body—everything was incorrect. More than incorrect. It was chaos, relentless and aggressive, a nightmarish, taunting prank of the objects come alive. An actual war, started up by the pencils, erasers, floor stains, window curtains, shadows on the walls.

After a few seconds of stillness—a white tank top, striped underpants, goose bumps on his skin—Sasha set to spastically putting things in order. Switching them around. Shifting just a centimeter over. A millimeter. Touching them.

"Why aren't you asleep at this hour? What's going on?" Mother stood in the doorway of his room, unkind and drained without her makeup.

"Looking for a notebook for a test," mumbled Sasha, barely audibly, and running up to Mother, he clung to her neck. He buried his cold lips in the bunch of her red hair, smelling of sweat and sour cabbage. With his hand, he discreetly fixed up her ugly beaded barrette. Delicately touched it with his finger on the left. Saved Mom.

Got into bed and half an hour later leaped out again—something else remained unfinished. Then he thought of Mother and Father, the way they slept in the other, probably faulty, room. He waited a while longer. Stepping with his icy feet on the parquet, he left his room.

Slowly opened their door. Turned on the light. And threw himself at the sideboard, at the bookshelves, at the pile of magazines—while there was still time, while Mother, shielding herself from the light, couldn't see what he was doing; while Father hadn't yet sprung up and yanked him—screaming, wet from tears and saliva—from the venetian blinds that had to be—it was imperative—ripped off the window.

— — —

Next morning Mother made him explain in detail about the Game. And her words—pitiful and tender words, confident words, the metallic resounding of her voice—somehow managed to drown the other silent Voice that Sasha had been listening to for over a year now. Shrinking from Mother's sticky kisses and niggling hands that kept trying to pat his cheek, Sasha, relieved, was agreeing that no, there weren't any Rules, he'd made them up himself. And now all he had to do was simply stop following them—that's all.

Without the Rules, the familiar cracked road to school seemed like an even bigger torture than it had been with them. Shriveling under his little backpack, Sasha was stepping on the crooked black lines and feeling like he was possibly killing someone, inevitably hastening some terrifying catastrophe. On the way back, it got easier. In another couple of days, the cracks hadn't yet become just cracks, but they already seemed like harmless, conquered enemies. He stepped on them with insolence and not without glee. He knew he was probably tormenting them by refusing to play. But the Judge, it seemed, had already awarded the unreserved victory in this Game to him. No one was punishing him for not following the Rules. There was no thunder. And no lightning.

The first night without the Rules Sasha felt anxious. No fewer than hundreds of objects huddled chaotically on top of the table, dresser, shelves, and windowsill, and, nonplussed by his neglect, assumed, with impunity, the most erroneous positions. As it got dark, they set about making threats. They were pulling faces and intimating that the big Violation had been committed already. And that its inevitable, irreversible result would follow soon, having monstrously distorted the world. It would not be one of those reasonable, cozy troubles that Mother said "come out of the blue." No. Quite simply, incidents—small at first sight, unimportant, and even pleasing— would fold any minute (have already started folding) into a horrible, snakelike fine chain that would lead to a Catastrophe, and then, to the End.

Sasha kicked off the blanket but remained in bed. To get up now would be to admit absolute defeat. Or, if he were to believe Mother, an ailment. His cowardice. Because, in essence, what could be more stupid than to jump out of a warm bed just to move a pencil box five or six centimeters?

To calm down, Sasha slipped his cold damp hand down his underwear. Slowly stroked his testicles. Counting to three. Stopped. Stroked again—stopping on "three." And again—one, two . . . And suddenly yanked out his hand in terror, shrank, swallowing tears and breathing rapidly. This part of the Game he'd forgotten to cancel. Counting to three was now completely unnecessary. Not allowed.

— — —

When Sasha came home from school, he first thought there was a dog whining in the kitchen—perhaps she had escaped from the neighbor again, the one that barely fed her, and in some manner penetrated their flat. He opened the door slightly, and cautiously peeked through the crack. Sasha was afraid of dogs. He never touched them—so that a tick, which could be found in a dog's fur, wouldn't climb up his fingers and paralyze him for life. And also—so that he wouldn't get rabies, which would make him forever foam at the mouth.

Through the crack, he couldn't see the dog. It had probably hidden in a corner. Or behind the refrigerator. Sasha opened the door a bit more and squeezed in sideways. There was no dog. In the corner, Mother sat behind the table. Her eyes were shut tightly; she was swaying from side to side in an odd way, smearing with her hand a moist pink lipstick stain around her lips, and whimpering.

Sasha got scared. Awkwardly jerked back toward the door, his elbow grazing a cup of tea on the table. Cold fallow liquid spilled over his hands and sweater. Mother opened her eyes, looked at the dull drops, and said:

"Our papa died."

Sasha turned and went to the bathroom. And very carefully, ten times, washed his hands with soap—even though he hadn't touched a dog.

At the funeral Mother didn't cry. Not later either. Sasha knew she was prevented from crying by the fact of the dead woman, whose warped body was extracted, along with Father's, from the wrecked car that smelled of perfume and blood.

Father was buried in a closed casket, and because of that, Sasha hadn't managed to check whether he lay there correctly.

On the way home, the Voice, which had been silent for half a year, spoke again. It was very soft. It felt sorry for Sasha. But said that it had all been Sasha's own fault. Sad and reproachful, it explained the new Game Rules to Sasha. They were much harder than before.

After the wake, after seeing off the guests, Mother sat down in an armchair and stayed there, still, until the evening. When the room grew dark, Sasha slowly—so that he could count to seven—approached her and said:

"Mom, you're sitting incorrectly."

She didn't move. And didn't answer.

Sasha went to the kitchen and fetched a knife from the drawer, the one to the left. With a wooden handle. Then returned to the room and said:

"Mom, you're sitting incorrectly."

THE SEVENTH TOAST
TO SNAILS

EKATERINA TARATUTA
Translation by James R. Russell

1. SAILING ALWAYS COMMENCES with notable events. As is my custom, I nailed to a tree a plaque stating that I beg the forgiveness of all in the world before whom I stand guilty, and forgive all who have brought me grief. The vessel *Zubatka*, my sister ship, after innumerable past lives, had lost all her former glories and become a rotten tub. So it was left to me to rely only on my own powers, just when the much mightier, massive ships of our city were saluting me in mockery as I set sail rocking cozily in the coastal waters, before heading out to the open gulfs of ocean.

2. Once they brought turtles. Yeah, live ones for soup.

Live?

Sure. If you kill them, they rot at once. So as not to confuse them, we named them after the clients who had ordered them: we painted Mr. or Mrs. So-and-so on their shells. Sometimes, you know, I had to note in the ship's log, "Mr. So-and-so died."

Was the client angry about it afterward?

Look, what are you supposed to do if it dies? In general we tried to keep alive the turtles with royal blood. Sailors are a superstitious lot, and we reckoned the death of a noble turtle might bring bad luck.

3. They say that at the equator there is a region that is uninhabitable on account of the ferocious heat. On old maps they sometimes signify it by the hand of Satan rising from the waters. It's true what they say. Cowardly crews approaching those parts demand that the ship turn around and sail back: they fear that if the vessel draws nearer they will find themselves in latitudes where the heat of the sun has made the waters of the sea boil.

So does it really boil, then?

I've never seen such a thing. But there are numerous maelstroms in those regions, and that could have given rise to the legend. It's a verifiable fact, at any rate, that the skin of the locals turns pitch-black, and there's no way of escaping the sun's glare. Your skin burns even under your shirt, because the rays of the sun in that part of the world are so greedy that they penetrate even the weave of fabric.

And what about the gold, Marianna?

The gold that the intense heat of the tropical sun extracts? I don't really know, my dear. All we know is that the souls of a white-skinned crew in those latitudes experience a sort of darkening and everybody becomes stupider and cruder than normal. Who knows? Perhaps the sun there distills all the gold right out of them . . . and somewhere in those parts that gold accumulates. Yes, it's possible.

4. Their captain proposed I drink with him to good fortune, but I declined.

How come?

I saw in my wineglass the reflection of a man who was at that moment nowhere to be seen.

Did you hide this from the captain?

On the contrary, I told him.

Do you know who it was whose visage illicitly manifested on the surface of your drink?

Yes. As soon as he heard the name, the captain repaired to his stateroom in silence.

What sort of wine was it?

There is an entirely black island by the name of Satanazes. Only grapes grow there: the local wine is sweet, but tastes of iodine and ashes, and one wants to salt it before drinking. This wine is helpful in wartime.

5. The smoked chicken was already past its freshness and smelled like an old rag. A woman with a big belly was eating it: she had been a beauty in her youth. She thought it a shame to throw out the chicken, so she tried to swallow at least a bit of it. She didn't let her kids try the meat, but declined their offers of fresh food—which was, incidentally, abundant.

6. There is a country called Kroraina or Kroran, but you can't get there by sea. This means that such a country is excessively mysterious and, in consequence, cannot last very long. They also have a migrating lake that changes its location every three years—so it is impossible to record it on any map. It is large, but no boats ply it, since its water seeps into any craft in the space of a few minutes, no matter how stoutly tarred the hull. Nor can one drink this water; so a traveler in those parts, unless he wants to die of thirst, must drink the blood of his horse. The districts of that country bear the names Chalmadana, Nina, and Sacha. They portray on their coins either a Bactrian camel or a horse. They write letters on wooden tablets shaped like thin ax heads that are called *kilamudra* and *likhitaka*. They tie two of these together with a string and then seal them, so the letter is on the inside; the address, on the outside.

7. In accordance with their Italian custom, she sent her beloved a lock of her hair. It was considered especially chic if a little blood adhered to the severed bang, so that is what the woman did.

How should a man feel upon receipt of such a gift?

I reckon he must consider himself flattered, but it seems to me also that scarcely any man will feel that way with an entirely pure heart. Yet when one is considering symbols of this kind, sincerity has nothing to do with it.

8. I once saw a captive wild man.

Where?

Right here. You know I don't sail to faraway climes the way you do.

It's not in the least surprising you saw him here. One can encounter wild men anywhere. Sometimes you can even catch them at sea.

9. Once, a demon appeared onboard. At the nearest port we summoned a priest to the ship. He climbed up on deck with the greatest difficulty and declared that before performing the exorcism it was necessary to read a sermon to the entire crew, at once. I collected the men and he set to. This priest was a lachrymose fellow and his tears flowed freely. About an hour into the sermon the demon whom he was preparing to expel appeared before him and all of us. The demon abused the priest, calling him a pompous windbag. Then he pissed blasphemously on the deck and vanished forever. My boys were so furious at the priest for this that I had to protect him from their anger. He was hastily bundled into a dinghy, sobbing loudly all the while, but looking perfectly delighted.

10. She was recalling the days spent at that school. According to her account, they went around all summer dressed only in frocks, barebreasted, while each tended to her assigned tasks.

What were they?

She had to sort out old compositions in the archive on rubbing salves.

11. Have you ever seen any foreign potentates?

Yes, a lot of them.

Are they any different from ours?

Yes, strikingly so.

In what way?

It is well known that the rulers of foreign lands can be recognized by the way they eat watermelons.

How do they eat them?

That's one thing I have never had occasion to observe.

12. In those parts people get terribly ill with fever. The four-day fevers are the most lethal. As one doctor wrote: The only cure is to administer a sudden fright. But the problem is that it's hard to scare someone that sick, since he's so seriously ill that he's already prepared for the worst. He's overwhelmed by weakness, so he greets with curiosity and hope everything that might otherwise hint of danger. He speaks in a funny, squeaky voice reminiscent of a child's, and his eyes are permanently inflamed. It seems to him that everyone's out to get him. One member of our crew in that grim condition even kept trying to publish articles in the newspapers about his suspicions—to no avail, since he was utterly illiterate. But all the rest just gulped down rum and never strayed from their bunks. They couldn't resist the powerful desire to sleep, yet whenever they nodded off, their slumber was so heavy that it was as though the night had been cored out of their heads with a knife.

13. After that he said, *She seized me with her legs and thus turned me upside down.* It actually seemed to him that she had done something of the sort intentionally, and ever since then he had wanted to call her.

And how about her?

She fell for him, too, but as it happened he was married and a man of honor. So he was very frightened of it all.

And what sort of man was he?

He was one of the kind who guffaw loudly in company, but never laugh when they're by themselves.

And what did she say?

Ah, I'm like a ship freighted with tons of iron from all the cannon balls shot into her. But sometimes such ships still manage to return to port.

14. At that time all the local cats gorged themselves and sat in the sun, their fur shining, sleek.

What color were they?

Various hues: they looked like stones on the seashore.

15. They call the local saint who is the protector of seamen Sophia: she presides over all the sea lanes, and her voice is as the voice of many waters. She manifests herself to every sailor once a year, on his appointed day. The extinction of the rays of heaven is the sign that precedes her appearance, and, in that way, every sailor is alerted to be prepared.

How is he supposed to prepare?

He has to be ready to render a full accounting of his business at sea for the past year.

16. She passed an entire week in expectation of the resolution of her fate. Her thoughts roiled, a swarm of ricocheting balls. But her heart was as cold as though it had fallen through a hole in the ice.

17. Drinking Song:
   You sailed away
   Unhurried and without delay
   Playing dances
   And avoiding parting glances
   And when you were tired
   You found something to do
   But no trip's in the offing for you
   So sit down and get warm
   Count your beads, sigh in calm
   After six shots, six hours
   Why wait any longer
   The seventh toast to her?
   To snails!

18. They like to hire lunatics to man the tugs.
   On dry land?
   Yes, the local pilots are just too taciturn.

19. Can it really be that nobody has yet attempted to reach the ocean floor?

Almost nobody. We heard Alexander the Great succeeded. But he didn't tell a soul what he saw down there.

Of course he didn't. Would you have told?

I don't know, my dear. Sometimes it happens that you do, and then nobody pays the slightest attention.

What disturbs me all the time is the possibility that I've already heard news of the ocean floor on numerous occasions throughout my life, without realizing it.

So shouldn't you perhaps try to dive down there yourself?

I think not.

20. She's a thief, like all the rest of them. Don't be fooled by her tenderness or gently bred forebears.

You know this for certain?

When she was a guest onboard our ship, the princess and her sister, taking advantage of some kind of commotion that had started for some reason or other, broke into the stateroom of one of the officers and filched two sheets. The very same evening, the two young ladies presented themselves in the high society of that country in white drapery.

21. Just before we were to go into battle against his men I had a dream that I had illicitly consumed the head of a fox. Inside the head one found three tiny bones, like date pits, and I wanted to offer them in my defense. But they fell from my palm into some limpid water near the well in the yard and—still in the dream—I was unable to locate them.

You can never domesticate a fox.

That's right, and you mustn't eat one, either, since anyone who desires its flesh will die. But, by the way, the battle ended in our favor.

22. When he said that, she became so furious she bit him under the arm, and so viciously that she almost tore off a piece of flesh. I saw the scar with my own eyes.

23. They say, don't they, that on the island of Sicily there's a path down to the valley of the hiding place of King Arthur?

Nothing of the kind. His hiding place is somewhere else entirely.

24. Actually, she was constantly conversing with herself out loud, usually without noticing she was doing so. Once her neighbor told her that he kept hearing some kind of muttering emanating from her room.

Well, and what of it?

She was really surprised. As for the neighbor, he was only trying to be sociable by asking indirectly what she was grumbling about all the time.

What was it about, then?

Oh, she didn't know what to answer.

25. That year they were without bread the whole time. They sowed the seed, but mice dug it up and gnawed all the kernels.

26. She didn't suffer too much from their separation; but, at the same time, all she wanted was to summon him back. His name resounded inside her head again and again and was ready to rip its way out, out loud. It seemed then to her that he was beside her.

27. But over there I was scrutinizing portraits: 1. The woman inn-keeper Susanna with a cigarette clenched in her teeth, lipstick, square buttons fastening her gown from top to bottom, hair gathered into a bun, a stoppered green bottle in her hands, and, on the little table placed before Susanna, a sizable gramophone. 2. Two old women in black frocks with splendidly flared shoulders, kerchiefs on their heads. Each has a gold ring on each of her hands, which makes a total of four. 3. Three little girls in children's bonnets of various styles, lined up strictly in order according to height, every one of the girls keeping her mouth tightly shut. 4. At a saloon, against the background of a frightfully beat-up swinging door, two apprentices in frock coats, with bright, thoughtful faces. 5. A clever lass with a ribbon in her hair and three lines of piping down the length of her dress and, also,

lace, a book, an armchair, a pendant, a ringlet, a corsage, and a straw boater. 6. Zina Alexandrovna, wife of Arthur Carlovich Arcabalst, who received a beauty prize in Odessa in the year . . . (the date has been rubbed out).

28. That day for the nth time I blessed both our harquebuses, designated *Wolf* and *Rhinoceros*. They were skillfully cast and more than once have saved us from certain doom.
Can you fire them yourself?
I rarely have occasion to.

29. The wife of this one writer was weaving a straw wall-covering for his study. She kept at it for some years and then died.
Did she manage to finish the job?
Of course not. But he soon remarried, and his second wife completed it. The straw is still nice to look at, though by now its color has quite faded.

30. They raise cheetahs for hunting. They suggested I purchase one of the beasts. I consented; but when they delivered the cheetah I saw it was in fact a leopard and told them it was unsuitable for me.
Why?
Nobody goes hunting with leopards.
How do you tell the difference?
A leopard has an elongated muzzle, like a dog's, and blue eyes. A cheetah's muzzle is rounded; and his eyes are black.

31. It's so humid in those parts that everything that breathes is instantly enervated. Everything in the houses is overgrown with a film of greenish slime, and the furniture comes unglued. The vegetative force is irresistible: insects molt from second to second. When we disembarked, we saw some people not too far off exhuming something: I went over and ascertained that they were preparing various roots and plants. Then I dug up some plant by the roots myself. We have no name for it in our language. I put it in a box.

32. Even when she was just writing a letter to him, her lips would redden without the application of any lipstick. What particularly attracted her to him was a singular facial expression that made her want to grab him by the chin.

33. This Pole wrote a primer for kids with the title *The World of Sentient Things in Pictures*. Mainly it was just a good textbook. One must consider whether adults ought to be allowed access to such books. As for children, this is exactly the sort of thing they need: the kids who learnt the alphabet from it worked afterward in the local map depository. Each would copy out a few lines with no idea of what they were about. This is the most reliable way to keep a secret and save the lives of the copyists as well.

34. Later on she told me not to believe a word he said.
    Why did she think so?
    When they were making love he always retained the ability to converse in her language, which was foreign to him.
    You think she's right?
    I don't know. I hope that he at least made some grammatical errors at such moments.
    Which languages did they usually employ?
    She says that at first it didn't matter, but when they felt themselves deeply in love, yet were still trying to resist their emotions, they fixed upon a neutral, third language, one that was neither hers nor his.

35. I took a look at her. She sat at the piano. *Play the Geography Waltz*, I said to her, and she replied with severity: *There is no geography. By tomorrow it will have been recognized to be pseudoscience.*
    Well, what's this waltz for, then?
    The waltz? It's simply too delightful.

36. This man was elevated to one of those middle ranks skilled boatmen attain. He was able to determine the course for a ship based simply on the smell of the silt drudged up from the bottom.
    Do you know this method?
    No.

37. We were once sitting in a coffeehouse whose doors, it seemed, never closed for even a second, so warm air was continuously colliding with cold on the threshold. A woman emerged at one point from the clouds of steam. She went up to the proprietor, who was seated at our table, and said: *Your coffee is smooth and black and bitter. All the local women will soon arrive and wreck your little den, since our men are wasting all their evenings here. Besides, just yesterday my husband burnt his tongue at this place.*

Having had her say, she picked up the owner's cup, emptied its contents on the floor, and made her exit holding on to it. At first the proprietor of the café sat dumbstruck, but he recovered and began smiling.

38. After that he sent her a portrait of himself stark naked.

Did she appreciate the gift?

For the most part she did. But it possessed one rather troublesome attribute: every time she looked at the canvas, it made her want to speed up the day, so that it might end as quickly as possible.

39. At first we couldn't see a thing around us except for little gulls feeding on the ice. When you're traveling between icebergs you can't afford to hesitate or make a mistake, so I made an effort not to be distracted by the gulls. But they became more and more numerous, and all seemed to be landing at once without a single one actually flying in; and soon there was no place to look away to distract one's vision from them. They began to confuse me so much that, fearing I might crash the ship, I summoned the sailor working the rudder to take the wheel. When I turned around, there he was leaning over the side with the rest of the crew, staring at the birds.

What gives? he asked.

Maybe they've just overbred, that's all.

Well, they're just about to overbreed some more, grumbled a seaman.

And sure enough, the birds multiplied yet again.

Take the wheel, I told the sailor, which he did, even, as it seemed, a little eagerly. But as soon as he began to steer the ship, the birds started to decrease at the same rate they had previously been multiplying, and very soon just a few remained—no more than normal.

40. The devil knows what . . .
   Yes, indeed. Devils have to keep their wits about them.

41. He had on a double suit of chain mail, and each suit was lined and trimmed with wool and rabbit fur.
   It must be hard to wear something so heavy.
   I'll say.

42. These people considered paying the slightest attention to the quality of the food one eats, or anything but cold indifference to the methods of its preparation, an indication of softness and effeminacy.

43. We stuffed ourselves on Christmas night and proceeded to Mass. It was very dark, and somewhere above us—invisibly, of course—the bells were clanging. It wasn't much brighter inside the church. Only twenty or so candles burned. One of the parishioners had let in a huge black dog, which was lying on the floor. When the priest entered, he petted the dog affectionately behind the ears; it stretched out with its nose to the ground. During the sermon there was some whispering back and forth in the pews. Girls with very stern expressions and loose, flowing tresses sat there, the golden adornments pinned to their coiffures glittering in the dark. The girls did not look at the men. At last a little organ started to play and the members of the congregation applied themselves to singing, after which they lined up for communion. The communion chalices were also bells set on tall stems. I was not too pleased when the priest lifted one of them right to my face. It turned out to contain white wine, and the glow at the bottom of the cup was so intense it made me dizzy. I concentrated my gaze on the wine and didn't hear a thing the priest was saying to me.

44. We visited the abandoned fishermen's shack: in the lot in back was a pile of sturgeon bones. The city itself was large and prosperous, even though the climate was extremely cold. But the place lasted only seventy years and then the inhabitants abandoned it.

45. Their door was made of iron, fitted to an iron frame, so it screeched mercilessly, banging in the wind even when locked. A man said to them, *You might at least glue a piece of cloth to it: otherwise, it makes such a racket that one would think the end of the world were approaching.* They asked him, *And what should we use for glue?* So he replied, *You might even try tar.*

46. This one professor was an exceptional bore. Whenever he talked, he nodded his head with a regular motion to which the modulation of his speech fluctuated accordingly, like a pattern of wavelets. As each wavelet receded he would pause briefly and quietly pronounce, *Yes*, and then continue. After listening to his lecture for half an hour, I had the feeling that any minute I might fall off my chair, as though I'd been slipped some sort of soporific drug.

And what about his pupils?

It's surprising, but they were scribbling down every word he said, and even laughed from time to time, when it seemed to them that the professor might be joking.

47. Be careful in places / Where undines leave their traces!

48. A famous ballerina happened to be among the passengers taking a pleasure excursion on that ship. They were begging her to do one of her most famous numbers, but she couldn't bring herself to, because the boat was rocking too strongly. The captain then ordered the speed reduced to a minimum and maneuvered the craft in such a way as to reduce the pitch and roll. The ballerina agreed to perform. They say the dance was something fantastic: the slight, fluctuating motion of the ship coupled with her renowned artistry created a sense of perfect triumph over the law of gravity.

49. When he was still very young, this man was already a well-known mathematician, as well as one of the Carbonari. He produced, notably, a formula for the solution of quadratic equations. His life proved to be very brief: he was killed at twenty-eight in a duel, not because

of mathematics or even revolution (which he enjoyed discussing when carousing with his friends). It was the fault of a woman who had almost no relationship at all to him.

50. I learned this game in China. It's by no means just a game. You need a board, pieces, and a magnetic spoon. This set of objects is used for predicting the weather, for prophecies concerning the fate of men and kingdoms, as well as for navigation, for the etiology and diagnosis of disease, for the reckoning of time, and for understanding when one should begin a matter—and when to bring it to an end.

D.O.B.

ALEKSANDER SNEGIREV
Translated by Mariya Gusev

TODAY IS Kostyan's birthday. Twenty-six years. He has his hands
full. He needs to make it over to Byelorusskaya station to pick up
a prescription note for his grandmother, stop by OVIR (or what is
it called now?) to pick up his international passport, and also stop
by the market to pick up the groceries. In the evening, friends are
coming to celebrate.

Kostyan received his first birthday greeting from an astrology site.
Last year, he ordered a year's worth of horoscopes, paid for it by SMS,
and now his phone displays a cheesy poem promising *a sea of happiness and the absence of bad weather* and, updated every two weeks, his
horoscope. Kostyan tries to decipher his future prospects. A sleepy
Katya comes out of the bedroom:

—Hello.

—Good morning . . .

Be careful with making decisions, obstacles in your way are possible . . .

The water turns on in the bathroom.

Saturn will place before you a choice . . .

Katya comes up from behind:

—I have a delay.

—A delay . . .

—Already the fifth day . . . Oh, happy birthday! Katya kisses
Kostyan on the neck.

Recently, they were making love, having drank a bottle of wine. Katya, in a fit of ecstasy, exclaimed: —I want you to finish in me! Kostyan paused, to confirm. —Yes, yes! I'm supposed to get my period if not today, tomorrow, don't stop! . . . So, he finished . . . And now the period is late . . . Quite a present, just in time for his birthday.

However, it is still too early to panic. Kostyan is trying to behave calmly, like a man. After all, they've been together for two years already, they sort of love each other, Katya, in principle, does want a child . . . Not right now, true, after some time, somehow, later . . . oh . . .

— — —

It's cold outside. "Cold" doesn't cover it anymore—it's bone-chilling. There is a dirty sticky mess under your feet. This is Moscow. The end of December.

His mobile rings. It's Mother.

—Volodya and I congratulate you. Volodya is Kostyan's father.

—Thank you, Mom . . .

—Did you buy the medicine for Grandma?

—I'm on my way to get the prescription right now . . .

Kostyan patiently listens to his mother's congratulations and directions, says something in return, then finally reminds her about the apartment:

—Mom, on Monday I'm going to call the agency, it's time to rent it out.

—Monday is not a good day, let's try a week from now. Mother is superstitious. Additionally, she is pathologically incapable of making decisions. She, for example, never knows what she should eat in the morning: fried eggs, yogurt, or nothing at all. It's been two months since the decision was made to rent out the bedroom willed to him by his late aunt, and still nothing. The keys and ownership certificate are stored at Mother's.

—If Monday is not a good day, let's try on Tuesday.

—On Tuesday I'm going to the doctor's.

—Are you going to spend the whole day at the doctor's? Kostyan begins to fume.

—I don't know, I can't run around like a soldier!

—Give me the documents and the keys, I will show it myself. The apartment was willed to me, after all!

—Why are you always in such a hurry all the time?!

—I'm not in a hurry, things are just not so good with money, I'm sick of borrowing!

—It's your own fault! You're not a baby anymore, get a real job! reprimands Mother.

Kostyan is a screenplay writer for TV. It's either feast or famine.

—Listen, let's not talk about this. I do what I love doing, and I'm pretty good at it. Everybody goes through difficult times.

—If you had gone to graduate school, you could be teaching right now.

—I just want to rent out my apartment. After all, I'm the owner . . . He gathers his remaining patience.

—Feel a little like you own everything, lately?

Kostyan contains his rage with great effort. He's silent for a few seconds, waiting for the wave to recede.

—So, here we go. He breaks it down, syllable by syllable. —On Monday, I'm calling the agency and asking for a realtor. Please kindly hand over the keys and the documents to me.

There is silence on the other end. He hangs up.

His parents are struggling themselves. Renting out the apartment would be beneficial for everyone, but Mother is being stubborn. She's afraid of crooks, unscrupulous tenants, and the devil knows what else. Just so that she doesn't have to make a decision. And also she likes power. Power over Kostyan. He comforts her, listens to her reprimands, visits like clockwork, helps out when he can with money. He even bought his parents a small German car. And now, when he's going through a difficult time, Mother doesn't want to meet him halfway . . . *Maybe I should lie that Katya and I split up?* he thinks. *Say that I have no place to go. Then mother will give me the keys. But what if she says: "Come back home, sonny, live with us"? That's the last thing I need . . .*

— — —

On Leningradsky Prospect, near the metro, there are endless rows of vendors selling souvenir rats. For a split second Kostyan is surprised by this deluge of toy rodents, but he immediately remembers: the year of the rat is about to begin, which means that everyone, for lack of anything better, will most likely gift their families rats on suction cups, a sitting rat, or a batteries-included rat. There is a wide variety of rodents, many dressed as recognizable characters. There is a rat-president, a rat-cop, a rat-prostitute. There is even a rat-zebra. Rats with batteries move, wave their "hands," shuffle their "feet," and intone *Happy New Year's, baby*, in a mechanical voice.

The vendors have situated their tables under the wall of a pompous Stalin-era building with a bumpy stone façade. Kostyan knows from childhood that this type of stone was brought here in '41 by the Germans to build a monument to Hitler, but the invasion was disrupted, and the supply of stone was used for city buildings. There are many houses with this stone in the city. Either the monument was meant to be enormous, or Kostyan is mixing up the facts . . . Deep in thought, he almost trips over a beggar woman standing on her knees on a piece of cardboard, bowing repetitively.

—Excuse me . . .

Just a few meters from the wall of the building, along the sidewalk, a rickety fence made from mesh has been installed, to cordon off construction work. They are widening the car lanes of the prospect. The drilling machines and jackhammers rumble away, covering the pedestrians in clouds of black, odorous soot.

Kostyan hurries, maneuvering around the slower ones. Enveloped in a warm cloud released directly at him by a yellow excavator, Kostyan jumps back toward the Hitler stones and immediately ends up in the middle of oncoming pedestrian traffic. In essence, not many of them are late, but all are running, for some reason. Kostyan is pushed, cursed at. Under his right heel, he feels a rolling, slippery, and taut lump.

—Gross! . . . Damn! . . . Mother! . . . curses Kostyan with disgust. A rat! A gray, tattered sausage with pink feet sticking up, and a long tail. So very much a real rat, a dead one.

A mixture of pity and disgust rises up inside Kostyan. Twisting around and raising his foot, he tries to see over his shoulder if his heel is smeared. Luckily, the sole of his shoe is smooth, had it been ribbed, most likely something would have caught in the tread. He'd have to pick it out with his hands at home! Kostyan, for some reason, also looks at the people around him. Did anyone see how he lost it and stepped on a rat? It could happen to anyone! He didn't do it on purpose . . . He doesn't catch anyone looking at him, everyone is walking with lowered heads. But he meets the gaze of many artificial eye-beads. The toy rats look on, without blinking. There is no reproach in these eyes, they couldn't give a shit about their real—not toy—sister.

— — —

A layer of snow crashes from above. A significant amount lands inside Kostyan's collar. Good thing it's not a giant icicle! Every winter a rumor goes around the city about the killer icicles, which fall off the roof and impale unsuspecting pedestrians. Kostyan straightens his coat, moves his shoulder blades, sticks his hand under his collar, trying to shake the unpleasant feeling. Lifts up his head. A Kurgyz wearing an orange jumpsuit is looking down at him, waving his hands and screaming. For some reason Kostyan is sure that the orange man is a Kurgyz, they say that all street sweeps in Moscow are now from Kurgyzstan. Came over here in a herd and began cleaning things up. This particular Kurgyz is not the sharpest one, picked a great time for cleaning off snow, when there are plenty of people below! It would be stupid to pick a fight, Kostyan says something under his breath instead.

Right in front of him is an archway—a calm place for a smoke. Kostyan takes a large drag, looks around. The space underneath the archway is occupied with a mural, executed with paint on plywood. It's got a military theme. In a naïve manner, there is a diligently executed map of the European-facing part of Russia, and also of Western and Central Europe. Large red arrows transverse everything. In the lower right corner of the mural, a tank glows green. Above it, in large letters, *The heroic battle passage of Marshal so-and-so*. The marshal himself is represented as a bronze large-cheeked head in a *papaha* hat, standing out from a weighty plate of the same material. The plate is bolted to a wall made from Hitler stones. Other than the head, the slab also contains an explanatory sign with the titles and regalia of the marshal. A really heavy mother. If it falls off the wall—will definitely kill you dead. Even if it only falls on your foot—for certain you will be left without a foot for the rest of your life.

Underneath the memorial plate, not afraid of it in the slightest, stands a glum little old lady with several clusters of small rats in her hands. The old lady shifts from foot to foot. Her coat is out of fashion, lilac-colored with a fur collar. It looks like the savvy vendors don't let her near the busiest spot, so she has to hang out in the archway, in the company of the bronze head.

The phone rings.

—Yello . . . hi, dear . . . thank you . . . see you tonight. An old friend has called to wish him happy birthday.

Kostyan perks up a little after the call and dives back into the human stream. Having jumped over black puddles, slipped on the stairs of the underpass, and walked over the boards covering the trenches dug out for the septic pipes, he finds himself on the other side of the prospect. And here is the turn onto the street, where, inside the clinic, his meeting with Galina, Grandmother's doctor, is scheduled.

— — —

He ends up having to wait, Galina is seeing a client, and seeing a client is sacred, one should not interrupt it. Galina is a psychotherapist. Or a psychologist. Or the first and the second together. To make the story short, right now someone is pouring out his or her soul to her, for one hundred dollars an hour. Kostyan sits in the hall and listens to a fat woman doctor scolding the receptionist for making an appointment for one pregnant woman in the spot already reserved for another pregnant woman. Kostyan's thoughts about a child return: *I'm not ready at all . . . we need to have an abortion. It is not dangerous at this early stage. All of those screams, the crying, sleepless nights, the washing of swaddling sheets . . . Or don't they use swaddling sheets anymore? Right, now there are diapers, but just the same . . . I'm not ready to bring up a child. To spend all my free time on it and all the other bullshit . . . And when it grows up, dealing with: for a guy not to get drafted, for a girl to make sure she doesn't get knocked up by the first stranger, to make sure he doesn't get hooked on drugs and that she doesn't come home too late . . .*

When Galina comes out of her office a quarter hour later, a pantomime takes place between her and Kostyan. He greets her with a friendly nod, making a motion to rise from his seat, Galina's face says that she remembers everything, she takes a blank receipt from the receptionist, writes something down, and stamps it.

—Well, how is she feeling? Are there still hallucinations? Galina inquires about Grandma's health, handing Kostyan the prescription.

—Seems a little better, recently. The drops are helping.

—Not good to take them for a long time—there are side effects. It's possible to have a stroke . . .

Kostyan promises to update Galina on Grandma's condition in a month. Grandma has seriously lost her mind in her old age. His parents were offered the option of having her institutionalized, but Mother refused. She felt bad for Grandmother.

The prescription is written out to some fictional woman. Galina doesn't remember his grandmother's name. However, it doesn't matter. Kostyan thanks her, says good-bye. Remembering, as he walks through the door, about the upcoming holidays, he yells to Galina:

—Happy New Year!

—Same to you.

He thinks about Grandma's illness. What would they do if her prescription was discontinued? A stroke is either death or paralysis. Death . . . not a good thing, of course, but death would be a relief . . . for everyone . . . But paralysis . . . Without the prescription Grandma will again become aggressive, will run away from home, scream . . . He wonders, could one inherit this? Galina had said that there are no confirmed cases, but still . . . What if he'll also lose his mind in his old age, stop recognizing relatives, dash around aimlessly in the street, drop his food before it reaches his mouth. He already pours his tea all over himself sometimes, when unfocused. Life flickers by quickly, before you can turn around, you'll already be a schizophrenic, in delirium . . .

Walking past the archway on his way back, Kostyan tries not to look in the direction of the dead rat, but his gaze is compelled in that direction on its own. He sees something new, something he hadn't noticed the first time. From underneath the long tail, there blooms a small bouquet of entrails. The insides have squirted out under someone's weight . . . Was it his weight? It seems doubtful, he would have noticed . . . The toy rats are still just as dispassionate, the bronze marshal with round cheeks is looking into the emptiness, the red arrows of encirclements and breaches are still sharp.

— — —

The entrance carousel in the metro squeaks in protest when Kostyan puts his fare card in. A glitch? Kostyan repeats his attempt. The mechanism makes an irritating noise and a red light on the turnstile glares at him. People keep slamming into his back, not expecting a delay at the turnstile. Put your card in—pass through, put it in—pass through. The metro passengers, like blind moles, hit the unexpected obstacle in the form of Kostyan, freeze, and then deflect around him, seeping through the neighboring turnstiles. Kostyan repeats his attempt with the card and scanner several more times, unsuccessfully.

—Why are you standing there! Don't hold the others up! screams a woman in a skirted, gray—as if dusty—uniform. A mouse, controlling the passage of moles into the underground kingdom.

Kostyan makes his way back through the crowd barging toward the turnstiles. He's out of rides on his card, needs a new one. Kostyan stands at the tail end of the long line to the cashier, digging through his pockets in search of money. He is suddenly covered with small beads of sweat—there is no money. He turns all of his pockets inside out again. Forgot. The news about Katya's pregnancy had startled him so. There is only a five-ruble coin. Luckily, a plastic card turns up, and here is a *bankomat*.

Kostyan dials the four digits of his pin code, and the monitor displays the words "wrong password." He dials it again. Same shit. Don't really want to repeat it the third time, after the third wrong attempt the *bankomat* will absorb the card—and try getting it back then. Turns out, he's forgotten not only cash but also the code for his own card. Kostyan calls home. Somewhere among his documents there should be a bank memo with the code.

Katya doesn't answer the phone right away. He gets irritated. He still has so much to do, it is, after all, his birthday, and she doesn't answer! And also got herself knocked up . . . Contrary to his precise instructions, Katya is not able to find any piece of paper with the code. Crazy! He'd always known the code for his card by heart, but this past summer he lost his card. Kostyan got a new one, made sure to memorize the new code extra well, and, following the instructions, destroyed the piece of paper on which this code was printed. However, a week later, when money was needed, it turned out that he didn't remember the code. Counted on his memory, and his memory let him down. Had to go back to the bank, ask for a new code. This was less than a month ago.

Kostyan memorized the third code as thoroughly as he could, using a system of associations, something like "the second year of the first World War and the year when I turned ten." Did not destroy the reminder slip, but hid it among his documents. Now it's clear that his associations aren't worth a damn, and the code has disappeared into the ether.

The awkwardness of this situation strikes Kostyan, and he again breaks a sweat; everything begins to itch: head, back. How can he get into the metro without money? Beg the dusty controller woman? She has already barked at him. She'll kill herself before she lets him through for free. Might also call the cops . . . He remembers how on his fifth birthday Mother gave Kostyan a ruble's worth of kopecks, he hid the coins in one of his little pockets. Once Mother was meeting with a girlfriend by the metro station, and little Kostyan was digging around in a freshly planted flower bed nearby. He had a great idea, to bury a treasure. Kostyan scraped out the coins together with bread crumbs and balls of lint and poured them into a little hole. Looking around—is anyone spying on him?—evened out the soil. Then mother beckoned him over, and they entered the metro together. Mother asked Kostyan for a ten-kopeck coin. Knowing that he carried coins around. Kostyan proudly told her about the buried treasure, expecting to be praised. Instead of that, mother unleashed on him a hailstorm of reprimands and accusations of stupidity. Turned out, she had forgotten her wallet at home. Mother demanded that Kostyan show her where the coins were buried. He began wailing and walked her over to the flower bed . . . Here a terrible thing became clear: there were several flower beds, and all of them were splitting in threes and blurring from his tears. Dragging Kostyan by the hand, Mother entered the metro and talked the loud woman in the skirted uniform into letting them in for free. Since that time Kostyan is very afraid to find himself in front of a turnstile without money.

Kostyan begins to dig through his pockets with renewed force—his coat, his jeans, his sports shirt. Receipts, his work ID, his phone, his passport . . . Here! There is a God! How could he not have noticed it earlier? There, between the pages of his passport, hid three rumpled, stuck together, new ten-ruble bills.

Kostyan's face shone with happiness. He experienced the feeling that a true miracle had taken place. A mundane miracle, but how pleasant! Especially on his birthday. He even looked around, wanting to share his happiness with the others. Proudly bought a card for one ride, figuring that the remaining thirteen rubles plus the five-ruble coin should be enough for the bus to OVIR.

— — —

Descended into the underpass. Two human streams separated by marble columns. One of the streams flows underground, the other to the surface. A young man is leaning against one of the columns. Younger than Kostyan by about five years. Blondish and without arms. The guy doesn't have arms at all. Neither the right nor the left one. Up to his shoulder.

Kostyan, without stopping, reads some words on the wooden sign hanging around the guy's neck. A plea to help out with expenses for prosthetics. It is as if the guy is standing on the bank of a turbulent river of the walking. Near him, the people are even speeding up. He's unpleasant. His stumps are repulsive, like an old lady's tits. Kostyan sticks his hand in his pocket, feels the ten . . . Stop. He's already past the guy. It would be stupid to backtrack. Kostyan takes another couple of steps and . . . turns around.

He sees a boy he hadn't noticed at first. Still very young, a child, with a school backpack behind his shoulders. Standing across from the armless one, studying him attentively and crunching on chips.

Kostyan puts the banknote into the small bag near the cripple's feet.

—Wishing you health, says the guy quietly.

—The same to you, manages Kostyan, catching the gaze of the inquisitive schoolboy. The eyes of the child contain nothing, but to Kostyan it seems that the boy is musing over his awkward answer.

I messed up . . . wished him health . . . So crazy, couldn't think of anything smarter to say! Kostyan berates himself. *Should have wished him luck, and not health! He took offense, I bet. Thought that it was a joke. What kind of health could he have without arms . . . What a retard I am . . . Should I go and apologize . . . No, that small one will laugh at me . . . Oh, and I no longer have any money. Now none at all! Damn! How am I going to get on the bus . . . I'm going to have to trudge from the metro on foot . . .*

An anxious male voice emanates from the loudspeakers on the escalator: "For the purpose of intercepting violations of the law, please let us know about the gatherings of suspicious characters, beggars, and persons in marring clothing . . ." Should he report the armless guy or no? Kostyan studies the stickers on the lampposts, which stick out like torches between the mechanized stairs. *A gothic party . . . Punks in the city . . . Stop the Islamization of Russia! . . . Death.* Part of the last sticker is torn off, and the question of who should be put to death is left for the Moscovites and guests of the capital to figure out on their own. The male voice becomes enraptured and with aplomb recites a poem about a sunny winter day, delicate ice-covered birch branches and the snow, crunching underfoot.

— — —

In the subway car, Kostyan suspends himself from the railing by his hand and, getting bored, studies the advertisement for some sort of book. The punch line states: *How to acquire a true church, a two-stage demise of America, Russia—the last abode of God on Earth* . . . At the next station, a confused-looking old lady sticks her head into the door.

—Will this train take me to station . . . the old lady looks into a crumpled piece of paper and recites: —New Slobodskaya? . . . and lifts her eyes to the man standing closest to her. He mumbles something unintelligible, the others remain silent. The old lady crumples the paper with the address in her fist. Kostyan remains silent along with everyone, the old lady, as if to spite him, is no longer asking anyone, and is just looking around in a diffused way. What a hat! Kostyan is almost ready to tell the old lady that she needs to ride until the next stop, then switch trains and ride for one more, and the station is actually called Novoslobodskaya, but the doors slam closed, and the train departs.

Always the same thing, as soon as you gather the courage to shake off this city paralysis, the indifference to everything happening around you, there you go, it's already too late. Kostyan calms himself down with the thought that he wasn't the one being asked, that he, in principle, doesn't need to worry about it at all. Her own fault, she can't even pronounce the name of the station correctly, and she picked a nonlocal idiot who doesn't know the city to ask for directions . . . Only now Kostyan notices the map of the subway, crossed out with a swastika. It's drawn in black marker, the lines are weak, faded, the pressure was wrong, the vandal/graffiti artist in a hurry. Kostyan studies the symbol, black lines covering the colorful lines of Moscow's underground. It begins to seem to him that the weave of the colored lines is not random but is also full of meaning, forming a different magical symbol. We ride around this labyrinth our whole lives, transfer from the red line to the green, from the green to the yellow, and there is no way out. We submit to the power of this symbol, we are its slaves. The swastika will be erased by the cleaning women, but this sign is not going anywhere . . .

— — —

From the metro, Kostyan shuffles forward. Sniffles. His nose is really running, there is no tissue. Wipes himself with his hand. Still running. Sucks it in as hard as he can. Tastes salt in his mouth, looks at his hand . . . Rusty dry lines on the back of his hand. Blood! Great. A bloody nose right in the middle of the street! Unbecoming . . .

Tilting his head back and covering his nose, Kostyan makes a stop near a telephone pole. What should he do? Turns out that his nose is smeared with blood. In perfect shape to receive his passport . . . At least the bleeding seems to have stopped. Probably from the cold. Kostyan sees a photo lab and looks inside. There should be a mirror here.

Nose turns out not to be smeared too badly, Kostyan rubs some spit with a finger near his nostril, scrapes a little with his nail. Smiles at his reflection. Now good enough to get the passport.

OVIR got renamed to FMS. On the floor—dirty linoleum with corners sticking up, along the walls—old safes, pulled out of offices when they were no longer needed. Like loyal soldiers, still standing, out of habit, near the walls of the barrack from which they were expunged. A line of several people. Kostyan sits in a chair with torn upholstery, begins to wait patiently. His parents had taught him, back in childhood, how to wait in federal offices. To just wait. Shouldn't argue, complain about delays. Wait, and sooner or later you will get yours. His parents' training comes in quite handy when the pudgy lady handing out the passports comes out of her office, locks the door, and leaves for tea break, waving the weighty hocks of her bottom. One of the men in line, who looks like a graying raccoon, is appalled. Naturally this brings no result.

— — —

Kostyan, however, is sitting there calmly, enjoying watching the line. Here a lady in a mink shrug coquettishly asks a man with a briefcase for a blank piece of paper. She forgot to write her statement. Here's a retiree in pants and a short orange suede *dublenka*. Each wrinkle on the pensioner's face is dutifully rubbed over with a tonal cream—in a way that one would polish a pair of favorite, worn-out shoes, her swollen lids are accented with eyeliner, dried-up lips painted brightly. Here's a gray, round-faced dame in a long coat, talking on her cell phone, trying to persuade her grandson to come pick up his passport in person. This, you see, is required by law. One can tell that the conversation taking place is with a grandson because of the special caring notes in her voice, by the mention of the words *university* and *exams*, and the question "Did you eat some cheese pancakes today?" which she repeats several times.

Having finally drank her fill of tea, the passport woman returns. The gray raccoon, huffing with indignation, pushes himself into the office behind her. He is thrown out with a scream: —Enter only when called! What, you don't know how to read?

Slowly, the line crawls ahead. Even though there are no windows in the ventricle in which they sit, one can still feel the advancement of evening. The chill is getting stronger.

— — —

In the office, Kostyan says hello loudly, sits down on a chair, and states his last name. He looks around while the lady searches for his passport. Bookcases with rolodexes, a paper portrait of the president.

—Ever been tried in a court of law? the clerk interrupts his thoughts.

—No.

—For some reason, I can't find you.

—I came in here last week, you had to annul my old passport.

—Yes, I remember! The office lady digs through a different drawer.

In the summer, together with the bank card, Kostyan also lost his international passport. This happened in Italy and turned into a real adventure. Because he also managed to lose Katya's passport. Feeling wary of Italian pickpockets, she had given him the documents for safekeeping, and he had fucked it up in Florence. He hadn't even been robbed. To get out of a foreign country without your documents is a complicated task. He had to make a trip to Rome. The Russian consulate is located inside a lush mansion, into which diplomats have brought the inimitable atmosphere of the Soviet polyclinic. Up and down the marble staircase, a consul was darting and, without any self-consciousness in front of the visitors, accusing his subordinates of taking small bribes. Entering the office of the consul's assistant, the first thing Kostyan did was stub the pinkie toe of his foot, clad in a flip-flop, on a car battery, sitting on the floor. In

Moscow, about twenty years ago, batteries used to be brought inside
in winter: they would lose their charge in the freezing cold, and
there was no way to get a new one. In Rome there is neither frost
nor a deficit of batteries, why the consul's assistant needed to drag
this heavy thing into the office was a puzzle.

— — —

The consul's assistant, a fidgety fatso, huffing and puffing, pardoned
himself and invited Kostyan and Katya to sit at the table, which
turned out to be a child's school desk. Having listened to the story
of how the documents were lost, the fatso believed Katya, a blonde
with a Slavic face, but doubted Kostyan's story. His appearance
caused the diplomat to feel mistrust.

—We need proof of your husband's identity. We'll give him a
document, and then some sort of Basayev will come over . . . said
the fatso to Katya, looking askance at Kostyan. Kostyan sighed heavily, his pinkie toe hurt, and from the wall the paper icons and the
president's portrait looked on suspiciously. Kostyan began to feel like
a criminal.

Luckily, friends were able to send a copy of his internal Russian
passport to the consul's assistant. His reputation as an honest citizen
was restored, and, for a moderate fee, they were given a set of temporary documents. Katya had behaved courageously then, and had not
even once reprimanded Kostyan for his absentmindedness.

The processing of a new passport after his return to the motherland had become a whole production. Kostyan had never been
drafted, and he wasn't yet twenty-eight. This meant that Kostyan was
still eligible for active duty in the army, which meant he needed a
certain certificate from the Ministry for War. At the ministry office
he was told that the army needs him like a dog needs a fifth leg, that
they don't give out any certificates, and that because of some sort
of stupid bitches sitting over in OVIR or whatever it's now called,
the country is in chaos. Kostyan returned to FMS again, relaying the
words of the army commander to them in the most diplomatic way.
The passport lady with the ham-hock ass convened with her boss

for a long time and finally accepted his application. But this was not the end of the story. When giving out a new passport, bureaucrats are supposed to annul the lost one. And they forgot to do this right away. Which is why Kostyan is here now, again. His passport finished processing a week ago already, but he could not receive it then. And now, since the old one has been annulled, he should receive it.

Everything is going smoothly as butter. Kostyan receives his new red document, puts down his signature . . . sees his own finger, smeared with dried blood . . . On his way out, he wishes the butt-heavy passport lady a Happy New Year. She raises her eyes in surprise.

—The same to you . . . Looks like he was the first to wish her this today.

— — —

His mood had improved significantly. A half hour walk home does not seem tiring. *A child, actually, is even great. If it's a boy, I will with pleasure play the railroad game with him, and if a girl, I will buy her dolls and various bows and outfits.*

At home, he shares all of these thoughts with Katya, showing off his new passport in between. Katya, on the contrary, is not inspired by thoughts about a baby. She actually has an interesting proposition at work and a pregnancy is not at all timely. Studying his photograph in the passport, Katya skeptically says:

—And you couldn't get a normal photograph done?

—Meaning? Kostyan is clueless.

—You look like an Arab terrorist, they don't like that at the consulate. They may not give you a visa.

—How? . . . Why? . . . He tears the passport out of her hands. Looks into it intensely. It's true, his cheeks are grizzled, his gaze unkind, his chin is sticking out forward, instead of a collared shirt and tie he is wearing some black T-shirt . . . He looked in a similar way when he lumbered into the consulate in Rome. An exterior appearance like this does not elicit trust from the average person.

—Why didn't you tell me this when I was getting the photographs done?

—How could I have imagined that you would dress like that! As if you were born yesterday! snaps Katya, and locks herself in the washroom.

Kostyan gets mad. *Things are great for her! She's already received her passport! No one's thrashed her because of the army, she looks like a movie star in her photograph . . . What does one need a life like this for!* His looks only cause problems. He's always taken for someone else. A quiet *intellectual*, who seems to everyone else a dangerous slaughterer. And all because, as a child, he hated red woolen trousers . . .

The connection here is a direct one. When in the winter they tried to make little Kostyan wear red trousers, he screamed like he was being murdered. It was both the color and the itchiness that irritated him. Then father thought of a trick—he showed Kostyan a picture from a book about the Crimean War. There, Turkish soldiers in red pants were entering, in a victorious march, the destroyed Sevastopol. A child's imagination couldn't take it anymore, Kostyan demanded that he be given the pants, scrambled into them, tucked the cuffs into his *valenki*, and felt himself to be a fierce Janissary. After a couple of years, his parents had a new problem on their hands: how to switch the attention of their firstborn onto any other pair of pants—the red ones were already barely covering his knees.

The pants had long since turned into rags and disintegrated, but the idea of them, their essence, had seeped into Kostyan permanently. He began looking like a Janissary in any getup, and even when he was completely naked. European visas are given to him with trepidation, his biography, residential registration, and place of work are checked and rechecked a hundred times. No one can even guess that underneath the aggressive appearance there hide numerous fears, which wear him out. For example, the fear of a Russian mutiny, the fear that one day the next crowd of sailors will burst into the capitol and he'll have to make tracks, and the Europeans will see the photo in his passport and turn him back around . . . Or the Iron Curtain will slam shut again, and with his physiognomy he won't even be able to ask for political asylum. No one will believe that he is a cultured, educated person. They'll say, "Go back to where you came from, into your wild Asia." But I am one of you guys, wait . . . Terror overwhelms him.

And if they won't let him out of here, whether he likes it or not, he'll have to become a freedom fighter. And with kids, it's very inconvenient, they could be taken as hostages. In other words, now is not yet the time to have a child.

— — —

Kostyan takes some money from Katya's wallet and leaves the apartment. Lately he lives off the support of his significant other.

The market is about a fifteen-minute walk. In the fish aisle, one of the vendor women winks conspiratorially at him. Kostyan approaches.

—Do we desire some black caviar?

There is a moratorium on selling black caviar these days, one can only buy these grains shining with golden slime illegally, but the vendor woman knows him. Several times, after receiving good commissions, he's bought a half kilo from her. He always thoroughly taste-tests it, squeezing the grains with his fingers, showing off the knowledge he picked up from an old cookbook. In other words, the vendor woman considers Kostyan to be one of her own. He smiles:

—We desire, but I'm low right now.

The vendor woman gifts him with the look of a prostitute who knows how to wait:

—When you have money—come by.

A half hour later, weighed down by heavy packages, Kostyan walks out onto the sidewalk to catch a taxi. He won't be able to drag all of it home on foot. *I wonder, will the birthday make the box office?* Kostyan has asked his friends to give him only money as gifts. It doesn't matter how much, even a mere hundred rubles. You never know what to do with presents, but with money there is never a question. It's especially relevant now, when there is not enough cash. Will the D.O.B. break even? Will the cost of wine, cognac, seafood, vegetables, fruits, cake be redeemed? And will there be a profit? *If it works out to zero, that's already great, and if it works out to a plus, it can be counted as a successful project,* thinks Kostyan, applying a movie-producer's logic.

Near the market's gates, a moustachioed policeman is feeding leftovers to a flock of homeless dogs. The dogs are wagging their tails. Kostyan lifts his arm. An elderly large-nosed gentleman driving a Ford stops for him. On the way, the man begins to make chummy talk with Kostyan. Again his looks play a role, the Armenian taxi driver mistakes Kostyan for one of his own. He's driving in an unhurried manner on purpose and in five minutes manages to relay everything one needs to know about the majesty of his people.

—We are the descendants of Noah! Even Peter the Great himself first summoned Armenians into Russia, because they are great builders. And during the war, there were so many marshals who were Armenian! Bagramyan was one! . . .

The list ends at Bagramyan. The man slows down on purpose, letting other cars pass, the pedestrians, the pigeons running around in the street. He still has a lot to talk about.

—When the trouble began in Karabakh, Armenian tanks had almost made it to Baku. But they got a call from Moscow, saying, "Enough" . . .

Kostyan's phone rings in his pocket. He pulls it out laboriously, untangling his palm from the package handles, which are digging into the skin. The display lights up with the number of a school friend, whom he hasn't seen in about five years. During their last meeting they had a drink, and he went at Kostyan with his fists. The friend's nervous system is unbalanced, his mother perished in the mountains. However, Kostyan's good-heartedness has a limit: How can one meet without having a drink? And he's not interested in getting into a fight. Kostyan doesn't pick up and sticks the phone back into his pocket.

—Could you stop right here, please.

Kostyan exchanges New Year's greetings with the large-nosed gentleman and climbs out of the car, his packages rustling.

— — —

—I was just trying to call you, to remind you to pick up the sour cream, Katya says first thing.

—Strange, I didn't hear it. Kostyan puts the packages on the floor, looks for his phone. The phone is not anywhere to be seen. Meaning, nowhere at all . . .

—Mother . . . it probably fell out in the car! He's in despair. This is all because of that idiot, the school friend—the phone disappeared after his call. And this one, too . . . with his great nation of Armenia! "Bagramyan is one" shit! . . . A chatterbox, he distracted me! *Stop, take a break . . . It's not good to think about people in this way. It's no one's fault that I lost my phone . . . God, please forgive me for these disgusting thoughts. Please help me find my phone! I'm not a bad guy! What did I do? . . . How am I going to receive my birthday greetings?! For sure someone will want to clarify the address . . . How many numbers won't I be able to restore, and the phone itself also costs money . . .*

And maybe I should just end everything at once? A thought about suicide is born calmly, without drama, just dry math. And it has nothing to do with the phone. It's just already clear that nothing cardinally new can be expected in his life. Sick of knocking heads with the family, straining to make money, being afraid because of an unflattering photograph in a passport . . . How can one bear a child into this incongruous world? . . . Now a subsidy is given out for each newborn, and what's the point? The money will evaporate, and the surrounding absurdity is not going anywhere . . . Kostyan goes down into the yard. Maybe the phone is lying on the sidewalk, in the spot where he got out of the car.

A guy has grandmother's tits in place of arms, and he still lives. Won't jump in front of a train, stands there begging. He can't even blend in, but still lives. And life—it's a pretty useless process. Especially when nothing interesting is happening. Here I walk down the same streets over and over, see the same faces. Get upset when there is no money, get happy when there is. I fall apart because of such ridiculousness like losing a phone! That one has no arms, and he . . .

To kill oneself is scary, of course, but possible. He'd feel bad for his parents, though, Kostyan is their only son. As soon as you imagine the elderly mom and dad, coming to visit his grave, tears stand in your eyes. He has no right to do that to them, suicide is too selfish a deed. And to be honest, he's simply scared of harming himself. Even if no maman and papan existed, he wouldn't be able to do it. Too scary, and he has inherited his mother's indecisiveness. Genes are a part of his fucked-up closed circuit.

It's stupid to kill yourself . . . Just need to shake it off . . . take a trip somewhere . . . see some new places, begin an affair . . . Kostyan is getting completely demoralized because of his own nonentity: the only things he can think about—to run away and start an affair! *That's what you mean by new? The only chance to renew your own life, to scrape the rust from it? The fantasy is just as banal as the reality. It's full of clichés. Maybe I should, after all, get a hold of myself and saw up the old veins? At least it'd be something new . . .*

The phone, of course, does not materialize on the sidewalk. Kostyan turns around to go back home.

What if the child is born deformed, an invalid? What if it's born without arms or with two faces, like those conjoined Filipino girls from the television? What if the son grows up to be a psycho, and the daughter a frigid gloomy? What if the other kids won't want to be friends with his child, will begin to taunt him? What if the child grows up to be a scum, and commits him, Kostyan, to a mental institution in his old age?

Kostyan remembers how bumblebees had made a nest under the roof of his summer home. In the cozy layers of insulation, between the corrugated sheets of roofing and the boards of the internal cladding of the garret. Mother-bumblebee picked an excellent place, she only neglected to take one thing into account—the newborns, one after another, were pushing their way not into the outdoors, but into the house. They buzzed, flew around the garret, too warm from the sun, slammed against the closed windows, and overheated to death. Sometimes Kostyan was able to release the next unlucky newborn into the garden, using a towel to move him closer to a wide open window. But he didn't visit the summer home regularly enough to be able to save all of them.

He also is slamming against the glass like the imprisoned bees, he can see the flowers and the trees clearly beyond it, but he will die, unable to ever reach them. Maybe he, like those bumblebees, was born into the wrong world? Instead of a fragrant garden, he landed in a stuffy little room? . . .

Having returned to the apartment, he dials his own cell phone number using the landline. Hears beeps on the other end. A shining of hope. It means the driver is not a thief. A thief would have turned it off right away. He waits one minute, at least. No one answers . . . a thief, after all . . . Kostyan almost hangs up, but then hears the familiar voice of the Armenian patriot:

—Was it you who forgot your phone with me?

—Yes . . . me . . . how great . . .

—Come out, I'll drive up.

Kostyan almost feels like flying. His dark thoughts are blown away, as if by wind. Another miracle! A second one today! He has never before lost a phone and gained it back in such a short time period. Grabbing the first thing he can find—a bottle of vodka—Kostyan hurries back into the street. Not waiting for the elevator, runs down the stairs. What if the Armenian doesn't wait for him, changes his mind and drives away.

After all, his world is still beautiful! People are kind! Again, he wants to live, wants a child . . . The Ford is already waiting for him.

—No need, no need, the Armenian declines the vodka gift.

—Take it. I drink this kind myself. Kostyan puts the bottle on the seat. —Happy New Year!

— — —

The display lights up with several unanswered calls from friends. Kostyan makes a final decision for himself: *No abortion, we're going to have a baby. Any child can be raised into a decent human being, after all, my genes and Katya's are not the worst. Father's cousin is a convict, it's true, and from Katya's mother's side not everything is clear—she's from an orphanage. But that's okay, we're not monsters, we are charismatic, intelligent people . . .*

At home, a joyful Katya throws herself at Kostyan:

—It started!

—What started?

—My period started! Yay! She hugs him, kisses him, twirls around. Kostyan stands in the hallway, awkwardly returning her affections.

—Sit down, rest. I'll start cooking!

—Everyone'll be here soon . . . chirps Katya, bouncing from happiness. —Oh, I totally forgot! I bought a little present for you! A symbolic one for now. Here! Katya pushes into Kostyan's hands something gray, soft. A rat. A souvenir-toy. A gray soft belly, gray feet, a long tail. The familiar eye beads look out intently. Katya kisses Kostyan and rushes to the kitchen.

Kostyan drops himself into an armchair. *We-e-ll . . . And I had already gotten excited . . . Thought to call her Valentina, if she turned out to be a girl . . .*

THE KILLER AND HIS LITTLE FRIEND

ZAKHAR PRILEPIN
Translated by Svetlana Ilinskaya and Douglas Robinson

THE THREE OF US reinforcements, Special Forces MPs, were standing on the highway to the capital: Seryoga, whose nickname was Primate, his friend Gnome, and, of course, me.

Primate had recently bought a pound of bullets from the boys and took along a handful with him now on every shift, like sunflower seeds. Jammed one in the breech and looked for something to shoot.

Sometime around 3:00 AM, when the traffic thinned out, Primate noticed a stray dog running across the road, whistled at it. The mutt gave him a distrustful look but then tried to sidle up to us, this group of humans who smelled of iron and evil, and of course immediately took a round in her side.

The dog didn't die at once, but went on squealing long enough to wake half the creatures of the forest.

The checkpoint was at the tree line.

I spat out my cigarette, sighed, and went to pour myself some tea.

I bet he'll finish her off with a head shot, I thought, tensing against the report—although I have been present at shootings, I don't know, ten thousand times probably. I flinched this time too, as the dog fell quiet.

I wasn't angry at Primate, and didn't feel sorry for the dog. So he killed it, so what. A guy likes to shoot, big deal.

"I wish somebody'd start a revolution," Primate said at some point.

"Are you serious?" I started happily. I wanted a revolution too.

"Why not? I could shoot as much as I wanted," he said. A second later I realized who exactly he wanted to shoot at.

I didn't get especially upset then either. As a matter of fact I liked Primate. Psychopaths posing as human beings are repellent. Primate was open and sincere in his passion. He didn't see anything wrong with his personal predilections. And anyway, he seemed like a good soldier. I sometimes think that soldiers should be like this, like Primate. Anybody else becomes completely unfit sooner or later.

Besides, his sense of humor was refreshing and good-natured. To be honest, this is the only thing I find attractive in men: the capability to be courageous and funny. Other talents don't do much for me.

Primate didn't take offense at his nickname, usually, especially after I explained to him that primates were originally thought to include human beings, apes, and Australian sloths. Primate himself had his own take: he insisted that all the other guys in the detachment had evolved from him.

"I'm your ancestor, tailless apes," Primate would say and laugh infectiously.

Gnome jokingly posed as Primate's father, though he was a good three times smaller.

Primate weighed maybe a hundred and twenty kilos, beat all our soldiers in arm wrestling; I personally didn't even dare compete with him. During the hand-to-hand combat training sessions he broke one soldier's rib and damaged something in the next guy's head in the first seconds of the fight.

Before Gnome joined the detachment, Primate didn't mix with that many people: he pumped his iron and guffawed, equally unfriendly with everybody.

But he and Gnome hit it off.

Gnome was the smallest guy in the detachment and why in the world they let him join up I never understood. We had several short guys, each one of them worth three muscleheads. But Gnome really was gnomelike. He had thin little arms and a birdhouse rib cage.

I tried not to stare when he arrived among us. At least I didn't fixate on him or anything. And Gnome didn't seem to give a shit whether anyone was looking. Maybe he was just careful to seem not to care. But then one day we were standing around smoking and got to talking, and it turned out Gnome's wife had recently left him. She was from an orphanage and couldn't stay put anywhere for very long, even in her marriage. But she left their six-year-old girl behind, and that's how they'd been living, father and daughter together. Fortunately, Gnome's mother lived next door and stopped by to feed the little one when her son went off to work.

Gnome didn't seem to be either crushed by all this or proud of it. He pulled extra hard on his cigarette, as if trying to suck it dead with one drag. He couldn't, of course. But it only took a few before he was grinding it under his heel.

I felt for the guy. And then watched the two of them with unflagging interest, Primate and Gnome: they chowed down together, lit up together, did everything but take a leak together. Pretty soon they were sneaking out of the barracks to pick up easy girls together, sometimes one girl for them both, other times a whole car full, squealing and laughing, impossible to count, never mind that Primate had a stout young wife waiting for him at home.

Despite his nickname, Primate had a big white hairless face, slightly bloated. When he smiled, though, he came into his own: his nose became more prominent, his eyes glittered attentively, his Adam's apple stuck out, his mouth was suddenly full of big yellow teeth that gleamed stubbornly.

Gnome didn't have a beard either, just this thin officer's mustache. Everything about his face was tiny, like some strange moustachioed doll. And when Gnome laughed, you couldn't make out his features at all. They immediately twisted all up, his eyes disappeared somewhere, and his mouth fidgeted, flashing tiny teeth.

Gnome didn't act as bloodthirsty as Primate. Everything about him said that he wasn't going to kill anyone himself. He just watched with interest, as if walking around and around a thing, contemplating it from all sides, as his big friend entertained himself.

I heard their agitated voices outside and left the checkpoint.

"Finished off the dog?" I asked.

"The bitch," Primate said with a satisfied smile.

He took out his gun as if it were itching, flipped off the safety, aimed point-blank at the wooden porch column, thick as a good-sized birch tree, and fired again.

"Look," he said, inspecting the column, "didn't go through. Gnome, stand on the other side, lemme try again."

"Put your hand there, try it on yourself," laughed Gnome, flashing his little teeth.

Primate put his hand on the wood and in an instant, before I could say anything in superstitious horror, fired once more, his gun right up against his huge paw. I didn't see if his hand jerked at the moment of the gunshot or not, because I flinched. When I opened my eyes, Primate was slowly taking his hand off the column and studying it closely.

It was white and clean.

In the morning Primate's wife found us at the base. Her face was gentle, damp, and sleepy, like a flower after a hard rain. She'd been crying a lot and hadn't slept much.

"Where have you been?" she asked, firing the stupid question at him, a warning shot from close range. They looked good together, big and leggy. Both of them built for plowing.

"Fishing, can't you see?" he chuckled, and slapped his holster.

His wife burst into tears again and, noticing Gnome, cried out:

"And he's here! It's all his fault!"

Gnome walked round the young woman with his face so tight it became even smaller. His head appeared to shrink to about the size of Primate's fist.

"What are you, nuts?" Primate asked indifferently. "What don't you like? That I go to work?"

"And you're going to Chechnya, too, you bastard," the wife said, ignoring his question.

Primate shrugged his shoulders and went to return his gun.

"You should say something to him!" she said to me.

"Like what?"

She was jealous, of course, that was clear, and not without reason. She didn't even believe that he was going to work. She assumed it was about carousing with girls, but, still, she made it about Chechnya. I answered her question with a question because, you know, what did Chechnya have to do with anything?

Primate's wife waved her arm with disgust, as if to knock my words out of the air, and walked away. Crossed the road slowly, without paying any attention to the cars, and stopped at the fence to the park with her back to the base. She stood and swayed a bit.

"She's waiting for him," I thought with some satisfaction, "but wants him to come to her first. Good woman."

Having returned his gun, Primate stood smoking for a while with Gnome, squinting at his wife's back. They laughed, remembered the shot bitch again, spat out their cigarette butts and ground them carefully with their shoes, lit up again, and finally parted.

Primate came up to his wife and stroked her back.

She said something to him, must have been something moderately unfriendly, and walked along the path without looking back. Primate followed her without hurrying much.

"They'll make up in about fifty meters," I decided. I was watching them out the window.

A minute later, Primate caught up with her again and put his arm around her shoulders. She didn't shake it off. Subtly her hips swayed a bit more, brushing against Primate with each step.

"They'll arrive home and ... everything will get better at once," I thought romantically, a little aroused at the sight of these two animals with their ancient scents.

Somehow I knew that Primate was filled with a rich male passion, stronger than anyone's. There was as much seed in him as there was the desire to shed someone's blood. Spill the one and spill the other and everything's fine, everything's in its place.

The first person killed was Primate's doing too.

He kept yearning all week: the blood wasn't coming his way. He kept scanning the Chechen scenery greedily—tempestuous wrecks, empty and obscure houses—every minute waiting with stern hope for a gunshot. Nobody shot at him. Primate was unhappy and irritated at almost everybody in the detachment.

Except Gnome, of course. When the two of them hung out, Primate's face warmed and clarified.

Our detachment practically prayed for bad luck to pass us by. Primate would always blow up at the guys:

"What, you want to come to the war and not see war?"

"What, you want to take a dirt nap?" they asked him.

"What the fuck difference does it make where I take my nap?" Primate answered with disgust.

There were constant shootings on nearby streets. Every day someone from neighboring Special Forces detachments would get killed, sometimes almost a whole detachment of drunken draftees was mowed down in a horrible absurd firefight. Only we were going around Grozny as if under a spell: our crew was responsible mostly for convoy and sometimes neighborhood sweeps.

As we rode around town in a beat-up pickup truck following not completely clear orders—go here, go there, go to some godforsaken place to take an assignment or a package or a case of cognac from this major to that full-bird colonel—Primate would demand that we turn off onto some neighboring street where the iron was zipping and crashing.

"What the fuck would we want to do that for?" I would ask.

"What if our boys are getting shot up there?" Primate curled his lip.

"Nobody's getting shot up there," I said, then added after a pause: "If they call us, we'll go." We weren't called, of course.

But on the third day of the third week during our morning sweep through the suburbs we finally picked up three nervous young guys, completely unarmed, in the attic of a five-story building. We'd gotten a tip about some shots fired from the attic at the nearest commandant's office.

"And why are you sleeping there?" the commander asked them.

"Our house was bombed. We've got nowhere to sleep," one of them answered.

At this point the commander ripped open one guy's sweater, and the bruise on his shoulder, the kind a rifle's kick might make, told its story.

But we didn't find any ammunition in the attic.

"Passports?"

"Burned in the fire, when we were bombed, yes!" The Chechens wouldn't crack.

"Well, they'll figure this out in the commandant's office," the commander nodded.

"Take them far away from each other so they won't tell each other anything," he added, "or they'll plan their answers."

Our camouflaged guys went into neighboring entrances and worked the building. From outside you could hear the doors flying off their hinges. When nobody answered, they battered down the doors. The three young guys were taken aside. Primate and Gnome remained standing by one of them.

To be on the safe side I walked three soldiers over to stand watch by two lines of little storage compartments. God save us from any dirty Chechen with a good eye and an itchy trigger finger crashing our party by climbing out of one of those little storage sheds.

Coming back, I lit a cigarette and it hit me: all of a sudden I remembered Primate's heavy blink when he took his prisoner by the collar, saying, "Let's go," and hauling him far from the building where the sweep was taking place. He took him to a small open space recently converted into a dump.

I hurried, and when I got behind the storage compartments, I saw Primate standing with his back to me and Gnome's ominous smile.

"Run!" Primate told the prisoner quietly but clearly, "or they'll shoot you. I'll tell them that you escaped. Run!"

"Stop!" I shouted, almost suffocating with horror.

My shout was what pushed the Chechen to run. He raced across the open space, fell down at once, got caught in some wire, stood again, made it a few steps more, and took a big fat bullet in the back of his head.

Primate turned to me. He had his gun in his hand.

I was quiet. There was nothing to say.

A commander sprinted up to us a minute later, a few of our meatheads trailing after him.

"What happened?" he asked, checking if any of our guys were hurt or down.

"While attempting to escape . . ." Primate began.

"Silence!" the commander said and stared into Primate's eyes for a second.

"You really are a primate, aren't you." He spat.

I remembered the damp spring night we readied for Chechnya. Receiving our guns, attaching underbarrel grenade launchers, wrapping clips with duct tape, packing our rucksacks, tightening field vests, smoking a lot, and laughing.

Primate's wife came in around 4:00 or 5:00 AM and stood there in the middle of the hall with black eyes.

As soon as he spotted her, Gnome disappeared into the locker room, sat there quiet and looking a bit down.

Primate came up to his wife. They stood there staring at each other without saying anything.

Even the wildest guys for some reason got quiet as they walked by.

I walked by quietly too. The woman saw me and nodded. All of a sudden I noticed that she was pregnant, not too far along but confidently and seriously pregnant, not someone likely to get rid of it.

Primate's face was calm and distant as if he were already hunting for prey in the mountains, had already flown across half of black-soiled Russia. Then he suddenly went down on one knee and pressed his ear to the swollen belly. Don't know what he heard there, but I remember the moment very well: the hall full of armed people, black iron and dark obscenities, and in the middle of all this, under a yellow lamp, a pale man kneeling with his ear to the hidden fruit.

"Primate, you ape," I thought, approaching the corpse, the back of whose head looked as if a big chunk had been bitten off.

Nobody said anything.

When they told us we were being shipped home, our little business trip became an excuse to get shitfaced. In the midst of the party the light went off in the barracks and Gnome made everybody laugh by chirping in this high and surprisingly sincere voice:

"I'm blind! I've gone blind!"

"Father, what's the matter?" Primate said.

"Son, is that you?" Gnome said. "Carry me out to the light, son. Away from the laughter of these jerks, to the last sun."

And then the light came on and everybody saw Primate carrying Gnome in his arms.

Later we remembered this story without laughing.

With only two days left in country, Primate and Gnome were part of a small group sent out to rescue a field commander who'd been captured, God knows how, from a checkpoint somewhere in the piedmont wilderness. They were dispatched on a helicopter with a couple of Special Forces guys from Lower Tagil or Upper Ufaley.

When they found the field commander, Primate loaded him into the helicopter personally. His face had been beaten in offhandedly with a boot and a club, but he was alive. Prolonging the game a little, the Special Forces guys—don't remember what city they were from—stood next to the helicopter with their guns pointing in different directions. They liked to pose: they were sure that nobody would shoot them down. Pretty common feeling at the end of a mission. Gnome stood there close by, flashing his little teeth.

That's when the guys from Lower Tagil or Upper Ufaley were felled by two single shots—boom, boom, down they went. Gnome dug into the grass like a little animal, and, under heavy fire, Primate shouted something at him, but he didn't reply. Primate himself had already climbed inside the helicopter by then, and the chopper was spinning its blades wildly in hopes of getting the fuck out of there as quickly as possible.

Primate jumped out into the bright light, sweating, his helmet off, and without even bending down squeezed off a round at whoever was shooting, then grabbed both of the wounded guys at the same time and threw them over his shoulders, took them to where the field commander lay fidgeting with his legs tied and his heavy eyelashes stuck together in blood like a butterfly unable to flap its wings.

Next Primate ran to get Gnome, pulled him from the grass, and carried him in his arms to the chopper.

Gnome had not a single scratch on him. While the chopper was taking off, he was sensing with his eyes closed where exactly in his body he'd been hit, but not a single part of him felt pain. Then Gnome opened his happy mouth to tell Primate about it.

Primate sat silently across from him in a black puddle, missing one eye. Later it was found that the second bullet had entered his leg, and the third right under his armpit where the armor didn't protect his white body.

A handful of bullets had also hit the armor and several of Primate's internal organs must have burst from the impact, but no one considered those organs: it was enough for Primate to have been rescuing everyone with a hot piece of lead in his eye socket .

The guys from either Lower Tagil or Upper Ufaley both survived, and Gnome was put forward for a decoration.

And so we returned home with Primate in a big zinc box.

His wife met the coffin with a furious face and banged the lid with her hands so hard that Primate must have blinked open that one eye he had left.

At the funeral she stood silently, not shedding a single tear, and when it was time to throw dirt into the grave she froze stiff with a red clod clasped in her fist. The others waited for her, but then began tossing their own clods. The dirt scattering over the coffin.

Gnome didn't even cry, but somehow whimpered, and his shoulders were jumping and his chest still looked like a pathetic birdhouse, as if someone was cooing and flapping quiet wings inside it.

Primate's wife kept clasping that dirt in her hand so hard that it squeezed through her fingers, leaving her palm sticky.

She even came to the wake with this dirty palm.

First we were drinking silently, then started talking as usual. I was still looking at Primate's wife, her petrified forehead and hardened lips. Couldn't help myself, came up to her and sat by her side.

"How are you?" I nodded at her stomach.

She didn't answer. Then unexpectedly stroked my hand.

"You know," she said, "he gave me a bad disease. When I was already pregnant. It was impossible to take care of it the right way, and it was impossible to stay diseased. But when he got killed, that very same day it went away. I went to the doctor's to check, and nothing, as if there had never been anything."

A few months later, while his widow was at the women's clinic, Primate's house was robbed. All the money was taken, a lot of it, the death benefits she'd received, and somebody had taken the car keys and driven the car right out of the garage.

The widow called me three days after the incident, asked me to come see her.

"Any news?" I asked when I got there.

She shrugged.

"I have . . . a suspicion," she said, stroking her huge stomach. "Let's go see this one woman, okay? She's a witch. She hasn't received anyone for a long time, says that her truth brings bad luck. But she owes my father, and that's why she's meeting with me."

I snorted a little: what next, witches, for God's sake. But we went there anyway. You can't say no to a widow.

The door was opened by a friendly and lucid woman, not old at all, and not dressed in black, and with no head scarf. Not at all what I had imagined: smiling, white teeth, in a sundress, beautiful.

"Would you like some tea?" she offered.

"We would," I said.

We sat down at the table, each of us took a chocolate off the plate, the tea was hot and fragrant, in potbellied cups.

"Looking for someone?" asked the witch.

"My house was robbed," the widow answered, "and everything was done so well that it must've been somebody we know. They didn't rummage around for anything. They knew where everything was."

The witch nodded.

"I've brought a picture," the widow said.

She took a photo out of her purse, and I remembered that nice Chechen day, when we were drinking and then the light went out, and then turned back on again, and we took this picture, everybody already drunk, the bunch of us, just barely squeezing into the picture, wide-shouldered as horses.

"This one robbed you," the witch said simply, and her light beautiful nail touched Gnome's face.

"See what he's like?" she added after a moment of silence. "He positioned himself so that he would seem taller than the rest. Look. He's small, right? But you can't tell here that he's small at all. Looks bigger than your husband, widow. Is he your husband?" She pointed at Primate. "He's already dead. But his children will be good. White. You have twins."

I was sitting there stunned, and the teaspoon even trembled in my hand.

Gnome had quit the detachment three months ago, and nobody had seen him since.

"Let's go to him!" I almost screamed when we got outside, trembling with fury. I was probably ready to kill him.

The widow nodded indifferently.

Gnome's little house was in the suburbs. We got there quickly and found the windows shuttered and a lock on the door, the heavy kind that people only use when they're leaving for good.

We went and talked to the neighbors, and they confirmed it: yes, he had left. Everybody had left: the mother, the daughter, and himself.

We got into the car, me hyped-up and angry, the widow calm and quiet.

"We should report it," I stormed, lighting up a cigarette and looking at the house with such hatred, like I was contemplating burning it down. "They'll find this bastard and lock him up."

"No," the widow said.

"What do you mean, no?" I choked.

"I can't. He was my Seryozhka's friend. I won't."

I started the car. We drove. The widow rode along smiling, with her hands on her huge belly.

ONE YEAR IN PARADISE

Natalya Klyuchareva
Translated by Mariya Gusev

MAY 9. I've asked to borrow a TV from a neighbor. He put on an *understanding* face, but luckily we managed without any questions. A week ago my mother-in-law came to pick up her things. Because of this, the whole building now knows that my wife has left me.

Running into me on the staircase, all women, including the four-year-old Marusya, whom I used to count among my friends, maintain a meaningful silence and turn away, and all men—as if on cue—make an *understanding* face.

But I needed a TV not because I was dying of melancholy, as my neighbor had, of course, assumed. Even though I am truly dying. Still, the last thing I'd look to for a cure would be television programming.

It's just that May 9 is the only day each year when I watch television. Films about war. They don't let me delude myself. Don't let me take everything, which we usually occupy ourselves with, for actual life.

The thing is, it's not about war itself. I'm a normal person, and mass killings elicit no delight from me. I use these movies, no matter what they are—naïve, full of pathos, sentimental, full of propaganda—to quench my thirst for the real. Everything in them is serious. "For reals," as Marusya would say.

Also, war movies always make me ashamed. In front of these kids (younger than me) who went to their deaths with no faith in their future lives, with only the hope that their grandchildren would be happy, I'm ashamed of the unhappiness I feel because of things that are, in essence, unimportant.

After I finished *Ascent* I couldn't take any more and walked down to the store. Even though I'd promised myself not to drink—at the very least, for now—I came back with two bottles under my arm. The neighbor, who was smoking on the stoop, followed me with an *understanding* gaze.

But during the whole evening I only thought about her once. Remembered her screaming: "If you like all of this military trash, you should sign up for some contract work in the army!" She believed I was nostalgic for gunfire, trench fleas, and hand-to-hand combat.

Drank, watched *A Ballad about a Soldier*, thought about my grandfather, who was declared missing near Smolensk. I only know about him from the stories I've heard from my grandma, who despised him. She was in love with a different man her whole life and married my grandfather out of spite after she had a fight with that one. But war evened everything out: neither of them came home.

Grandpa loved her like crazy. Although sometimes he couldn't take it. And without saying a word would go into the woods for a few days. And that's how he perished: went into the woods on a surveillance mission, and no one has seen him since. Neither dead nor alive.

This is also my story. To the point. Just without the war.

Suddenly, I wanted to visit those woods. And since I was already sufficiently drunk, I decided not to think about it for too long and simply returned the television to my neighbor, slammed the door shut, and walked toward the train station.

The whole way there I drank, toasted the telephone poles, talked to my grandfather, and yelled, "One victory is all we need today." In other words, I acted silly and stupid, like I always do. On the train, I passed out right away. And in the morning, my curiosity rising, I saw the word *Smolensk* through the window on the gray terminal wall.

Decided to walk around the city. Kremlin and poured-concrete Kruschev-era apartments, same as everywhere. Came across a bus terminal. Got onto the first bus I saw without even asking where it was going. The back of the bus smelled like diesel, it was stuffy,

and on each bump my insides jumped into my throat. About forty
minutes later I was completely shaken up and nauseated. I asked the
driver to stop.

Walked through a field for a long time; it was full of dandelions.
The sky looked like a battle mural. The clouds were crowding each
other, attacking, intercepting. I watched until my neck got stiff.
There is no sky in the city, after all.

Ended up in some village. Sat down to rest. Lit a smoke in the
sun's warmth. A man looked at me from a leaning house. And, of
course, came over to bum a light, even though a lighter was poking
out of his chest pocket.

I asked what the name of the village was. The man said, "Paradise"
and spit into the bushes. I decided that he was making a joke, and
asked again.

The man suddenly lost it. Ran into the house, immediately
jumped back out, and stuck a pile of notarized papers in my face. In
the spot where his black finger furiously pointed, it said: "Smolensk
Borough, Gryazev District, Village Paradise."

—Cool, I said. —You live in Paradise.

—Yep, he spit again. —It doesn't get any cooler than this!

I decided not to argue, finished my cigarette, and got up to go.

—Hey, the nervous man called to me. —Want a house on the
very edge of Paradise?

—I don't understand.

—This house there.

—This house what?

—What in the butt! Buy it, I'm telling you. It's a worthwhile dig.
It will stand for another hundred years.

—How much? I asked, partially from curiosity, and partially leery
of angering him by declining too fast.

—Just a box of fuel.

While I was trying to figure out what he was talking about, the
man dragged me inside, choppily and incoherently explaining something about the fireplace, the basement, and a rake. On the wall hung
a big map of the Russian Federation.

—Left over from the teach. She ran off to the city, when the
school was closed. My sis, damn her!

—I think I will be going, I said. At this point I didn't know how to get away from him.

—You lost your mind? It's a seven-kilometer schlep! We'll get there on my buttshaker faster than a fly!

I thought he was offering to give me a lift to the highway. And only after some incoherent snippets of conversation as his Zaporozhets, roaring like a fighter jet, tore out onto the intercountry road, did I finally gather that we were driving to officiate the purchase of my house. This did not fit into my plans in any way.

—Listen, man, what is your name? Lyokha? You know what, Lyokha, why don't I just give you some money for booze? Let's not get into this production with documents, all right?

Immediately I was swept away by a deluge of irreplicable cursing, which basically came down to how honest and businesslike he had been with me, and how I was taking him for a lush and a beggar. At full speed, Lyokha spun the steering wheel wildly after each word. Probably for extra expressiveness.

At first I lost my cool. I got scared that I was going to, so stupidly and unglamorously, die on the same soil where my grandfather fell to a courageous death. And then I became ashamed. I had indeed offended him.

—All right, don't storm, I screamed to Lyokha. —I was just testing you. Because who knows.

This completely nonsensical phrase suddenly had an effect. Lyokha calmed down and stopped talking. The car continued skidding in all directions, and I suddenly saw that he was simply navigating around the potholes rather than trying to kill me. Fear has big eyes.

In the city center of Gryazevo we loudly slowed down next to a two-story merchant's home. On the doors of this operation there hung a large lock. All of a sudden, I had hope of absolution. But this was not to be. Lyokha, cursing continuously, ran to somewhere inside the yard and, before I could descend the stairs, came back escorted by a pudgy functionary with small violet curls.

The woman silently looked me up and down. Then opened the lock, continuing to ogle me, then began lumbering up a steep wooden staircase to the second floor. Even while walking up, she managed to keep looking back at me. I was worried that she was going to twist her neck.

Inside the office Lyokha began an incomprehensible social inter-action with the functionary, whom he called "Tanyuha-tart'uha" in his own hopped-up language.

—Are you not yet tired of this monstrosity? He seemed to be referring to her husband or cohabitant.

—What could I possibly do with him? Tanyuha flashed her gold tooth in a coquettish way while pulling the stamp out of the drawer.

—Just stick him into your vegetable patch instead of the scare-crow! Lyokha, I was beginning to suspect, had a man's interest toward this paper pusher. But from the subsequent conversation I gathered that Tanyuha's "monstrosity" was his own blood son.

After a half hour, I descended from the office porch holding the ownership documents to a house in Village Paradise. Lyokha, having received his eight hundred rubles, quickly said good-bye, jumped into his fighter jet, and promptly sped away toward the store.

I got on the bus going toward Smolensk and the whole way there thought about how my wife was right to leave me. I'm not a person, just a complete idiot. Dashing God knows where while drunk, buy-ing a house . . . What silliness!

— — —

On the first day of my vacation, I had a strange dream. As if I'm walking, tripping over myself, across a gray field. Dry prickles cling-ing to a military overcoat, something I've never worn in my life. In the forest's clearing I meet another soldier. I recognize him as my grandfather. But for some reason, I'm not supposed to tell him who I am. He asks me for a smoke. We sit down in the hills, warmed by the sun. Grandfather, laughing, tells me that the Germans fired two rounds directly at him:

—My chest is like a sieve! As if it matters! Everything just con-tinues!

He's covered in blood. I can see that he's dead, but for some rea-son, he doesn't understand this. And I don't know how to explain it to him. And whether or not I should explain it to him.

—Let's go to paradise! he suddenly suggests. —Drink our fill of fresh milk!

We go through the small forest and walk out to a wooden house. Grandpa disappears somewhere. I peer into the window, see the map of Russia on the wall—and remember. And become terribly joyous, as if some torturous secret has just been solved. And feel—in my sleep—a huge relief and even possibly happiness.

In the morning, I took from the crawl space Grandpa's ancient backpack, in which tools were stored. Cleaned it up a little and began loading it with books. Without them, I couldn't imagine a life, even in Paradise. The backpack turned out to be terribly heavy. I struggled to get it onto my shoulders and set out for the train station.

As I walked, I imagined that I wasn't leaving for a month but forever. Just like that, without saying a word to anyone, with a bag of books. These thoughts made me feel joyful and light. A long-forgotten feeling.

Back in Paradise, I was again convinced of my incurable impracticality. Of course instead of books, I should have brought kitchenware, some type of grain, salt. The house contained nothing, not even matches. And I had lost my lighter somewhere.

So I had to visit the neighbors. The first living being I met in Paradise was a large smoky cat on the stoop of the house across the way. Where there are animals, there are people, I concluded, and, stepping over the cat, which didn't even move, I knocked. There was no answer.

I entered. In the middle of the room there sat a fallen ceiling support beam. Grass grew through holes in the floor. There was the stuffy smell of a dwelling that has not been lived in for a long time, something rotten and moist. On the buckling wallpaper hung a reproduction of Raphael's *Madonna*, faded nearly into oblivion. This was the only remaining evidence of any human presence.

Checked out several more houses; the scene was the same everywhere. The only difference was the degree of decrepitude. So when I saw two little old women, who were digging in a garden, I was as happy to see them as if they were family.

Toma and Lucia—they insisted that I should address them exactly like this—were sisters. They talked nonstop and often uttered whole phrases in chorus. Each time this happened they would grow amazed and triumphant, as if something unbelievable was happening.

After a half hour, I knew the entire history of Paradise. The cat on the stoop—his name is Vasily. His owners left several years ago, but he didn't want to go—climbed out of the basket in which he was being transported and came back. Keeps living like this in the empty house.

Toma and Lucia were born here. In their youth, they were accepted to a technical college in Smolensk and so they moved to the city. They still had a two-bedroom apartment there. They came to Paradise for the summer. In winter it was too hard for them in the country.

—And you will of course live here permanently? asked one of the sisters.

—Yes, I answered suddenly, surprising myself.

—Oh, how great, it's just fantastic! exclaimed Toma and Lucia in unison and laughed joyfully. —You can take care of our house. Otherwise, each winter Cherenok breaks into it; it's impossible to leave anything here. We have to bring everything to the city with us. But he, that devil, will always find something to steal. And if he doesn't, he'll just break the windows and take a dump in the middle of the room, like a mischievous dog. He's some punk from Gryazevo. He finished his prison term and now doesn't know what to do with himself, odd thing!

The sisters fed me boiled potatoes and generously gifted me various housewares. I promised to till them a row for planting garlic the next day. After I returned to the house, I discovered that Russia had lost the Far East. The map was disintegrating and falling apart at the creases.

And so it began like this. I would help the sisters with their garden. Every once in a while walk to Gryazevo for groceries. Toma and Lucia fed me, took care of me, gave me advice, and every evening told me a story about Kostya.

—Oh, our Kostya was such a tall stately hunk! one of them would begin, folding her hands on her apron endearingly.

—A smoking brunet! picked up the other. —The exact likeness of Lev Frichinsky!

—What are you saying! Yevgeniy Urbansky! the first would take offense.

—Gerard Philippe! the sisters made up instantly and continued.
—Oh, no one else could dance the waltz like our Kostya!

—He was the most enviable partner!

—But he only asked us to dance! Alternating: Lucia, Toma, Lucia, Toma . . .

—He was just crazy about us!

—And he couldn't make up his mind!

—And then he got reprimanded at the Party meeting!

—They told him that love between three people is bourgeois excess!

—He looked so upset!

—He came over and said: *I love the two of you equally!*

—Yes! *And I'm proposing to both of you!*

—*And which one shall marry me is up to you, sisters!*

—We cried all night long!

—And in the morning, we both declined him!

—Because we also loved him equally!

—And we also could not make a choice.

— — —

I walked around the neighboring forests. Gazed into the large puddles, where black moss stood. Jumped over the flooded passages. Slipped on wet roots. Watched, for a long time, throwing my head back, the tips of the birch trees bowing in the faraway sky. And I myself began to waver to their rhythm, becoming a tree.

Then I would scramble onto the road that led to Paradise, completely drunk—from the air, the scent of the forest, the birch seesaw. I walked and I sang, scaring away the crows:

"*Our Kostya, it seems, is in love!* screamed the dockhands at the port . . ."

A week later, I ran into two more inhabitants of Paradise. At first I noticed a goat. She was looking at me intensely from the tall grass. On a nearby log sat a fierce old woman in a puffy coat and *valenki*.

As opposed to the curious goat, she didn't even turn around. I came over and greeted her.

—*Beh-eh-eh!* replied the goat. She was much more friendly than her owner.

—What are you called? I asked.

—Where is he intending to call us to? the old lady suddenly spoke angrily to the goat. —To teatime with those city fufus? I've already said I won't go! No business of yours! You've flattened all my grass! Shoo, get away from here!

The goat lowered her horned head and walked toward me aggressively.

In the evening, I asked the sisters about the old lady.

—Oh, that's Auntie Montie! Toma and Lucia burst into giggles, just like little girls.

—She's a savage!

—Is not friendly with anybody!

—Except for her goat!

— — —

A month passed. Kamchatka quietly fell off the map. My vacation time was about to end. A decision had ripened inside of me a long time ago. Probably it was there from the very beginning. Considering how, on my way to the train station, I had dreamed of never returning to the city and, having arrived in Paradise, on my very first day, had declared to the sisters that I was here to stay . . .

And so all that I could do was take everything as an already committed-to eventuality. Because in secret, I'd thought about something like this for a long time. About an escape. About a different life, where everything is for real. But this seemed impossible. And consciously, I would have never had the courage for such a step. Everything had happened on its own. Without any action on my part. All that was required from me was to agree, and not to resist my fate.

However, a day before I was supposed to return to work I loaded my books into grandfather's backpack—books that I hadn't touched once—swept the floor, closed and latched the window shutters, and began walking toward the highway. I didn't say anything to Toma and Lucia. And they were busy with weeding and did not notice me.

I dragged my feet, telling myself that the backpack with the books was too heavy and so I could not walk any faster. I even sat down on a tree stump and had a smoke, even though I didn't at all want one. And when, having walked up the last hill, I saw the bus leaving the terminal, for some reason I even put on a whole performance: ran after it, waved my hands (I of course knew that the driver couldn't see me), and then—as if frustrated down to my heart—threw the backpack with the books into the dust, stamped my foot.

Only then did I burst into laughter. And I couldn't stop for about ten minutes. My stomach even started hurting, and my jaw tightened. The last time I had laughed like this was in sixth grade. I returned to the village the back way, through the vegetable patches, so I wouldn't have to explain anything to anybody.

— — —

Once, in the woods, I tripped over an old soldier's helmet. At its bottom pooled rainwater, in which swam the sky and a black last-year's leaf. Carefully, I untangled the grass, dug out the earth from around the helmet with my hands, and freed it. Immediately, water flowed out all over me. The helmet had been shot through in two places.

The soldier who had worn it must have been lying somewhere near. I turned over the whole clearing. Without result. I only gathered a handful of spent ammo shells. I decided to return the next day with a shovel and begin my search for real.

But when I went back, the clearing had disappeared as if it was wiped away. Together with the crooked tree stump and the anthills. I wandered around the forest for a whole week, falling into small swamps, bursting through the undergrowth, and cursing my city-dweller's uselessness with the worst language I could muster.

Having lost hope of finding the place where the soldier had perished, I decided to at least bury the helmet and shells, which I had brought with me. Behind the settlement line of Paradise, on a sunny half hill, there was an old cemetery without a fence, open completely to the surrounding fields.

Toma and Lucia put a bouquet of field bluebells on the small bump, which looked like a newborn's grave, and had a small cry while I nailed a piece of crooked plywood to a pole that read: *Unknown soldier, year 1941.* In vain, I tried to get away from thoughts of my grandfather, repeating to myself that life is not a sentimental novel, and coincidences like these just cannot exist.

The next morning I, for some reason, headed to the cemetery again. And stopped in awe. In front of our handmade burial had grown a strong wooden cross, as tall as myself. I turned around and ran back to Paradise as fast as I could.

—It's the mute carpenter from Gryazevo. The sisters' words— after they'd had their fill of laughter at my mystical terror—calmed me down. —He sells coffins. And the crosses—he has this quirk, likes to put them everywhere. Who knows why?

Soon after, I saw the carpenter himself. Wearing camouflage, with a gray prophet's beard covering his entire chest. He was dragging, heaved onto his shoulder, another cross. For a moment I wanted to catch up to him and help. But for some reason I didn't move an inch. It seemed that he didn't notice me. When I came home I was in a bad mood. In the evening, a piece of Taymir fell off the map.

— — —

The freeze began. In the morning, the grass in tire tracks and ditches glistened with ice. I burned summer's trash in the sisters' garden while Toma and Lucia, with four hands, cooked apple preserves in the laundry tub and chatted. The magpies on the fence harmonized with them.

On the last evening before their departure to the city they told me the story of how once, a long time ago—even before they went off to school—a fighter plane crashed in the field behind Paradise. And they were in such a rush to see it that they both fell into the same ditch. And Toma broke her right arm, and Lucia, her left.

The sisters walked to the bus stop with almost no luggage. All of their belongings, all of the priceless plates, forks, and pots were left as my responsibility. Of course I had promised to keep their little house safe from the Gryazevo punks.

Toma rolled a cart with the squash while Lucia carried a huge bouquet of golden heliopsis. They waved to me for a long time from the bus window. I stood on the side of the road, in clouds of dust, and felt suddenly orphaned.

That day, Auntie Montie spoke to me for the first time. She angrily put a one-liter jar of goat's milk on the table, suspiciously eyed the pile of books in the corner, petted the cold stove, and said, in a hoarse, rusty voice:

—So they've rolled away, have they, your fashionista chatterboxes? And they've left the rowan berries to the jackdaws, I see? Why don't you go shake them down, don't let a good thing go to waste. I will, if the day is right, churn up some rowan-berry liqueur, and here Auntie Montie, suddenly agile, winked and clicked her tongue. —My liqueur puts your city thingamajigs to shame—it will get you down to your bones!

I gathered the red berries. Chopped some wood for the winter for Auntie Montie and myself. Tried to glue Yakutiya back to the map, but it stayed on the wall for less than a minute, and I gave up. Right outside my window there grew a stout birch. While falling asleep, I listened to the lullaby of rustling leaves. Each day, the lullaby became more dry and rarefied.

One chilly morning I discovered Vasily the cat croaked on my porch. Probably, having sensed his death approaching, he was instinctively drawn to be near a human being. But this hadn't saved him. I wrapped the cat in an old tablecloth, carried him to the cemetery hill, and buried him next to the unknown soldier. In the evening, Auntie Montie and I toasted the both of them with nuclear rowan-berry liqueur. That night, the first snow fell.

Auntie Montie's basement contained one-pound burlap bags with an endless supply of grain, sugar, and peas. As soon as darkness fell, I went to her house to "evening over." We had a supper of buckwheat. Then sat with our backs to the stove. I smoked up, Auntie Montie sewed something, and the goat, with her front hooves on the bench, gazed out the window with a tense and almost intelligent melancholy. She now lived right here in the house and had somehow become completely human.

We were spending longer periods of time in silence. Auntie Montie answered my questions unwillingly and dryly. I was able to find out that she had a daughter who lived somewhere on the Kolsky peninsula with her husband, a military man.

—She used to send me postcards on New Year's. The pictures on them were different, but the writing was always the same: "Health, happiness, many long years." As if she couldn't write a word of her own. I wrote to her and told her not to waste any more money on stamps. On New Year's, I'll pull out your old "Health, happiness, many long years" from the dresser and will marvel at that. Same difference . . . and that's all. Since that time I've heard and seen nothing of my dear daughter.

— — —

Alarming, foreign noises populated my sleep. I tried to wake myself up several times, but kept falling back into swampy, squelching thoughtlessness. Woke up with an aching head and a premonition of some sort of menace. While I was getting dressed, the south of Siberia peeled off the map and slowly drifted to the floor.

I walked outside and immediately heard that sound. It was the unlocked door, rhythmically slamming in the wind. The broken windows of Toma and Lucia's house looked at me with surprise. As if asking: "How could this be?" Tire tracks blackened the snow near the porch.

All this notwithstanding, I didn't anticipate what I found inside. The house contained ab-so-lute-ly nothing. The robbers got away with everything: from the tall iron-post bed to the very last knife. They even peeled the faded wallpaper with pink flowers off the walls.

—Did you hear them operating in here? I asked Auntie Montie.

—Maybe I did hear it.

—So why didn't you stop them?!

—Have you lost your mind?! They'd stick a fist in my forehead— and good-bye. No one would notice I was gone. I trembled the whole night, hoping the devil wouldn't drag you out to get in their way! Thank God you've got enough wits to sit it out.

—Sleeping! I was sleeping! Not sitting it out! . . .

—Where are you going?!

—To Gryazevo, of course! To that bastard! I'll make him drag everything back for me! On his own hump! And he'll put the windows back in, stupid swine!

—Don't you dare! I won't let you! Auntie Montie jumped into the doorway and jabbed an oven fork toward me. The goat appeared next to her and threateningly lowered her horns.

—All right, move away, I said silently, and began shaking.

After running all the way to Gryazevo, I cooled down a bit. The gray February sky was almost low enough to settle onto the roofs. The crows screamed bloody murder. There was no one around. Only two disheveled strays conducted their business in front of the grocery store doors. I thought about it a bit, then I headed to the police station.

—Well, write a statement, since you're up for it, sighed the young, round-faced sergeant with a full-cheek, rosy glow. —But you really shouldn't bother—we won't find it.

—Will you look for it?

—Well, we'll look for it, of course . . . the sergeant stretched his answer out noncommittally.

I threw the pen down:

—Does he share it with you, or something?!

—If he was sharing, I would have married Lyubka, the sergeant chuckled mirthlessly. —Otherwise, I'm living on one salary—who needs somebody like me . . . Do you want some pierogies? My mammy baked them. Well, as you wish. But I will have some, I think. Oh life . . .

—I could see right away that you're new, he continued with a full mouth. —You don't know the local ways. Stick your nose where you shouldn't. No one deals with Vasyukhin. With Cherenok, I mean. He's completely frozen off. Has got no brains.

—Well, how can you be like this! One ex-con has the whole borough quaking in its boots! And you call yourself the police!

—Exactly right, the police! Cherenok chopped up the pope! The pope! And I'm a cop! Get it?

—So you're afraid, is that right?

—My mammy is old. And I want to marry Lyubka. I'm still young.

—Well, you could call for reinforcements, hero!

—Are you kidding? Who will give them to me?! They've busted into a house! Big deal! How many houses are busted into every day?!

I looked around the room. Pierogies, a rosy glow, a dusty fichus snoozing in a pot. And understood that it was completely useless. I crumpled up the unfinished statement, threw it into the corner, and walked out, slamming the door. I was choking with rage. I knew that I wouldn't be able to change anything.

Cherenok was waiting for me on the porch. Even though I had imagined him to be completely different, I recognized him instantly. He was a short, patchy chap with a gray face and unexpressive little eyes. He stood there with his hands deep in the pockets of his track pants, rocking on his heels.

—Whoa, homie, swilling tea with the sergeant? Cherenok inquired colorlessly and grinned with half his mouth.

Suddenly I didn't feel well. Once in my childhood I got pushed into an open grave that had been torn up by vandals. It was a trend, back then—digging up and breaking open old coffins, looking for treasures. My friends and I would run to the cemetery—to watch.

I fell into the grave and my hands felt some sort of clay-smeared rags. The smell of rot and cold hit my face. I couldn't even scream. Everything that was alive in me convulsed with sorrow and in unconscious terror turned inside out, straining to escape the proximity to death, to survive.

I experienced the same thing now. Cherenok monotonously rocked on his heels and senselessly repeated the putrid word *homie*. And nothing else. I quickly walked off the porch. And almost ran down the deserted street. Behind my back, someone barked. It was Cherenok, laughing. I couldn't give a shit. *Justice, humiliation, virtue*—these words were foreign to me in that moment.

I only wanted one thing: to get back to my house as quickly as possible and to bolt closed the door. There even flickered the thought to just drop everything and go directly back to Moscow.

I lit a smoke and my panic subsided a little. It was getting dark. To walk would be unreasonable. A bus that passed the turn to Paradise departed in a half hour.

I stopped by the post office and ordered three minutes to call Smolensk. Knowing the sisters' chattiness, I was worried that it wouldn't be enough time. And I barely had enough money. Toma picked up the phone. She heard me out. And didn't ask me a single question.

—No big deal, I stated with a fake cheerfulness. —I will lend you my bed. And we'll also deal with the rest of it, somehow!

—I probably won't come there any longer, said Toma bleakly.

—Huh . . . ? I began, and in the same second understood everything and stopped short.

—Yes, confirmed Toma. —Lucia passed away.

I remained silent. Toma hung up the phone.

— — —

After I went to Gryazevo Auntie Montie stopped talking to me again. The deceitful spring winds began blowing. I would walk into the fields, stand on the thawing hill, and watch the columns of light propping up the gashes in the clouds. Every once in a while, the sun would peek out right above my head, and I would find myself inside a beam. And it seemed to me that between myself and the faraway, invisible sky there appeared a momentary unbreakable connection. But the clouds drew closer together, the sunbeam broke, and I remained alone on the estranged frozen earth.

Sometimes I would utter aloud some word. Just to remember what my voice sounded like. My lips moved unsteadily and unwillingly. The entire Urals had fallen off the map. At night, something was sighing, slapping around, mumbling behind the windows.

On one of these restless nights, all of the wires disappeared off the telephone poles. The lights went off in Paradise. The wires were cut all the way to the highway. I didn't even bother going to Gryazevo to figure it out. I knew that no one would install new electrical lines for the sake of one old woman.

Auntie Montie produced a dozen paraffin candles from her supplies. Silently separated one half for me. We began going to bed at dawn and getting up at dusk. *Why am I here? What am I doing here?* I thought more and more often.

I wanted to believe that by staying in Paradise I was doing the right thing. That this was how it was supposed to be. But after my run-in with Cherenok my feeling of alignment with fate began to subside, and by spring it had left me completely. And again, as had happened often in the city, I stopped understanding which actions life required of me. I was melancholy, grew scruffy, and couldn't make myself crawl out from the old padded jackets under which I slept until midday.

— — —

One day, while gruffly digging into the floor with a balding broom, I heard joyful voices outside my window. Among them, a bell-like girl's voice especially stood out. Carefully and warily I peered outside. In the middle of Paradise, looking around and giggling, stood two guys in tall boots and one girl in a smartly tied red bandanna. I felt as if I'd been stranded for a year on an uninhabited island and had just seen a boat.

Her name was Lesya. The guys, who couldn't tear their lovelorn eyes away from her, one was Mitya, and the other one was Dima. My feral house was filled with backpacks, sleeping bags, wild activity, and Lesya's voice.

—We're from Smolensk. Students, she said, peeling the potatoes quickly. —It's boring to be stuck in the city. We're always taking trips somewhere. On the weekends, on holidays . . .

—And is now a weekend or a holiday?

—What's wrong with you?! Tomorrow is May 9! Lesya burst out laughing, a potato slipped from her hands and rolled to Mitya's feet. —So, we're taking trips. But to just take trips is boring, also. So we try to do something useful during each trip.

—For example?

—Well, anything you want! Most often we help grandmothers with their house chores.

—Are you Timurites? I asked with vitriol, getting ready to start hating my sudden guests.

—No way! she gaily dismissed me. —We're un-idealists!

I was again filled with sympathy toward Lesya and her posse. Asked more questions. She merrily and gladly answered. The guys suspiciously huffed in the corners. Lesya dug out a thick notebook from her bag and trustingly showed me the various odd words eavesdropped in villages, domestic stories and fairy tales, requests from and errands for the grandmothers that she'd been writing down in it. Usually they asked her to buy some sort of magical herbs from the city, about which they'd heard on the radio, and to find out if godmother so-and-so still lived in the next village.

The same notebook contained quotes from books of regional studies. Lesya endearingly prepared for each trip at the library.

—Can you imagine, Princess Ulita was born in Gryazevo, the wife of Vasily, who was blinded by his brothers! I love that name so much: Ulita! I would like to name my daughter that. And they, Lesya threw a quick, laughing look at Mitya and Dima, —are teasing me! Saying: "Snailita, show your horns!" . . . And also nearby there lived monk Illarion, right in the ground, in a cave. And during the war there were battles in these places . . .

Having eaten, they headed to Gryazevo. I wandered around Paradise all day, couldn't find a place for myself. It began to get dark. I started to think they would not return. I smoked continuously, and my lips were bitter from tar. Suddenly I imagined that Lesya had been killed by Cherenok. Immediately, I flew into some sort of frenzy. But then I heard her sonorous voice beyond the fence.

—We were painting a war obelisk, growled Mitya or Dima. —From the twenty casualties fourteen were Vasily's—imagine!

—And there were crosses everywhere! continued Lesya. —Where the monk had lived and where Ulita was born and where the battle was! We later found Stephan, the carpenter, who installs them, and chatted with him until dark. He's such an interesting person! A philosopher!

—Chatted with whom? I was amazed. —He's mute!

—What do you mean, mute? Lesya was amazed in turn.

At night she sat on the stoop and, smiling, jotted things down in her notebook. One night I looked over her shoulder. Lesya had written:

We will go to village Paradise
In our tall boots.
One shed stands there,
Tangled in grass roots.

In the shed sleeps tractor driver
Drunken and blue.
Yellow leaves are falling,
And the cows moo.

I sat down next to her, for some reason feeling embarrassed.

—So is it me, the tractor driver?

—Don't be silly! It's an image! Lesya explained, as if to a child.

—Look, you don't have cows here, either. Or leaves. Especially yellow ones.

We were silent for a while. Lesya looked up at the stars. Shivered. I wanted to cover her shoulders with my sweater, but didn't dare to.

—Back to the city tomorrow, sighed Lesya. —I really don't want to . . .

—Stay, I offered and, surprising myself, added, —You'll get married to me. We'll have a daughter, Ulita. I won't tease you. I give my word.

Lesya stopped smiling and lowered her eyes onto her notebook, like a valedictorian who didn't study for her exam.

—Well, I first need to finish school. I'm still neither this nor that, unskilled . . .

—How much longer do you have?

—Three more years.

This is when Mitya and Dima returned from gathering firewood. And this was the last time that Lesya and I were alone. In the morning, I saw them off to the bus station.

—Come back! I yelled when the doors slammed shut.

Lesya nodded and smiled through the dusty glass.

— — —

I was planting potatoes when the goat flew, bewildered, into the vegetable patch. And began bleating in despair. For some reason I immediately guessed what was going on. I threw the shovel down and followed her, wiping my hands on my pants on the way. The goat jogged down the only street in Paradise, turning around every once in a while and continuing to bleat.

Auntie Montie lay on the very same hill where she'd spent all her days with the goat. She was still alive. Inside her chest, something bubbled and hissed.

—The Sweeps are sweeping, she mouthed. I didn't understand.

—I leaned Auntie Montie against a tree stump, got down on my haunches, grasped her under her knees, and heaved her onto my back.

—Hold on tight, I'll fly you home like the wind! Then we'll call a doctor. Don't be afraid. Everything will be all right!

I was carrying Auntie Montie. Irrelevant thoughts kept forcing their way into my head. I unfortunately remembered how I had dragged my grandfather's pack with the books—since covered with dust in the corner—here. For some reason, I thought about my wife. If only she could see me now!

What an idiot! Left his prestigious job and apartment in Moscow so he can drag peasant hags around on his back! is what she would probably have said.

Auntie Montie began sliding off to the side.

—Hey, Mother, hang on! I called to her.

A dried-up little lady, who weighed about as much as a child, had suddenly become unbearably heavy. The goat was no longer bleating, but screaming, with a voice that was human. I awkwardly tried to rebalance Auntie Montie, who continued sliding down. My hands slipped. And she fell to the ground.

In that very same second I understood that she didn't care any longer. The goat came closer, looked Auntie Montie in the face. And suddenly jumped back. And sped away like a hurricane. I haven't seen her since. Probably the wolves butchered her in the forest.

I dragged Auntie Montie to her house and laid her down on the table. I began looking for documents since I didn't even know her last name. But the dresser only contained bundles of string, patches of cloth, buttons, and various other nonsense. I couldn't even find her daughter's postcards. I turned the whole house upside down. Nothing. No passport, no pension book.

The house had been cleaned. All of the jars and cans, usually filling the table, were gone. On the bed there was a clean, homemade robe. I understood what was required of me. Went and got a bucket of water. Hesitated for a moment. I felt a little out of sorts. I'd never dealt with the dead before. But there was no one else who could do it.

I took a pair of large rusty scissors from the dresser and cut apart Auntie Montie's skirt and sweater. Took a clean towel and began to wash her down. Joyful rivulets of water dripped onto the floor. My consciousness moved into the most remote corner of my brain. I wasn't thinking. Just doing.

I then dressed the deceased in the clean robe. Folded her hands on her chest. Closed her eyelids. Went outside for a smoke, thinking about which boards would be best for nailing together a coffin. It was very quiet out in the world. Or did it only seem that way to me?

With effort, I was able to crack open the shed door, which had grown into the earth. Pulled out the tools. The second half of the shed was always locked. Suddenly—another foreign thought—I became curious about what was inside. Not spending too much time thinking further, I opened the dried-up door with an axe—and staggered away.

In the shed stood a coffin. Auntie Montie had taken care of everything ahead of time. And, seemingly, a long time ago: the coffin was completely covered in cobwebs.

I buried her next to the nameless soldier and Vasily the cat. And wrote on the sign just that: "Auntie Montie." I couldn't even invent a full name for her. I stood above the fresh grave and couldn't make myself leave, feeling that I had not yet done everything.

Suddenly I thought about Gogol's Homa Brut, and I had an epiphany. But it was useless to look for religious literature in Auntie Montie's house. She had been an atheist. And I myself did not know a single prayer by heart but this . . .

—Our father . . . I said tenuously. And suddenly I remembered the second line somehow: —Who art in heaven . . .

How does the rest go? I stiffened. My head was empty. Then I stopped trying to remember. And immediately, without any effort, recited the whole prayer. Then again, one more time. And again. Three times. It started drizzling. I felt that I could now go.

As soon as I stepped through the doorway, what was left of the map of Russia, as if it had been waiting for me, began slowly peeling off the wall. I ran over and held it up with my hands. The urge to smoke was unbearable. I turned around in a way such that the map lay across my shoulders; I pushed it against the wall with my back and took the cigarettes out of my pocket.

Outside the window, darkness was falling quickly. I smoked, holding up the motherland. I wasn't in a hurry to be anywhere.

CONTRIBUTORS

AUTHORS

EVGENI ALYOKHIN was born in 1985 in the town of Kemerovo. His first story was published in the journal *October* in 2005, and he was a finalist for the annual Debut literary award in 2004. He tries to write in the genre he defines for himself as "children's literature for adults." He lives and works in St. Petersburg.

ARKADY BABCHENKO, born in 1977 and winner of the Debut prize, is a rising star in Russian literature. He is mainly known for his cycle of firsthand accounts of the Chechnya war, which can be viewed both as fictionalized documentary and narrative nonfiction. His memoir, *A Soldier's War*, was published in the United States in 2008 and won the English PEN Award. He was drafted from the Law Department of Moscow University and sent to Chechnya after only elementary military training. Upon discharge he finished his education and wrote a cycle of stories about his war experiences so as "to get the war out of his system." He lives in Moscow and is currently working as a columnist on the opposition paper *Novaya Gazeta*. He received special commendation from the Frontline Club for his outstanding coverage of the conflict in South Ossetia and Georgia in 2008.

ALEKSANDER BEZZUBTSEV-KONDAKOV was born in 1980 in Leningrad. He is the author of numerous historical novels, which have won many literary prizes. He currently works in administration for the office of the governor of St. Petersburg.

MARIA BOTEVA was born in 1980. She graduated from the Ural State University in Ekaterinburg with a degree in journalism and the Ekaterinburg State Theater Institute dramaturgy seminar with Nikolai Kolyada. She is the author of the book *The Light Alphabet, Two Sisters*, and *Two Winds* (NLA, 2005), and her work has appeared in the journals *New World, October, Ural, Air*, and *Babylon*. In 2005 she was a finalist for the Debut literary prize and the Triumph award. She lives in Vyatka and works as a journalist.

DMITRY DANILOV was born in 1969 in Moscow where he currently lives. He is a writer of prose and the author of the books *Black and Green* (Red Sailor, 2004) and *House Ten* (Raketa, 2006). His work has been published in the journals *New World, Russian Life, Yang* (Belgium), and other print journals as well as in numerous literary Internet resources. His work has been translated into

English, Italian, and Dutch. In 2008 he traveled to the United States as a fellow in the Open World program. He works as a journalist, and his personal Web site is http://ddanilov.ru.

NIKOLAI EPIKHIN was born in 1982 in the city of Voronezh. In 2003 he won the Debut literary prize in the category of short prose. He graduated from Voronezh State University with a degree in journalism in 2005 and currently works as a correspondent in Moscow.

MARIANNA GEIDE was born in 1980. She graduated with a degree in philosophy from the Russian State University of the Humanities and lives in Moscow. She has won Russian and international literary prizes. She is the author of two books of poems (*Time of the Dusting of the Thing* and *The Slugs of the Garrote*), a book of prose (*Lantern of Dead Men*), as well as of the critical papers of Thomas Aquinas, whose texts she translates into Russian. Her poems and prose are translated into Italian, Macedonian, Ukrainian, English, Estonian, French, Turkish, and Romanian.

LINOR GORALIK was born in 1975 in Dnepropetrovsk. She lived and studied in Israel for many years, working in the area of "hi-tech." In the late nineties she began working as a poet and journalist for many publications in Russia. Since 2001 she's lived and worked in Moscow. She is the author of a wide range of novels, including *No* with Sergei Kuznetsov and *Half of the Sky* with Stanislav Lvovsky; two collections of short prose; a collection of poems; the monograph *Hollow Woman: The World of Barbie Inside and Out*; two children's books; and a range of translations from English and Hebrew. She has won several literary prizes including the Triumph award.

VADIM KALININ was born in 1973. He graduated from the Moscow State Forestry University with a concentration in landscape design and currently works in Moscow. He was one of the founders in 1989 of the Union of Young Literateurs, *Babylon*. His poetry and prose have appeared in publications such as *Babylon, Solo, RISK, Mitin's Journal, Avtornik, Day and Night*, and others, and also in two anthologies of new prose edited by Max Frye, *A Book of Vulgarities* and *A Book of Perversions*. He's published one book of prose, *A Kilogram of Explosives and a Train Car of Cocaine* (2002; also published in Italian in 2005), and a collection of poems and graphic art, *Poka* (2004). As a graphic designer, he has designed several dozen books for ARGO–RISK publishers, including books by G. Sapgir, N. Gorbanevskaya, N. Iskrenko, A. Ozhiganova, and others.

MARIA KAMENETSKAYA was born in 1981 and lives in St. Petersburg. In 2003 she graduated from the journalism program at St. Petersburg State

University and in 2006 completed two years of screenwriting workshops at the "Shoot" studios of Lenfilm. She works as a journalist as well as on various Internet projects and in arts culture management. Her professional interests center on literature, theater, photography, and restoration. As a manager and press secretary, she has participated in numerous international education projects and photo exhibitions. She is the author of many articles, essays, stories, and film scripts.

NATALYA KLYUCHAREVA was born in 1981 in the city of Perm. She graduated from Yaroslaval State University with a degree in philology. She currently works in Moscow as a journalist. In 2002 she was named to the shortlist for the Debut literary award in the category of poetry. Her books include a collection of poems, *White Pioneers* (ARGO-Risk, 2006), and the novel *Russia on Wheels* first published in the journal *New World* and later reprinted by Limbus Press and nominated for the literary award National Bestseller. Her story published here, "One Year in Paradise" won the 2007 Yuri Kazakov award and the Eureka prize.

ILYA KOCHERGIN was born in 1970 and studied geology and Chinese at Moscow State University and the Institute of Asian and African Countries, and in 2004 he graduated from the Maxim Gorky Literary Institute. He's taken part in multiple expeditions in the Russian Far East, where he worked for three years as a forester in Altai State Nature Reserve (Siberia). He has many publications in Russian literary magazines. His first book, *Assistant to a Chinaman*, was published in Russia and in France (Actes Sud, 2004) and won the Globus international literary award for promoting closer ties between people and cultures. His most recent book, *I'm Your Grandson*, will be published simultaneously in Russia and France in 2009. In 2000 he won the Debut literary award and in 2001 the Eureka prize. He has won the Moscow Government Literary Prize and received scholarships from the Russian Ministry of Culture. He has appeared in literary festivals and cultural programs in the United States, France, Germany, Belgium, and Russia.

VLADIMIR KOZLOV was born in 1972 in Mogilev, an industrial city in the eastern part of what was then the Belorussian Soviet Socialist Republic. He is a graduate of the Minsk State Linguistics University and the Indiana University School of Journalism. Kozlov has worked as a reporter, newspaper editor, translator, screenwriter, and documentary filmmaker. He has lived in Moscow since 2000. He is the author of the story collection *Hoods* (2002) and the novels *School* (2003), *Warsaw* (2004), *Second Class* (2006), *Pops* (2007), *USSR* (2008), and *Back Home* (2008), as well as several nonfiction books. *Hoods* was named one of the year's two best prose books by the *Ex Libris* literary review and was published in France in early 2009. In 2007 Kozlov won the Tamizdat contest

CONTRIBUTORS

sponsored by Summer Literary Seminars, Inc., with the short story published here, "Drill and Song Day."

ZAKHAR PRILEPIN was born in 1975 in the village of Ilyinka in the Ryazan region. He graduated with a degree in philology from Lobachevski State University in Nizhny Novgorod and the school of public politics in the program "Open Russia." He took part in the military operations in Chechnya with the special operations division of the Russian Army in 1996 and 1999. Since 2000 he has worked as a journalist, critic for Russian publications (*Spark*, *Russian Life*, and others), and general director for the Nizhny Novgorod edition of *New Newspaper*. He has been an active participant in the Russian left-wing radical opposition and an activist in the banned National-Bolshevik party and cochairman of the All-Russia movement "People." He is the author of the novels *Pathology* and *Sanka*, the story collections *Sin* and *Boots, Half-full with Hot Vodka*, and the essay collection *I Came From Russia*. He has won numerous literary awards, including the National Bestseller prize, Clear Glade, Russia's Faithful Sons, and others. His work has been a finalist for the Russian Booker prize. His books have been translated into Chinese (*Sanka* won China's Best Foreign Novel of the Year), Polish, and French; his shorter works into Bulgarian, German, Latvian, Czech, and others. He lives in Nizhny Novgorod with his wife and three children.

KIRILL RYABOV was born in 1983 in Leningrad. He started writing prose when he was thirteen years old and started publishing at eighteen. In 2005 he won special literary citation at the Northwest conference of young writers, and in 2007 he was named to the longlist for the Debut literary prize. His work has been published in the journals *Russian Invalid*, *Northern Lights*, *Bear Songs*, *Main Entrance*, and *Train Station* and in the anthology *Young Petersburg*. He lives in St. Petersburg.

Born in 1973 to a Chechen father and Russian mother, **GERMAN SADU-LAEV** grew up in the Chechen village of Shali. At sixteen, before the start of the first Chechen war, he left his homeland to study law in Leningrad and never went back. Sadulaev's second book *I Am a Chechen!* was highly acclaimed and nominated for the National Bestseller prize. *Snowstorm, or the Myth of the End of the World* won the Eureka prize; his most recent book, *The Tablet*, has been short-listed for the 2008 Russian Booker. He lives in St Petersburg. "Why the Sky Doesn't Fall" is an excerpt from *I Am a Chechen!* to be published in the United Kingdom by Harvill Secker in 2010.

ROMAN SENCHIN was born in 1971 in Kyzyl in the Republic of Tuva. He served in the boundary armies in Kareli and in 2001 graduated from the

368

Literary Institute. His work has been published in the literary journals *Banner*, *New World*, *Friendship of Peoples*, and others. He is the author of six books of prose and one book of literary criticism. His novel *Minus* was published in the United States and United Kingdom in 2008 by Glas and has also been published in Germany. He's been awarded literary prizes such as the Eureka prize and an award from the journal *Banner*.

ALEKSANDER SNEGIREV was born in 1981. He is the author of the collection of stories *Russian Size* and the novels *How We Bombed America* (Limbus Press) and *Oil Venus* (AST, 2009), and his work has been published in the Limbus Press *Anthology of Twentysomething Prose No. 3*. He is the winner of the Debut literary prize (2005), the Wreath award (2007), and Eureka (2008).

ANNA STAROBINETS was born in 1978. She is a journalist and writes on cultural issues for a number of respectable magazines, such as *Expert* and *Russian Reporter*. She is also a scriptwriter. Her collection of short stories, *The Awkward Age*, has been translated into a number of languages. She is also the author of the novel *Refuge F/A*. All of her books have been nominated for the National Bestseller prize. She lives in Moscow with her daughter and husband, Alexander Garros, author of the international bestseller *Headcrusher*. "Rules" appears in the collection *The Awkward Age*, published in the United Kingdom by Hesperus Press in 2009.

EKATERINA TARATUTA was born in 1976 in Novosibirsk. She studied philosophy and philology at the Novosibirsk State University and received her PhD from St. Petersburg State University, where she currently teaches in the philosophy department. She is the author of the prose works *101 Minutes* and *The Philosophy of Virtual Reality*, as well as numerous academic articles.

OLEG ZOBERN was born in 1980 in Moscow. He is a graduate student in twentieth-century literature at the Maxim Gorky Literary Institute. His stories have been published in *New World*, *October*, *Banner*, *Friendship of Peoples*, *Neva*, *Siberian Lights*, *North*, *Don*, *Esquire* (Russian Edition), *Passionate* (Netherlands), *Yang* (Belgium), and in other magazines and anthologies. He was awarded the Debut prize in 2004. In 2007 his book *Silent Jericho* was published in the Netherlands (Douane) and in Russia (Vagrius). In 2008 his book *Funeral Feast for Yann Volkers* was published in the Netherlands.

OLGA ZONDBERG was born in 1972 in Moscow. She graduated with a degree in chemistry from Moscow State University. She's worked as a schoolteacher, secretary, and advertising manager. Currently she is an editor in a legal and technological publishing house. Her poems and prose have been published in many journals and anthologies, including *Babylon*, *Nine Measurements*, *Paragraph*, *TextOnly*, and others. She is the author of the book of poems *Book of Recognitions* (1997) and *Seven Hours and One Minute* (2007), the collection of stories *The Winter Company of Year Zero*, later included in the book *Very Quiet Story*. Her poems have been translated into English and Italian. Two stories in English translation recently appeared in the New York journal *A Public Space*. From 1999 to 2001 she was the curator of the Web site *Young Russian Literature*. In April 2008 she participated in the "Open World" sponsored by CEC ArtsLink in New York and Oxford, Mississippi.

TRANSLATORS

NICK ALLEN is a British citizen who studied Russian at the University of Bath, UK, and worked in Russia for the *Moscow Times* and the German press agency DPA (Deutsche Presse-Agentur GmbH) from 1996 to 2006 before moving to head the dpa Islamabad bureau until the end 2007. He translated Arkady Babchenko's memoir, *One Soldier's War*, into English and is currently working on a book about the conflict in Afghanistan.

KEITH GESSEN was born in Moscow in 1975 and moved to the United States in 1981. He is a cofounder of the magazine *n+1* and author of *All the Sad Young Literary Men*. His translation of Ludmilla Petrushevskaya's *Scary Fairy Tales* will be published by Penguin in 2009.

ANDREA GREGOVICH's translations have appeared in *Tin House*, *Cafe Irreal*, *AGNI Review*, and the Dalkey Archive Press collection *Amerika: Russian Writers View the United States*. She is currently translating a collection of Vladimir Kozlov's short stories. Her own novel, *Martyred Cars*, is a finalist in the Liberty in Fiction Contest. She lives in Anchorage, Alaska.

ANNA GUNIN is a translator and interpreter who studied Russian at Bristol University. Her translation of German Sadulaev's *I Am a Chechen!* will be published by Harvill Secker in 2010. She lives in Somerset, England, with her Russian husband and son.

MARIYA GUSEV is a freelance translator and editor living in New York City. Currently, she is associate editor for the *St. Petersburg Review* and has been on the staff of Summer Literary Seminars since 2003. Her recent projects include interviews for two chapters on Russia included in *Poor People* by William Vollmann (HarperCollins, 2007) and works by Leonid Kostyukov, Maria Kamenetskaya, and Marina Temkina for the *St. Petersburg Review*. She is currently translating Natalya Klyuchareva's first novel, *Russia on Wheels*, into English.

SVETLANA ILINSKAYA is an instructor in English at the University of Mississippi and coauthor with Douglas Robinson of the first-year writing textbook *Writing as Drama*. Prior to coming to the United States she was an instructor in English at Voronezh State Pedagogical University in Voronezh, Russia, and a freelance interpreter. She and Douglas Robinson are co-coordinators of the annual visit of Russian writers to Ole Miss through the Open World Cultural Leaders Program.

ELLEN LITMAN is the author of a novel in stories, *The Last Chicken in America*, which was a finalist for the 2007 Los Angeles Times Art Seidenbaum Award for First Fiction and the 2008 New York Public Library Young Lions Award. A native of Moscow, she immigrated to the United States in 1992. She currently teaches at the University of Connecticut.

VICTORIA MESOPIR was born in Leningrad, USSR, and grew up in Nairobi, Kenya, before coming to the United States in 1991 to continue her university education. She has a master's degree in education and a bachelor's in political science, with a minor concentration in African Studies and Russian Literature. Her translations of contemporary stories in Russian are forthcoming in a number of publications. She lives in Montreal, where she teaches English and works as a freelance literary translator.

JULIA MIKHAILOVA is the Language Program Coordinator in the Department of Slavic Languages and Literatures at the University of Toronto.

DOUGLAS ROBINSON is professor of English at the University of Mississippi and author of *The Translator's Turn*, *Translation and Taboo*, *What Is Translation?*, *Who Translates?*, *Translation and Empire*, and *Becoming a Translator*. He is also editor of *Western Translation Theory from Herodotus to Nietzsche* and coauthor with Svetlana Ilinskaya of the first-year writing textbook *Writing as Drama*. He and Svetlana Ilinskaya are co-coordinators of the annual visit of Russian writers to Ole Miss through the Open World Cultural Leaders Program.

JAMES R. RUSSELL is Mashtots Professor of Armenian Studies and a member of the Executive Committee of the Davis Center for Russian and Eurasian Studies at Harvard. His recent books include *Bosphorus Nights: The Complete Lyric Poetry of Bedros Tourian* and a translation of Derenik Demirjian's *Book of Flowers*. He has also published articles recently on cosmology in the prologue to *Ruslan and Ludmila*, on the Indo-Mongol material in the ballad of Ilya of Murom and the Nightingale Robber, and on the ancient Iranian sources of the old Russian Book of the Dove. His translations of Vera Kobets's stories have appeared in WordsWithoutBorders (www.WordsWithoutBorders.org).

ACKNOWLEDGMENTS

The editors are grateful to the following individuals and organizations for their help in assembling the roster of writers and translators in this anthology: CEC ArtsLink's Open World Cultural Leaders Program, Robert Chandler, Dmitry Danilov, Glas Publishers, Dmitry Kuzmin, Leonid Kostyukov, Limbus Press, Natasha Perova, Maria Pyshkina, and Alexander Troitsky.

Thanks to Liana Loshniy for her work as an editorial assistant in reading both Russian and English versions of these texts. Thanks also to John Goldbach for feedback on translations.

Thanks are due to the staff, participants, and faculty members who participated in the Summer Literary Seminars program in St. Petersburg, Russia, over the years for their interest in and enthusiasm for contemporary Russian literature. And thanks to editors Jessica Bomarito and Dwayne D. Hayes at *Absinthe: New European Writing* and Elizabeth Hodges at the *St. Petersburg Review* for their support of this anthology and the good work they do in publishing Russian writers in North America.

Special thanks to everyone at Tin House Books, particularly Lee Montgomery and Meg Storey, for the invaluable editorial work and for making this project happen.

And thanks to Ellen Levine and Alanna Ramirez at Trident Media.

MIKHAIL IOSSEL was born in Leningrad, USSR, where he worked as an electromagnetic engineer and night guard and belonged to a circle of underground ("samizdat") writers. He emigrated to the United States in 1986 and currently serves on the faculty of Concordia University in Montreal, Canada, where he is the coordinator of the creative writing program. He is the author of *Every Hunter Wants to Know* (W.W. Norton), a collection of stories, and coeditor of *Amerika: Russian Writers View the United States* (Dalkey Archive). His fiction has been published in Russian in the Soviet Union and in English in literary magazines in the United States, Canada, and abroad; translated into several foreign languages; and anthologized in *The Best American Short Stories* and elsewhere. He has received fellowships from the NEA, the Guggenheim Foundation, and Stanford University, among other literary awards. In 1998 he founded Summer Literary Seminars, Inc.—one of the world's largest international literary conferences: www.sumlitsem.org.

JEFF PARKER is the author of the novel *Ovenman* (Tin House Books) and, with artist William Powhida, the collection of stories and images *The Back of the Line* (DECODE). He previously coedited the anthology *Amerika: Russian Writers View the United States* (Dalkey Archive) and has written about Russian literature, music, and culture for the *Walrus*, *Spin*, *Poets & Writers*, and *Billiards Digest*. He served as the Russia Program Director of Summer Literary Seminars in St. Petersburg for many years. Currently, he is the Acting Director of the Master's Program in the Field of Creative Writing at the University of Toronto.